TALES OF SHUB-NIGGURATH

A CTHULHU MYTHOS ANTHOLOGY

FEATURING STORIES BY

C. T. PHIPPS ~ DAVID HAMBLING ~ ANDREA PEARSON
DAVID J. WEST ~ MATTHEW DAVENPORT
JESSI VASQUEZ ~ PATRICIA LEE MACOMBER
TIM MENDEES ~ ERIC MALIKYTE

I was in love.

A love that would surely doom me.

It was nothing so pedestrian as the fact that the woman I loved was married. My father had kept a mistress as did his father before him. No, it was the nature of the woman who was to be my doom. She was my Eve, Salome and Delilah all in one. It was to satisfy my mad passion for her that I was following her up the accursed slopes of Sentinel Hill. Dunwich was not the sort of place any respectable Arkham gentleman visited, any more than the ruined hellscape of Innsmouth. The rotted inbred families were descended from the worst of England's religious fanatics, still clinging to superstitions about Old Scratch in an age of electricity and motor cars.

Nonsense.

But Sentinel Hill made you *believe*.

The woman in question was dark, smallish, and very good-looking except for her protuberant eyes. It was a quality common among the Innsmouth folk but seemed more striking than nausea-inducing as I'd seen in some of that foul community's ranks. My companion's beauty, however, came primarily from her sharp and forceful personality as much as what nature had bestowed her, though. Tonight, she was dressed in men's breaches and a button-down dress shirt with a leather jacket. A lovely, perfumed scarf was around her neck. The androgyny of it only increased her appeal to me.

"Are we almost there?" I finally spoke up, as much to distract myself from my surroundings as anything else.

"Are you afraid of a midnight stroll, Wentworth?" my companion asked, mockingly. Always mockingly. Her ability to tear down men's pride and reduce them to sobbing ruin was well known on campus.

"No, Asenath," I lied. "It's just Professor Armitage spoke of Sentinel Hill as a, uh… well, cursed place."

Contents

Contents

Foreword

By C.T. Phipps

Ever Their praises, and abundance to the Black Goat of the Woods. Iä! Shub-Niggurath!

Iä! Shub-Niggurath! The Black Goat of the Woods with a Thousand Young!

—The Whisperer in the Darkness, H.P. Lovecraft

The desert creatures will meet with hyenas, and one wild goat will call to another; there the night creature will settle and find her place of repose.

—Isaiah 34:14

Shub-Niggurath, she of the unfortunate name.

I kid.

Sort of.

The Black Goat of the Woods with a Thousand Young, the wife of The-Not-To-Be-Named One, and one of HP Lovecraft's rare female characters. She is a fertility goddess, associated with Cybele and Attis ("The Rats in the Walls"), a kind of sophisticated Astarte ("The Mound"), worshiped by beings as far off as the Mi-Go ("The Whisperer in Darkness"), and as close by as the K'n-yanian ("The Mound"). She never appears on-screen, so to speak, but is frequently referenced in the chants of various supernatural spells and invocations.

H.P. Lovecraft seemed to have an especial fondness for Shub-Niggurath and even has a few semi-benevolent individuals harness her power. In "Out of the Aeons", her power is wielded against the demon Ghatanothoa. However, it is within other fiction by later authors that Shub-Niggurath has achieved her biggest fame. Perhaps because while

HP Lovecraft was from the Puritan homeland, it was others who were willing to tackle the idea that she represents. A terror that HP Lovecraft faced and fell prey to himself.

Yes, I speak of the primal feminine.

Anima.

Shub-Niggurath is a figure associated with sex, birth, witchcraft, cyclic blood, woods, and all the things that seem to have a fundamental ability to terrify certain parts of the population while also being seized as power among other parts. It is easy to imagine her as the patron deity of individuals like Keziah Mason (alongside Nyarlathotep as the Black Man of Salem folklore), the Lilith worshiped by the cultists in Red Hook, and perhaps the patron of the Medusan Marcelaine, the witch who made the mistake of marrying into a Confederate family. These stories weren't necessarily linked together in the original Lovecraft canon but it is easy to imagine they could be.

The Black Goat of the Woods with a Thousand Young is a goddess, not just a Great Old One, and the odd-woman out in the Unholy Trinity of Azathoth, Yog-Sothoth, and Nyarlathotep. A figure far more physical and earthly than those transcendental beings that Randolph Carter encountered in the Dreamlands. Fertility goddesses and expressions of gynophobia are far more elemental and materialist than the secrets found within the *Necronomicon* or *Book of Eibon*. No, Shub-Niggurath is the kind of goddess who can only be experienced in the kind of rituals performed by the cult of Cthulhu in Louisiana swamps or amid the dark corners of the Earth.

Tales of the Shub-Nigguarth is an anthology of short stories and novelettes based around the aforementioned goddess. We'll have our usual mixture of pulp heroism and horror but this time around, we'll also be incorporating a slightly more witchy edge to things. I hope you enjoy this walk on the wild side. Fans of the previous Books of Cthulhu will see many returning faces while also meeting some fantastic new authors who add a bit more perspective on just why Shub-Niggurath is so terrifying. Also, perhaps, why women might turn to her.

Prologue

The Mother of a Thousand Stories

By C.T. Phipps

I was in love.

A love that would surely doom me.

It was nothing so pedestrian as the fact that the woman I loved was married. My father had kept a mistress as did his father before him. No, it was the nature of the woman who was to be my doom. She was my Eve, Salome and Delilah all in one. It was to satisfy my mad passion for her that I was following her up the accursed slopes of Sentinel Hill. Dunwich was not the sort of place any respectable Arkham gentleman visited, any more than the ruined hellscape of Innsmouth. The rotted inbred families were descended from the worst of England's religious fanatics, still clinging to superstitions about Old Scratch in an age of electricity and motor cars.

Nonsense.

But Sentinel Hill made you *believe*.

The woman in question was dark, smallish, and very good-looking except for her protuberant eyes. It was a quality common among the Innsmouth folk but seemed more striking than nausea-inducing as I'd seen in some of that foul community's ranks. My companion's beauty, however, came primarily from her sharp and forceful personality as much as what nature had bestowed her, though. Tonight, she was dressed in men's breaches and a button-down dress shirt with a leather jacket. A lovely, perfumed scarf was around her neck. The androgyny of it only increased her appeal to me.

"Are we almost there?" I finally spoke up, as much to distract myself from my surroundings as anything else.

"Are you afraid of a midnight stroll, Wentworth?" my companion asked, mockingly. Always mockingly. Her ability to tear down men's pride and reduce them to sobbing ruin was well known on campus.

"No, Asenath," I lied. "It's just Professor Armitage spoke of Sentinel Hill as a, uh... well, cursed place."

The night air was uncommonly foul and there was a stink to the area that I could not get away from, more noxious than burning sulfur or corpse flowers. It infected my lungs, and I couldn't help but feel an intense sense of unease as I saw the strangely formed plants and deformed animals that seemed to lurk around us as we made our ascent.

The animals had no fear of man and were covered in thick cancerous sores and odd growths. Elk, rabbits, and even squirrels had eyes that seemed to glow in the night. Worse, they seemed to be watching me, and I understood why so many had deemed this place to be unnatural. The cicadas made an eerie noise, quite unlike anything else I'd heard in New England, sounding more like a siren warning away travelers.

"Professor Armitage thinks of this place as the manger of the Antichrist," Asenath said, as if describing a local tourist spot.

"Perhaps he's right," I muttered.

Asenath laughed. "Perhaps he is. However, the monoliths here were constructed by people who long predated the natives. The ol' goddess worshipers of Neolithic times would cavort here with monsters to guarantee powerful babes. They would offer the deformed and inhuman—the ones who could not pass for human—as sacrifices."

"You are speaking of old wives' tales," I said, frowning. "Witch stories and fairy tales."

Asenath smiled, her teeth barely visible in the moonlight. "Of course. What other tales would a wicked woman like me tell?"

Asenath was wicked, truly. She was one of those dangerous femme fatales that always seem to be lurking in the dark imaginations of Pulp writers, waiting to lead stoic heroes to their doom. I'd always been skeptical of the lurid depictions therein and thought myself a modern, enlightened man. Suffragettes were not going to be the end of men nor did I believe there was a Lady Macbeth standing behind every fool that brought about his ruination.

Gods, what a woman! It would be unfair to say she was not like other women. I had met proud, intelligent, and even fierce members of the fairer sex in the past. However, there was something about Edward Derby's wife that defied conventional classification. Asenath possessed an ancientness to her soul and contempt for civilized mores that awakened primal feelings within.

And the sex, *dear God.*

No lover had ever known my darkest fantasies or secret cravings as a man. Nor had I paid so dearly for them to be satiated. The pain and humiliation had made me want her more. I was her slave.

But a disobedient one. At least tonight. "Tell me Asenath, where are we going?"

"So eager to find out where we're going to perform some pagan ritual in the nude and fornicate under the moon?" Asenath asked.

I turned red with embarrassment. That was another quality of Asenath: she did not talk like a proper woman. When Derby had decided to make her his bride, many men had said he was marrying a woman with the mouth of a whore and the mind of a man. Some had even suggested the insults were more than mere hyperbole and alluded to indecent behavior at Halls School for Women. That, too, intrigued as much as repelled.

"I, uh, well, I…" My speech trailed off to gibberish.

"Oh, you silly boy," Asenath said, chuckling. "Wentworth, what do you know of Shub-Niggurath?"

That, at least, was a subject I could speak upon with some authority. Anthropology was a hobby of mine even if I had no intention of making it a vocation.

"Shub-Niggurath, also known as the Black Mother and the Goat with a Thousand Young. She is one of the deities mentioned within the *Necronomicon* and *Liber Ivonis*," I said, giving the textbook answer. "A maternal figure speculated by some anthropologists to date back to

Neolithic times through some rather sketchy linkage of idols and funerary practices. Professor Wilmarth stated he believed that she was the precursor to such figures as Tiamat, Ishtar, and Isis. That there was a connection to the demon Lilith that has no orthodox basis but showed up repeatedly in folklore."

I tried not to think of one of Asenath's old lovers, the much older corpulent Robert Suydam, who had been quite Lilith-mad. The New Yorker had been a visitor to Arkham's Ivy League for only a short time before his indiscreet liaisons and assault of an Irish maid had driven him from polite society. Robert had simply uprooted himself back to his home state and settled in Red Hook. Supposedly, he had styled himself as an American Crowley and taken to cavorting with foreigners in basements. Last I'd heard, he'd died on a cruise before a building code accident had killed most of his followers.

Good riddance.

"Indeed, as well as Ceres and Cybele," Asenath said. "The Romans built multi-breasted centipede-like statues to both goddesses. Some believed her to be an Outer God. Others believe her to be a Great Old One like the Cthulhuoids. That whore-nun Brianna Lethder made up a whole genealogy of her as the consort of Hastur and having bred with Yog-Sothoth to create an alchemical pantheon from the Great Old Ones."

"Contradictory mythologies are to be expected when dealing with such a long-worshiped figure," I replied, having no real belief in the supernatural. I was a Jungian in my beliefs and thought obsession with the primal inhuman gods of humanity's distant past had more to do with cultural development than any greater cosmic truth.

"But do you see what the strangest quality of Shub-Niggurath is?" Asenath asked as we reached the summit of Sentinel Hill and its strange collection of standing stones.

The stone monoliths were arranged in a circle not unlike Stonehenge with a large, presumably sacrificial altar in the center. The inky black rocks were of a type that had baffled many a geologist as the only similar ones that had ever been found were in such curious places as the South Pacific and as far off as Antarctica. Most scientists agreed they were probably volcanic in origin as that was the only way they could end up in such wildly different locales.

"She's... uh, a woman?" I ventured a guess that I worried would mark me as a fool.

"Yes!" Asenath said, removing her scarf and beginning to unbutton her dress shirt. "The Black Goat with a Thousand Young is not the only one of the female Great Old Ones. There is Mother Hydra of the Deep Ones, Cthylla if you believe in the de Marigny Manuscripts, and the Unimaginable Horror. Yet, she is the only one who is of true prominence. In so much as the Great Old Ones have genders, I believe that is cosmically significant."

My heart rate quickened and I began to undress myself. "Yes, that sounds fascinating."

Asenath, now in her undergarments, shook her head. "You don't understand but I don't expect you to. Magic has long been segregated by sex among human practitioners. The Ordo Templi Orientis would only allow this body to be a scarlet woman or vessel of divine power yet some mysteries are only accessible to women in other societies. A difference between witchcraft and wizardry is nearly universal in all human civilizations from the barbarian to the civilized. I believe for true everlasting power, one must be able to cross the threshold of man and woman to access both. To be as Adam before God took his rib to create Eve and split the Fruit of Knowledge but not Life between them."

I had long since ceased listening and instead stared at Asenath's skyclad form. She was overwhelming in every way, both beauty and intellect. "Yes, I see. No, wait, I don't. What does this have to do with sex?"

Asenath gestured to the altar. "We shall unite man and woman there. Magic shall happen."

"Ah," I said, understanding that quite well. I was naked now, and cold, but my lust kept me warm. "Err, who shall be on top?"

"I will," Asenath said, calmly. "Lie down."

I swiftly obeyed. Lying prone, I stared up into the stars above and thought they looked *different* on Sentinel Hill. "I must say this is a strange ritual you have concocted, Asenath but I've seen worse—"

What followed was horrifying, agonizing pain. I tried to scream but Asenath's left hand was already over my mouth, tighter and stronger than any woman's grip should have been possible to achieve. In her right hand, there was a small piece of inky black stone that had been shaped into a crude knife. That object was tearing through my intestines.

"Shub-Niggurath, wife of the Not-to-Be-Named One and Yog-Sothoth, Mother of Nug and Yeb, I call upon thee with this blood offering! With the words of T'Yog of K'naa and through the speech of the fungi of Yuggoth, I bring forth thine avatar to show me thine secrets! Come forth and spew thine dark young upon this world, o mighty Black Goat! Feast upon this meal and reward me with knowledge of spheres beyond! Iä! Shub-Niggurath! Iä! Astarte-Lilith! Iä! Cybele and Attis!"

If only God had mercy, if he cared or existed—if *any* human-like God cared or existed—then I might have been spared what came next. I would have mercifully gone to my death believing Asenath was merely a madwoman, some twisted modern-day Lizzie Borden or Erzsébet Bathory. Instead, I was cursed with my final moments spent being exposed to a horrifying truth that reduced my last moments to gibbering madness.

In the skies above Sentinel Hill, red storm clouds formed into a spinning vortex that was visible with an ambient crimson light that seemed to eat the darkness but provided no comfort. From its eye belched an enormous cloud-like entity that extruded black tentacles, slime-dripping mouths, and short-writhing goat-like legs from its back. From porous holes across its body, I saw misshapen things pouring out and slithering across the ground as they made noises akin to mewling babes. A single beautiful, closed flower bud grew in the center of its mass which opened like a primrose at night. That exposed a human face within.

Asenath's face.

"Hello, Father," the monstrous thing said to Asenath. "It has been a long time."

I did not have a chance to ponder what that statement meant because the misshapen things had crawled upon the altar, little goat-headed babes with all-too-human teeth. They surrounded me, eight or nine of them, and began to feast.

That was when I was allowed to scream.

Mother of Darkness

A *#SAVANT* weird western adventure

By David J. West

1875, Ottoman Empire—Turkey

Crows cawed and flapped their wings amidst the wreckage. Their incessant cacophony roused Porter from his unbidden slumber. His head ached and his limbs were as sore as they had been in weeks. It took him a long moment to realize where he was lying: the ground.

He blinked and tried to understand what he was looking at. Everything was wrong. The bolted stools were horizontal to his view, the sky loomed sideways, and the floor was the wall. The gondola was on its side and the airship's envelope was deflated and still being picked up by the light wind, creating a canopy of shade from the rising sun. Where was he?

Looking the other way, he saw barren brown land stretched out level to the horizon. Shattered crockery and foodstuffs from the kitchen were scattered all around Porter. He put a hand to the ground to get up but drew back as he touched broken glass. He still felt dazed and tried to remember how he came here.

This was all a surprise as his last memories were when the big zeppelin, *Atlas*, was still airborne in the storm clouds. There was lightning, but then what? Had they been struck down? They were clearly on the ground now.

Then panic stricken, he gazed around for Elizabeth. "Liz!" he called, realizing he was far hoarser than he would have guessed. He wiped at his eyes and glanced at the broken bottles hoping one had survived. He was feeling the need for a stiff drink. It was a lot harder to avoid now than it used to be.

"Liz, you all right? Where are you?"

He thought he heard a moan from behind a collection of smashed furniture.

Elizabeth was not far away, sprawled out in her long dress and coat, damp from last night's rain. But at the least she did not appear to be in a terribly injured state. She was breathing.

They had been through a lot together these last few weeks, ranging across the entire United States, over to England, down to Egypt and now here, wherever here was. She was young enough to be his daughter, and in a way, he thought of her as such. They had been brought together by her great-great-great-grandfather John Dee, the English mystic magician, for the purpose of helping him find a way to die. There probably wasn't a stranger circumstance of bringing people together that Porter knew of than this, but they had accomplished their goals and were now on their way home. Taking the long scenic way as he thought of it. Liz was something special as she found out that she had magical powers as well, and Porter was quite fond of her.

Finally getting up, he headed over to her fallen form. Porter gently roused her, and she stretched and sat up as if she had spent the night in a royal suite rather than a storm damaged gondola.

"Where are we?" Elizabeth asked.

Porter could only shrug. "I thought the steward said last night that we were likely over Ottoman territory."

Checking beyond the sides of the crashed airship, Porter saw low brown hills covered in scattered small shrubs and rocks. "My understanding is that the Ottoman Empire is pretty big."

Clumps of tall grasses that sprouted up here and there across an arid landscape seemingly following a serpentine pattern. There was a small, nearly dry stream snaking its way across the land.

"Least we won't die of thirst here," Liz said hopefully, coming up behind him.

Porter glanced at the broken whisky bottles, "Speak for yourself," he lamented under his breath.

In a few moments they found the rest of the crew of the *Atlas*. They were on the other side of the overturned airship, attempting to work on the damaged envelope. The wind was causing problems pulling it away from them whenever they thought they could grasp it for repairing. Captain Gordon had a bandage on his scalp but was otherwise unhurt. One of the other crewman might have broken an arm and had it in a sling while the others only had bumps and bruises.

"I'm afraid we will need to spend some time patching the spot where lightning burnt through the envelope," said Captain Gordon. "It would be easier if we could get this damned wind to settle for half a moment."

Elizabeth asked, "Have you done this before?"

Gordon shook his head. "I have not myself, but yeoman Daniels has. He is the lead mechanic and at one time or another has done a little spot of everything."

"Is there anything we can do?" she asked.

"I'm afraid at this point, it is probably just a waiting game, although we will want to be as quick as possible. This is Ottoman territory, and I fear we could be vulnerable to bandits or worse."

"What's worse mean?" asked Porter.

Gordon frowned and said, "Frankly, I don't trust the locals. I've flown here before when I was transporting an archaeologist named Wood. He excavated an old temple, said it used to be one of the Seven Wonders of the World."

"The Temple of Ephesus?" Elizabeth exclaimed.

"That's it," Gordon agreed. "I don't think we are too far off."

Porter growled, "That still doesn't explain your worries."

"I only spent a night near here for Wood's sake. It gave me the willies."

"What did?"

Gordon shook his head. "The night here. Something isn't right, especially at night. I'm hoping Daniels can get us airborne before then, but I'm not sure. It's a very big hole on the starboard."

Elizabeth said, "Well, Porter and I will make sure you don't have any troubles from the locals while you're working."

Gordon nodded dubiously at that and got back to directing the crew.

"He didn't believe me," Elizabeth said to Porter angrily.

"Why should he?"

"I guess after everything I've been through lately," she said, "I forget that everyone isn't in on the joke."

"Joke?"

"You know what I mean. I feel like I should have a little more notoriety with some good guys instead of just the bad."

"Not everyone can know everything," Porter said, "and who would believe half of what we've seen these last few weeks? Not me if I hadn't been experiencing it myself."

Elizabeth frowned and sat down on a broken chair that had come from the upper deck of the gondola.

Porter shielded his eyes from the sun and pointed out toward the east. "Looks like a welcome wagon is heading our way."

Liz knew she couldn't see quite as good as the frontiersman and asked, "Who are they?"

"It's some woman, all wrapped up in her blankets from the sun. Bedouin or something. No wait, there are three of them."

"They're not Bedouins," said Captain Gordon. "They're Turks."

They waited as an old woman followed by two younger women made their way, guiding a camel. They were in no hurry and watched the foreigners apprehensively as they came closer. Finally, the old woman shouted when she was more than a hundred feet away. "Are you Englishmen? I speak good English."

"Sure, you do," answered Porter, "But we're American."

"I'm English," answered Gordon. "She looks like a beggar, but they might be spies for bandits. Get rid of them in a friendly manner if you can. Make them think we're better armed than we really are, that way they shan't think we are worth the fight."

"That won't be a problem," Porter said as he strode toward the old woman.

Porter tipped back his hat, letting the warm sunshine splash across his face. He smiled hoping he would look friendly to the women, and he raised his hand in a friendly gesture. It took him a moment squinting against the sun to realize that Liz was beside him, also giving a wave to the women who came no closer.

The three of them had steely dark eyes and were shielded from the sun in faded black kaftans. The elder held the reins of the camel in one hand and long staff from which dangled a few bizarre trinkets of metal and a feather or two.

"Howdy," Porter said as he stopped a few paces away.

"They may speak English but won't know howdy," Liz chided under her breath. "Hello, we are working at repairing our airship and then will be on our way. I hope we haven't inconvenienced you with our arrival."

The women looked at one another.

"They don't know what that meant either," Porter muttered softly.

"The storm," the old woman answered after a long pause. "It brought you to us for help."

"Help?" Liz asked. "The storm bringing us was a coincidence. But how can we help you?"

The old woman again pointed at the sky answering, "You will help us, the Goddess, the Mother, she brought you to aid us. A bad man has taken our..." she paused as if searching for the word. "Treasure. You help us get back and we will aid you in repairs."

Liz whispered to Porter, "That doesn't sound like anything a Muslim would say to me. They must be some kind of pagans."

"I think Captain Gordon has it under control," Porter answered. "We're good, thanks anyway."

Liz asked, "What do you need help with?"

"Very bad man took our treasure from the temple," one of the younger women said. "The bad man has it. We must get back or terrible destruction will fall upon us."

The old one gave her a stern look, and the young one went silent once more. "It is irreplaceable, from the lost city of Irad."

"Treasure?" Porter asked brightening.

Liz smacked a hand across his shoulder. "She didn't know the right word for a relic they need. I can sense that. From the temple?"

"You are near Ephesus, where the Atrium once stood. Englishman came here to dig and found the temple among the ruins. But we who abide here have always known and preserved the law since time began. This place used to be named Harag-Kolath."

"She must be talking about what Gordon told us. The archeologist took something, and they want it back," Porter said to Liz. Turning back to the native ladies, "He's not with us. Sorry, but he's gone back to England with it. The old woman shook her head, "No, no, he is here still—there in the house of the magician beyond the hill." A faint trail of smoke rose in the morning sky, denoting a small fire that Porter guessed would be someone cooking.

"You want us to get back a relic?" Liz asked unsteadily.

The old woman nodded emphatically. "Please, you must help us. The Great Mother brought you to help us."

"How can we know it is yours?" Liz asked.

The old woman drew her hand forth out of the sun-bleached garment and revealed a strange tattoo on the underside of her forearm. It was a chaos of lines and not unlike Liz's crosshatch sigil when she worked her magics. Liz had only recently discovered that she was the thrice great, great granddaughter of famous English mystic John Dee, and subsequently was endowed with more than a few arcane powers herself. Determining the best way to use these sorcerous powers, well, that was still an ongoing adventure in itself.

The old woman said, "I am Lamia, a daughter of Hecate and I sense that you are a powerful sister, you must help us. I know all the old magics and serve the Great Mother of a Thousand Young. But the magician holds the relic, and it must be returned for our salvation. Soon, the new moon is reborn. The stars are right tonight, the dead ones and the living."

Liz looked at her own sign, burned on to her palm. Her power was enabled in part by use of the hand motion that resembled the crosshatch sign. "Porter, maybe she is a sister of sorts to me in my own magical workings. I sense she holds power, but I don't know why she can't get the relic for herself?"

"Just ask her," he prodded.

"Why can't you retrieve the relic," Liz asked. "I can feel you have magical power too." She mimicked the symbol on the woman's arm with her finger in the air.

"You are daughter of the goddess too," the old woman said. "You can open the gate and will aid us. The magician has a ward against me and my daughters, a curse binding us from his home. But you can recover it, you and your man. You are not bound by his curse."

"I ain't her man," Porter said, "Just a friend."

Liz gave him a "hush now" look, signaling the old woman to continue.

The old woman wrinkled her nose at Porter, directing her words to Liz. "Please, you are not here by accident. The Great Mother with a Thousand Young brought you here now to help against our enemy, the magician. Please, sister, and we will help you with your machine."

"An evil magician, just great," Porter murmured as he instinctively felt for his gun in his vest pocket.

"Easy," Liz said. "I think we need to help them get it back."

"What about Gordon and the airship? We can't just go galavanting off."

"We'll talk to him. It doesn't look like this magician is very far away. Besides, they said they could help with repairs."

"Them? How? They don't know these machines any better than you do."

The old woman smiled and swirled her hands in the air, the two other women joined her and instantly a dust devil rose up beside them, swirling dust in a brown vortex. The woman moved her arm this way and that, showing that she controlled the direction and force of the dust devil.

"It seems she has some powers of the air and could help liberate our airship from the ground and make it easier for the crew to work on their repairs."

Porter was dubious but had to acknowledge the old woman's abilities. "I suppose so."

"All right we'll go get this relic," Liz said to Lamia. "What is it?"

The old woman drew the figure of a candelabra in the sand and said, "It is a gold-covered artifact to light the fire for the gate of the Great Mother. It is the opener of the way, the key to the silver door, the door that is between us and that of the Great Mother. It is presently locked. Quarinah will guide you there," she said gesturing to one of the young women beside her.

Porter shook his head at that. "Bunch of nonsense."

"It matters to them," Liz said. "Why shouldn't we assist those who need our help along the path of our way? Good karma, I should think."

"Karma," Porter sniffed.

They made themselves ready with minor provisions, more ammunition for Porter and several canteens for water. It was warm and would be hot by midday as they made their way out into the arid terrain. There were hills and scrub brush amidst the desert landscape, but Porter also noticed olive trees and the dry stream bed from before. It was not too unlike back home in the southwest United States.

The young woman, Quarinah, was acting as their guide. Her dark ebony hair spilled out from beneath her hood, and she did not adjust it back to how she had it earlier in front of Lamia. She cast hungry eyes at Porter several times and Liz was slightly suspicious of the woman's intent, but that was not the focus now. Quarinah spoke little besides mentioning that the house of the magician wasn't more than a mile or so beyond the hillside where the airship had crashed and that she believed they would reach it within the hour.

"There will likely be several men with guns protecting the magician," she told them.

Porter responded with, "Of course, all magicians have gunmen watching their backs these days," Porter said.

"We are almost there, just on the other side of this hill," Quarinah said. They rounded the small red hill and saw the house of the magician only a few hundred yards away. It was small, reminding Porter of a one-room schoolhouse. It was rectangular, about thirty feet long and twenty feet wide, and was made of wood which was visible where the brown plaster had broken off, the same color as the earth surrounding the building. The house was on flat terrain, but there were wavy, low-slung piles of dirt mounded nearby like dunes blown in from the desert. The building was topped with a thatched roof and a jagged stone chimney jutting overhead on its backside.

"If that's a bandit hideout, I'm a schoolmaster," Porter muttered at the sight.

"He doesn't have to be a bandit to be a thief," Liz said.

"These women folk seemed capable enough what with that wind magic. I don't know why they'd need us to take back a sacred key or whatever they called it."

"Sometimes it takes a new way of looking at things to get it done."

"True enough," Porter answered as he walked suspiciously from Liz to make sure someone wasn't watching from the far side of the house to possibly ambush them. "Keep back a bit until I get the lay of the land."

As Porter walked far enough to see around the corner of the house there was a man standing there, dressed in a long, flowing kaftan. He was taken by surprise by Porter's sudden appearance. He shouted something in alarm and picked up a long rifle that had been hidden in the folds of his robe.

"Easy," Porter said, holding his hands up, but the dark clad man tensed, and Porter guessed he was about to pull the trigger.

Porter dropped low and drew his own pistol as the man fired. Before the man could take aim again amidst the cloud of gun smoke, Porter put him down with a quick shot of his Browning automatic.

"Get down Liz, I think there are more," Porter shouted as he crouched beside a knee-high bit of brush and rocks to hide his presence. It wouldn't provide any true cover but the less exposed he was, the better. Quarinah moved in behind Porter, keeping low to avoid any possible incoming bullets.

"You should stay back, sister," Porter warned her.

Quarinah shook her head and crawled closer, as if she wanted to see everything that happened, and even help rush and attack the house.

Liz started to trot forward, watching anxiously, when another robed man sprang forward from a hiding place behind some barren rocks and started shooting at her. Bullets kicked up dirt not three feet in front of her.

A third, white-robed Turk rushed around the side of the building and fired a rifle at Porter and Quarinah

Liz started to work her magic to send a windstorm to repel the bullets from her direction, but something didn't work. She did the crosshatch sign and a glow formed in the air from her personal sigil. A wave of energy snapped forward and struck an invisible wall and dissipated. She wondered if she'd miscast while being distracted by the incoming bullets.

Porter shot the man firing at Liz first because he wasn't about to let anything happen to her. Then he pulled his second pistol and opened with both of them at the other opponent.

A fourth Turk came around the opposite side of the house and fired at Porter, catching him in a crossfire. The shot came dangerously close, whistling past Porter's ear before he returned fire. Porter's bullets caught the Turk in the chest, and he grunted loudly as he fell forward with blood flowing red onto his tan kaftan.

"Why are there so many at this little house?" Porter asked as he reloaded both pistols.

Quarinah answered, "Guards of the magician."

The final Turk raced back inside the house and fired again from a small trapdoor beside the stone chimney on the back wall.

Porter fired multiple times trying to create enough of a diversion so that he, Quarinah and Liz could find cover.

"You were saying something about these wouldn't be bandits?" Liz shouted.

Porter spat and reloaded his pistols before opening another barrage of lead at the shooter inside.

Liz called upon her powers with her crosshatch sign and sent a whirling dust devil at the house. But before it could reach the building it dissipated once more as if hitting an invisible wall of counter-magic. Liz was flummoxed. "That's twice now, I haven't seen anything like this before."

"It's all right, I'll get him," Porter said as he fired both his Browning automatic pistols in quick succession and rushed around the back side of the house and was right beside the spider-hole through which the Turk was firing.

"Be careful, there is something strange going on here," called Liz.

The Turk inside fired once more but this time Porter was beside the opening and as the rifle poked out a few inches. He had an idea and holstered his pistols. As the sniper poked his rifle out the spider-hole once more, Porter grabbed the end of the hot rifle barrel, yanking it through the door and disarming the shooter.

"Ow, that was hot!" Porter cried, waving his burned hand.

There was a cry of alarm from inside and a shout that sounded like a curse or threat.

Porter shook his head, grabbed his guns and wondering what they were yelling about. "I'll get to you soon enough, less'n you want to come out and surrender."

He saw Liz reach the side of the low dune not thirty feet from him.

"Stay put, can't have you getting hit with anything," he ordered.

"My powers don't work here," she said in obvious frustration. "It's like I'm nullified."

"What?"

"I can't use my magics to help," she shouted before ducking back down behind a low dune as a bullet ripped through the earth beside her, causing a cloud of dirt to fly into her eyes, obscuring her sight.

"Liz! You hit?"

"No, but that was awful close."

Porter shouted back, "Stay down, I'll handle this. Promise."

"I promise, but we should…"

"I got it, stay down!" Porter maneuvered back and forth, watching around the corners of the house.

"Wait!" Liz called out. "If my powers are dampened, there is magic afoot here. There must be a powerful sorcerer in there!"

"We already knew that!" Porter answered.

"I will help your friend," said Quarinah as she rushed forward to assist Porter.

"No just have him get back here!" Liz shouted as she ran.

A pistol fired from within the spider-hole and Porter could not fire back as the tiny door dropped down once more. He decided he would have to do the worst thing and rush the door. That was awfully dangerous but what else could he do? He looked at the roof. The jagged stones making up the chimney stuck out just enough that he dared climb them. He swiftly went up to the roof, watchful in case one of the Turks should come out with a gun again. Given they were up to four Turks and possibly the magician, there had to be a basement or they'd been awfully cramped in that one room house.

Quarinah followed Porter, climbing up the outside of the stone fireplace, sullying her robe, wary and silent though her look was hopeful and even pleased that he was attempting this unusual attack.

"Why is she climbing up with him? Why am I sitting here?" Liz muttered. She tried her magic again, and once more the powerful force of wind she attempted was dissipated in a counterspell. "Maybe I'll have to help the old-fashioned way."

Porter was at the top of the roof, carefully moving his feet on hidden wooden beams under the thatch to avoid falling through, and watching the shadows on either side of the house to be wary of anyone coming back out the front door. Quarinah made it up and stood beside Porter.

"You shouldn't have come up here," he whispered.

Shots rang out from the spider-hole toward Liz and Porter cursed, "Damnit." He fired straight down the chimney, knowing that while he couldn't see anything, the bullets would cause enough mayhem to confuse and slow down the shooter inside.

The shooting stopped.

Quarinah was grinning like she was enraptured staring at Porter, "You are wonderful," she said reaching out and wrapping her arms around him.

"No, you got the wrong idea, now ain't the time," Porter said as she stepped beside him and then there was a loud crack as the section of roof they were standing on buckled and broke.

They fell inside the house with a terrible crash.

Liz saw them fall through the roof and since the shooting had stopped, she ran forward with all haste and reached the front door and threw it open. She half expected the thunder of guns to be her welcome but there was only silence.

It was dim inside and it took a moment for her eyes to adjust. The place was full of bizarre curios and Middle Eastern décor. Carpets were across the floor and walls. A pair of hanging lamps were lit, but the shaft of sunlight from the hole in the roof was the source of most of the light inside.

Porter was in a tangle of thatch and on top of another person. Liz feared it was Quarinah until she saw that the ebony-haired woman was beside someone else in the corner.

"Porter, are you okay?" she asked.

"Got the wind knocked out of me, I think I've crushed Quarinah."

"No, she is fine, I think. Quarinah?"

"Here," said the woman as she stepped into the light, holding the golden candelabra. "It is done. You have helped us so much my friends," she said sounding triumphant.

"The magician?" Liz asked.

"He is dead," Quarinah said matter-of-factly, as she put away a bloody dagger.

Porter struggled to his knees and Liz bent to help him up while also watching Quarinah suspiciously. "Is there anyone else in here?

"Porter took care of the last man by landing on him."

Porter stood shakily, saying, "Yeah, I planned that all along," as he coughed and then took in a deep breath.

"What did you do?" Liz asked Quarinah.

"I landed on top of Porter and was unhurt, then I attacked the magician before he could cast a spell on us. I had to do it. It is done and justice is restored to this land," she said as she turned and looked at the magician and then spit upon him with obvious hatred.

Liz and Porter looked to one another.

"Now what?" Porter asked.

"Hopefully Lamia has been able to help Captain Gordon, and we can be on our way shortly."

Quarinah said, "They are not yet finished. Tomorrow you may go. Tonight, we celebrate our victory." She then liberated a large bottle of wine from beside a bookcase heavily weighted down with a variety of scrolls. "You will like this very much my friend," she said to Porter.

"How do you know that?" asked Liz.

"Can you not feel it? The magician is dead and his hold over this house is gone, I can now commune with Lamia, my mother."

"She is your mother?"

Quarinah nodded passionately.

"Like I asked before, now what should we do about this place?" Porter asked.

"It should be burnt. I will help you put the bodies in and we will torch this evil house."

Liz reached for her magics and could feel that the dampening force was gone. She decided she could give Quarinah the benefit of the doubt now, though there was something distasteful about how this adventure had turned out. Was she becoming numb to violence because of her continued association with Porter? She hoped she never became as numb to death as he and Quarinah seemed to be.

They dragged the fallen men back inside the house and Porter prepared an oil lamp to be tossed onto a pile of scrolls and other papers. Fire would cleanse this place. Quarinah insisted they need not worry over bandits or anyone else seeing the smoke and causing problems, this was a good day.

Porter lingered at the threshold for a moment. Quarinah and Liz were outside and beginning to walk back toward the airship when Porter heard a man coughing.

He gingerly put the lamp down and cautiously looked for the source of the cough with his gun drawn.

The old magician lay in a pool of his own blood. Quarinah had stabbed him viciously, but he had just regained consciousness and was not yet dead, though with this amount of blood loss, Porter knew the magician would not last long.

"Sorry old man, but when you wrestle the bull, you get the horns," Porter said.

The old man smiled grimly, "It is the way of the eternal round, but I ask you take this for your own protection from the Mothers of Darkness," he said holding out a small necklace. At the end of the chain was a golden trinket with a strange crosshatch mark that Porter had seen before though he could not remember where.

"What's this?" Porter gasped as the pendant burned his palm, and he tossed it aside. Looking at his palm, the sign was scorched there like a brand, though none was too bad. "Why you!" Porter snarled, glaring daggers at the magician.

"For your protection… in the night to come," said the old magician, as he coughed and visibly sagged, nearly finished by his final exertions. Blood was pooling ever larger beneath him.

"Who are you?" Porter asked.

"I was… the guardian of the gate. I held the door shut… so that the Great Mother of Darkness… could not come through. Now her… daughters… will open it… and you… will have… to close it." He breathed once more and was gone.

Porter wondered at the truth of things. He would ask Liz later what kind of magic she felt from the sign, without anyone else about.

Quarinah was at the door, "What happened? I heard you cry out."

"Nothing, I burnt my hand on the lamp. Let's go," he said as he tossed the lamp, and it caught fire to all the papers and rugs. Soon a black cloud roiled up and consumed the house of the magician.

It felt like a long dusty walk back to the airship and by the time they got there Porter was so parched he was ready to have that wine Quarinah offered, and he forgot his suspicions and telling Liz about the burnt sign on his palm.

Back at the airship, Captain Gordon and his crew had made progress, in part thanks to Lamia and her power of keeping the wind in just the right place to hold the envelope of the airship and allow them to work unencumbered.

"I believe we should be able to leave by late tomorrow morning," said Gordon.

"That's perfect," Liz said. "We got to help these people and, in the process, saw a brand-new place in the world."

"New?" he said. "This area is downright ancient. The Great Temple of Artemis was here, probably not more than half a league beyond those hills. Once this was a great city. Now it's just a great ruin."

"Is there anything to see over there now?"

Captain Gordon scratched at his chin and said, "Well, since you already made friends with some locals it is probably safe enough, and if I remember correctly there would be the ruin of the Artemision temple. Though there are only a few columns standing now."

Lamia said, "I would be honored to show you the temple."

Liz nodded excitedly. "I would like to see it. Porter, would you?"

Porter was already celebrating with the liberated bottle of wine and Quarinah. "I think I'm occupied. Just stay here, it's safer. Promise?"

"Promise," Liz lied.

Porter drank a conqueror's portion with Quarinah who was more than happy to keep refilling his cup. The wine was potent and tasted so good. Liz smelled it at one point but firmly declined having any herself. Soon darkness fell and Porter was asleep early with Quarinah lying in his arms. Liz didn't like that. Not from a romantic perspective, Porter was a father figure or maybe uncle. There was something she didn't trust about the ebony-haired woman. But it seemed harmless enough at this point.

Lamia and the other daughter stood before Liz. She said, "The stars are right, we should go to the temple, and you will see the great unveiling in the night."

"Do you mean like a constellation?"

"Yes, of course, it is the least I can do for you since you rescued the key for us. It is a great honor we have to show you."

Her English was slightly flawed, but Liz was sure she was grateful and excited to show her some mystical scene at the temple. She glanced at Porter, snoring away drunk with Quarinah in his arms. "All right, I'll go but let us be back by morning." All reservations were gone now that she saw Porter curl over and nuzzle Quarinah.

"Most assuredly," replied Lamia.

Liz looked up and saw the new moon hiding behind a wide bank of clouds. "Maybe we won't be able to see anything with these clouds. What am I saying? You have the power of the winds and can move the clouds away."

"Yes, we can. Come with us. You don't want to be late for the opening of the way," said the younger woman as she blew a cloud of dust into Liz's face and then smiled. The cantrip worked and Liz was neither threatened nor offended. She drowsily nodded.

"I'm getting sleepy," Liz said, briefly halting in her walk as if she might turn around and remain at the airship.

"The stars are never sleeping, the dead ones and the living," said Lamia, repeating the curious phrase from before. "Let us go." She tugged on Liz's sleeve guiding her away.

Quarinah's eyes shot open as she knew her mother and the others walked away with Liz. She had been playing possum and could now enact the other half of their plan. Tonight was the night, the stars were right, the dead ones and the living.

She reached into her girdle and withdrew the very same dagger she had used to murder the magician. She murmured her private invocation to the Mother of Darkness, offering up the blood of this man who had been used as a tool to enact their revenge against the forces of Nodens. She raised the dagger…

In the midst of a dream, Porter wandered a strange landscape. Colors and terrain were different here and though it was all new to him, it was not disturbing or unsettling. A voice called to him from across the waters of a sunlit sea…

"Awake Porter and know this is the time to act. Use the symbol as a key, a key to lock the door again."

The symbol that had been burned on his palm floated in the air, growing and shimmering, strange and powerful. The voice echoing, emanated from the massive floating glyph.

Just before Quarinah plunged the dagger down, Porter blinked awake and raised his hands, the burned palm sigil struck Quarinah on the forehead and burned with the fire of ages. She screamed in wretched fear and dropped the dagger. Red light shot from her eyes and mouth as scintillating power flowed like a river from the sigil.

Porter was as dumbfounded as she was, though he did not feel the burning sensation.

Quarinah fell dead, smoke issuing from her sockets.

"Liz!" he got up and glanced around their encampment. She was nowhere to be found.

"That girl, she went with the women folk off toward the Temple of Artemis, just beyond that hill there," said one of the workman, roused by Porter's shouting.

Not waiting for any more information, Porter ran toward the glow he could see from the cleft of the distant hillside.

Life moved like a dream, and Liz was led on flowery paths through towering marble ruins and fluted columns until they reached the sunken floor of a great amphitheater. An altar of stone was at the head of the sunken platform, and she felt firm hands guide her to the altar and lay her down upon it. Then these same hands put stout ropes on her limbs and drew them tight stretching her body between them. She was still in a dreamlike state and felt no awareness of danger or fear. It just was.

The candelabra that she had helped retrieve from the old magician was placed in a socket on the side of the altar as if it were made for that exact spot. Lamia anointed it with oil and muttered over it, running her hands across its spindly form.

A half dozen unfamiliar faces leered at her and joined in chant. The words now grew ominous, and Liz sensed that this was not a safe meeting of the minds. Grim portents fouled the air as braziers were lit and pungent incense was burned amid the droning of the cultist's veneration of their evil goddess.

"Ia! Shub-Niggurath! Almighty Goat with a Thousand Young! Come to us! We the Black Mothers invoke you!" the chanters cried out in an alien language that somehow they all understood. A pinprick of deepness formed and swirled not a dozen strides from the altar. Winds blasted as the gate grew exponentially larger. The awareness of impending dread brought Liz back to reality, and then the fear took hold as she saw the cultists invoke and summon her doom.

Somewhere in the world beyond the gate stirred a titanic infernal thing. Hooves stepped in a chaotic, misshapen gait, coming closer to the doorway between worlds waiting for it to open wide enough that it might step through into our realm. The bleating of its young was deafening. Rancid odors filled Liz's nostrils, and she screamed mutely while the witches finalized their dark invocation.

Porter moved soft as a cat, stepping on dry grass and avoiding those sharp, grasping branches of olive trees. But one misstep and he trod on a rotted branch that snapped like a dry bone.

Cursing softly, he was almost glad when he became aware of the ruckus down in the sunken amphitheater. A wind was picking up amid the chanting of cultists and the fires would make them night blind.

The firelight put an orange, rusty glow over everything in the clearing, even the standing stones, which leaned like mute sentinels over the circular depression.

Winds whipped about and the clouds in the sky were moving far too fast. He had seen twisters before out on the prairies crossing the states, but this was different. There wasn't a shaft of whirlwind reaching from the horizon to the sky. Instead it was like it was on its side and facing toward himself and the rest of the people gathered at the temple base. A vortex threatening to suck them all in to God knew where. That should be impossible, but he had seen enough strange things in his time to know this must be dark sorcery.

The light and darkness, the very coloration at the mouth of this wind was unnatural, too. It seemed like a doorway open to a different world where it was not night as it was here. The arid land here had its own smell and dryness, while the portal exuded a wretched, fungal scent. Movement caught his eye as if bats or some night birds had ventured across that wicked threshold and were rapidly approaching. Instinct guided his hands as he reached for his pistols.

He didn't want to give away his position or reveal himself to the witches just yet, but he had little choice. The flying things were heading straight for him as if they were black winged moths and he was the flame. But though they resembled gigantic insects, they were not moths. A droning buzz emanated from their wings, and they had sinister-looking pincers, and a large black stinger curling forward from their abdomen like they were flying scorpions.

Porter drew both Browning automatic pistols, aimed and fired. The buzzing things were close and menacing but he did not miss. His shots echoed in the night, muzzle flashes sending up a signal as to his exact location. He warily ceased after striking down a half-dozen buzzing things and changed position, moving down three of the great pillars just in case any of the human opponents were coming, so he would not be standing where they had last seen the muzzle reports.

The giant flying insects were not so easily fooled, seeing in the darkness far better than any human could. They followed Porter and he was forced to almost immediately open fire again. As one zoomed past him, he felt its stinger shear across his coat. It was like a knife caught the heavy wool and tugged. It yanked him off balance for a half second. This was ultimately a good thing as an acolyte of the witch priestess sent an arrow his way. It bounced off the stone pillar and shattered right where he had just been.

Porter rounded the great column and took aim at the new opponents as well as those flying about. There had to be at least a dozen and only the first acolyte was armed with a bow, the others had old single-shot smoothbore muskets, remainders from the Crimean War. These sent out piercing loud shots that crackled on the stone around him. At least he had good cover, unless they reconnoitered and surrounded him. But they may have also been distracted as the opening doorway grew larger and the winds cascaded from the elemental plane opening intensified to gale force.

Porter dared a glance down into the abyss toward Liz. She looked awake now but had been bound as tight as a wrapped mummy. He had to reach her soon before that dark gulf opened entirely and the giant hulking thing beyond could traverse the edge.

He dodged quickly as one of the giant insect things buzzed past him. He turned and shot the thing, foul ichor splashing across the stone pavers, sizzling as it hit the marble. Another arrow whipped past and then a volley of shots. There had to be no less than a dozen guardsmen all focusing on him now instead of the ritual. They were moving, working at getting him caught in a crossfire and he didn't have anywhere else to hide now.

Liz was groggy but felt like she might be coming around. The horrifying chanting continued. Whatever they had done to her had worked. Her head throbbed, and her thoughts were muddy. But she knew she didn't like being bound and laying on an altar. She knew that sure as shooting.

Shooting? Someone was shooting. Porter? She tried to call out to him to help her, but only a gurgle issued forth. Then she became aware that part of her confusion was because of the gale force winds surrounding her, that and the strange droning of the witches that stood over her.

She strained at the bindings. They itched and were tight as anything, her hands were turning blue. What could she do? Thoughts flowed slowly like molasses, but she knew she didn't want to be there. She would try her own spells, her own power. She couldn't perform the crosshatch with her hands fully, but her fingers—numb as they were—could still move. She waved them in the pattern as she mumbled her own counteroffensive spell.

She caused a blast of air, which bowled the witches over. They had been standing fast against the rift that was growing, and Liz's gust had come from the opposite direction. Instantly Liz felt some of the grogginess dissipate. They were causing her mind-numbness. Now, she could at least shout her defiance. She shouted more loudly than she ever had since the disaster in London.

The altar beneath her cracked and broke in half. The magical candelabra—the key between worlds—slipped from its socket and tilted awkwardly, allowing her to slip from half of her bindings. Her hands were still held above her head, but her feet kicked free from the rotting rope. She rolled off the altar and stood on unsteady legs, her hands still bound, facing the witches who were themselves getting up and dusting themselves off.

Hateful eyes glared at Liz.

"I'm not one to take this kindly," Liz said, as she drew forth her own magical working. She burned away her bonds and was free.

The old crone wearing Lamia's face flared in anger as she squinted and pointed a long crooked wand toward Liz, but Liz shouted once more and sent it flying away.

Another barrage of counterspells sent the witches tumbling over one another. This time the old crone did not get up. She looked broken, hanging limp over a slab of Roman carved stone.

Porter was racing toward her, firing wildly into the air.

"Porter! I think I got them!"

"Not yet," he shouted as he almost knocked her down and had her take cover beside the altar. It was only then she realized he wasn't wildly shooting in the air but was taking down some kind of birds that were swooping and diving toward them. Then as he shot one that was perilously close, she realized with horror that they were not birds but gigantic wasp-like creatures with bulbous eyes, furiously beating wings and stingers as big as ink quills.

"Whatever gate they opened, you've gotta shut Liz!" he roared against the howling winds.

"I don't know how! I'm only just waking up to this!"

He held up a hand and she saw the burn on his palm.

"Where did you get that?" Liz called.

"The mark? The old magician wasn't quite dead and handed me a necklace. It burned this sign on my hand," he paused to aim and shoot a pair of the cultist soldiers that ran between the columns. "He said it was a key to shutting the door, but I ain't no magician. I don't know how to use it."

"I think I do," Liz said, as she traced the sign in the air before her repeatedly, then turned and faced the swirling gateway. The colossal behemoth beyond was at the threshold. It was a cloudy, swirling thing like the darkest thunderhead, and innumerable hooved feet rolled beneath like a millipede rushing ever closer. Dark tentacles shot out and retracted from the cloudlike form, gyrating and pulsing in a gross hypnotic dance.

Porter cursed and reloaded his guns as he placed himself between Liz and the attacking cultists. They were getting bolder, running forward shouting an unintelligible war cry. He snapped the magazines into the Browning automatics and fired, gunning down a trio of the acolytes.

Liz made the new sign, and a glow formed in the air from her powerful sigil. A wave of energy snapped forward and struck the gateway and the gigantic thing beyond made a thunderous gurgle and pushed against the now closing portal.

It shrank and diminished and yet the thing on the other side pushed and roared. A dozen of the tentacles came through and flailed wildly to reach its antagonists, but Liz stepped behind Porter and the altar for shelter and was just beyond their reach. Then the portal winked out of existence with a staccato crack and the winds that had been so powerful vanished. The dull absence of sound was itself disturbing and the final pair of acolyte guardsman saw themselves alone.

The gate was closed, the dark priestess Lamia was dead, and their gambit gone with her. They turned and fled into the night, Porter sending a few pieces of lead at their heels.

"I think I've learned a valuable lesson about people that want my help," Liz said.

"Oh?" Porter grunted in response.

"I'll be just a little more hesitant if something seems too coincidental."

Porter laughed and said, "Now you're sounding like me."

A Drive in the Goat Woods

A Captain Cross Adventure

By David Hambling

They spoke of old Keziah Mason, and Elwood agreed that Gilman had good scientific grounds for thinking she might have stumbled on strange and significant information. The hidden cults to which these witches belonged often guarded and handed down surprising secrets from elder, forgotten aeons; and it was by no means impossible that Keziah had actually mastered the art of passing through dimensional gates. Tradition emphasizes the uselessness of material barriers in halting a witch's motions; and who can say what underlies the old tales of broomstick rides through the night?

—HP Lovecraft, "Dreams in the Witch House"

Tam saw an unco sight!
Warlocks and witches in a dance.
Nae cotillion brent-new frae France,
But hornpipes, jigs, strathspeys, and reels
Put life and mettle in their heels.
A winnock bunker in the east,
There sat Auld Nick in shape o' beast

—Robert Burns, "Tam O'Shanter"

Chapter One

London, 1928

Captain Cross could not get over his surprise that Cranley had picked him up in a brand-new motor car. Cranley, the most retired and bookish of men, had rarely been known to venture out into the open air. He had been seen in the back of a cab, but driving was a complete departure for him. And yet, Cross found himself in the passenger seat of a shiny Austin Seven four-seater, which his friend, resplendent in a car coat, was piloting with more enthusiasm than skill.

A change had come over Cranley, and Cross was still trying to fathom it. With his thinning hair and unhealthy pale complexion, Cranley did not resemble the hearty fellows directing their new machines about the streets of London and talking loudly about crank horsepower and overhead valves. But there was a glow to him, a newfound zest. Mr. Toad was not more pleased with his new car than Cranley.

"When did you become a motorist?" Cross asked.

"Just lately," said Cranley. "And for a good reason. All will become clear in due course."

Cranley had been deucedly mysterious about the whole matter. He had engaged Cross to assist in collecting a book, without saying why he needed assistance.

Cross was in the business of hunting down books. In his more self-pitying moments, he saw himself as a broken-down, one-legged ex-officer pursuing ridiculous errands to stave off melancholy. Generally though, he saw himself as an adventurer, on intriguing quests—more often successful than not—to find and retrieve mysterious books which others did not even believe existed. Only the man who Cross always mentally referred to as The Turk could match him when it came to esoteric and occult works. If a collector sought an arcane book which nobody else could track down, Cross was their man.

Cross had never stolen a book and would never do so. He had helped return one to its rightful owner using direct methods though, and a gun could be useful to emphasize the point. Cross had shot, or shot at, what might be termed for want of a better coinage supernatural creatures, and he knew the limitations of firearms even against apparently human beings.

Nothing had killed him so far, despite the machinations of The Turk. Cross had been able to relish his life of danger, getting close—but never too close—to death.

"Did you notice the mascot?" asked Cranley.

There was a little silver statue over the car radiator. There was a fashion for custom hood ornaments reflecting their owners' interests.

"It's St. Dunstan," said Cranley. "He who defeated the Devil."

"Very apt, I'm sure," said Cross, though the modernist, stylized design could have been anyone. "You could at least tell me what you brought me along for."

"There's a street map on the shelf by your feet," said Cranley. "If you could guide us towards Norwood that would be topping. I'm not much good south of the river."

"You're not much good out of your front door, old man," said Cross, unfolding the map. "Go down Park Lane for Vauxhall Bridge, that's what the cabbies do."

Cross, formerly a dedicated cavalryman, had never been fond of internal combustion engines. The Austin was a flimsy, lightweight vehicle, little more than a four-wheeled motorcycle with a tent over it, decidedly less comfortable than the grander roadsters. And yet, seeing Cranley gamely struggling with the double clutch, feeling the thrum of the engine as the world went past in a blur, he understood the appeal of fast machines.

Once they had navigated the worst of the traffic, conversation resumed.

"You trust my judgement, don't you, Cross? You know I'm not mad."

"You've been mad for as long as I've known you," said Cross. "Your peculiar interest in—nay fascination with—the occult has confirmed you as at least 'eccentric'. The condition has progressed to the point where you've shunned the company of your fellow men and surrounded yourself with books. You've been frittering away your fortune in the futile pursuit of a crazed theory about an ancient witch cult instead of enjoying yourself."

Cranley had been contributing his modest addenda to an academic project. He had helped trace out the descent from the Hebrew Azazel and Pharaonic Banebdjedet, to the Celtic Cernunnos and the Basque Aberbeltz, and even Shub-Niggurath of the *Necronomicon*, each taking the form of a black goat, and weaving them all into an aboriginal, pagan religion. Eliphas Levi had popularized the occult Sabbatic Goat as a cosmic force a generation earlier, now his disciples were fleshing out his theories.

Cross found it all highly dubious. He suspected the truth was darker and more complex, and probably beyond the comprehension of human minds. But scholars always wanted to tidy things up.

"When you put it like that, old man, I sound bonkers," said Cranley, with a rueful laugh.

"Almost as deranged, in fact, as myself. And we have now the emergence of a full-blown Don Quixote Complex," Cross continued. "When you—who I've never seen breathe fresh air—venture out, I assume you've been gripped by the same mania. Too many books and you're off chasing windmills!"

"That I won't allow," said Cranley. "My plan of action is concrete and directed to specific goals, driven by robust logical reasoning."

"If it's like the rest of your work, it's as flimsy as the garments of the showgirls in those West End productions you used to enjoy," said Cross. "Before you took your vows and pledged yourself to books."

"As a matter of fact, I have been seeing women. One woman. We're engaged to be married."

That was quite a thunderbolt. And perhaps the explanation for Cranley's unusual glow and cheerful mood.

"Good Lord! Congratulations to you both. Who's the lucky lady?"

Cranley's previous relationships had been with eminently suitable, if dull young ladies, as he lacked the skills to corner unsuitable ones.

"More on her anon," said Cranley. "Ellen is the pivot on which this whole matter turns."

"The plot thickens!"

"It does. But, by and large, you trust me when I tell you that a certain book surely exists?"

"By and large, I would."

"And if I told you that this book is priceless and can only be acquired with a certain degree of personal risk?"

Cross smoothed his moustaches. Cranley was a scholar, a book collector, a good customer, and a friend of some years standing. He was not a man of action. A weak chest had left him unfit for service in the War. Cranley had never participated in riding, hunting, shooting or even angling so far as Cross knew.

"I'd say you were poaching on my territory, old boy," he said.

"Haha! Yes, well, it's a two-man job. I can do the driving and get us where we need to go—hence this fine machine!" He patted the steering wheel. "But I will need you for some of the practical aspects."

Cross cocked an eyebrow, but Cranley, intent on the road, did not see. What with the noise and the lack of eye contact, conversations in cars were unsatisfactory.

"I believe this is the approach to Norwood Bus Garage—yes indeed. Our first stop, if I can just park this thing."

After finally fitting the Austin into a parking space, but without any explanation, Cranley approached a conductor as he got off the number 46 bus. The man was finishing his shift and looked up at the tall, thin scholar warily.

"Excuse me, is your name Deakins?" Cranley asked.

The man's weary countenance did not convey enthusiasm for a continuation of his working day, but he forced a pleasant smile.

"Yes sir, it is," he said. "May I help you at all?"

"I think you can," said Cranley. "It's a question of business. I'm a book collector, you see...."

"If it's the Lost Property Office, they're on the first floor," said the conductor. "It'll be open tomorrow at ten a.m."

"Nothing like that. I believe you have something I'd like to buy, Deakins. I'd like to make an offer."

"I think you're mistaken, sir," Deakins said, moving to depart. "I'm afraid I have to go."

"This is a business matter," said Cross, taking the man's sleeve. "Cash on the nail, and all perfectly legitimate."

Cross did not know whether this was true, but the mention of the word "cash" acted like a charm. And while Deakins might have brushed off one gentleman as an eccentric, the presence of two of them made the thing look more businesslike.

"Obviously I'll help if I can," Deakins said.

"Josiah Deakins was your great-uncle, I believe?" asked Cranley.

"Why yes, that he was, sir."

"I say," said Cranley "Is there somewhere I can buy you a cup of tea rather than the three of us standing out on the street?"

Deakins was not slow to spot an opening.

"There's a perfectly good pub just here," he said, nodding to a building opposite. "No sense in drinking tea like a lot of old women when the Horns is open."

Deakins improved further inside when refreshment was provided. He loosened his tie, sat back and raised his glass, happy to rent out his attention for a pint.

"Thing is, Mr. Cranley, Great-uncle Josiah didn't leave me a thing, and certainly not any books," Deakins said, with an imitation of polite regret. "So, I'm afraid I don't have anything for you."

Cranley was not fazed in the slightest.

"He was something of a rogue, Josiah Deakins," said Cranley, "according to rumor."

"More than a rogue, I'd say! A regular black sheep. He ran with a gang of roughs off in the woods, back in the day when there were woods to run around in. There are stories about them. They'd take anything that wasn't nailed down. Stole piglets from farms and roasted 'em on a fire. Burned down barns for the fun of it. And women weren't safe!" Deakins shook his head, wondering at how this suburban district had once been a shadowy woodland where the police hardly ventured. "I can tell you a parcel of stories, if that's what you're after."

"Did you ever hear tell," said Cranley, licking his lips. "Of dark rituals, pagan practices...."

"Oh yes! Bonfires and goats and altars and all that. Devil worship! Three parts messing around to one part acting up to scare people."

Deakins swigged his beer. "Josiah and his mates got up to some pranks all right."

"But he was really a diabolist?" Cranley asked.

"So they say. The vicar whipped him when he was a boy, and old Josiah hated the church his whole life." Deakins' beer was going down fast. He was not expecting the conversation to last long. "They say he couldn't open his mouth without blaspheming. All that devil-worship stuff was just out of spite."

This was clearly old family lore to Deakins, who seemed to rather enjoy the infamy of his relative from a safe distance. Josiah Deakins was a cherished villain rather than an embarrassing secret.

"Until he was murdered."

"When you knock about with that sort of crowd it's all stabbings and whatnot," Deakins said, philosophically. "Being on the buses is hard work, but nobody tries to knife you over a sixpenny fare."

"They say he had a book," said Cranley, "where he kept the names of those who had made a pact."

"That's not the half of it," said Deakins, happy to contribute his expertise. He leaned forward confidentially. "What they say is that when the gang initiated a new member, they'd all get up in cloaks and hoods and sit around a fire. And one of them would dress up as the Devil, with a mask and horns, and after a lot of tomfoolery, including drinking seven times seven, the new man would have to sign his name to a contract in a big book like you said. And then the Devil put his mark on the contract, and on the man too, to remind him—branded him with a hot iron!"

Deakins made a branding gesture with both hands.

"Good grief," said Cross.

"A devil's mark was a common identifying feature in many European witch trials," said Cranley.

"The thing was," said Deakins, "it meant they could never deny being one of the gang, not with the devil's mark branded on them. They were in it for life—name in the book, mark on the arm. Deakins had them on the hook... so, being an old book collector, you're after that book, are you?"

"I am."

"Like I told you, I haven't got it—never saw it, never heard anyone say who might have got it." Deakins drained the last of his beer and shrugged. "And that's all I can tell you about it."

Cross knew of Faustian contracts in various occult collections. Some were obvious fabrications, like the one used to convict the French priest Urbain Grandier. Some had been drawn up in good faith by men who wanted to get whatever they could for their souls and hoped to attract the attention of the Evil One. Many, like Christoph Haizmann's crazed tract written in his own blood, were the work of obvious lunatics. Dr. Freud had made a good case out of Haizmann's "demoniacal neurosis."

An entire book of such contracts would certainly be a valuable item.

"According to my research, the book would fall to you if it was found," said Cranley. "It's your inheritance."

"Doesn't do me much good, does it?" Deakins eyed his empty glass. "Could be anywhere."

"But you can sell me the title to it. Here, I'll give you a pound for it." Cranley had his wallet out and extracted a pound note which he displayed. "Cross, if you'll write up a receipt for legal title to Josiah Deakins' *Book of Names*—"

"I've told you I can't give it to you," cautioned Deakins.

From the receipt pad he carried with him, Cross quickly jotted out in a neat hand.

"'If and when found,'" said Cross, writing it in. "It's all correct. Just sign here."

Deakins tried not to look at the money. A cleverer or greedier man might have bargained.

Deakins seemed more worried that this unexpected windfall would vanish before he could get his hands on it.

"Here, you two aren't devil worshippers, are you?" he said as he took the pen.

Money for nothing was too good to be true. Deakins was trying to work out what the catch was.

"Far from it ," said Cranley, placing the pound note on the table and slipping a black book from his pocket. "I can swear on the Bible if you'd like."

"No need," said Deakins, signing his name quickly, and they closed the deal with a handshake. "I hope you gentlemen find Josiah's book, and it's worth the money. But you watch yourselves. I'm not superstitious... but I wouldn't go messing about with the Devil myself."

With this sage advice he made his way to the bar to spend some of his unexpected bounty.

Chapter Two

"Sorry old man, but I smell a rat," said Cross when they were back in the car. "A whole nest of 'em. Firstly, when did you ever 'hear rumors' about anyone or anything? Secondly, what would you know about gangs in Victorian South London? And thirdly —and majorly—what in blue blazes inspired you to buy a car and come and investigate in person?"

"Aren't you a little impressed?" said Cranley. "I've just bought a priceless book for one pound."

"You could have got it for two shillings and a couple of whiskies," said Cross, "assuming it exists. I'm not letting you off the hook. Let me guess, it's this Helen, isn't it?"

"You have an uncanny knack. As a matter of fact, it is. You see, her great-grandfather signed his name in that book. He pledged not just his own soul, but the souls of his children and their children, 'unto the seventh generation'."

"And why does she want the book?"

"To void the pact. Burning the book will invalidate the Devil's bargain and save her soul."

Cross cocked a skeptical eyebrow.

"That's a new one on me, old man."

"It's a legal contract. As with a will or any other piece of legal work, if you can't produce the signed paper, legally speaking there is no pact. The Devil is an absolute stickler on points of law and loopholes. *Faust* is clear on that."

"You of all people should know how unreliable *Faust* is," said Cross. "Folklore is a pretty screen, placed to hide ugly truths."

Cross had frequently regaled Cranley with tales of his exploits. Cranley listened with interest but took them with a pinch of salt. Anything not written in a book—preferably one a century or two old— was just hearsay as far as he was concerned.

"Ellen believes it to be true. And, as her fiancé, I am determined that her wish will be carried out. I told her I would do it! Hence the new motor car, and my sparing no expense in getting you to assist."

Suddenly, it all made a great deal of sense. Cranley was an intelligent man, but an innocent in the ways of the world.

"Let me make a guess," said Cross. "Your inamorata is at least ten years younger, and rather better looking than you. She dresses fashionably, not that you'd know. You met her somewhere completely by chance, and not too long ago. Somehow, you fell to talking, and you bonded immediately when you discovered—*quelle surprise!*—a shared interest in books relating to diabolism."

Cranley's face colored.

"I've seen less plausible plots in musical comedies," Cross went on, "but seldom in real life. It's a set-up, old man."

"It's true that everything I know about Josiah Deakins came from her, but I'm not sure what you're insinuating." Cranley's knuckles gripping the wheel were white.

"That you're being played like a fiddle. This girl, or perhaps her employer, wants this book. You are their means of getting it."

"If that's the way you feel about it, I shall drop you off at Tulse Hill Station. You are talking about the woman I love."

"Oh, don't take on, Cranley. Airs don't suit you. I never said I wouldn't do it, I just want to see how the ground lies. "

"You are mistaken about Ellen," said Cranley, coldly.

"I assure you, I'll apologize fully if I am—to her face, if you like—but you cannot be too cautious in this business. There is trickery at every turn."

Cranley's expression softened.

"Huh. You are a hopeless paranoid, Cross. I suppose that's understandable given how often people try to defraud you. Your world may be full of trickery, but you'll find my Ellen is unimpeachable."

"Wait a minute, wait a minute," said Cross. "Did you say her name was 'Ellen' or 'Helen'?"

"The former."

"And her great-grandfather signed a pact with the Devil, in Norwood?" It was too much to be a coincidence. "Tell me, Cranley, does this young lady happen to have a tattoo on her ankle?"

Cranley almost ran over a cyclist.

"How the devil do you know that?"

"I knew it was Ellen Edmonds! I met her over those Apophis scrolls."

He was referring to Cranley's efforts to make connections between the pharaoh Neferkara and the Black man of European witch cults. Cranley had been in possession of two of the scrolls; the Edmonds family had the rest of the set. "I visited the family home to take a *shufti*. She's the family librarian... or was."

Cross was a middleman, seeking out rare books for people willing to pay large sums for them. If he put buyers and sellers in touch with each other without any prior negotiation, he would quickly be cut out of any deals. Yet, somehow, Miss Edmonds and Cranley had made contact.

"Yes, she told me all about that."

Cross opened his mouth wordlessly. The visit had culminated in several deaths and Ellen Edmonds making a decisive break with her family. When Cross last saw her, she was supposed to be fleeing the country. How much had she told Cranley? And how much of that bizarre tale would he believe?

"If you know about her family...."

"She is a rose growing from a dunghill," said Cranley. "You cannot compare her to them."

Miss Edmonds was a genuine initiate into the dark arts, born into a family which carried out practices imported from Egypt, which would do more than raise eyebrows if they were known. He believed she was now on the straight and narrow, but she had been exposed to dark things.

"Indeed not. Drive on, Macduff!" said Cross. "But you haven't told me where we're going. Who has the book?"

"It's more a matter of where," said Cranley, recovering his previous jauntily mysterious manner. "We're going to the library for a map."

A dark green car pulled out in front of them, causing Cranley to swerve and brake, and Cross to grab the dashboard.

"Road hog!" shouted Cranley, leaning on the horn.

"Appalling driving," said Cross.

The green car had stopped directly in front of them and two young men stepped out, dressed in matching check suits and caps. For a moment Cross wondered whether this might be an ambush.

But the star tattoos on his wrist, which burned at any supernatural hazard, were quiescent. And before they had taken two steps, Cross had the measure of the two men: athletic, boorish and irate. The sort of men who jokingly called their cars "Hellflether" or "Hensdeath" but took great pride in their driving. Their hands were already balled into fists as they strode toward the Austin.

"Oh no," said Cranley, shrinking away at the chance of an altercation.

Cross opened his door to meet them.

"What the devil do you mean by that?" asked one, pink with rage. "'Road hog', eh?"

He seemed genuinely outraged to have his driving skill publicly called into question, even though he was obviously in the wrong,

"Blasted tin toys shouldn't be on the road," said the other, giving the Austin a hefty shove so it rocked back and forth. "Or their idiot drivers."

"No need to get over-exercised now, chaps," said Cross, leaning on his stick, giving them a chance to register his friendly manner and his regimental tie. "Just a near miss, no harm done. My friend is new to driving, you see, and he was a bit startled."

"Your friend needs to get out and apologize," snapped the driver. Cranley seemed to be trying to disappear behind the wheel. "Or he'll have some dented panels to remember us by—and a dented face."

He gave the bodywork an experimental thump, looking at Cranley. The men were too young to have served in the War, and they did not have the manners of ex-soldiers. Other measures were needed. Pistols weighed down the pockets of his long coat and Cross reached into the right-hand one.

"Not unless you want a couple of flat tires," he said, pointing the Mauser casually at the nearest wheel on the green car.

Both men registered shock.

Cross pressed the advantage before they could recover. "Now, why don't you two boys just shove off before things turn nasty, eh?"

Cross had dealt with many bullies. He was quite prepared to back up the threat if he had to, and face the consequences, legal and otherwise. It was rarely necessary. This type crumbled when they met resistance, and the pair turned tail and got back into their machine at speed, taking off with a screech of tires.

"I was flustered there," said Cranley. "Brought back my days at public school. Those fellows looked like brutes."

"They're quite common in my world," said Cross. "One learns to handle them."

It was late opening at the library. Normally there would only be a harried assistant on duty to stamp books out and take tickets, but they were met practically at the door by Hoade, the Assistant Head Librarian.

"Captain Cross, nice to see you again," he said, shaking hands. "And Mr. Cranley, I believe?"

"You know each other?" Cranley asked.

"Hoade is the essential archivist for local Norwood matters," said the Captain. "Our paths have crossed."

"I believe you were looking for the Goat House, Mr. Cranley," said Hoade, leading them to a side table where yellowed maps were laid out. "I couldn't find any reference further back than 1678, which I believe was the same as your source."

"Curious name," said Cross, casting an eye over a map, careful not to touch it.

"Just there," said Hoade, indicating with a wooden pointer. "Our eminent local historian, J. Corbet Anderson, opines that the Goat House was originally a deer-house or hunting box."

"That's a hunting lodge," Cross explained to Cranley. "For weary huntsmen to get a bite and take their repose."

"Though that's supposition," Hoade said. "Afterwards it was a farm, and for the past sixty years or so it's been a hotel. The Goat House Hotel. I believe they keep still goats in the back garden to amuse the children."

Hoade did not look like the sort of man who spent much time in pubs and likely had extracted the information from the books around him as a tree draws in water. Like Cranley, his only acquaintance with actual forests was after they had been cut down, pulped and converted into books.

"It is somewhere very close to the Goat House," said Cranley confidently, looking from the old map of the area to the new. "Everywhere in the world, it starts deep in the woods with goats, and it spreads to humans."

"This is the goddess Astarte, is it?" asked Hoade innocently.

"Astarte my foot," Cranley snapped. "Or perhaps you haven't seen Stafford's work on the Magna Mater and meteorite cults? No, they're a different breed, chalk and cheese."

"It's easy to lose track of what is heresy and what is orthodoxy in your world," said Cross, "It changes with every new paper."

But Cranley was lost in contemplation of the map. "Not much woodland left, is there?"

"There are stands of trees here, and here," said Hoade. "I haven't been able to find your ancient oak, but if there is anything left, it'll be there. We have a few named trees in Norwood. I can show you the site of the Vicar's Oak and the Elder Oak, the Turkey Oak and even the misnamed Oak of Arnon. But the Black Goat or Goat's Oak never made it to the cartographers."

"How far could you go back?"

"We have the most complete account of the area. Nothing noteworthy I'm afraid. But," said Hoade, brightening, "there is something from the earlier days. The Goat House area was known as Chelmerden, Shelmerdines, or Shelverdine. Which derives from the Old English name Ceolmer and the Old English Dun, meaning a hill. It was Ceolmer's Hill."

"Ceolmer," said Cranley. "Could it have originally been Cernun? Cernun's Hill?"

"Perhaps," said Hoade. "Names change. Croydon was once Crog Denu."

"Cernun as in Cernunnos," inferred Cross. "He being the great horned god of the Celts, Lord of the Woods et cetera. Sometimes depicted with goat horns."

"That's my theory," said Cranley.

As with Cranley's other theories, it allowed him to trace a continuous thread from pagan times to the present day, if you squinted a bit. It might even be correct, but it would never convince a serious historian.

"Only if you can make Ceolmer equal Cernun," said Cross. "But you might as well claim it was Cthulhu."

Cranley shot him a dirty look. He had no sense of humor about his subject.

"The *Black Goat Oak* must be here, or here," Cranley said, finger hovering over the area.

"I've hand-drawn you a copy," said Hoade, interposing a sheet of paper between Cranley and the precious map. "With the modern street names for reference."

"Excellent," said Cranley, taking it. "Shouldn't take too long to find it."

"Good, good," said Hoade. "I'm sure you know what you're doing."

But Hoade raised a quizzical eyebrow at Cross when Cranley was not looking.

Cross raised his hands in surrender.

They were soon back in the car. The daylight was draining away fast, and this time Cross insisted that they make a stop, partly for some food but mainly for another purpose.

"Listen to me, Cranley," said Cross, placing a hand on his friend's shoulder as they stood outside the cafe. "I want you to take what I tell you seriously."

"Of course."

"We are about to visit a place unfamiliar to you, where you do not know the rules of conduct and might give offence without meaning to. Here is my guide: imagine that we are entering some windswept mountain cave in Corsica or Sardinia, and that the men we meet are all mustachioed brigands with bandoliers over their chests and daggers at their belts—cheerful fellows, but quick to anger if they think they are being mocked or spurned. They might not greatly care for the sound of your voice, so keep it low and humble."

Cranley nodded, drinking it in. He had clearly never been to a workman's café.

"Listen," Cross repeated. "Maintain a somber expression and don't look any of them in the eye. And when we meet their chieftain, as I hope we shall, remember that in this place he has the power of life and death. Or at any rate, one word from him and you'll never see that car again."

"I say!" Cranley protested, looking nervously back to where he had parked.

Nobody would steal a car around here without approval, or at least a license, from Arthur Renville. But its presence would already have been noted and interested parties would be assessing the opportunity, maybe getting estimates for how much a silver hood ornament would fetch.

"Are we clear?"

"Crystalline, Cross," said Cranley.

Cross entered the Electric Café, moving between the tables with a quietly confident step, doffing his hat and finding an unoccupied space.

He sensed Cranley duck his head as a dozen sets of curious—and by no means friendly—eyes were turned towards them. The place had an atmosphere. Cross ignored it and found an empty table.

"Wotcher, Captain!" hailed a cheery voice.

It was Charlie Baxter, the plumber who had been the instigator in the case of the ghost door. A friend.

"Evening!" Cross called back.

"That's a fine automobile you got there," said an American voice, and Cross turned to see Bear passing with a cup of coffee in his hand. Bear, a driver by trade, had been a great asset in the *Al-Azif* case. Another friend.

"Thank you," said Cross,

"For a British car," added Bear, winking. "Why, it's almost as good as Ford's last model but one."

Cranley was about to object when they were interrupted by the waitress, an efficient woman of middle years, who never forgot a good tipper.

"Hullo, Captain," she said, offering a menu card.

"Sausage, mash and gravy twice, if you please, Betty," he said, waving it away.

"And two teas," she said, jotting on a pad, correcting his omission.

"Of course, thank you," said Cross.

"Coming right up."

The room seemed to turn away from them. The two strangers were not unwelcome upper-class tourists come slumming it, nor agents of officialdom. The Captain was known. Any questions about his visit would be revealed in time.

"Capital little place this," Cross said to Cranley in an undertone. "The kitchen is clean, and the food is as wholesome and tasty as you could wish. You won't get a carafe of Bordeaux, but I think you'll be pleasantly surprised. The bangers are a house specialty."

He indicated an enameled advertising sign: "We only serve Stubbs Celebrated Sausages. Never Settle for Less!"

Cranley looked around nervously at the other men in their overalls and work-boots. A few were digging into plates of food; more were smoking, sipping at almost-empty teacups and conversing. They looked like they were waiting.

As a distraction, Cross asked about the Austin Seven, and Cranley was soon explaining with the zeal of a new convert about the four-cylinder engine and how the gearbox ratio could be adjusted to four different settings, for touring, sports, racing or trials. The sausage and mash arrived as Cranley was describing his experiences of driving around London, and how he had got the car up to well over forty miles an hour on the open road near Watford.

Cross sensed the change in the room before he saw anything. A ripple passed through the cafe like a kennel of hunting hounds becoming alert as the master approached.

"Evening, Captain," said Arthur Renville, affably. His coat was well-cut, and his shoes were handmade, but this mild, middle-aged fellow did not stand out except, perhaps, for something deep behind his eyes.

"Good evening," said the Captain, rising. "May I present my friend, Mr. Cranley—Mr. Renville. Cranley collects books."

"Cranley," said Renville, with the briefest of handshakes. Cross sensed the name and image being stamped, annotated and filed for reference. "Owner of a new Austin Seven, I believe."

"He is!" said Cross, smiling as though the observation held no implications. "I trust your good lady and children are well?"

"Can't complain. And Mrs. Cross and your daughter?"

If Renville was willing to indulge in small talk, he was in a good mood.

"Both thriving," said Cross. "I say, Cranley and I are just on our way to pick up a book."

Recognizing a minor business matter that needed resolving punctually, Renville made a signal to a confederate. He took up a chair next to Cross which someone pulled up for him. In the background, men shuffled impatiently, waiting their turns for an audience.

"I don't suppose you ever heard of a fellow called Josiah Deakins, from forty years back?" said Cross.

Renville's expression showed amusement.

"That delinquent with the Goat House Gang? Yes, I suppose it would be forty years ago, now. Before my time."

"It seems he left a book, which my friend here has recently bought and plans to take possession of. Show him the receipt, Cranley."

Cranley was fumbling in his pocket but Renville was well ahead.

"Except it won't be a simple transaction," he said. "Else you wouldn't be talking to me."

"Oh, we're very much hoping it will be simple," said Cranley.

Renville ignored him.

"We wanted you to be aware," said Cross. "Is there any remnant of this Goat House Gang who might also claim the book?"

Arthur Renville was lifted by a wave of nostalgia.

"Back in the day, Captain, you'd need a troop of your cavalry to chase down that lot—and even then, you'd never find them. They could just vanish into the wood." He made a circle gesture with his right hand. "Them and their drunken antics... there were young gentlemen among them for the thrill of it, and their women. Not what you'd call 'career criminals.' More your actual 'hellraisers.'

"But Deakins was out of step with the times. The law was starting to mean something around here. Deakins wanted midnight rides through the streets, burning down people's houses when they offended him, bursting mob-handed into pubs to steal brandy casks. Attracting too much attention. So, the others murdered him—throat cut, a goat's horn stuck through his heart, and sundry other mutilations—and left his body at the crossroads by All Saints Church.

"After that, they say the gang still danced round bonfires in the wood and had their drunken revels—orgies and whatnot. But they kept themselves to themselves and didn't bother honest folk."

Things had changed in Norwood, but maybe even someone so dedicated to keeping order as Renville missed the wild romance of the old days. The Devil had left the forests of Norwood for the lights of the city, and the outlaws were gone.

"So, no more gang?" Cross concluded.

Renville shook his head, an authority on every crime in a five-mile radius.

"People say there was a bonfire round that way at Hallowe'en; some of the boys had a look in the woods and didn't find anything. But if they've stolen so much as a racing-pigeon or a rabbit, I've never heard of it in twenty years or more."

"There is at least some remnant," said Cranley, "and I mean to go and talk to them about this book."

"Please yourself," said Renville.

"I thought I'd let you know I'm armed," said Cross.

Renville generally took a dim view of Cross bringing firearms into his peaceful neighborhood. He cut up very rough when Cross had been involved in a gunfight with some anarchists. Now he seemed unconcerned.

"Nobody will be much bothered by a bit of shooting practice in the wood," he said. "Keep it away from human habitation and deaf ears will be turned."

"You won't send Harry Stubbs to nursemaid me again?"

Stubbs was a former heavyweight boxer and sometime odd-job man for Renville. On previous occasions he has been tasked with checking Cross's tendency to pull out a gun, and the two had become friends.

"Certainly not. Stubbsy is out a-courting this evening—taking his young lady to the pictures." Renville gave a wink. "We wouldn't want to stand in the way of young love."

"Well, then," said Cross. "Thank you kindly. We won't take up any more of your valuable."

Renville had already risen, and, with a lordly wave, he moved to consult with his ministers and captains about arrangements for the night's work.

Chapter Three

Cross was getting used to the routine of starting the car. At least it did not need to be cranked every time. Soon they were heading down the road again, stopping at a new automated traffic light across the road from a fine Victorian church which Cranley observed critically.

"All church territory now," he said. "A few hundred years ago this would have been woodland under the sway of the Black Goat."

"Hardly, old man," said Cross. "Country's been Christian since the sixth century."

"The old ways have always existed alongside the official state religion." Cranley was an authority on his topic. "The Hebrew priests worshipped Jehovah, but Azazel persisted in the countryside with his goats. Athens and Sparta worshipped the new gods of Olympus, but the country people still paid homage to the ancient goat-god Pan, guardian of the herds. It was the Puritans who broke the peace. They came with a Bible in one hand and an axe in the other, declared that common woods were evil because they promoted idleness and vice."

"I've enjoyed some idleness and vice in woods," said Cross fondly, but Cranley was in another world.

"People could gather firewood for nothing, and graze their pigs on acorns, and did not need to work. So the Puritans cut down the woods and ploughed the fields and enclosed them. They told the people that man had to earn his bread by the sweat of his brow, and repent. That was the end of the Great North Wood... and the Puritans turned the harmless goat god into a devil."

Cross had his own ideas which had less to do with religion.

"You can't help suspecting an economic motive," he said. "Someone got some free land out of it when they took it away from the commons,"

"That's Bolshevism," said Cranley. Cross recalled that the Cranley family owned some vast acreage in Sussex and wondered how much of that had come of the Enclosure Acts. Maybe Cranley was trying to make restitution to the woods' original owners through his work.

They drove past the Goat House Hotel—ablaze with lights and thronged with drinkers—and found their way to a street adjoining the nearest remaining patch of woodland.

"Therein lies the Black Goat Oak stump, I wager," said Cranley. "If we can find that, we will find the book. I guarantee it."

"In a witch's cottage in the woods?" asked Cross.

"Ah, well, no. Actually, there will be more than one witch," said Cranley.

Cross sighed. It was as he had suspected. He leaned over to get a better view of the sky through the side window until he could see a butter-yellow disk peeking through the foliage. The full moon rose at sunset and set at dawn. It reached its height at midnight, the exact counterpoint to midday, and the traditional hour.

The book would be there because it was being used in a ritual.

"A witches' Sabbat," said Cross.

"Well, yes."

That would mean a gathering of a coven of twelve witches and warlocks, possibly with their patron—whatever grim form it might take—in attendance.

Cross wondered if he should have brought more ammunition. He also recalled a print of Browning's *Tam O'Shanter* in Cranley's study, pursued by a pack of witches and warlocks. That was the inspiration: not Don Quixote on his Rocinante, but Tam galloping away on his mare.

"That explains the sudden enthusiasm for cars," said Cross. "You thought we'd drop in on the sabbat, grab the book, and make a quick getaway.

"Well, yes," Cranley repeated.

On the other hand, it was unlikely such a tiny patch of woodland could host a sabbat.

"Not much room in there," said Cross, squinting at the shadowy copse. "You couldn't swing a black cat in that."

"You are forgetting folk-geometry," said Cranley.

"Ah yes, Armstrong's theory of mystic dimensions and all that Yog-Sothothery."

"If herbalism is folk-botany, and wise women were folk-psychologists centuries ahead of their time, then the survival of a folk-geometric knowledge which transcends modern mathematics is equally plausible," said Cranley, ignoring his friend's flippant tone.

Cross, who had some experience of how space could be warped, did not question that such geometry existed. Accessing it was another matter, requiring capabilities few humans possessed.

"Don't you need to know a spell or something?" Cross asked.

"Or something," said Cranley, producing a thermos flask and unscrewing the lid. A wisp of steam escaped, along with a foul aroma.

"Oho," said Cross.

Cranley had an extensive collection of manuscripts relating to witchcraft, including recipes of all sorts. He had never, so far as Cross knew, been tempted to try any of them. This was another radical departure, like leaving his library and taking to the motor car. A testament to the power of romantic love, perhaps.

"According to the best authorities, witches travelled to the sabbat with the aid of a special potion. In some versions this was applied to a broomstick, but that is a corruption of the original. There are many recipes, but most include the dried powder of a particular toadstool."

He held up the thermos reverently and poured a tot into the cap which doubled as a cup. Cross was not specifically opposed to the use of ancient formulae, but he well knew the risks, especially for amateurs. Cranley was strictly a book learner. As far as Cross knew, he had never strayed into the practical side of the dark arts before. That was a curious departure, and also dangerous.

"Others say the narcotic potion gave the witches bizarre hallucinations," Cross warned. "They only believed they had flown to sabbats and seen impossible things. You have to know what you're doing with toadstools."

"The concoction opens the third eye, and allows one to see Beyond," said Cranley between small sips. "Only those with it can find their way to the sabbat, which remains hidden from outsiders." He made a face to indicate how vile the potion was. "This is the first time I've tried it, but my method is sound."

"Stop if it makes your mouth numb," said Cross, who knew something of toxic fungi. "That's enough. Wait to see if it has any effect, you can always have more."

The game was on, and they were headed into what looked very much like a trap. He needed to brief his friend.

"If you're expecting the Sabbat to be gaggle of old ladies chatting, you're going to be disappointed. They may not be the Black Goat Oak gang anymore, but it will be dangerous."

"Possibly a little," said Cranley. "But these days, as Renville said, it's all a lot more genteel."

All the people Cranley knew who were involved in occult research were scholars of the same stripe as himself: respectable men and women, mainly middle-aged or older, with the money and leisure to pursue their interests.

"You don't see them as fundamentally evil."

"Of course not," said Cranley. "As you well know, it's a nature religion drawing on the life force of the forest. Nature cannot be good nor evil, it just is—church propaganda notwithstanding."

Witches were being rehabilitated. The popular media liked to play them as comical figures. That book about the daffy *Lolly Willowes* and her misadventures as she learns to use her powers and falls into the arms of a charming Satan did not square with the Captain's experience of the type. Nor did the benevolent Pan of *The Wind in the Willows*.

Cross snorted. "Long story short, a warlock had a pretty good stab at killing me not six months ago. He decided it was easier than paying me for a book I found him. I came out on top, but it was a damned close-run thing." Cross suppressed a small shudder at the recollection. The man's name has been Phillips and he had not died easily, assuming he actually was dead, though decapitation was usually pretty reliable. "You know they practice human sacrifice?"

"Only a few covens, and even then only on rare occasions. Mainly unbaptized babies," said Cranley, "and occasional virgins."

It might have been undiplomatic to ask whether Cranley fell into the latter category, but it sharpened Cross's sense of danger and made him wonder why someone might lure his friend into a trap.

"People join a coven because they want power, or revenge, or because they lust after someone who is out of their reach," said Cross. "Like nature, they think nothing of killing."

"Well, yes, to a degree," Cranley agreed. "Which is why I brought you along, with a revolver and everything."

That reminded Cross of something else. He started looking though his pocket change but found only coppers.

"Have you any silver coins? I assume there's a spanner in your repair kit?"

Cranley passed him a three-penny bit. Cross checked the date: 1917, three years before the Mint started using nickel alloy instead of silver. The coin was half an inch across and thin enough to bend in half with a few blows of the spanner. A bit more battering crumpled it into a ball little larger than a pea. At home, Cross could cast bullets in his shed, but needs must when the Devil drives. He had been driven to similar measures before and knew the drill.

"A silver bullet – who's being superstitious now?" said Cranley. "The belief that only a silver bullet could harm witches did not exist before the seventeenth century."

"Neither did bullets," said Cross, fudging the timeline a bit.

Unlike Cranley, Cross had field experience. He knew that against certain individuals a gun might mysteriously jam or misfire. Silver seemed to break the curse and many still believed in it. In backwoods America just a few years previously, Cross had met individuals who still carried one silver bullet as a charm, "just in case."

With a bit of help from a pocket knife and Deakin's toolkit he fitted the crumpled ball of silver on to a Mauser round to replace the lead. The silver bullet was too small and light, the ballistics would be terrible, and it would need to be loaded manually. But it would do the job. He placed it carefully in a back pocket. Hopefully, no gunplay would be needed.

"There's something else to consider," said Cross. "The Black Goat of the Woods. The animating All-spirit of the forest from aeons past. The Lord of the Woods. The One with a Thousand Young."

Cranley half-laughed, then nodded. He had seemed ambiguous when it came to the reality of the occult and treated most of the Captain's stories as tall tales. It seemed he did not entirely rule out the supernatural.

"I accept there may be something to be worried about," he said. "That's why I have St. Dunstan, and my Bible and my crucifix. There's a spare in the glove box in case you wanted one."

Cross shook his head. "I don't know if my faith is strong enough, old man."

"That's not a factor," Cranley replied. "What matters is what *they* believe. Centuries of witch-burnings by Christians have left them with a deeply ingrained phobia, an involuntary reaction. The psychology of curses works both ways, what they call the 'placebo effect'."

"There is also the Black Goat to consider," said Cross.

"According to reports, holy symbols are an effective repellent… the metaphysics are obscure."

Cross was less worried by metaphysics than practical implications. "I don't think you'll find the Black Goat quite such an amusing character as the bumbling folk devil of the old fables. Nothing human will keep it at bay for long. Be prepared for something more… alien."

Cranley swallowed and nodded.

"I said I would get that *Book of Names*, and so I will," he said gamely.

Cross had to admire the man's pluck. He could have wished that for Cranley's first venture into the unknown he had chosen something less daunting than a possible encounter with a Great Old One.

"But why are you helping if it's so dangerous?" Cranley asked.

"Mainly for my morning toast and marmalade," said Cross.

"How's that?"

"Nothing improves breakfast as much as knowing it might be your last."

Without the risk of danger and death, life rapidly became intolerably dull. Even the slightest risk to life and limb gave everything zest, meaning he could crunch his toast with enthusiasm. Also, every time he could get his hands on a rare book before the Turk was a day worth celebrating.

"Is your potion working?" he asked.

"Yes, I rather think it is," said Cranley. "Things look… different."

"Then screw your courage to the sticking place and we'll not fail."

Cranley threw the engine into gear, ignited the headlights, and they rolled on to a patch of grass under the trees. The lights revealed a pair of ancient gateposts which Cross had not noticed before. They drove between them onto a muddy track leading uphill through the trees.

Chapter Four

"Do you see the path?" said Cranley. "It's like… a higher shade of black. I mean, a further shade."

Cross could not see anything except darkness and occasional patches of leaves in the dappled moonlight.

Cranley turned the wheel one way and then the other. Cross thought they would run into the trees, but the path bent ahead of them as though seen through a distorting lens. They kept going around to the left until Cross was sure they had covered a full circle. Except they had not returned to their starting point. Not a circle: a spiral. A gyre.

The path seemed to terminate at a pair of tree-trunks. But by some trick of perspective the narrow gap widened as they approached and the car passed through easily.

"Good heavens," said Cranley. "Did you see that?"

A lifetime of reading about such things was one thing. Witnessing for yourself was something else.

"Keep going, slow and steady," said Cross. The stars on his wrist felt as though he was holding his arm over a fire. Eldritch forces were at work, and they were dangerous,

The track levelled out, twisted, became narrower, until they were driving through a tunnel of foliage. Odd shadows thrown by the headlights danced ahead of them as the car lurched through puddles and potholes. The engine growled as though uncertain of its surroundings.

A pair of eyes glowed in the headlights then vanished. Probably a cat, or perhaps a fox. In half a minute they should have been back out on the road on the other side, but the woods stretched unendingly ahead. The trees seemed older here, the vegetation thicker. Something flitted in front of them and was gone. It looked bigger than the bats Cross has seen in the jungles of Central America, which was of course impossible. But not unlikely.

"Did you see—"

"Just keep going, old man," said Cross.

They bumped onwards in silence for some distance. The undergrowth began to thin, and now the headlights showed the trunks of ancient oak and beech trees.

"The primeval wood," said Cranley. "A mother then devours all her young. Everything that dies here is reabsorbed into the whole. The eternal cycle of nature... perfect balance."

Cross suppressed a comment that Cranley's only experience of woods was when they were rendered into pulp and turned into books. His friend seemed to be finding his own way of processing his first experience of the uncanny.

"Did your sources give any idea how far it might be?" Cross asked.

"It's no distance at all if you know the way," said Cranley. "Having a passenger may be making it harder, but—Oh! Can you see that?"

They had come over a low rise, and flickering orange light showed through the foliage. Cranley cut the engine, and as it died they heard music.

It was strange but familiar, thrumming and skirling with a rhythm but no obvious melody. Nothing like the music that Berlioz had imagined for a sabbat in his *Symphonie Fantastique*, nor Mussorgsky's *Night on Bald Mountain*. Something simple and yet still intensely powerful.

The celebrants could not have heard them. Opening the car door, Cross heard the roaring and crackling of a great bonfire under the music. It was no more than fifty yards away, and the track ran downhill. Cross, however, did not intend to stray so far from his means of retreat.

"Just take off the handbrake and we'll roll as close as we can," he said. "Whenever you feel ready."

Cranley swallowed. "Perfectly ready," he said, and the car trundled downhill at a slow walking pace. Cross signaled Cranley to stop before they came into direct line of sight. He had been keeping an eye out for sentries, but it seemed there were none. Now where would Josiah Deakins' book be?

They stepped out, leaving the car doors open. The pungent odors of woodland enfolded them, with top notes of woodsmoke. The leaf mold was spongy underfoot. Cross felt exposed, but forced himself to stroll into the firelight with Cranley beside him

The music and the fire's crackle were louder here. Cranley stopped, open-mouthed, beholding things he had read about for years. It must have been like seeing the illustrations from all those old books coming to life.

There was the bonfire that drew the eye, and the dancers that circled it. The fire was huge, piled more than head-high, with flames at least twice that height lashing upwards throwing streamers of sparks into the night sky.

The brilliance of the fire threw everything else into shadow or half-light, including the figures capering and prancing to the beat of the music. They were all robed—full nudity would come later according to the usual order of service.

Cross glimpsed some faces, including a woman he thought he recognized from one of his wife's magazines, and a man who was a minor politician. As he had observed before, covens had changed. The village wise women and cunning men had been elbowed aside by wealthy urbanites greedy for power.

Further from the flames was a second ring of dancers, prancing and capering. They were harder to make out, mere shadows, but for a moment it seemed to Cross the flitting silhouettes looked like goats.

"There's the Black Goat Oak," said Cranley, pointing.

Tearing his eyes from the dancers, Cross saw the stump of a great oak at the center of the clearing. It was laid out as an altar, with candlesticks, a goblet and other indistinct objects arrayed.

A black goat was tethered by the stump: a glossy, healthy-looking beast with black ribbons tied to its horns. Adherents of one religion are saved by the blood of the lamb; others choose the blood of the goat. A feathery shape in a wicker basket suggested that the traditional black cockerel would also be slaughtered.

His eyes flicked about—checking for danger or opportunity—and found a cauldron set over a small fire. Across from it and partly shielded from the dancers by a screen of vegetation were five musicians. They were also robed and played with the passion of a jazz band. They did not need sheet music; the music seemed to rise and fall on its own with a terrible inevitability, the rhythms of the forest, the pulsing heartbeats of every living thing merged into one.

Nobody paid any attention to the two interlopers. The musicians and dancers were lost in the wild music, and probably under the influence of stronger narcotic brews than Cranley's.

Finding the book would be difficult in the flickering shadows, with the pulsating music tearing at his brain. Direct action was needed. Cross closed one eye, drew a fat-barreled pistol from his left-hand side and fired upward.

The flare was designed to rise high into the air; instead it stuck in the branches overhead, bathing the whole clearing in harsh, white light. It was like suddenly opening the curtains in a darkened room on a sunny day. Cross had often found the flare pistol useful for creating distractions, though the smoke and fire were usually the most dramatic effects. It had never worked as well as it did now.

The music played two beats, faltered and died. The dancers, released from its spell, looked around in amazement. Some gawped up at the flare as though it were a new star, others looked about at their fellow revelers. The goats circled, confused.

"Sorry to butt in on you, as it were," yelled Cross, moving quickly towards the Black Goat Oak. "We just came to pick up Josiah Deakin's book. My associate has the receipt."

As he moved Cross scanned the robed figures, looking for any telltale movement to indicate one of them was going for a weapon. They seemed paralyzed by the light, which was better than he had hoped for. He had about six seconds before the flare burned out.

On the wooden altar were a tall goblet, some ornate candlesticks, a ritual sword, a whitened skull minus jawbone, sundry odd implements, a curious bundle wrapped in cloth. And a small book, bound in brown leather. Sweeping up the book with his free hand, he hastened back towards the car. Cranley, with two good legs, was already running.

"Stop!"

The flare sputtered and faded, and firelight and shadow fell back into place. Cross opened the eye he had closed to retain his night vision and saw the robed figures rushing at him.

Cross threw himself aside and felt a body hurtle past. Lying down, he waved his stick in a wide arc to catch any assailant while he drew the Mauser. The book fell out of his hands. A confusion of legs and bodies, human or goat, seemed to pass by in a rugby scrum. Hands grasped for him and he beat them away, but when he felt for the book on the ground it was gone.

A robed figure kicked at him, and Cross struck back at the kneecap with this stick. Something jumped over Cross, then, in the glare of headlights, a car horn beeped angrily, scattering the human and goat figures around him.

Cross was momentarily distracted by the bonfire. Something large and dark was moving inside the flames like a huge horned head thrust up from below. Something in Cross' brain wanted to make connections with the burning wood, the cycle of renewal, but he thrust it aside.

"Get in," Cranley urged from behind the wheel. Cross was already clambering in beside him.

Before Cross was properly inside, the car accelerated ahead. He saw then that Cranley's goal was not escape but pursuit. A robed figure was hurrying down the track away from them, leaving the clearing behind, the book in one hand and the bundle from the altar tucked under their other arm.

The fleeing figure looked back as they saw the car, but instead of turning aside ran faster down the track. Cranley swerved to overtake them.

"Excuse me," said Cross, pointing the Mauser out the window. "The book, if you please."

The figured looked up, and he saw the face inside the hood.

It was Ellen Edmonds.

"Let me in!" she shouted, opening the door and throwing herself on top of Cross. "Drive!"

"Ellen!" shouted Cranley.

"Drive!" said Miss Edmonds and the Captain in unison, and Cranley—in automatic obedience—put his foot down.

"Small world," said Cross, as she adjusted her robes. "Fancy meeting you, et cetera."

"What are you doing here?" she asked, brushing hair out her eyes. She had the same bobbed hair and heavy kohl eyeliner he remembered.

"The Captain's helping me," said Cranley. "But what are *you* doing here?"

"The only way I could find out when and where they met," Ellen said, "was to agree to become initiated myself tonight."

"You didn't tell me," Cranley accused.

"Darling, I couldn't." Ellen handed the book to Cross. "You take this."

"What have you got there?" he asked, as she inspected the bundle. It was only when he saw the face he realized it was a baby.

"She's been drugged, poor thing," Ellen said. "They were going to sacrifice her for my initiation."

"But what were you going to do?" asked Cranley, still bewildered.

"I was going to distract them and send them chasing me the wrong way," Ellen said. "Then, when there was that tussle, I thought if I took the book you'd be able to get away."

It did not sound quite right to Cross, but he was embarrassed that he had failed to recognize the baby.

"Well done rescuing the little one," said Cross. "Whose is she?"

"I don't know. They just kidnap them," Miss Edmonds said. "She can't be more than a few weeks old."

Cross guessed the baby would have been stolen from one of the more impoverished streets around there, from a family with several children already. The sort of place where the parents would not be blamed for the disappearance of an extra mouth.

"We need to turn around," said Cross. "Unless you know another way out of the wood, Miss Edmonds."

"I don't even know where this is," said Miss Edmonds. "They led me here blindfold from the Goat House. All I know is that this is a witch-wood, beyond our world."

She sounded sincere but Cross noted inconsistencies in her story.

"Technically," said Cross, "doesn't your soul already belong to them?"

"Mine, yes," she said. "But if I pledged another seven generations, that's three more for them. A large proportion of the coven are in the same boat."

Cross had to admit it was a sale scheme worthy of the Devil himself. People whose souls were already forfeited had nothing to lose, except the welfare of future generations. Also, like Miss Edmonds, they were likely to come from families where black magic ran in their veins.

"I can see a way," said Cranley, and made a left turn into a pool of darkness which turned into another path stretching ahead.

The vegetation around them had changed subtly. Cross did not look too closely.

They drove on through the winding green tunnel for some distance, and Cranley slowed to a crawl as jagged rocks appeared along the path.

"Better mind those," said Cross, "We don't want a puncture now."

"It's a bit narrow," said Cranley.

"Let me drive, darling," said Miss Edmonds. "You're still new to this."

Cranley, who had been visibly struggling, did not argue. The party swapped places, with Miss Edmonds driving, Cranley in the back holding the sleeping baby, and Cross in the passenger seat, the Mauser cradled in his lap.

Cross glimpsed lights in the woods around them, blue and green, too bright to be phosphorescent fungus, but too dim for anything else.

"No sign of pursuit yet," said Cross. "Do they have any weapons that you saw?"

"Just ritual ones," she said. "I'm more worried about other things."

"You mean—demons or spirits?" asked Cranley.

For a man who had spent the better part of a decade studying the occult, Cranley seemed to have an atrophied imagination.

"All the hordes of Hell," said Cross. "Or, if you prefer, every inhabitant of extra-dimensional reality in reasonably close proximity through Pythagorean space."

"That reminds me," Cranley said, "Cross, give Ellen the spare crucifix."

Cross retrieved the silver cross from the glove compartment. She duly put the chain around her neck, as she guided the Austin, jolting and rattling, down the uneven path back towards the Sabbat.

Interesting, thought Cross, as she straightened the crucifix, clearly unafraid to touch it. Cranley's mad scheme of using a motor car for a quick getaway appeared to be working. They were going much faster now. The car bucked and skidded, and there was a thump and "Ow!" from the back, but Miss Edmonds kept it on track.

"Sorry," she said.

"Don't go too fast," Cranley warned. "If we get stuck, we might not be able to get out."

"Is the baby...?" Cross asked.

"Baby is fine," said Cranley. "Baby wasn't the one who got a bump on the head."

"Steady as she goes," said Cross. Miss Edmonds was driving as though the Devil was after her. She probably had good reason.

"Bear left," said Cranley.

Miss Edmonds followed his instructions, and the path unfurled before them.

As there was a lull, Cross flicked through the book, but it was too dark to ready anything. The first few pages were text and pictures, the rest just had a few lines on each page with a mark below. It looked like the right book, but in the jolting car, even with a light, he would not have been able to read it.

Miss Edmonds gasped, seeing something in the rear-view mirror.

"What was it?" asked Cranley, turning to look through the back window.

"I don't know," she said.

Cross had his window wound down and the pistol in his right hand, ready to fire on anything that threatened them.

"I think I see something," said Cross.

"My god!" exclaimed Cranley.

It raced past them in the dark like a torpedo. To Cross, it was formless, like grey spindrift, the foam blown off wavetops in a storm. Cranley, with his vision enhanced by the drug must have seen something very different.

A second later the dark bubbles inverted themselves into a shadowy, robed figure, standing, arms outstretched, in the road ahead. One pale wrist was adorned with a bracelet of large, white shells.

The car jerked to a sudden halt and Cross caught himself on the dashboard.

"Drive on," he urged. "Run her over."

"I can't," Miss Edmonds said through gritted teeth.

Cross felt it too: the net of paralysis thrown over him. Somehow he was still able to open the door and step out, but it was as though he were underwater. A powerful current swept him forwards. He could walk with, but not against it towards the woman, but not away.

It was the witch he had noted earlier whose face looked familiar.

Two steps closer, and Cross was finally able to place her. He *had* seen her picture in a magazine. A noted society hostess whose dinner parties were the talk of London. The great and the good contorted themselves to get invitations to her soirees. Her husband was extremely wealthy and successful.

Of course he was.

She looked as relaxed and in charge as she would in her own living room.

Cross kept his hand on the gun in his lap. It was not loaded with the silver bullet, and if anyone was protected by charms it was this woman. Lead bullets might be as useless as spitting at her, but he would go down fighting.

"Well, you've certainly got a nerve, barging in like that," she said irritably, but with laughter dancing behind her eyes. Her eyes were still on Miss Edmonds, pinning her and Cranley in place. "Now, give me the book."

"As I mentioned, madam, I believe we have a right to it," Cross said calmly. "Please step out of the way before there is an accident."

He smiled. Cross hoped the witch had been charmed by his courage and dash, and he spoke pleasantly.

"I'm afraid not. I'm also taking back the offering which you stole." She had the modulated tones of a matriarch of the drawing room. "And her." She indicated Miss Edmonds. "She belongs to us, too."

When she moved her arm, the bracelet rattled. It was not made of white sea-shells as Cross had thought, but the skulls of babies. Perhaps shrunk or scaled copies, though Cross put nothing beyond this woman.

"In fairness," Cross said, "her soul was sold without her consent. She is hoping to get it back."

He was hoping that if he distracted the witch enough, Miss Edmonds would be able to free herself of the paralysis enough to put her foot down. In his experience, once the initial shock wore off victims could manage some small movement. Then, when the witch shifted her attention to the car, he would shoot her as many times as he could.

"Having your soul absorbed into the Eternal Mother, becoming one with nature, is not the fiery damnation the cross-wavers would have you believe," said the woman. "As you may shortly discover."

"We just want one page," Cross said. "You can have the rest of the book back. If you're not initiating Miss Edmonds into the coven, you won't need a sacrifice tonight, so nobody gets hurt and we all go home happy. Be reasonable."

The witch, however, also seemed to be aware of the limitations of her power.

"I'm afraid I'm not a reasonable person," she said, "Now, give me the book!"

This time, Cross felt his hand moving of its own volition. He stopped it with an effort of will, and she seemed to notice the check. He strained to hear the revving of the Austin's little engine but there was nothing.

"Resist me and I will break you," said the woman, as though warning that a cup of tea was too hot to drink.

Cross tried to draw his gun, but could not, while his other hand held out the book. Her lips twitched as she watched him struggle with himself.

Something moving behind her caught the Captain's eye.

"We can work out an exchange," said Cross quickly, "There might be other books you are interested in. I specialize in finding occult books."

"I hardly think—what?"

She turned at a figure emerging from the darkness. The moonlight caught Cranley as he rushed forward, wielding a stick in both hands. The witch made a warding gesture but whatever protection she invoked had no effect. The cudgel connected squarely, striking her head with the sound of a cricket bat hitting a ball, and she crumpled to the ground.

"Good show," said Cross, finding he could move again.

Cranley tossed the stick aside and looked at the fallen woman. He was breathing heavily. It was probably the first act of physical violence he had ever carried out.

"I wasn't sure," said Cranley, "but I thought I had a chance with elder wood. Should we... finish her off? Shoot her?"

"Not unless you want a blood-feud with the coven," said Cross. "Just get her out of the road."

Cranley dragged her aside with some effort, revealing more skin than was modest, including a mark shaped like a cloven hoof on one thigh.

"Can you still drive?" Cross asked Miss Edmonds as they climbed back in.

"I think so," she said, dazed but determined, and the car nosed ahead. "I feel sort of numbed but... Well done, darling."

"I couldn't just let her get you, darling," said Cranley.

She swallowed, and the car edged forward again.

"I silently recited the Twenty-third Psalm," he went on. "That gave me the strength to touch my crucifix, which restored my mobility. When I got out of the car I practically tripped over that elder branch. As you know, elder wood is a powerful counter to witches. Thank the Lord it was handy."

"A friend of mine would be quoting Paracelsus now, about how curative herbs always grow in the places a disease occurs," said Cross. "But I'm happy to give the Lord credit."

Cranley clearly had not realized what might have happened had he tried to attack her with anything less efficacious. On the other hand, it was exactly what Cross would have done himself in the situation.

"Oh no," said Miss Edmonds looking in the rear-view mirror. The car leapt forwards. "She is pointing at us."

"A curse, or a summoning?" mused Cranley.

"The Dark Young… but I can't see anything," said Miss Edmonds, eyes glued to the rear-view mirror. "Is the baby alright?"

"Still fast asleep," said Cranley. "Lucky thing."

"Please look at the road," said Cross, as the car lurched through a pothole. "Cranley and I will keep an eye out."

They strained to see what was behind them in the dark as the car bumped along. It had seemed fast enough before, now it was agonizingly slow.

"I can't pin it down," said Cranley. "First, it's here and then it's there. The whole forest is alive with moving shadows."

"So long as it doesn't gain on us, it hardly matters," said Cross.

The Austin continued its jolting way under Miss Edmonds' direction. If they could just keep going at this speed they might make it to the exit ahead of whatever was behind. Curious as he was to know what the witch might have called, Cross would happily forego the opportunity of seeing it.

"Faces," said Cranley. "I thought I saw faces in the moonlight—and horns."

Cross said nothing.

"Can you shoot them?" Miss Edmonds asked, her voice verging on panic.

"We can't even see them," said Cranley.

"There's a clearing here," she said,

White moonlight flashed through the car as they passed through an open space. Cross raised his gun, ready to shoot their pursuer once he could see them.

Then, a mass of black goats raced into the moonlit glade, filling the whole width of the path, dozens of them matching the speed of the car.

At first, they mainly looked like normal goats, though the bearded faces were disconcerting. Below that though, the goat bodies had undergone a range of transformations, stretched and warped out of shape. Some had long, spindly spider legs, some had thick limbs with too many joints, some were longer than any goat had a right to be... but mercifully the cavalcade was only briefly visible before they plunged back into the dark.

Chapter Five

"Good lord," said Cranley.

"Black goats of the wood," said Miss Edmonds, looking in the mirror. "You know how they say goats will eat anything? These do."

Cross could feel their presence, and his tattoo throbbed in time, like the drumming of hoofbeats.

Their deity was the Black Goat of the Wood with a Thousand Young, and these were the young.

The Old Gods, as they were known, were infamous for interbreeding with humans. According to unreliable accounts, some of their offspring seemed quite normal. Others were wholly monstrous and made more so by the traces of humanity that showed through.

But who said that They only bred with humans? Some might prefer other species. Each of the goat things was a reflection of some facet of their progenitor, a being too multitudinous to be contained in one earthly creature.

"They can't catch us," said Cranley. "Can they?"

"Miss Edmonds, would you happen to know any invocations to drive off the spawn of Banebdjedet?" Cross asked hopefully.

The goat-god Banebdjedet was one of Egypt's original deities, predating the nine gods of the Osiris pantheon, but which clung on for centuries in wilderness areas after the new religion took over. As a keeper of a stock of occult Egyptian wisdom, there was every chance that Miss Edmonds might have encountered a means of dealing with rival sects.

"I'm only really a student of the writings," she said. "I know a hieroglyph that might keep them at bay—not much good in a moving vehicle, I'm afraid!"

Cross was only too aware that, even executed flawlessly by a master, such wards only gave temporary protection. That had saved his bacon more than once, on one occasion giving him time to exit a tomb and reach daylight before the unholy occupant could get to him.

"We do have St. Dunstan," said Cranley.

Cross had never been one to rely on saints. He scanned the path ahead , puzzled by the way it meandered.

"This isn't the right way," he said.

"But there is only one path," Miss Edmonds said. "I'm following it."

"Cranley, where should we be going?"

"I-I'm not sure. I can't see," admitted Cranley. "Pass me the Thermos."

They continued at a steady clip, keeping ahead of the pursuit. Was there another exit to the woods which would take them out somewhere very different? Or were the woods quasi-infinite, meaning they would run out of fuel before they found the end of the track? If so, it would be a question of whether it was the Black Goats or something else that found them first.

Having refreshed himself, Cranley looked forward again, casting from left to right. There was no specific reason to believe the magic which had guided them here would also work for the return journey, but like a bloodhound finding a trail, he fixed on one direction.

"Turn left here, darling," he said.

"There's nowhere to turn."

Cautiously she veered to the left, and what had previously looked like shadows in the foliage opened into an uphill fork. The engine rattled alarmingly, then resumed its usual tone as she changed gears.

The headlights picked out two robed figures running down the path ahead of them. The guitar case revealed them to be two of the musicians, seemingly fleeing as fast as they could.

When they heard the car, one of them turned and stooped to take a stick which he threw at the windscreen. Miss Edmonds yelped slightly when it hit, then sounded the horn and put her foot down, forcing the two to jump out of the way.

"Why are you speeding up?" Cross asked after they had passed.

"Maybe we should offer them a lift," she suggested. "If they're running away too—"

"Good God!" exclaimed Cranley as the black herd rushed forward into the moonlight.

The goats' mouths opened wider than they should, and the inside was filled with black teeth like shards of onyx. Before the astonished musicians could react the goats were on them, biting, trampling and tearing. Cross caught a glimpse of the nearest one, half his face torn off, before the animal wave engulfed him entirely.

"Drive," urged Cross, and they sped away.

"Good God," Cranley repeated, quietly, still looking out the black window. Surely, he could not still see what was happening… unless the toadstool potion allowed him to see other things as well. "Good… God."

"It was a quick death," said Cross.

"Like a pack of sharks," muttered Miss Edmonds.

"Steady as she goes," Cross warned, as she started to accelerate. "We just need to stay ahead of them. If we have a spill it's all over."

As they drove through another glade, Cross saw that an animal faster than the others was making its way through the pack. It leapt like a hare to clear the others, then came towards them in great bounds through the dark.

"Oh no," said Miss Edmonds as the thing landed behind them. Cross had a glimpse of malicious eyes with bar pupils, then it leapt again, and landed, scrambling on the car's canvas roof. Four hooves were clearly visible through the material as it began tearing a hole with its teeth.

Miss Edmonds let out a yelp and hit the brake. The goat-thing was flung forward and rolled off the bonnet. The car lurched forward again.

As the creature scrambled upright Cross shot it twice, once through the body and once through the head. It fell back, spraying black blood that steamed when it touched the air.

At least bullets could hurt them. The Mauser held twenty rounds, and Cross had just fired two. There were dozens more of the creatures back there. Maybe if he killed the leaders the rest would flee. If there were leaders.

"There, there," Cranley said to the baby.

"Ferocious teeth those things have," said Cross, looking at the hole in the roof.

"Do you think we can lose them, darling?" asked Cranley.

"I'm trying my best," said Miss Edmonds.

They would be fine just so long as the track's condition did not get any worse.

As soon as Cross thought this, the car bounced in the air and came down with a splash into thick mud, slowing to a halt, then stalling. The headlights went out and they were plunged into almost complete darkness.

"Damn," said Miss Edmonds.

Cross, ignorant of cars, had no advice to offer.

"I can't see them," said Cranley quietly, his face against the back window. "Or hear them. Maybe we lost them at one of those turns."

There had been no obvious forks in the path. But by now it was obvious that the convolutions of their trail were invisible to Cross.

"Maybe," said Cross. "But it would be a good idea to get us going again as soon as possible."

The engine sputtered and caught, the headlights came on. Like moths to a flame, a black tide surged towards them, seemingly from all directions.

"It's the light, it's the light!" said Cranley. "Kill the engine."

Miss Edmonds cut the engine and the headlights went out.

The goats had formed a circle several deep around the car, none approaching closer than six feet. In this light they were a ring of horned shadows.

"Get away!" shouted Cross and fired an experimental shot in the air.

There was no reaction to the gunshot. Instead, the animals seemed to press closer.

"I think St. Dunstan is keeping them back," Cranley said, in an undertone.

A shaft of moonlight had caught the silver ornament over the radiator, and it seemed to glow. One of the goats reared up on its hind legs, lunged forward and bit at the statue, only to recoil as though burned. A second goat tried the same, and then a third, bigger creature tugged at the saint with huge, misshapen black teeth, leaving it bent at an angle before it had to let go.

St. Dunstan did not look as though he could take much more of this. Already the dark circle was closing in, shaggy forms making a wall around them, topped with horns like spikes on a palisade.

"They are attracted to light," said Cranley.

"The full moon—the bonfire—the torches," said Cross, recalling the paraphernalia of the coven. "Goats cannot see in the dark."

The dark, bearded faces pressed in on them from all sides.

"Do you have a knife and some matches?" Miss Edmonds asked.

Cross unfolded the blade of his pocketknife and passed it. She reached up and slashed a rectangular opening in the canvas roof above her, then took the book of matches he offered.

"I'm going to lure them away. You must get out of here—look after the baby." She had maneuvered so she was kneeling on the car seat, facing Cranley in the back. "Destroy that contract! And remember me always, darling."

They kissed, then she scrambled up through the hole and, bracing her feet on the roof frame, made a lunge upwards. She pulled herself up on to an overhanging bough with remarkable agility.

Modern women, thought Cross ruefully. He should have been the one to create a diversion, but he could not match her mobility. And Cranley, bless him, had not thought of offering to go instead.

One of the goats had wrenched the silver statuette from the bonnet, but the dozens of shaggy heads were distracted, looking at the woman making her way along the branch in the moonlight.

"Be ready to move as soon as she distracts them," said Cross. "And make sure the head lights don't come on this time."

Cranley clambered awkwardly from the back and struggled into the driver's seat while Cross surveyed the shadows outside. He thought he could hear their breathing. They were as disconcerting in the dark as they were when partially visible. An indistinct movement in the branches told him Miss Edmonds was continuing her progress.

"What is she going to do?" Cranley asked when he was finally in place.

As if in reply, a match flared up in the branches, and there was a rush of hooves as the goats stampeded over towards it. The area around the car actually seemed lighter when they had gone.

The flame brightened as she lit another match from it. She was kneeling on a branch with forms below her leaping up wildly like a bubbling cauldron of black liquid.

"Start the car," said Cross.

The car engine fired up again, and Cranley gunned it before easing backwards. The flame went out, but a second later another one was struck and Cross glimpsed Miss Edmonds' pale features—and, beneath her on the ground, a crowd of upturned animal faces, firelight glinting from their eyes.

One leaped up and caught hold of her robe in its sharp teeth, coming away with a mouthful.

Other goats were scrambling around, trying to clamber over each other to get at her.

Cranley was trying to maneuver the car, wrestling with the wheel and switching between forward and reverse gears.

Somehow one of the goat creatures had hauled itself up the tree and scuttled towards Miss Edmonds along the branch with terrifying speed. Rather than screaming and fainting, she grabbed it by one horn and, bringing the clasp knife up, slashed its throat in one quick move.

Blood spurted, and she threw the thing down. There was a terrible commotion below. Were its fellows eating it?

Cranley finally succeeded in getting the Austin free, but two yards clear he hesitated, looking towards where Miss Edmonds had struck another match and was looking about in all directions, as though she might be attacked from above, even as the dark shapes leaped up, one snapping at her foot.

"We can't leave her," Cranley said.

If only I had brought more flares, thought Cross, feeling in his coat pocket. And there, at the bottom were two more flare cartridges. Amanda, ever thoughtful—and ever the better planner—must have slipped them in before he left.

Mrs. Cross was quite a treasure.

"We won't," said Cross.

Aiming the flare pistol backwards through the hole in the roof, Cross hoped Miss Edmonds would take her cue.

As the car rolled forwards, the flare lodged in the canopy fifty yards behind them, partly shaded but still casting a flickering, electric light over the forest floor. The goats rushed towards the source of the illumination and the trembling shadows underneath it. It seemed there were hundreds of them now.

"Come on!" shouted Cranley and a second later the car rocked as Miss Edmonds jumped on to the running board, gripping the roof frame.

"Good show!" said Cross. "But mind how you go."

They were moving more slowly now, but still at a decent clip. Maybe not as fast as their pursuers could run, but the herd were well behind them and no longer had the running lights to home in on.

"I'm minding," said Cranley.

"Whew," said Miss Edmonds, as she regained a seat. "That was clever with the flare."

"It would have been a sight cleverer before you decided to sacrifice yourself. Not that Cranley would agree to leave you anyway."

"Then you're an idiot, darling" she said, patting his shoulder. "But, thank you."

"The baby is still asleep," Cross reported. "Breathing, anyway"

Cranley fixed his gaze on the rear-view mirror.

"Nothing behind us that I can see," he said. "Would you mind driving again darling? I'm a bit woozy."

He stopped and changed places with Miss Edmonds while Cross looked back anxiously into the utter black behind them. It took just a few seconds but felt like minutes.

"Are you all right, old man?" asked Cross.

"This stuff," said Cranley, taking another sip from his thermos. "I need to keep topping up so I can navigate—further to the left here, darling—it's not so much a matter of seeing but *feeling* the way."

Cross loaded the last flare into his pistol.

Miss Edmonds practically had her nose pressed against the windscreen. It was dark out there, but the track ahead of them showed as a paler darkness, while the branches moved past against the sky above. Cranley directed her in the places where absolutely nothing was visible, and, by whatever power, they always stayed on the path.

"Slow and steady, and we will make it out of here," said Cross. "We just have to keep moving."

"I can't see it," said Cranley. "I can't see the way."

"Have another swig of your toadstool-juice."

In reply, Cranley upended the empty thermos. From here on they were navigating blind.

"I'll just keep going then, shall I?" said Miss Edmonds.

"Follow the moon," said Cross, pointing up at it.

They drove interminably, through long dark tunnels, through dappled glades of moonlight, through avenues of impossibly tall trees.

"Just keep your eyes fixed on the road ahead," said Cross. He did not want her to be distracted by the tall column they had just passed: the thing that looked like a tree trunk but was not.

"Turn right," said Cranley, gesturing as they passed through another patch of pale light.

He was right; the moon seemed to be playing hide and seek with them, appearing in one direction and then another. Once they passed a ruined cottage whose architecture was not at all familiar, and once Cross thought he saw something long slithering through the undergrowth. He had his guns ready, but whatever it was had not seen them.

It occurred to him that if there was any intelligence guiding the pack, taking the wrong path would have thrown them off the scent. Certainly, they did not seem to have any followers now.

"What if we can't find the way out?" asked Miss Edmonds, with the slightest quaver in her voice.

"Of course we'll find the way," said Cross.

"We will," said Cranley, with some assurance. "We do not belong here. The woods do not want us. They will eject us, sooner or later."

"I wish they'd hurry up," she said.

If there had been more light, Cross might have been tempted to try and read the book, see if there was anything there that might help them make sense of the place's geometry. When he looked around, Cross noticed Cranley's lips moving silently, as if in prayer.

"You know, I think this is the right way," said Miss Edmonds, a minute later. "I think we're getting very close to the edge of the wood."

The vegetation became less thick and patches of dappled moonlight appeared here and there. There were still twisted stumps with alarmingly suggestive shapes, and bushes that writhed like living things, but it seemed that the worst of it was behind them.

Cranley let out an audible sigh.

"Baby has slept through it all," he said.

"One thing I'm not quite clear on," Cross said, to break the silence. "How did you two actually meet and come up with this scheme."

"Oh, it turns out we have a mutual friend," said Miss Edmonds.

"It's that other fellow in the book business," said Cranley. "A foreign gentleman. I think you may know him."

Cold realization hit Cross like a bucket of icy water. It was a set up. It had always been a set-up, just as he suspected. Cranley and Miss Edmonds had been introduced deliberately, to make this happen.

At exactly that moment, headlights came on in front of them, and Miss Edmonds was forced to swerve to avoid hitting a limousine blocking the road ahead. They ran into an earth bank, hard enough to break a headlight and throw the passengers violently forward.

Off the road they were out of the direct glare of the headlights. The first thing that drew Cross' attention was the Lewis light machinegun, which the man standing on the limousine's passenger seat was resting on the top of the windscreen and aiming directly at him. There was another man beside the car, armed with a submachine gun. Both were aiming at Cross, ready to blast him into bloody rags.

The ornament above the limousine's radiator was a silver Byzantine cross.

A man stepped out, in a neat pinstripe suit and fedora.

Naturally, it was the Turk.

The Turk and Cross had many things in common. Both were deeply involved in the occult book trade. In the War, Cross lost his leg as well as his vocation when machine guns and barbed wire erased cavalry from the army forever. The Turk had lost his country, an exile once the Sultan was deposed and Ataturk's radical progressives had taken over.

Cross and the Turk could speak cordially on matters of mutual interest, but they were still enemies.

The Turk was smoking a narrow cigarette in an ebony holder. He made a polite gesture inviting Cross to dismount. His bodyguards watched impassively. Cross noted a fourth man, a chauffeur, in the car.

"Good evening Captain, Mr. Cranley, Miss Edmonds. I am pleased and surprised to see you all," said the Turk. "I thought there might be less of you by now."

"You arranged this," said Cross.

"I located the coven six months ago, after years of searching, but retrieving the *Book of Names* was beyond my poor resources," said the Turk modestly. "So, I recruited Miss Edmonds, who at my suggestion recruited Mr. Cranley, who of course brought you into it."

"What is this?" Cranley said, looking into the machine gun.

"A precaution after my last meeting with the Captain. Overwhelming firepower might prompt him to behave."

"Are you going to kill us?" asked Miss Edmonds.

"Of course not," said Cross, taking out the book. "He just wants this. Though even *he* doesn't usually stoop to highway robbery."

"Please," said the Turk. "You still think it belonged to Deakins and now belongs to you? Have you looked at it?"

Cross flipped through the pages. It was a fine volume, with good parchment pages, the parchment being the scraped skin of calf, sheep… or goat. He had assumed it would be a notebook from Deakins' time, but it was far older. Paper had largely superseded parchment by the fifteenth century.

"The story about Deakins owning it was a ruse for Cranley," Cross said. People could easily be led to believe what benefited them.

"Legally speaking, as church property, Deakins was just holding it in trust. And, legally speaking, I feel on safe ground stealing from the Devil."

"You're stealing from Cranley. That's low, even for you," said Cross, handing the book over.

"Nonsense. I only want one page, which is a reasonable percentage for all my work." He flipped rapidly through the book, located a page near the front, and, with horrifying casualness for one handling a priceless antique, ripped it out before passing the book back. "You can keep the rest."

"Vandalism!" muttered Cross, staring at the maimed volume. It might be the Devil's own book, but he did not like to see any work defaced.

"Miss Edmonds plans to take a page herself," said the Turk, slipping the folded page into an inner pocket. "I'm just, you might say, 'taking a leaf out of her book.' In my case, I am dealing with a rather stubborn gentleman with a very important volume, and finally I have an exchange he will be interested in."

"Why are you giving the book back?" Cranley asked, suspiciously.

"I am not greedy." The Turk drew lightly on his cigarette. "As you know, the coven has ways of finding things, and they will find that book. I will stay, as you say, out of the picture, leaving you, Mr. Cranley, as the…"

He left the word hanging for Cross to pronounce.

"…scapegoat."

The Turk shrugged apologetically.

"Now, I will be leaving. I would not advise you to follow. There was a gathering of… beings in the woods close to the entrance. They will let us pass, but I fear they may be alert to you. I suggest you go back into the woods."

Cross was unsurprised that the pack which had been behind them was now in front of them. Such places had a geometry of their own.

"We can't go back!" said Cranley.

"That's very unfortunate," said the Turk.

"You're a wicked man," said Miss Edmonds.

The Turk shrugged again.

"I have another idea," said Cross, walking slowly down the path.

The two bodyguards were keeping a close eye on him, gun barrels following his movement. There was no sign of anything down the path as far as he could tell, but the Turk rarely told actual lies. Also, his tattoo was buzzing like a hive of hornets.

"What are you doing?" asked the Turk.

Cross slowly drew the flare pistol, pointing it upwards as though about to surrender it, then fired into canopy. The flare lit up the whole area around them with harsh white illumination.

The darkness seemed to rush like a great torrent down the track towards them, galloping towards the light. The goat-things were clearer now, more sharply deformed, more grotesque and less animal-like. They moved with jagged articulation, like menacing puppets, mouths open to show long, pointed teeth.

"*Aman Tanrım!*" shouted the bodyguard with the Lewis gun.

The Turk made the smallest gesture. The Lewis gunner opened, followed a moment later by the bodyguard with the tommy gun. Cross had already unholstered his Mauser and fired a burst at the nearest beasts. The chauffeur was out of the car too, firing into the advancing horde with a pump-action shotgun.

The goat-things made no sound even as the bullets threw them back, scythed them down and drilled through them. They raced forward into the light with seemingly unquenchable fury—until the bullets struck and they stumbled, gushing steam like broken locomotives. Even as they died, they tumbled forward and rolled, more leaping over the falling bodies. The bullets did their work, and the Turk's bodyguards proved efficient killers, untroubled by the sight of the charging monsters.

The Turk watched cooly as the charge stretched towards them over a breaking wave of falling bodies. The cloud of steam from so much black blood was so dense that the horde now seemed to be rushing out of thick fog.

Cross was aware that behind him, Miss Edmonds was scratching at the ground with a long stick.

Something powered along on the ground, curving towards them under the leaves and leaf mold like a shark beneath the surface. As the goat head broke out into the air Cross shot it dead, not pausing to look at the worm-like body.

Cross was counting his bullets, making every one count, but he still ran out of ammunition in seconds. All he had left was the silver bullet, and they were still coming.

The two machine guns stopped firing as they, too, emptied their magazines.

A fresh wave of goat things, led by one like a Giacometti creation as tall as a giraffe and another galloped forward, a rhinoceros of a beast with a body like a barrel.

"Back!" shouted Cranley, hurling his bible at the giraffe thing as its head dipped toward him. The book struck its target, and the thing fell backward as though poleaxed, but the rest kept coming.

Cross, fumbling to load the last bullet, felt a tug at his sleeve as Miss Edmonds pulled him back towards the car.

The goat-things seemed to run into an invisible barrier. The hieroglyph which Miss Edmonds had scrawled in the ground was weak, but it slowed them down like running into quicksand. They strained forward inch by inch, mouths opening much wider than goat mouths should, showing far too many of those massive black teeth.

Their feet were scuffing the edges of the symbol, wearing it away, pushing forward.

Cross raised his gun. He would use the last bullet on the first creature that got close enough to bite him or Miss Edmonds.

Then the Lewis gunner finally finished reloading and started firing again, destroying the barrel-bodied thing and shooting the next three or four animals with short, controlled bursts. The Captain and Miss Edmunds threw themselves flat as the tommy gunner started again, too, sweeping across the herd, scything down a row of the beasts.

Cross had a horrible vision from his past: men and horses trapped in barbed wire while the guns stuttered, a glorious charge ending in a massacre. Something in him was on the side of primal nature against the machines. Cross felt momentary dizziness, a blurring, and his tattoo flamed.

The bullets kept flying and something crumbled in the goat-things. A light seemed to go out of their eyes, and Cross came back to himself. Like the bullies Cross had faced down, the goat-things were unused to resistance, and being allowed to get so close before being gunned down must have disconcerted them.

Dozens of dead goat-things littered the track. The nearest was about the size of a pony, with horns like black scythes. Dead, the bearded face looked practically human. The creatures turned. They did not run away so much as fragment and melt into shadows, becoming one again with the dark wood as the echoes of gunfire died away. The Turk took a couple of steps forward to regard the steaming remains thoughtfully, each step scattering the tinkling brass cartridge cases which littered the ground.

"The Thousand Young, just as Al-Hazred describes them," he said into the silence. "Interesting."

Captain Cross was, for a moment, without words. The Turk's bodyguards were swiftly piling into the limousine, and the chauffeur gunned the engine.

"Well played, Captain," said the Turk, with an ironic bow. "Til we meet again. And Miss Edmonds, Mr. Cranley. *Au revoir.*"

Miss Edmonds was in the car checking on the baby. Cranley was standing still, looking poleaxed. The taillights of the limousine disappeared down the track.

"We're not out of danger," said Cross, taking Cranley by the elbow. He sensed rather than saw the Thousand Young regathering. They had been stung but they were not defeated.

"Get in!" shouted Miss Edmonds. Cross was barely in before he was thrown back in his seat with all the acceleration the little car could muster.

The only thought now was the desperate urge to escape, to get away as fast as possible. Cross could feel the danger behind them, all around them, suffusing the forest. The omnivorous dark was reaching out to enfold them. Cross sensed the enormous, organic form, the entire forest fused into a single being, seeking to absorb the intruders as though it was a living thing and they were just bacteria.

The car jolted and came out under streetlights. Miss Edmonds swore, the Austin swerved, tires skidding, then she had it back under control and was slowing down on the smooth tarmac road.

They were out of the wild wood, back to the mundane suburbia of South Norwood, with its road signs and pillar boxes, lampposts and hedges, even a late delivery van trundling past: the ordered land the Puritans had taken from the pagans and claimed as their own. They were outside the reach of nightmares.

"Well driven, darling," said Cranley as she pulled the car over.

All of them looked back towards the lane, as though the horde might burst forth from it.

Under the streetlight Cross was able to look at the *Book of Names* at last. The first few pages were taken up with invocations, fragments of garbled text that might come to mean something if you studied them closely enough. There were geometric diagrams, including one showing a normal goat next to what might be the same animal after a mathematical transformation.

Those first few pages looked like they had been cribbed directly from the *Necronomicon*. After that, the format was simpler. Each page was a contract, with a list of requests by the person being inducted and, at the bottom, a scrawled signature in blood and the imprint of a hoof.

Towards the end, he came across a page with the name Phillips, the warlock he had dispatched. The man whose death had left a place in the coven empty for Miss Edmonds.

Small world, he thought.

Cross soon found the page he was looking for.

"Just one small thing we need to clear up, old man," he said, turning to Cranley. "You know I was worried about your fiancée—it seemed to me rather as though Miss Edmonds had lured you into a trap."

"Oh no," she said quickly. "It was just that I couldn't—"

"I understand that now," said Cross. "You didn't tell Cranley you would be here because you thought he'd forbid it. Too dangerous."

"Of course I would," said Cranley.

"No, Miss Edmonds, I don't doubt your integrity at all. Especially not after you tried to sacrifice yourself to save us. I fully apologize for any suspicions I harbored about you. I don't see *you* as a Machiavellian schemer at all."

"No, the scheming was all your Turkish friend," said Cranley.

"What's the matter?" she asked, catching his tone.

"I understand perfectly your motives. Your great-grandfather's name is in the book, just as you said, and seven generations of Edmonds are owed to the Dark One according to his contract. But," looking to Cranley "things are a little less clear with you."

"He was helping me!" Miss Edmonds protested.

"He was helping himself," said Cross, levelling his gun at Cranley. "The Turk may have brought him into it, but he had his own plans."

"You're making a big mistake," said Cranley.

"This book has the invocations to summon Shub-Niggurath or whatever you want to call it. Isn't that what you wanted all these years? To have that knowledge yourself?"

"My interest is purely academic, as you well know. "

"Oh, it started out as academic," Cross said. "But you would not be the first to be sucked in. This whole escapade has been very out of character for the old Cranley. You say you escaped the influence of the evil eye with the twenty-third Psalm, or was it some counter-spell? Your mascot might have been St. Dunstan, but I rather doubt it. And you say you're wearing a crucifix, but I've never seen it. I noticed you did not touch the one you gave to Miss Edmonds."

Cranley gulped.

"And throwing your family Bible — that's more the sort of thing the other side would do, eh?"

"Please don't shoot me," said Cranley.

"He's not one of them... he can't be," said Miss Edmonds.

"I don't doubt that you love him," said Cross. "That was another thing that puzzled me. Why would a beautiful young woman fall for an old library fixture like Cranley?"

"That's a bit thick, old man," Cranley protested.

"Cranley has quite a collection of recipes for potions." Cross tapped the thermos. "I'm sure he has plenty of love potions in his collection. A good way of getting you to play along."

"Except it isn't true," Miss Edmonds snapped.

"I know you may think your feelings arise from natural causes—"

"I know they do, because I bloody checked," she said sharply. She glanced, embarrassedly at Cranley. "I'm sorry darling. I carried out a divination to determine if I was bewitched in any way. And of course I'm not,"

"Oh," said Cross.

Cranley gave a short laugh of relief mingled with something else.

"Oh dear! Darling, I have a confession too. I did the same. You see, I'd never felt this way before, and I wondered..."

"At least you didn't point a gun at me!" she said.

"Now, if you could just not shoot me for a second, Captain," said Cranley, more confident and fumbling under his collar. "Look!"

He held up the small silver cross.

"I know my redeemer liveth," said Cranley. "You know, Our Lord, one who can tell the sheep from the goats—even if some others can't."

An awkward silence descended. The lovers were holding hands, beaming at each other.

It had been a perfectly good theory. A solid theory that accounted for all the facts. That Cranley and Miss Edmonds should have fallen in love with each other with no self-interest on either side seemed a far less likely explanation. It just happened to be true.

Cranley was not the only one with plausible but erroneous ideas. Cross, all too aware of the corrupting power of occult knowledge, had underestimated the redeeming power of love,

Then again Cross had to admit that people had found his engagement to the lovely Amanda—now Mrs. Cross—equally unlikely. Maybe every love story looked implausible to outsiders.

"Fair enough," he said, lowering his gun and ejecting the bullet into his palm. "May I offer you two a small wedding present? You can show this souvenir to your grandchildren."

Miss Edmonds burst out laughing again. Cranley merely let out an exasperated snort.

"Fine thing it would have been if you'd shot me, eh, Cross?" he muttered, but Miss Edmonds laughed even harder. "But, damn it all, we're alive and we've got the book. You deserve some credit—even if you're just as a paranoid as I said."

Not many men would have been so forgiving. But Cranley had known Cross longer than most.

"Very handsome of you," said Cross offering his hand, and they solemnly shook. "No hard feelings."

"None," said Cranley. "But I'd be obliged, if, by way of reparation, you might have some advice on how to escape from a coven. I thought crossing the Thames would be enough but now I'm not so sure."

Running water was traditionally supposed to stop witches. In this case it seemed unlikely, given that several of them lived north of the river.

"Do you have a can of petrol?" Cross asked. "The first thing is to destroy the book."

"Why?" asked Cranley.

"Let's do what he says," said Miss Edmonds

Stepping out under the light, the car was very much the worse for wear, the panels battered and dented, the roof torn, bullet holes in the corner of the windscreen. Both overtaking mirrors were gone, and in one place the bodywork showed the clear imprint of a pair of horns. Extensive repair work would be needed; it was a wonder the thing still drove.

Cranley retrieved the can, and sloshed petrol over the book which Cross had placed on the road. Cross patted his pocket for matches, which Miss Edmonds produced, and lighting four at a time, ignited the *Book of Names* which went up with a satisfactory whoosh.

It was a unique and priceless work, moreover one with the actual mark of Shub-Niggurath on every page. But Cranley, bibliophile that he was, was happy to see it burn, throwing up tall yellow flames.

"We're saving all of the rest of the coven's souls too," said Cranley, squeezing Miss Edmonds' hand. "But why?"

"The other side of the contract," said Cross. "As soon as it is invalidated, they lose whatever benefits and powers that the goat-being—Azazel or Pan, Shub-Niggurath, Cernunnos, whatever you call it—gives them."

The coven would still be dangerous without any supernatural powers. But they might have come to rely on occult forces to do their dirtiest work for them, and suddenly being stripped of power would be a blow.

"Couldn't they sign up again?" said Miss Edmonds.

Cranley chuckled and shook his head.

"Easier said than done, darling," he said. "According to accepted lore, someone first must summon Shub-Niggurath and they become coven leader and sign up more witches. Sort of like bishops in the Church of England making other bishops. Without the book I don't think they can call up anything."

"Unless they made a copy," said Miss Edmonds, but Cranley and Cross shook their heads as one. Covens were fanatical about secrets. Which was why true grimoires were rare and valuable.

"But even without that they are still quite formidable people," she went on. "You're not supposed to know names, but one of them is an MP and I think one is in the Lords."

"Oh, they're dangerous all right," said Cross. "But don't you think the *Daily Mail* would be very interested to hear one of regulars in their Society pages is a paid-up witch."

"Who would have thought that the *Mail* might be useful for something?" wondered Miss Edmonds.

"Haven't we just destroyed the evidence?" asked Cranley, as the pages crumbled to ashes one by one.

"A contract could be faked, and she would deny it anyway," said Cross. "What will hang her in the eyes of the newspapers is all the ancillary evidence."

"But nobody is going to demand to see her thigh looking for the mark," said Cranley. "This is not the Middle Ages."

"Don't be too sure," said Cross.

"Anyone can check and see that she's had a gap in her engagements diary every single time there was a full moon," said Miss Edmonds. "And has never been seen in a church."

"And there is the question of crucifixes," said Cross.

"It's not as though anyone is going to thrust a cross in her face," said Cranley. "Or splash her with Holy Water and see if it blisters."

"You don't read the papers, do you?" said Miss Edmonds. "That's exactly what they'd do for a stunt. And they'd bring a photographer"

"Fleet Street isn't quite as scrupulous as it was," said Cross. "And there is nothing more they love than a witch hunt."

"I suppose she'll be forced into hiding?"

"Remember what happened to Josiah Deakins," said Cross. "The one thing the coven cannot tolerate is being brought into the light."

"That's rather fiendish," said Cranley appreciatively.

There was a wailing from somewhere inside the car, a ghastly, miserable sound. Cross and Cranley stood transfixed, unsure what this new horror could be. It was Miss Edmonds who moved quickly to comfort the crying baby.

"There, there! What are we going to do with her?" she said, cradling the babe in her arms.

"Do we drop her off at a church or a hospital, or something?" asked Cranley.

"We return her to her parents," said Cross. "If a child has disappeared in the area, Arthur Renville will know about it. The anxious father will probably be at the Electric Café talking to him right now."

"But how on earth will we explain it?"

"That's the thing about Arthur Renville," said Cross. "He knows when not to ask questions."

"How do you stop them crying?" asked Miss Edmonds, and Cross realized that he was the only one present with experience of child rearing. With some reluctance he took the child and sat in the back for the short journey,

"You can drop me off at Norwood Junction," said Cross, checking his watch. He would be in good time for the last train home. "I would advise you two to leave the country in the morning. Get married, take a honeymoon or something. Avoid having adventures."

"What about you?" asked Miss Edmonds. "That coven..."

"They won't bother with me," he said. While they may well be able to identify Miss Edmonds, and Cranley by the car, Cross was confident they were unlikely to make the necessary effort to find him. They would probably assume he was in league with The Turk, who they would not want to tangle with. And if they did show up—he had plenty of silver bullets at home.

Cross yawned, suddenly feeling very tired. It had been rather a long evening. He was looking forward to the comfort of a railway tearoom, and a chance to quietly digest the evening's adventure.

The forces of chaos had been pushed back, a little. But the goat cult had survived for thousands of years in the shadows, despite all attempts to suppress it. And now, it seemed, it was moving up the social scale. There could be more trouble ahead... that could wait.

More worryingly, he had been tricked into dancing to the Turk's tune and retrieving a book under false pretenses. But he had pulled off a final trick himself, and forced the Turk to save him and his friends. Call it even honors on that one. And tomorrow would be another day and another chance to come out ahead.

Hollow Dollies

A Eugene Angove Adventure

By Tim Mendees

Weak shafts of sunlight filtered through the gently swaying branches of a nearby hawthorn tree as a sprinkle of pinkish blossom drifted onto the freshly cut grass. Spring aromas of pungent pollen and sickly-sweet berries combined to concoct a heady perfume that tickled the nostrils of the sweaty man currently hiding in the shade. It was unseasonably warm, more like July or August than late April. Even the wind whistling in off the nearby coastline had lost its bite. The local fauna seemed to be enjoying it, but Albert wasn't sold. Maybe if he was able to just lounge around like the owner of the garden he toiled in, not pull weeds, he may have been better disposed towards the heatwave.

Removing his flat cap and mopping his lined brow with his sleeve, the elder Mr. Weston let out a sigh and made a decision. "That's it, I'm done for the day, and if *he* doesn't like it... he can go and whistle!"

Albert Weston had been in the employ of the Angove family since he was little more than a boy. His father had been in service likewise and it was something of a family tradition. He was well looked after and, on the whole, had little to complain about in the grand scheme of things. That said, it was hard graft, and he got the distinct impression that the current master of the house, Eugene, couldn't give a single fig if his hedges were manicured and his flowerbeds free of hogweed and nettles. It often felt like they were both going through the motions for the benefit of people who were no longer on the mortal plane. Still, it was work, and he was far too old to go down a tin or arsenic mine and that's all the nearby village of Hollowhills had to offer as an alternative.

Gathering up his tools and placing them in his wheelbarrow on top of a pile of uprooted interlopers, he grabbed the wooden handles, lifted, and began trundling towards the shed. The ground was hard under his feet and his calves barked as he navigated a slight declivity between two raised beds housing brightly colored blooms that teemed with striped and spotted denizens that buzzed and munched with gleeful abandon. Rounding the eastern bed, he joined the path at the bottom, reducing the friction on the wheel and taking some of the strain off his back. He wanted to take a break but it wasn't far to his wooden sanctuary so he decided to press on, the promise of a glass of lemonade at the end of his trudge buoying his spirits. He may even put gin in it. After all, by that time in the afternoon his employer was most-likely half-cut.

Albert parked his barrow next to the shed and transferred the trowels, forks, and pruning shears inside. He looked down at his padded lawn-chair and let out another heavy sigh. He had one more job to do before he could relax. Luckily, it wasn't too arduous, he just had to take the weeds to the compost heap over by the boundary fence backing onto the woodland behind the Angove estate. Leaving his cap on the workbench next to his glass and leather tobacco pouch, he left the coolness of the shed and stepped back out into the stifling heat. The air between his position and the towering rear wall of Angove Hall shimmered, and the cacophony of insects seemed to increase in volume to greet him. Damn, it was hot.

Placing the weeds in a sack which he then dragged along the ground behind him, Albert cursed his decision to leave his balding pate exposed. He'd walked mere feet before he could feel his pale skin begin to sear. Quickening his pace, he reached the shade created by the towering trees beyond the fence. Oaks, elms, birches, and yews, it was an ancient place, more-or-less, untouched by humanity. Blanketed by moss, deadfall leaves and branches, and clumps of exotic-looking fungi, it had an abandoned, neglected feel to it that appealed to his solitary spirit. It felt like the world at large had forgotten its existence.

Only the odd track and snapped branch would let one know that a single soul had planted a foot within its confines in decades. Albert found it a peaceful place. Some of the more superstitious in the area found it eerie.

A centipede and a bevy of bloated beetles skittered for cover as Albert removed the planks of wood on the top of the compost heap. Foul aromas of decaying matter drifted into the air as he averted his nose and upended the bag of weeds. Poking them down into the rotting mass, he replaced the planks and gave them a good stomp with his size twelves to ensure they were firmly in place.

"Right, that's it, I'm done," he smiled, giving his brow another mop. "Reckon I'll wait for the sun to go down a bit before heading home." The walk from Angove Hall back to the hamlet of High Bend where he shared a cottage with his wife of thirty years wasn't a long one but the road offered no shade whatsoever. He'd be the color of a boiled lobster by the time he put his key in the door.

Albert was turning from the compost heap when a strange sound from the trees made him stop in his tracks. It was carried by a chill gust of wind and distorted by both distance and obstruction. Despite the oppressive warmth, he felt a shiver trace its way from his lower back all the way to the nape of his neck. It sounded like a scream. He turned in the approximate direction and approached the fence, straining his ears. Draping his weed bag over the wooden beams, he leaned forward and listened for what felt like several minutes, though, in reality, it was more like thirty seconds. When he heard nothing more, he straightened up and shook his head.

"Probably a fox."

No sooner had he uttered his statement of wishful thinking, another sound came from the darkness between the trunks. It was faint again, though much clearer. Two distinct words were audible. Breathy and appearing to drift on the wind. "Help Me!"

"Hold on," Albert called out, imploring the girl—or it could have been a young boy. He nimbly mounted the fence and was over in one fluid motion. "Where are you?"

"Help me…"

The voice seemed to come from a westerly direction. Albert winced. Typically, this was the densest part of the wood and festooned with nettles, thistles, and other aggressive foliage. Looking around, he snatched up a large stick and started swinging it at the green barrier.

"Hold on, I'm coming. Keep talking so I can follow yer voice, lass!"

"Over here…" The voice sounded both closer and more distant, as though it was part of the breeze itself. The Cornish winds played havoc with the senses at the best of times, but you add trees to the mix and you haven't a hope in pinpointing sound.

Once a path between the weeds had been cleared, Albert broke into a jog and crossed the threshold of shadow into the trees. Instantly, the temperature dropped a couple of degrees but the humidity remained, giving the woods an oppressive, subtropical feel. His brow poured with sweat as he hopped a fallen tree limb and crushed a wilting daffodil. A few more paces and the ground became clearer. The greenery gradually receded, leaving only a blanket of dull brown and the occasional muted orange. Spiders' webs crisscrossed between swollen boles and branches, glistening with moisture that twinkled with the kiss of the sun's rays that infiltrated the canopy.

"Over here…"

Albert stopped dead, the direction of the voice had shifted. It was now to his right, deeper into the woods. By his reckoning, the distressed girl was somewhere in the direction of Hollowhills. This gave him an anxious pause. The village was named for the many natural caverns that lay below it. These had been expanded somewhat in the last century or so by extensive mining. Sadly, cave-ins were not uncommon, and reports of people, pets, and livestock being lost down freshly-opened maws in the earth came with alarming regularity. In fact, at an earlier point in his lifetime, an entire house along with its owner had been sucked below. He wished he had darted back to the shed and grabbed a rope.

"Where are you? Have you fallen down a shaft?"

"Over here…"

The voice in the wilderness was louder now, yet still wraithlike and spectral. Albert pointed himself in the general direction of its source and pressed on. After a hundred yards or so, he stopped again and called out. This time there was no response. He tried again and again, all to no avail. It was pointless to carry on without anything to home in on. He spat a bitter curse to the heavens and threw his stick into a patch of yellow scrub grass. As he did, another sound came to his ears. It sounded like laughter. High and girlish, like his eight-year-old niece when she had liberated a treat from the biscuit tin. His brow furrowed. Was this all some kind of game?

"Right, you can come out now. You've had yer fun, you little scamp. It ain't safe to be muckin' about in 'ere."

Another giggle came from his left, accompanied by the crack of a twig.

"Come back here," Albert growled.

This time, the response came in mocking tones. "Can't catch me, old man."

"We'll just see about that, ye little tyke." Charging off in pursuit, Albert nearly legged himself up on his discarded stick as he plunged through the dry grass towards a cluster of densely packed trees. Turning sideways, he shuffled crab-like between them and, upon reaching the other side, instantly lost his footing. The soil below him was loose and his left foot went from under him eliciting a yelp of surprise from his weathered lips. Landing hard on his coccyx, he slid down a steep bank before going into a roll, coming to a sharp halt at the bottom. Landing flat on his belly, the wind was driven from his body as pinpricks of bright light exploded before his eyes. Groaning and panting, Albert rolled onto his back and stared up at the canopy in sheer bewilderment. Above him, gently twisting and swaying, were hundreds of misshapen corn dollies.

"What in God's name?"

"Which god, yours or mine?"

Albert cried out in surprise as the voice whispered into his right ear. Turning his head, he found himself staring at a grotesquely twisted corn effigy of something that no sane hands could have crafted. Quadrupedal with what looked like tentacles sprouting from its back, the "animal" seemed to glower back at him. Sitting upright and reaching out a hand tentatively, he quickly recoiled as his fingers brushed the tip of one of the strange appendages. It was warm to the touch and strangely fluid, as though it was composed of jelly and not corn. All around him, shrill, unnatural voices began to titter and giggle, rising and lowering in pitch creating a disturbing kind of music that made his skin crawl and his teeth itch.

Scrambling to his feet as the daemonic din echoed around him, Albert searched for a swift exit. Eyes darting left and right, he found himself in a perfectly circular hollow, almost a crater, which was entirely circled by twisted yew trees that looked like a procession of bent crones on their way to a sabbat. As his pulse went from a steady march to a sprint, the entire area began to be smothered by darkness. Above him, the pinpricks of light began to die like stars in the night sky occluded by clouds. The breeze became a gale that whipped leaves at his legs and grit into his watering eyes. All the while, the myriad corn dollies bounced on their strings as their mirth grew into mania. The cacophony was almost too much to bear. Covering his ears with his hands and screwing his eyes shut, he tipped his head back and roared.

When he opened his eyes, he found that he could see very little, the circle was now in complete darkness. Removing his hands, Albert was relieved to find that the dolls were now silent. This brief moment of reprieve was fleeting, however, as it was swiftly replaced by irregular heavy steps from his rear. Something was behind him. Something fairly large. He didn't want to turn around but he forced his legs into motion. What met his eyes snapped the threads holding his fragile sanity together. Unravelling in an instant, merciful madness took him as he was unceremoniously separated from the land of the living.

Door chimes echoed throughout the wood-paneled corridors of Angove Hall. At the rear of the grand old pile, a sigh drifted from the parlor adjacent to the kitchen as its occupant put down the candlestick he was polishing, removed his apron and gloves, and strode towards the door with his spine straight and his shoulders back. The man in the immaculately pressed suit hadn't made it five meters before the bell rang again, then again a second or two later. He rolled his eyes.

"Forgotten our keys again, have we, sir?"

Turning the key in the heavy oak door and sliding aside the deadbolt, Hampton prepared himself to meet his employer with one of his patented withering looks. As the door opened to allow a fresh breeze into the stuffy entrance hall, he was shocked to see a distressed-looking woman standing on the doorstep, not a half-sozzled chap in an ill-fitting tweed suit and his current lady friend. It took a second for recognition to dawn. Once it had, he smiled and purred a greeting.

"Good day, "

"Oh, Hampton," Angela Weston trilled, her voice high and her eyes red, "have you seen my Albert?"

"Today? I'm afraid not, madam. He didn't arrive for duty this morning, I assumed he was feeling under the weather."

Angela crossed herself. "Oh, Lord, what could possibly have happened to him. He never came home last night. When did you last see him?"

Hampton thought for a moment. "Around fifteen-hundred hours. He was pulling weeds on the north lawn as I drove Mr. Angove and Miss Green into Betyls Cove. There was no sign of him when we returned later that evening."

"Good grief," Angela started to hyperventilate, her face flushing and her hands fluttering at her cheeks like puffy pink butterflies. "Something ghastly has happened, I can feel it in my bones."

Hampton sprang into action, putting a strong arm around her waist and leading her into the hall. Directing her to an upholstered chair, he sat her down and turned towards the kitchen. "Try to calm down, I'll fetch you a glass of water."

"I'd prefer a brandy."

Smiling and changing direction, Hampton nodded. "Of course. Just one moment, I'll be right back." Heading to the drawing room, he approached his employer's drinks globe and retrieved the crystal decanter containing the fortifying liquid. Pouring two fingers, he returned to the distraught woman in the summer frock. "Here, take this. It should serve to steady the nerves."

"Thank you, Hampton." Angela forced a smile then knocked it back in one gulp.

Hampton cocked an eyebrow.

"That's better. Now, where's Mr. Angove? Perhaps he has sent him on an errand?"

"It's possible, I suppose. Though, he usually directs things of that nature through me." Hampton was almost certain it would be futile but acquiesced all the same. "Very well, we shall go and speak with Mr. Angove. I believe he is in the gazebo. If you would like to follow me, we will take the rear entrance. Are you well enough to walk."

Angela stood, wobbled for a second, then centered herself. "Yes, fighting fit. That brandy has done the trick."

"It usually does, madam. Very well, this way." With a sweeping gesture towards the kitchen, Hampton steered their guest through the working areas of Angove Hall.

Flies buzzed around the receding waters of the ornamental pond in the well-tended rose garden as Hampton and Mrs. Weston approached the gazebo. From inside the stone structure, the unmistakable tones of Eugene Angove could be heard. He sounded in good spirits, though Hampton suspected that the various bottles of spirits that Mr. Angove kept squirrelled away in his varied outdoor bolt-holes may have had something to do with the mirth that rode the wind. Since he had struck up his recent relationship with the comely Miss Green, his employer had been seldom sober. It was something of a concern. He had always liked lashings of the sauce, but this was getting a tad extreme. The sun was barely over the yardarm.

Clearing his throat with a discreet cough, Hampton called out a greeting. "Apologies for disturbing you, sir, we have a guest that needs to speak to you urgently."

An exclamation of surprise, muttered grumbles, a girlish giggle, and the sound of hurried straightening of attire followed as Eugene put his glass down, took his hand off Miss Green's knee, and rose from his wicker chair. "Blast it, Hampton, you certainly know how to make an entrance. I nearly dropped my gin and tonic! Can't you whistle, or something, so I know you're coming?"

"That wouldn't be seemly, sir."

Wobbling ever-so-slightly, Eugene moved to the arched wooden entrance and shielded his eyes from the dazzling rays. "I suppose not. Right, what's all the flap about?" As his eyes adjusted to the change in light, he recognized his gardener's better half. "Ah, Mrs. Weston, what brings you all the way out here in such ghastly heat?"

"It's my Albert, he never came home last night."

"Oh, is that all, he's probably on a spree."

Hampton balled his fist, pressed it to his lips, and coughed.

"I mean," Eugene's glassy eyes darted from his valet back to Angela, "it's probably nothing to concern yourself with. A chap can get caught up in things, isn't that right, Hampton?"

Glancing sideways at the attractive woman in equestrian attire appearing behind his employer, he tried his damnedest not to roll his eyes. "Indeed, sir."

"Oh, not my Albert, it's so very unlike him. I fear he has keeled over from the heat. Have you not seen him today?"

"I'm afraid not," Eugene thought for a second then raised a finger. "I know that he kept a fine bottle of gin in his little shed. Perhaps he took shelter and had one snifter too many. Come, let's have a look. I could do with stretching the old legs. Come along, Cynthia. Afterwards, we can take a stroll over to The Rat and Raven for a spot of lunch, if you fancy?"

Cynthia Green smiled as she brushed a wayward curl of strawberry-blonde hair from her eyes. "Oh, what a spiffing idea. I hear they do a smashing rabbit pie." Her voice was refined and plummy in contrast to Mrs. Weston's Cornish burr. As heiress to the Green shipping fortune, she had been privileged to attend the finest schools and had a regal bearing, despite her reputation as something of a party-girl and socialite. She stopped and regarded Angela from top to tail, her nose wrinkling at the state of her rumpled dress. Had the woman never heard of an iron?

For her part, Angela found the idea of a thirty-something woman parading around in full riding garb like she was going fox hunting on the hottest day of the year so far faintly ridiculous.

Eugene spotted the frostiness creeping across the path and leapt into action. "Ladies, my apology, I don't believe you have been introduced. Cynthia, may I introduce Mrs. Angela Weston. She's the wife of my gardener, Albert. Mrs. Weston, meet Lady Cynthia Green of the Betyls Cove Greens."

"Delighted," Cynthia flashed her perfect teeth and fluttered her lashes.

"Likewise," Angela's face remained locked in a worried expression.

Hampton, sensing that Angela couldn't give two toffees who his employer's lady friend was, gave a sweeping motion over towards the back lawn. "Shall we press on, sir. I feel this is a matter of some urgency."

"Yes, yes." Eugene batted away a fly. "Lead on, Hampton." He fell into step leaving the two ladies behind them. "What do you think of all this, my dear chap?"

"I don't know what to think, sir. I'm hoping for a happy outcome. Your *spree*, perhaps."

"No need to snipe. I didn't mean to be insensitive. I merely wanted to placate the woman. She looks like she is going to have an attack of the vapors."

"Indeed, I had to give her a stiff drink to steady the nerves."

"Good thinking."

Behind them, the two women walked in silence. As they left the path and stepped onto the lawn, Angela stumbled and became short of breath. The dual shocks of the extreme heat and her husband's absence had taken a toll on her.

Cynthia rushed to her side and took her by the arm. "Here, allow me."

Angela smiled, her demeanor softening. "Thank you. I just came over all faint for a moment."

"Oh, you poor thing. I'm sure Eugene will find your husband."

"It's just so unlike him. He's never done this sort of thing before..."

"Never?" Cynthia cocked an eyebrow in surprise. "In my experience, men are prone to wander."

"Not my Albert. I can't help thinking the worst."

As the duo fell into an uncomfortable silence, Eugene Angove and Hampton reached the shed. The door was pinned open and it was deserted.

"Hmm, that is odd, I'll grant you that," Eugene mused as he looked at the tableaux before him. It was like a strangely bucolic Mary Celeste or Flannan Isle. A newspaper sat next to a glass and a couple of bottles, the cushion on the deck-chair was plumped and ready to receive a tired posterior, and various articles of clothing shed throughout the day hung on a nail next to the door. "It looks like he stepped out for a moment and never returned. What did you say he was doing when we left, old chap?"

"Weeding, I believe, sir."

Eugene exited the shed and walked around the side. "The barrow is here, can you see his weed bag?"

"Not in here, sir," Hampton called out before also leaving the shed. "Perhaps he went to the compost heap."

"Good thinking. Come along," he lowered his voice so as not to alarm Mrs. Weston. "I'm starting to fear the worst myself."

Hampton nodded and took off with great strides across the lawn. Eugene followed, again leaving the two ladies trailing in their wake.

"I don't like this one bit," Angela whispered, barely audible over the drone of insects and twitter of overheated birds.

Cynthia gave a weak smile and squeezed her hand. "Never give up hope. There could still be a happy outcome."

"I hope you're right. I've just had such a feeling of dread ever since I awoke and found the bed still empty. Then I found that *thing* on the doorstep..."

"What thing?" Cynthia raised an immaculately plucked eyebrow.

Angela dipped a hand into the white crocheted bag hanging over her right shoulder and pulled out a mangled corn doll. "This. Isn't it foul?"

Cynthia took it, eyes widening. "It's certainly peculiar. Did you twist it up?"

"No, I found it like that. I think that's how it was made."

"Well, whoever made it has a rather warped eye for art. I have no idea what it's supposed to be. I *think* these four stumps are legs… What the things sprouting out of its back are is anyone's guess. Here, take it back, it's making me come over all wobbly. Of course, that could be the gin."

Angela smiled for the first time that morning. She was warming to her haughty new friend. As she slipped the doll back into her bag, the two men reached the compost heap.

"Here's his bag," Eugene exclaimed. "Where the ruddy hell has he got to?"

Hampton approached the fence and scanned the tree line. Spotting fresh tracks and trampled weeds, he pointed towards a new opening. "I think he went into the woods over there, sir."

"Why in all that is sane would he have gone wandering off in the blasted woods?"

"Beats me, sir. Though, I dare say, he must have had his reasons. The whims of gardeners are not something one is taught when training to be a gentleman's personal gentleman, sir. Nor did they come up in basic training during the war. Perhaps, he went foraging for berries or fungi?"

"Perhaps…" Eugene looked longingly at his gazebo, small and pointy on the horizon, then sighed. "Right, help me over the fence, would you? These tight trousers were built for decorative purposes, not action, and I don't want to do myself a mischief."

Hampton rolled his eyes. "Very good, sir."

A few paces behind them, Angela looked confused. "What the devil are they doing now? Surely, my Albert wouldn't have been so foolish to have gone mucking around in there!"

"Oh, why's that?" Cynthia asked.

"Well, the wood is haunted, isn't it?"

Cynthia was taken aback by Mrs. Weston's matter-of-fact tone. "Haunted? Surely, you don't believe all that superstitious twaddle?"

"Don't you?" Mrs. Weston asked.

"Not at all. I've walked these woods ever since I was a girl. They are beautiful and peaceful. Granted, I haven't gone that deep into them, only skirted them on the Hollowhills side, but I've seen nary a spook nor specter."

"Ah, that's it, then," Angela raised a hand to the crucifix on a train of pearls around her neck. "It's the heart of the woods that you have to steer clear of. There is talk hereabouts of strange sightings, disappearances, even a group of ne'er-do-wells that…"

Angela was cut off by Eugene bellowing an expletive as he split a seam in his riding britches. Once back on *terra firma*, he whispered an instruction in Hampton's ear and watched as he ambled over to the two women.

Hampton was doing his level best to appear unruffled, though in truth, he had started to experience the unnerving prick of something sinister that he had experienced several times since meeting his employer in the trenches.

"Mr. Angove suggests that you both return to the house and call for the constable. I believe he will be in The Rat and Raven at this hour, and they have a telephone. The number is in the little black book on the side."

"A constable," Angela wailed. "Oh, Albert!"

"Calm yourself, madam," Hampton said, "it's just that we are going to need help searching the woods. It's a vast area and neither Mr. Angove nor I have a map and compass to hand. We fear he may have gone in search of fungi and become lost. It is so easy to get oneself turned around."

Whether Angela was buying what the valet was selling is anyone's guess, but his reasoned words and smooth delivery did a fine job of calming her down. "Very well. That makes sense."

"Come along, dear," Cynthia cooed, "let's get you out of the sun and another brandy inside you. I'd like to hear more of the stories about the woods. I find this kind of thing fascinating."

Watching the two walk off arm-in-arm, Hampton felt that he may have misjudged Miss Green. Maybe, like his employer, there was a tender side to her nature that was often suppressed beneath a shroud of bluster and obstreperousness. Turning away, he hurried back to the fence and nimbly hopped over. Unlike Eugene, he hadn't let himself go to seed since leaving the army and had kept himself in reasonable condition. Following what were presumably Albert's tracks, he joined Eugene at the gaping black hole in the wall of green.

"I think he went this way, Hampton. Look, you can see where his boots have scuffed the soil. Of course, that could have been made by a fox, hare, or pheasant."

"Wearing hobnail boots, sir?"

"Oh, very droll, Hampton. If you're such an expert tracker, you can lead the way."

"Very good, sir." Picking up a stick, he batted a bramble aside and entered the woods. Keeping his eyes lowered, he followed the tracks to the best of his ability while Eugene hummed a ribald music hall ditty to keep their spirits up. They carried on like this for several minutes until they encountered a fallen log. Hampton checked all sides and eventually picked up the tracks again. As he turned to Eugene and opened his mouth to speak, a rustle in the bushes to their left had them both jumping in alarm.

"What the blazes," Eugene yelped as a large black shape emerged from the undergrowth and regarded them with baleful yellow eyes.

Hampton smiled. "It's just a goat, sir."

"I can see that, Hampton, the blasted thing nearly gave me a coronary." Picking up a branch festooned with dried leaves, he rustled it at the interloper. "Go on, bugger off back to whatever farm you have escaped from, you daft so-and-so!"

The goat glared at Eugene, not moving an inch.

"Go on, get off with you!" Eugene waved the stick at the goat's face.

With startling quickness, their caprine friend snapped its teeth around the leaves, yanked the stick out of his hand, and began eating.

"This doesn't seem to be working, sir."

"I can see that, Hampton."

"Maybe, we should leave Billy here to his snack and press on?"

"Yes. Yes. Very well. Just remind me to put a note in the post office window that somebody's goat is loose."

Nodding, Hampton resumed his search. The deeper into the woods the men tramped, the looser and more pungent the earth became. This made tracking easier, but ambulation more treacherous. Despite the weather, the area was something of a mud bath with a steady descent leading towards the valley that housed the village of Hollowhills. As it began to level out, Hampton spotted something odd lying under a bush. Stooping down, he picked it up and waved it at his employer. "I've found something, sir!"

Eugene hurried over. "What in blazes is it?"

"It appears to be a corn doll, sir. You know, like the ones superstitious folk make at harvest to ensure a good crop and ward off the Corn Man."

"I can see it's a corn dolly, Hampton, but what the deuce is it supposed to be. I've never seen the like. It looks like it was crafted by a raving lunatic that had just sunk his body weight in grain spirit!"

"It's certainly a strange object, sir." Hampton turned it over in his hands and hummed thoughtfully. "I wonder… I've heard tell of similar effigies being made in Eastern Europe. A fellow I met in the trenches told me that pagan worshippers crafted all kinds of strange totems to appease their myriad gods. It could be something along those lines, don't you think?"

"Possible, I suppose. Maybe it has something to do with, what my father called, the Frisky Sisters."

Hampton's left eyebrow lifted in confusion. "Pardon, sir?"

"I always thought they were one of his tall tales, you know, to stop us youngsters wandering in the woods. He told us of a 'sisterhood' of witches that gathered on moonlit nights to conduct 'fertility' rites. He reckoned that they were responsible for the high birth rate in the area.

Utter nonsense, of course. Anyway, he used to spook us by saying that any man caught in their sacred ground would be used for their diabolical rites."

"Diabolical rites?"

"He didn't go into detail. Back then, I assumed human sacrifice. Now I think about it, as they were interested in fertility, he could have meant rumpy-pumpy... Though, that doesn't sound too diabolical to me!" Eugene let out a roar of mirth that startled two pheasants, a wood pigeon, and a crow, all of which had been having a nice snooze out of the sun.

Hampton rolled his eyes and tossed the doll back into the bushes. "I'm sure it has no bearing on the matter at hand. Should we press on, sir?"

"Indeed. The quicker we find the wretched fellow, the quicker I can get back to wooing Miss Green. She is a delight, isn't she, Hampton?"

The valet still wasn't convinced and crossed his fingers behind his back. "Indeed, sir." Since Hampton had reconnected with Eugene Angove after the war and took the recently opened post of valet, his former Captain had embarked on a grand total of six romantic entanglements, none of which had ended at all well. Hampton feared this one was to go the same way in the end. You mix alcohol and hormones in massive doses, and you have a recipe for disaster. If they could only stay off the sauce long enough to realize that they had absolutely zero in common.

Nearing the foot of the hill, Hampton noticed several patches of soil that looked like something had been dragged or fallen along its path. "Over here, sir. I fear Mr. Weston took something of a tumble. It looks like he went crashing through those bushes over yonder."

"Come along, Hampton. The poor chap may have brained himself on a rock and been knocked insensible." Eugene stumbled on the steep slope, nearly landing on his rump, but he managed to right himself on a stout oak.

"Careful, sir. The last thing we need is you coming a cropper."

Eugene managed to get himself down without incident. He reached the bush and sniffed. His nose wrinkled and his face darkened.

"There's something foul here, Hampton. I fear the worst." The unmistakable stench of death drifted on the breeze.

Hampton approached and pushed his way through the brush. His heart was in his mouth, expecting to find the missing employee with his head split open and his liquified brain fertilizing the soil. What he found, though strange and unnerving, came as a relief. "It's an animal of some sort. Maybe a shrew or mouse. But…"

Eugene bristled. He hated it when Hampton paused for effect. "Spit it out, man," he grumbled as he pushed on through. "But what?"

"I'm not sure how to describe it, sir. Look."

Standing shoulder to shoulder with Hampton, his tweed jacket clashing against Hampton's formal black, he looked down and gagged. "Bugger me." The body of a small quadruped, minus its skin, appeared to be encased in the abdomen of one of the strange corn dollies. The only reason they could see the pathetic remains was that it had been split open by a heavy boot. Ends of dried corn jutted into the spine of the carcass, leading up into the odd appendages of the doll. "Well, I've seen some things in my time but this takes not only the biscuit but the whole barrel. Only a mind fit for Bedlam would conjure up such a horror. To think this insanity has been happening right on my doorstep."

"It gets worse, sir."

"Worse, how?"

Hampton nudged Eugene with an elbow and pointed up to the gently drifting treetops.

Looking aloft, Eugene gasped. Every branch of every tree had one of the strange dolls twisting on a length of twine. They ranged in size from that of a field mouse to that of a hare, cat, or smallish dog. In short, as big as could be suspended without snapping wood.

"Good God in heaven. There must be a thousand of the hateful things. Do you think?" It was his turn to trail off.

"I fear so, sir." This implication made him grimace. The chances were good that the one he had handled also contained a flayed mammal.

"Oh, good grief," Eugene pointed over to the bushes ringing the clearing. "Could those be sheep?"

"They certainly look to be the right size, sir."

Eugene had to choke back a wave of nausea, replacing it with anger, first at the perpetrator of such an atrocity, then at the fact that they were alone in a madman's playground. What followed was absolute chaos as they waited for a response to the outrage and for matters to settle.

Eugene cursed. "Where in Hades is that blasted constable? Surely he should be here by now."

"That's if he was, indeed, in The Rat and Raven, sir. No, I think it's safe to assume we are alone for now."

"Thank you for that, Hampton. Reassuring as ever. What is this hellhole, anyway?"

For the first time since stumbling across this scene of horror, they examined their location rather than its grisly contents. Hampton turned a complete circle. They were in a natural clearing with a bowl-like terrain leading to a raised circular mound at the center. To him, it looked like a ritual space of some kind. The pyramidal mounds of stone that ringed what he assumed was a dais added credence to his assumption.

Silently, Eugene walked towards the center, muttering oaths that turned the air blue. "Maybe Father was right after all. But, it seemed like such a tall tale."

"Sir!" Hampton yelped, waving his stick to a smaller clearing to their extreme right. It had been occluded by vegetation and only now became visible. There were more strange dolls. Though, these were larger. One would say *man-size*.

"Please, no," Eugene hissed under his breath as he fished his trusty pen-knife from his inside pocket and extended the main blade. "Don't tell me there's people in there."

Flies buzzed and flitted from doll to doll. Hampton counted an even six as he raced over with Mr. Angove. "Be careful, sir. Lord knows what pestilence you are about to uncover."

Eugene nodded and paused before the pile. Taking a handkerchief and his omnipresent hip-flask from his pocket, he wet the fabric and held it to his nose. Once shielded from the malodorous aroma, he selected the newest-looking weave. Crouching, he slid his blade under the threads of the head end and began to slice. Once the corn started to separate, he gingerly put his hankie away and gripped each side of the cut. With a sudden burst of strength, he wrenched the doll open. Gasping and falling back onto his haunches, he returned the brandy-soaked rag to his airways and looked up at Hampton with wide eyes.

"Well, sir" Hampton blanched and looked away. "We have found our missing gardener. Just be grateful he still has his skin."

Eugene scrambled to his feet. "Only on his face, Hampton, only his face! Look below the neck."

Hampton glanced, saw maggots wriggling onto the dead man's cheek, and looked away again. "I'd rather not, if it's all the same to you, sir."

"Let's get out of here. By my reckoning, if we head that way," Eugene pointed in the opposite direction from which they had come, "we should come to Hollowhills in short order. Then, we find the constable, and hand this dreadful ordeal over to the authorities."

Hampton nodded before a rustling from his left made him brandish his stick like a rapier. The next second a familiar visage put in a return appearance. It was the goat. It had followed them. Hampton's guts lurched as he looked at the hunger in the animal's eyes. "They will eat *anything…*"

"Get out of here, you bloody gannet!" Eugene flapped his arms like a portly pigeon attempting lift-off. "You can't eat any of this. Go and find some berries, for Heaven's sake!"

Once again, it wasn't working. The goat opened its mouth and unleashed a garbled bleating noise that sounded like someone in the grip of celestial mania speaking in tongues. Hampton took a step back as a harsh wind burst from the trees, whipping their faces with dead leaves, dry sticks, and clumps of soil. The sky darkened and the trees shook as the belligerent bovid wiggled its tongue and emptied its lungs of air. Its eyes were ablaze and its hooves stamped the ground in menacing fashion.

Hampton started to back away. "I don't know what's happening here, sir, but one thinks we should run." Just to put an exclamation point on that notion, one-by-one the dolls dropped from the trees, the once lifeless effigies twisting and writhing with torturous life.

Eugene was agog with terror as even the sheep-sized cocoons started to twitch. When the late Mr. Weston opened his eyes, Eugene was running as fast as he could with a piercing scream escaping his lips. Hampton was in close pursuit as the woods continued to darken and the strange noises emanating from the fallen dolls twisted into a deranged parody of childlike laughter. It was horrible to hear. A noise associated with joy and hope becoming one of death and horror. It was a mockery of nature and it had shaken both men, who had endured horrors to their very cores in the past. As they reached the perimeter, Eugene risked a backwards glance and wished that he hadn't. The unholy things were starting to follow on stubby little legs as tentacular growths on their spines licked the air.

Ploughing through the bushes with their hearts hammering, Eugene and Hampton ran until their lungs burned and their knees jellified. As the trees started to thin out and wisps of chimney smoke became visible on the horizon, Eugene crumbled, collapsing to the ground on his hands and knees. Hampton stood over him, stick ready to at least attempt to fend off their reanimated pursuers as he scanned the woodland for signs of movement. All was now still and the wind had dropped. The cloud that had seemingly eclipsed the sun for a brief moment had passed. Once he was halfway convinced they were safe, he, too, sank to his knees.

"Apologies, sir," Hampton panted.

"What for?"

"I'm going to have to… there!" Hampton unbuttoned his collar and sucked oxygen.

Eugene smiled. "Don't fret, old man, I'll not inform the Junior Ganymede Club."

"Thank you, sir. Also, please pardon this next outburst, but what in God's name just happened?"

"I have no inkling of an idea." Eugene took out his flask and emptied half of its contents down his gullet in one mighty gulp. He offered it to his compatriot.

Hampton shook his head.

Just as his pulse rate began to return to a regular seventy beats-per-minute, Eugene got another shock that sent it galloping back into the hundreds. The tall grass to his side rustled as something small and furtive came snuffling in his direction. He raised a fist to ward off what he assumed was one of the doll creatures but dropped it again when a playful Yorkshire terrier appeared with its eyes bright and tail wagging.

Seconds later, a middle-aged woman wearing a headscarf to shield herself from the sun appeared clutching a lead. She too got a shock to find the two men lolling on the grass. "Oh, Mr. Angove, what are you doing down there?"

Angove rolled his eyes. Of all the people to bump into, it had to be Miss Weatherall, the church organist. She only had to catch a whiff of alcohol on his breath and she would deliver a fire and brimstone sermon on temperance as quickly as you could say Pontius Pilate!

"Oh, hello, Ms. Weatherall. Do excuse us. We have been out for a run. You know, got to keep in shape, and all that. Isn't that right, Hampton?"

Hampton looked at him askance. "Um, yes, sir, that's most correct." He was breaking the valet's code left, right and center, and he didn't like it one bit.

"I wonder," Eugene continued, "have you seen Constable Fowler today?"

"Oh, yes." Weatherall replied, disapproval dripping of every syllable. "He's in that den of iniquity again."

"The public house, you mean?"

"You know where I mean. I'm surprised you're not in there sucking ale beside him."

"Well, some of us have had a busy day. Thank you, Miss Weatherall."

Tilting her nose to the sky and puffing out her chest, she clicked her bony fingers at her dog and returned the way she had come. The dog, Timmy, followed meekly behind.

"I bloody knew he'd be in there. Damn the fellow's eyes! Come along, Hampton. Let's give that raw lobster a piece of our minds. The sooner we get reinforcements from Betyls Cove or Boscastle, the sooner we can clear this mess up.

Standing, buttoning his collar, and brushing grass seed from his jacket, Hampton nodded. "Very good, sir…"

PC Fowler stared across the table at the glassy-eyed farmer before taking a mouthful of ale. "Once again, when was the last time you saw Flossie?"

As the bewhiskered man with rosy cheeks and shaky hands opened his mouth, the door to The Rat and Raven burst open to admit Eugene Angove and his valet, Hampton. Making a beeline for the bar, Angove barked for a large brandy which he gulped back with one fluid motion before turning to face the saloon. His eyes landing on Fowler, he jabbed a finger in the young officer's direction and roared, "There you are, you work-shy bounder! Where the bloody hell were you when we needed you?"

Fowler, affronted, rose from his seat. "How dare you? I've been doing my blasted job, that's where I've been."

Eugene snorted. "Work? What bloody work can you do in here?"

"If it's any business of yours, which it isn't, I've been interviewing Roger here about his missing sheep. He's lost four this week."

Hampton dug an elbow into his employer's ribs. "If I may, constable, did you not receive our urgent summons?"

"Summons, what blasted summons?"

Hampton and Eugene shared an uneasy glance.

"Come on, Mr. Angove, what's so important that you barge in here raving like a wild boar?"

Hampton interjected. "I'm afraid, it's a rather delicate matter. Can we go outside?"

Fowler huffed, puffed, and drained his glass. "Very well, but this had better be good."

Stepping outside, Eugene led them over towards the road and out of earshot. "Please excuse my bluster. We've had a hell of a day."

Nodding to accept the apology, Fowler took out his notebook and pencil stub.

"Do the honors, Hampton," Eugene continued. "I don't think I can adequately put our ordeal into words."

Hampton sighed then proceeded to deliver chapter and verse in graphic detail, leaving the listener with an unbelieving look and his mouth agape.

"Human bodies wrapped up like corn dollies? It's just so... It's absolutely..."

"We know," Eugene smiled, offering him his hip flask, "but we assure you every word of it is true."

Fowler puffed out his cheeks and shook his head

"Am I to take it that nobody telephoned from Angove Hall?" Eugene asked.

"I'm afraid not, Mr. Angove. The line has been down all day. Lord knows when it will get repaired."

"Damn it," Eugene shared a worried glance with Hampton. "Cynthia and Angela are alone up there. I don't like this one little bit."

"Agreed, sir. We need to get back there post haste."

"Constable, is there any chance that you are sober enough to drive?"

Fowler was about to become affronted but remembered who he was talking to. There is no way Angove would rebuke a chap for having a tipple. No, this was simply a matter of safety. He thought for a moment, then nodded. "Come on, we can borrow the bakery van. We can't very well all cram on the back of my bicycle, can we?"

Eugene smiled and followed Fowler towards the center of the village.

Dusk was approaching as the bakery van rattled along the driveway towards Angove Hall, yet the temperature remained extreme. The interior of their ride had become increasingly uncomfortable with every passing yard, despite the windows being open. Sweat and stale bread had mingled to concoct a scent that rivalled that of Mr. Weston's cocoon deep in the woods. Pulling up next to the ornamental fountain outside the grand pile, Fowler stepped out first and regarded the windows.

"No lights... Maybe they got tired of waiting and followed you?"

"Good God, I hope not," Eugene muttered as he tried to get the kink out of his spine. "Come along, chaps, we don't have a moment to lose." His feet crunching in the gravel, he led the trio to the front entrance. Reaching the steps, he stopped them with a raised hand, his old officer training kicking in subconsciously. "Look," he pointed to a familiar-looking bundle on the doorstep. It was the corn doll that Angela had shown Cynthia that morning.

Hampton shuddered.

"Is that one of the dolls?" Fowler asked, instinctively stooping to pick it up.

Hampton gripped him by the shoulder and shook his head. "I wouldn't if I were you, sir." Looking for a handy implement, he returned to the van and produced a flour-caked broom. Gingerly, he held it before him and swept the doll off the step and into a plant pot housing a wilted, presumed dead, daffodil. "There. At least it didn't twitch. Shall we go inside, sirs?"

As Eugene and Hampton mounted the steps, PC Fowler couldn't resist having a look at the doll. It was certainly odd, and the faint gamy smell gave veracity as to its contents, but he still didn't believe that it could move. No, it was far simpler to put their story down to shock over finding the variegated cadavers, alcohol, or both. Corpses trussed up like harvest totems were one thing, but *walking* corpses trussed up like harvest totems something else entirely.

"Come along, Fowler, we don't have time to gawk!" Eugene opened the door and was hit squarely in the nose by the wafting odor of decaying animals. In a line, like grisly versions of breadcrumbs in a Grimm fairy tale, corn dolls were evenly spaced, leading along the entrance hall towards the kitchen. "Not good. Not good at all. Hampton."

"Yes, sir."

"Fetch my revolver from the library, there's a good chap."

"Very good, sir." Hampton left the other two standing in the weak cone of light from the waning moon that was raising its head above the trees.

Fowler produced his wooden truncheon from its belt hook and hefted it against his left hand.

"That's the spirit, constable." Eugene smiled, desperately trying to hide the notes of panic in his voice. Though they had only recently begun stepping out, he really was fond of Cynthia. The thought of some maniac skinning her and mummifying her in corn made his blood boil. No, if he had to, he would put a bullet between the bounder's eyes before they had a chance. "Come on, Hampton," he muttered, beginning to pace like a caged animal.

Momentarily, his valet returned holding Eugene's service revolver and a box of ammunition. He had also taken the precaution of securing his trusty butterfly knife from its hiding place behind a history book about the Philippines. It had been a trusty companion throughout the Great War and had saved him from more scrapes than he cared to remember, and hiding it behind a book about its place of origin made him smile. Not that he hid it from Eugene, who was well aware of its presence. No, it was from the charwoman's boy who tended to have sticky fingers where sharp and shiny objects were involved.

Eugene snatched the gun and ammunition from his valet's gloved hands and made for the kitchen. "Come on," he commanded, following the dolls to the back door. It was ajar, swinging gently on the breeze, each movement eliciting a faint squeak from the aged hinges. Eugene couldn't help injecting a moment of levity, if only for his own sake. "I thought I told you to have them oiled, Hampton? Tsk, tsk, what do I pay you for.

Taking the lead, Hampton tutted and pulled the door aside so the others could exit. As soon as they stepped outside, a chill fell over them. Dolls stretched the entire way from the rear entrance to the gazebo. It was lit by candlelight which flickered ominously in the distance.

"I think we are being led into a trap, sir."

Eugene set his jaw firm, squared his shoulders, and held the gun at waist level as he adopted a slow march towards their intended destination. Fowler's eyes darted hither and yon as he kept a close eye on the hedges and shrubs for any movement. Hampton adopted an air of nonchalance as he followed on at the rear. Though, in truth, he was the most capable of the trio if it boiled down to fisticuffs. He had done things in the killing fields of France that haunted his dreams. It had been do or die.. and he had done what he had to do to survive. He was more than willing to do it again, should it come down to it.

Nearing the gazebo, Eugene could feel his stomach churn at the grisly tableaux that awaited them. He couldn't make it out, due to the bulk of the horror being inside, but he could see blood. Lots of blood.

Hampton stopped him with a hand on the shoulder. "Allow me, sir." He took the lead while Eugene covered him. The steps leading to the gazebo were dappled red and a slogan reading "Iä Shub-Niggurath Iä The Black Goat Of The Woods" had been daubed across the top step. He stepped around the strange writing and peered inside. "Oh, Good Lord!" He turned sharply away, pressing his fist to his lips.

"Is it?" Eugene asked.

Hampton shook his head, rapidly turning green around the gills. "It's Mrs. Weston... I think."

"What do you mean, *you think?*"

"Going off the clothes, it's her, but... her head." Hampton wobbled down the steps dry heaving over privet hedge.

"Allow me, Mr. Angove," Fowler asserted, before anyone could stop him. He got as far as the door, turned, and let out a sob. "It's gone... It's been replaced!"

"Replaced?" Eugene asked, his patience wearing thin. "What are you babbling about, man?"

By now, Hampton had recovered enough to elaborate. "I'm afraid Mrs. Weston's head has been removed, sir. Removed and replaced."

"Replaced by what?"

"Remember that goat we met in the woods?"

"You can't be serious?"

Hampton nodded. "Sewed on with lengths of corn like some grisly scarecrow."

"That's it," Eugene held up his hands. "There is no way it's just one rogue lunatic doing this. We are so far out of our depth that we're bloody drowning! Fowler, go inside and try the phone. I should have thought to do that earlier. If it, too, is out of commission, take the van over to High Bend. They have a telephone in the Ram's Head. Get as many men as you can muster."

Fowler nodded. "What will you do in the meantime?"

"Check the area."

"Be careful, Mr. Angove."

Eugene checked the cylinder of his revolver and nodded in response. "Go!"

By now, Hampton had steeled himself enough to peer into the gazebo. "Sir. You need to see this. There's a note."

"What does it say?"

"Ahem. It reads: 'Mr. Angoove.'"

"Angoove?"

"That's how it's written, sir. The author's grammar is atrocious. 'Mr. Angoove. If tha' wants to see thee strumpet again, come to the Place of Dolls. Don't bring no Peelers. I'll hung her from a tree an' slit her belly open if ye do.'"

"Place of Dolls? That has to be the clearing in the woods, correct?"

"I would have thought so, sir."

"Well, let's go."

"Now, sir? Do you not want to wait for reinforcements? You must know that this has all been an elaborate trap?"

"You read what that unmitigated bounder wrote. No police." Eugene paced up and down outside the gazebo for a moment. "You're right about it all being a trap. Is it big-headed of me to assume that all of this slaughter has been for my benefit?"

"Not at all, sir, that's the way it appears. Let's face it, you've made no shortage of enemies—both natural and otherwise—since returning from France. I can well imagine that any number of miscreants want to get some kind of revenge on you."

"Exactly my thoughts. With that said, I intend to give them exactly what they want. Are you coming?"

Hampton took his knife from his pocket, stooped, and rolled up his trouser leg. Slipping it into his sock, he smoothed down the starched fabric over it, stood, and nodded. "I shall take the liberty of retrieving your wind-up lamp from the library drawer."

He left and quickly returned with the object in hand before he passed it to his employer.

Eugene turned it over in his hand, and grinned. "Capital!"

Eugene switched off the weak electric light and slipped it into his pocket. The moonlight was sufficiently bright to illuminate the final few yards of their journey. In this part of the forest, it poured through the leaves and branches, projecting a tapestry of waving shadow on the soil below.

Eugene took out his handkerchief and dabbed at the perspiration beading his brow. It was still uncommonly hot. The extreme humidity and lack of wind made it stifling and hard to breathe. They had made good time retracing their earlier steps and were doing their best to traverse the muddy slope down to the ritual space without breaking their necks.

"I've been thinking, sir." Hampton said in hushed tones. "About the letter, I mean. There's something *off* about it."

"Stating the obvious again, old chap. Of course there is something *off* about it. It was obviously written by someone who is as mad as a sack full of March hares."

"That's just it, sir. I think that is what we are supposed to think. There's something about the spelling and grammatical errors. They seem forced, inauthentic somehow. As though written by someone with a perfect grip on the English language who wants us to believe that they are illiterate."

"To what end?"

"Misdirection."

"You could be right, Hampton, but it changes nothing. We go as Judas goats without a flock of sheep to leave in our place..."

Upon reaching the point where Mr. Weston had come a cropper and kickstarted the chain of events that led them to this tainted spot, Hampton put a hand on Eugene's shoulder and whispered in his ear. "Do you have a plan, sir?"

"Why, yes, I do, Hampton. I intend on blasting the bugger to kingdom come." Producing his revolver, Angove crashed through the bushes without a single ounce of stealth. Several small fires had been ignited around the circumference of the earthen dais. A figure in a hooded robe stood in the center with arms aloft. As far as they could tell, they were alone. None of the hideous dolls were visible... and there was no sign of Cynthia. Eugene raised his gun to the sky and squeezed the trigger. A deafening crack shattered the stillness, sending bats wheeling from the branches in a dense cloud of teeth and wings.

"Alright, you bastard," Eugene snarled, levelling the weapon at the figure. "I won't hesitate to shoot should you try anything. Where's Miss Green?"

The figure, who had its back to the two men, said nothing, but its shoulders started to shake rhythmically as though in fits of amusement.

"What's so damn funny, you swine?"

Holding arms out in a mockery of the crucifixion, the figure spun and faced them. Eugene tried to see the face under the heavy red fabric to no avail. Before he could speak again, the figure spoke. "You really are as pig-headed as we thought." The voice was all too familiar.

Indeed, it had been whispering sweet nothings in his ear that very morning.

Eugene gasped. "Cynthia?"

Removing her hood, it was confirmed. Her hair cascaded down the front of her robe and her scarlet lips twisted into a sardonic smile. Looking beyond the two men with their mouths agape like beached cod, she looked to the tree line and spoke. "Take them. The Goat Mother demands blood."

Before Hampton and Eugene could retaliate, five similarly-hooded figures swept from the shadows and surrounded them. Three of them wrestled Hampton to the ground and began binding his arms with coarse rope, while the remaining two fought with Mr. Angove. He did his best to ward them off but was quickly overcome. As he was gripped from behind by one, he managed to pull the hood down on the other. What he saw made him gasp?

"Miss Weatherall?"

The church organist grinned and brought her knee up sharply, connecting with his crotch. Eugene let out a groan, dropped the revolver, and sank to his knees.

"Good work, ladies," Cynthia applauded. "Now, keep them still while I prepare the ritual." Raising her hands aloft once more, she spoke to the sky. "Thousand Young, come forth and prepare to welcome the Black Goat of the Woods."

There was rustling followed by the strange stamp of corn-wrapped hooves, paws, and feet as the diabolical horde emerged and formed an impenetrable barrier around the clearing.

"For God's sake, Cynthia," Eugene cried once he could speak again. "What is the meaning of this madness?"

Cynthia turned and glared at him. "Meaning? You foolish man. That's exactly what this is all about. Meaning. I'm giving meaning back to myself and my new sisters."

"What the devil are you talking about?"

"Look around you. Look at the faces of the women before you. Do you not see?"

As the women removed their hoods, Eugene looked from face to face. Each one was familiar, but he couldn't see what Cynthia was driving at. "I don't understand."

"You really are a tiresome oaf, aren't you? You see before you a group of women without meaning or purpose. The overlooked and abandoned, the barren and infertile, unmarried, unloved. Spinsters all. While their peers and siblings have been married off and escaped this dreary backwater, it is we that remain. We have no use in society, so society has chosen to make us outcasts. Three years ago, I had a horse-riding accident which left me unable to bear fruit, as it were. From that moment, I was thrown on the scrapheap. Daddy lost interest in one who couldn't provide an heir. I became depressed. I contemplated joining the choir invisible. Then, by a quirk of fate, I met the sisterhood."

"This bunch?"

"They dabbled in pagan fertility rites. Unsuccessfully, I might add, but it got me thinking. When I was younger, Daddy had me work in the office of his shipping business. All kinds of strange artifacts came in and out of Cornwall. My brother, Arthur, an antique dealer in Betyls Cove, had an interest in, let's say the more esoteric end of the cargo. He told me of what will be our redemption. He told me of an ancient and powerful deity associated with rites of fertility. He told me about Shub-Niggurath!"

The women spoke in unison. "Iä! Shub-Niggurath! Iä! The Black Goat Of The Woods with a Thousand Young!"

"When we spill the fertile blood of man, the Goat Mother will grant us an issue. We will birth her young onto Earth and a glorious matriarchy will be established!"

"Have you not spilt enough blood?" Eugene asked.

"Not the right blood," Cynthia sighed. "Those withered prunes of men were no more fertile than I. We need virility."

Hampton looked at the assembled dolls. "Pardon me, Lady Green, but just what are those abominations?"

"They are representations of the Dark Young. Mere poppets given life as servitors. Soon, they will be replaced by the entities they represent. Hideous and beautiful in perfect symmetry, the spawn of the Goat Mother will rise!"

"You're as mad as a blasted badger! Every damn one of you is utterly cracked."

"Are we?" Cynthia smirked, unruffled by his outburst. "What use does society have for a barren woman? We are seen as nothing more than breeding stock. Cattle to be branded with diamond rings and paraded in front of leering crowds like cows at the market. That is a woman's lot. Without that, we are nothing."

"What utter rot!"

"Is it?" She fixed Eugene with a stare that burned deep into his soul.

Eugene looked away. There was an awful truth in her words. "Cynthia. This is not the way."

"What other way is there? Like it or not, even now we live in a male dominated society. If *they* see us as useless, then useless we are."

"But… I would have loved you. I have no wish for blasted children, and there has to be others that feel the same."

"Enough. You could never love a barren woman. It is not in the brute man's nature. You mount, impregnate, and control. You see us only as human flower beds to sprinkle your filthy seed upon. That will soon change. The balance of power will shift. You will become the breeding stock. Let's see how you like it. Our destiny is already in motion… the ritual has begun." Cynthia took a wavy-bladed dagger from the sleeves of her robe and sliced her left palm. Spinning anti-clockwise, she sprinkled her blood upon the soil. Instantly, the wind started to rise. She tipped her head back and started to chant. *"Nog uh'enythnah fhalma. Nog Shub-Niggurath!"*

Clouds wheeled overhead and the assembled dolls began to titter and wail. The air grew heavier still and the fires burst into great columns that reached almost to the tops of the trees. Eugene's eyes grew as above Cynthia the air started to ripple and discolor and reality began to tear. He had seen similar things before and knew that it often ended in two ways. Madness or death. He didn't fancy either and began to struggle. Hampton remained in place and managed to slip his knife from his sock.

"Now," Cynthia demanded. "Spill the blood of the oppressor: man!"

Miss Weatherall grabbed Eugene by the hair and yanked his head back to expose his throat while the other woman produced another blade. As the trio attempted to do the same to Hampton, he finally managed to cut his bindings and slashed one of his captors with his blade. She screamed and dropped to the floor clutching her calf as blood jetted from a deep wound. Fighting off the other two robed women, he shouldered them aside and took down the one about to slice Eugene's neck with a flawless tackle.

The rift began to swirl as particles crackled and spat like lightning. Cynthia looked aghast. "No! That is not how it should be. She demands male blood. Kill them. Kill them now!"

Leaving his foe dazed and winded, Hampton snatched the fallen revolver and shot Miss Weatherall. She dropped like a stone with a surprised grunt. Turning, he pointed the barrel at Miss Green.

"No!" Eugene bellowed. "Don't!"

Hampton turned, a puzzled expression on his face. "Sir?"

"There may be…" His sentence was cut short by the rift opening with an unnerving rip.

As he watched, a protoplasmic appendage dropped through and encircled Cynthia Green's waist. As it began to lift her and take her to Lord-knows-where, she gave one last defiant smirk.

"How does it feel to be powerless, Mr. Angove?"

As her body was sucked into the void, the four remaining women scattered as the dolls began to disintegrate and melt into foul pools of gore. Hampton cut Eugene's bonds and helped him to his feet. Racing into the bushes to escape the tragic scene, they nearly collided with seven men in blue uniforms carrying bulls-eye lamps.

"Ah, Fowler," Eugene panted. "You took your bloody time."

"What the hell has been happening?" Fowler replied, shrugging off Angove's rebuke.

"It's a long story. There are four murderers in robes running around in the woods. You might want to catch them first. I'll explain all later."

"Very good, Mr. Angove. Come along, boys!"

As the heavy stomp of police-issue boots faded into the distance, Eugene's expression darkened. "Was she right? Cynthia, I mean?"

"In a way… Yes, I believe she was. Though, the way she went about it was far from righteous. Her motives were sound enough, but her means left a lot to be desired."

"Poor women. I can't help feeling sorry for all of them. Do you think society will ever change?"

"I hope so. In time."

Eugene sighed. "What a damn senseless waste of life."

"Isn't it always?"

"True." Taking out his fob watch, he checked the time. "Rats! All the blessed hostelries in the area will be closed by now, and I need a blasted drink."

Hampton rolled his eyes one more time. "Come along home, sir. I'll pour you a brandy."

Andrew Doran and the Blessings of the Black Goat

An Andrew Doran Adventure

By Matthew Davenport

Chapter One

On a rare occasion, I have free time. It never comes in large chunks and is quite frequently usurped by chaos. The problem that I have comes down to filling the time. My hobbies are minimal at best. Sometimes, I will catch a baseball game or try to slow my mind enough to read a book, but most of the time any empty slots on my calendar were for grading homework. Any rest for Professor Andrew Doran tended to be sleep brought on by whiskey.

The quiet hours are when the ghosts haunt me.

Not literal ghosts, although that is not unheard of. These ghosts are the memories of the people who I have failed and will never again have the chance to apologize to for letting them down so thoroughly. I had only just accepted that my previous assistant, friend—and maybe more—Nancy Dyer, was on that list. She had been pulled through a closing portal to Hyperborea, and after too many long nights interrogating witches, reading grimoires, and almost melting my mind trying to open a new gate, I have been forced to conclude that she will forever be lost to this world. While I had added her ghost to my memory-fueled nightmares, I had also managed to quiet one of them.

My sister, Mary Doran, and I had been estranged from each other for many years until recently. Last year we had resumed contact after years of blaming each other for a tragedy that had befallen our parents.

Now I was forcing myself to make some of that "free time" for a short vacation with her to a cabin owned by a mutual friend. Mary wanted to get back into feeling like siblings again, and I just wanted to catch up with everything that I have missed in our years of not talking.

Maybe that's the same thing, maybe not. The difference is that I never saw her as not being my sister so much as I saw her as having cut me out of her life. Different approaches to the same heartbreak that I hoped we were well away from. This is what was running through my mind as she threw her bags in the back and climbed into the cab of the Miskatonic University pickup truck that I had procured for a weekend at a cabin in the woods with my sister.

I didn't own a truck, and not everyone at my job hated me as much as the dean did, so the truck was on a temporary—but almost permanent—loan from the maintenance team whenever I needed a ride.

Mary lived in the small Adirondack town of Harrisville, New York. She was a schoolteacher in the large brick building in the middle of town. It was a quaint place where I could easily see myself retiring if I ever thought I would still be alive in my retirement years.

The moment that Mary slammed the truck door shut, she twisted and pulled me into a tight hug.

"Ready to set sail, captain!" She laughed as we broke, and I shifted the truck into gear.

I laughed and felt a wave of stress that I hadn't realized I had been holding onto release.

"Are you ready for hot dogs, nature, and mosquitos?" Mary joined in by saying the "and mosquitos" part with me. We went camping a few times when we were kids, and Mom always said that line every time we got into the car. She had not been an advocate of the outdoors.

Mary added, "We need to stop by Bear's place first." She held up a pie pan that I hadn't noticed she had been carrying. "I want to thank him."

The cabin was also on loan, but Miskatonic had nothing to do with it. The same happenstance that managed to bridge the expanse between Mary and I also introduced us to an old soldier turned hermit, for lack of a better word: Donny Bear. Donny was a well-travelled man who had decided to spend his retirement mostly alone and in the woods. While there, he had found that he wasn't the only thing enjoying the solitude of nature. He became aware of darker forces and educated himself enough, as any good soldier would, to hold the line and defend his home. We had worked with Donny to stop a curse from the *Al-Azif* that was making people go missing. He had been instrumental in us locating the cult responsible and stopping them. Since then he had become like family to Mary.

The cabin that she and I were going to was deeper in the hills than Donny's home was, and he only ever used it when he wanted to switch up his hunting places.

I nodded, excited to see my friend, but I was also wary. The reason that I didn't take time off was because the world always seemed to be under attack from alien or occult forces, and going to visit Donny— who was in my life specifically because of one of those reasons— seemed like I was inviting more opportunity to spoil this trip.

As we pulled away and headed in the direction of Donny's place, Mary was catching up on the events in her life.

"So, it looks like I will be moving on to third grade education starting in the next semester," she said.

"Why is that?" I asked, struggling to remember which grade my sister was leaving.

Mary must have seen my face, because she laughed and said, "I teach second grade."

We turned onto a dirt road surrounded by tall pines, and she continued. "Clarence Barlow, the current third grade teacher is retiring, and it is cheaper to hire my replacement than his." Mary frowned at that. "Which makes no sense, but I get a raise and am not interested in questioning their decisions as long as I get paid more for it."

"Is that something that you want to do? Third grade?" I asked. "That's great about the money, but if it's a few pennies and you prefer staying put, then what's the point?"

I was the last person who should be giving my sister career advice. I never wanted to work for my school and had found myself tricked into being the dean, losing the job to the worst person I'd ever met (and I'd known Nazis) just to secure the dangerous secrets that were hidden there. I was officially a professor at Miskatonic University but did very little teaching. My duties trying to keep the world from being eaten by the Great Old Ones prevented much in the way of education. Which I suppose made me a research professor.

"Because of the timing, I'll have most of the same children that I have now," Mary explained. "That makes this a known quantity. I'll be stepping into doing the same thing that I did this year, but with a new curriculum and more money. Additionally, there's another reason this move had to happen that you and I will need to talk about."

"Oh?" I asked as we pulled into Donny Bear's makeshift driveway. His cabin that he chose to live in was a standard Adirondack log cabin with three rooms. It was one floor and mostly blended into the forest. If it wasn't for the dirt road that Mary made him put in so that she could visit, no one would ever find this place.

Before she could explain further, Donny stood from where he had been sitting on the porch and started in our direction.

Donny was an older man who had served during the Great War. He had a grizzled look with a more-salt-than-pepper beard and an old hunting cap that he wore everywhere. His clothing, much like my own, was devoid of any bright colors. He preferred the dark browns and greens of both his surroundings and his past military career.

After a youth of fighting overseas, Donny had wanted to see some of what he had been fighting for and had chosen to do odd jobs and tour Europe for a few years. When he finally settled down and returned to the states, he had chosen to return to one of his more youthful skills and spend his days closer to nature, with a bow in his hand and fresh meat on the stove.

It was a simple life that he had hoped for and never fully achieved. When we met Donny, he helped us to defend the local area from occult gatherings, alien invasions, and disappearing townspeople. Since that day, we have had numerous conversations with him that demonstrated that his entire life, much like mine, had been a steady trickle of supernatural and wholly unnatural events.

I saw our friend as the quiet guardian of the woods, even if he would loudly disagree.

After Donny hugged Mary, he spun to me, and we clasped hands.

"What's the report, soldier?" I asked as we broke.

Donny's smile wavered only slightly and then he nodded toward his home. "Let's go in. I want to talk to you about the place, give you the keys, and catch up. Mary here has kept me mostly up to date on your life, but she leaves out the fun bits."

"If you have coffee, I can stay indefinitely." I laughed and followed our friend inside.

The inside of the cabin was designed much as anyone having met Donny would have assumed. It was neat, to an almost militant level, with sparse furniture, a few books near the only comfortable looking chair, and a table with four wooden stools in a kitchen. The kitchen looked like something from a wild west novel, with a large wood stove and pans hanging on the walls. On the stove was a coffee pot.

To my satisfaction, it was percolating.

As I took a seat at the table, Mary grabbed us tin cups from wherever Donny kept them and the old soldier took the coffee off the stove. As he poured, he tossed the key down on the table.

"I won't beat around the bush," he said as he poured the hot contents of the percolator into our mugs. "Be careful out there."

"That's the worst effort to be direct that I've ever heard," I smirked. "Can you give me a little more?"

He shrugged, "I really don't know too much." He put the pitcher on the stove and took a seat across from us. "For starters, the cabin you're going to be staying at is further in the hills. It's more removed than even my place. After we broke up that, uh…" he trailed off trying to find the word.

"Bug thing," Mary said. "I just keep thinking of it as the bug thing."

He nodded and continued. "After we broke up that bug thing last year, it didn't frighten off many of the wackies. If they were already in the hills and we didn't scare them away, then we drove them deeper. Loggers that come through here have been telling me stories."

"Like what?" Mary pressed.

Bear lifted his head toward the ceiling. "They don't like to log near dusk. They said the stars won't come out on clear nights and that they hear... something... howling. Like a bluejay. It isn't howling because it's hunting, it's howling because you entered its territory."

I understood the reference, but less because of my wonderful skills at nature and more because I had been hounded by a bluejay as a child. Basically, when you enter their territory, they get really loud.

"You think more cultists are in the woods, uh, howling?" Mary asked.

"Or they got another thing like that space bug they pulled here last time," Bear said.

I shook my head. "That would be impossible without a copy of the *Al-Azif*. They don't have that."

I knew because I made it my job to know.

"What else have you seen?" Mary blew on her cup to cool it before taking a sip. She seemed intrigued by this stuff that she normally avoided talking about with me.

"The woods are filled with odd things, but as of late, I've also seen goats and that's not something you see a lot of in the Adirondacks. They're farming animals, but I have seen at least four different black goats here in the last month." I could see his eyes falling into a memory, but he came out of it and returned his attention to us. "Honestly, it reminds me of a thing that happened when I was younger, but that was an ocean away." He shook his head to clear it. "Anyway, I don't want to scare either of you. I just want you both to be careful out there." He looked directly at me when he added, "The cabin is protected, so nothing should bother you." He was telling me that he had warded the place with runes from the *Al-Azif*. Nothing supernatural would get into his cabin.

Donny turned to Mary, "I'll be coming to check on you both Sunday morning. I'll bring fresh eggs, but no heroics. I know you're capable, but we both know the weird kinds of things your brother gets into, so let him be the big scary man this weekend, please."

Mary smirked, "I'm more stubborn than he is, so that bet is already out the window."

We talked some more, catching each other up on the big stories in our lives. I stayed away from some of the darker events that had happened recently in my life, as I didn't want to sour the mood, but I spoke of how falling into teaching had been an interesting challenge, only to be scoffed at by my sister.

Bear hadn't had too much in the way of life changes, either. His hermit lifestyle had only been interrupted about once per month by the regular visit from my sister and to get goods in town. As a matter of fact, the movement of what he considered to potentially be cultists had almost become a hobby of his. He hoped that whatever they were doing was more akin to dancing naked in the moonlight than bringing alien bugs into our world, but he would rather be prepared than not and had kept his attention on them.

That was when Mary finally told me the news that she had been originally planning on telling me when we were unpacked and relaxing in the cabin.

"We're all here now, so I might as well tell you," she explained. "I am getting married." She reached for her neck and tugged at a chain I had known was holding Mom's cross, but when it came out from behind her shirt, it also had on it an engagement ring. "I can't wear it at school because the children can't mind their own business."

I was floored. Excited for my sister, as well, but also flummoxed. "I didn't even know that you were seeing anyone." I was smiling as I said it, so Mary continued to beam like a ray of sunshine without a cloud in the sky.

"Well, that," she seemed mildly embarrassed, "is for a few reasons. The first of which being, we only just reconnected, and you never asked."

Huffing, I said, "That's hardly fair."

Mary ignored my rebuke and continued. "The second is that he's the third-grade teacher that is leaving. We thought it improper to share with anyone, as the school has had an odd history on whether that is frowned upon. Once he was able to line up a new job, which didn't happen until last week, we decided that it was safe to announce it.

I thought back to the drive over. "Barlow. You said his name was Barlow?"

Mary nodded. "Clarence. You will have to meet him. He's quite the gentleman."

I looked at Donny who hadn't asked any questions. "Have you met him already, then?"

He nodded, a smile across his face. "I investigated him for you, big brother. He's clean and seems to compliment your sister nicely."

"And when do I get to meet him?" I demanded.

"When our trip is done, if you like." Mary's smile showed me that I hadn't screwed this up yet, and I hoped not to. "I have some more things I want to talk to you about this weekend and then you can meet him any time."

Now to screw it up. "Mary," I said it a little quieter than I had been talking, letting the excitement leave my voice in place of concern, "I am not going to be the brother who acts like he has any right to tell you how to live your life when you've spent the entirety of your adulthood making those decisions yourself."

"But," Mary winked at Donny.

"But," I said, "I wouldn't be a brother at all if I didn't ask, are you sure that's what you want for him?"

"Wait," Mary's face blanched with confusion. "What?"

"He is asking if you really want your brother in your life as you start a new life with your beau given, well, everything that seems to follow in his wake," Donny explained.

Mary let out a sigh. "You have a unique perspective, Andy," she said quietly before letting out a laugh. "We have met on several occasions since the bug thing and nothing has come out of the stars to claim me or one of my students since. I think we might be safe from the weird."

Bear was the one who explained it a little better for me.

"That's not what he means," he said. "When you see the things that he has, or that I have, they attach to you. A kind of shellshock of the soul. These things never go away, and they only keep coming back."

"Were these things here before Andy found them?" Mary's voice shifted to what I assumed was the voice she used when discussing things with her students. "Did Andy become a magnet for these things, or have they always been there? Because here's the truth: you can choose to see the world for what it is, or you can choose to put on blinders and only look straight ahead. These things are horrible and terrifying and, yes, you and Andy keep bumping into them, but isn't that a great thing? Isn't it a great thing that there are people in the world who see it for all of its contents and stand against it? Why wouldn't I want that kind of person in my life, or in my future husband's life?"

It was a profound statement, and I was proud of the stance she took, but I had to add a harsh reminder. "What about Mom and Dad?"

"What about them?" Mary demanded, suddenly angry. "Don't you get it? It's already in our lives and not having you know about it led them to ruin. I have what they didn't. I have Professor Andrew Doran standing between me and the monsters." Quieter, she added. "I just got you back, Andy. Most families have problems. At least you can shoot ours."

My heart welled with emotion, but I kept it in and nodded my thanks to her before she leaped on me with a hug. It stopped me from saying that most of the things I dealt with couldn't be stopped by mere guns.

"You will like him," Mary continued. We spent another hour sipping and refilling our coffees before saying our farewell to the old soldier.

Once Mary was in the car, Donny grabbed me by the arm with an iron grip.

"What I didn't say is that the goats seem intelligent," he said. It took me a moment to remember what he was referencing. "I have never seen them moving, eating, or anything else. One moment they are just standing there and staring at you. It'll go on for any length of time, but then when you aren't looking, they just disappear."

"I appreciate it," I said tugging at my arm.

Donny, my friend, pulled me in tighter. "I never see the goats leave, but I don't think they are alone. There's always something else moving.

I don't see it, but I hear it. Two days shouldn't be a problem, but what do I know."

I meet his eyes with all the respect that I had for the man who had saved both mine and my sister's life. "You know plenty. I trust you. If you're afraid, we won't go. Or maybe we can look into it."

"Go, have fun with your sister, but keep an eye open. Not everything in the woods is out to get us." He let go of my arm. "And if the great big brother of Mary Doran happens to figure out what's going on so that he can calm down a superstitious old man, then all the better."

"It isn't superstition if it's trying to kill you." I smiled. "I'll look into it. I didn't bring any of my usual tools, is there anything I might find in there?"

"Chest under the bed," Donny nodded. "You will know it when you see it."

Thanking our friend again, we bid him a final goodbye and headed in the direction of our cabin for the weekend.

While I had never been there before, Mary had a map in hand drawn by Bear that led us. We wouldn't be able to drive the car the entire way, but there was a place to park and then we had a hike of about a mile or so to travel.

It was about fifteen minutes of driving before we parked in an open area. It looked like a parking area for hiking trails. We unloaded everything we could carry, including our groceries, and clothing, and then we started our march.

Mary stayed in the lead with her head in the map while I kept my eyes on our surroundings.

It might have only been Bear's warning, but I felt like we were being watched, and history had convinced me to trust those feelings.

It was mid-afternoon when Mary shouted that it was up ahead. The break in the silence made me jump, but I recovered enough to notice the smaller copy of Donny Bear's home.

The sun cut through the trees about a hundred feet above our heads while the cabin was nestled in a shadow cast by the hills and the forest.

Mary wasted no time collapsing on the porch into one of Donny's rocking chairs.

"You have the key," Mary wheezed.

I smiled and dug around in my pocket before producing the item. Within seconds I was in the cabin and unloading my bags on the table in what I would be referring to as the dining area. Much like his home that we had left only an hour or so before, this cabin was minimally furnished, but that suited us just fine.

We were here to sit in front of a fire, catch up on lost time, and sleep. If we could start a fire, the camping experience would complete itself.

With only one room, I had already planned to take the couch. There was a bottle in my bag that promised that it didn't matter where I rested my head. To that point, the couch looked more comfortable than the bed did, and I didn't regret my choice.

"Want to trade?" Mary asked after she had already emptied her bag onto the bed.

I shook my head. "And take the only bed in miles from my baby sister? No, I'm not a monster."

We spent the next hour or so unpacking our bags, claiming our spaces, making coffee, and adding our own special liquor to it before I decided to go outside and gather some wood for the fireplace.

The forest was both quiet and full of noise, as a soft breeze blew, bending pines gently in its passing.

Donny wasn't the kind of person to call fire in a theater. Why would he mention cultists up here to me if he didn't expect it to be a problem?

During that quiet moment alone was when I decided to really take a look at my surroundings. When I reached the log pile, I continued past it and turned around, first taking in the cabin with all my experiences in mind.

It was just like his home, except slightly older with grayer wood and weathering on the roof. The roof, though. That had something to it. Stepping carefully and holding onto a smaller tree, I climbed up the wood pile to look at the angle of the roof.

Sap or tar, or something was painted on top in the shape of some sort of symbol. I didn't know that specific symbol of swirls and crosshatching with several small dots, but the basic shape was like protection sigils I had seen in both the *Necronomicon* and along the edge of the *Scroll of Eibon*.

The sounds of the forest retreated to almost nothing, like a tide pulling away from the shore. I focused my attention in an attempt to hear whatever it was I was missing. Not for the first time in my life, I wondered if I was beginning to go deaf.

A goat bleated from somewhere incredibly close behind me.

The sudden noise in all the silence startled me and I went down hard onto the wood pile.

As I recovered, I looked in every direction. I was entirely alone.

Chapter Two

As we were here to relax, and I felt Donny's warnings were more than enough stress for the evening, I decided against mentioning the goat I had heard while outside. Once the fire was roaring, we got the old stove up and running and worked together on dinner.

The initial small talk was slow, as we avoided talking about family, monsters, or almost anything that we had in common just because those commonalities were also tragedies.

So, we talked about work.

Mary let me know about small changes in her teaching position. The students would be the same, as she had said, but the curriculum was more advanced, and she was looking forward to the challenge. I had always thought she was better suited toward teaching than I was, and it filled my soul to see her light up as she told me about her more colorful students and their advances and struggles.

On the other hand, I couldn't talk about work without diving more into the monster side of things, but if I stayed on the periphery I assumed that I was safe. I recounted a few, half-censored anecdotes from my most recent travels. How I had been asked to "consult" on a museum exhibit at the Arkham Historical Society, of my recent mingling with Arkham's social elite at an antiquities auction, and my having gotten "stabbed by a mummy" in Vienna. I left out the part that the blade was of phantom energies meant to pierce the soul rather than the flesh, but she was more hung up on the fact that I had gone to Vienna.

"Maybe you should slow down a bit, Andy," Mary said after a bit. "Get a girl, or something. You're not getting any younger."

I laughed softly. "That's rich, coming from you."

Mary smiled and the conversation slowly changed to more generic topics again. We returned our focus to the food, and soon we sat down to beans, salted pork, and small glasses of whiskey.

"Alright," Mary said slowly as she pushed her plate away, "I guess I'll ask: how has Dad been?"

The sun had just been setting as we finished our meals and I slowly poured more whiskey into my glass. I noticed that Mary hadn't touched hers as I prepared myself to answer her.

I had been wondering if Mary was going to bring up our father. Until recently, we had assumed he was missing. Then, several months before Mary and I had reconnected, she had received a letter from him. He had been in Arkham Asylum, a mile from my apartment, and I had never known. I had told her that I would begin checking on him, but I had yet to amass the courage to do so.

Before I could explain that, we were both startled by a thunderous pounding on the front door of the cabin.

Mary startled like a normal person. She spilled her drink as her arms jolted and over-recovered, falling from her chair with a short yelp.

I was startled like an old soldier. In a way, I was. The monsters, ghosts, and goblins I had come across over the years seemed to never let up, and I was always trying to fight or think my way out of a scenario.

When I was startled, my hand slapped at my hip in search of my pistol.

Except that I was on a harmless vacation with my sister, and for reasons that I will never recall, I chose not to bring my gun with me.

Mistake number one, I thought to myself.

Only one person knew that we were here, but if it was Donny, he would have called out.

Holding up my hand, I mimed for Mary to be quiet and to get behind the table, while I stepped to the door.

Reaching up, I unlatched it. Donny's stories had put us on edge, so we had chosen to latch the door just in case. Clearly, with the force that was hitting the thin wooden portal, it had been a good idea.

I cast one more look back at Mary to make sure that she was in a safe enough place and then I slowly unlatched the door and pulled it open.

Nothing was there.

I stared out into the night, taking a step onto the small porch to look around in the waning light. I saw and heard nothing.

Mary was suddenly beside me.

"Get back in the house," I hissed.

"No," she sounded almost bored with me. "Do you see anything?"

I shook my head. The silence was almost oppressive.

"I saw something," Mary grew excited and began pointing into the woods. "Movement over there. I swear, I saw—"

She was interrupted as something large as a bear and just as black ran in front of us and the porch. We heard hooves or paws hitting the ground with speed and force, but in the darkening evening, we couldn't make out what it was. It was gone as quickly as it had appeared.

"What was—" Mary started, but this time I cut her off.

"Get in the house," I grabbed her shoulder and started to shove my sister. She couldn't take her eyes off what I had just noticed.

Two eyes, glowing like coals in a fire, just beyond the tree line. A large black mass stepped into view. From what I could see, it had large, curved horns, four legs and the eyes continued to glow. Comparing it to a bear hadn't been far off. It was huge.

"Inside," I hissed again. "Now!" This time, I shoved Mary inside and spun to shut the door just as I saw the creature pawing at the ground. I witnessed its first steps in its charge before I slammed the door shut and grabbed Mary's chair, slamming it in place to hold the door.

As big as that thing had been, I couldn't imagine that the door—even with the chair—was going to be much help, but it might buy us time to come up with a better plan.

I slammed my body against the top of the door to brace it further.

The impact shook the entire cabin. The door flexed under the force and propelled me back and onto the floor.

Luckily, the door held.

I was gasping for air. The force of the door had bounced me back, but I had felt something else hit me in the chest.

Mary screamed and rushed to my side, helping me up as I clutched at my chest.

"Andy! Are you alright?"

"I felt that," I answered as I got to my feet. "That thing hit more than just the door."

She was still holding my arm as I tried to catch my breath. "What was that?"

"I don't know. A goat I think," I said, "but it wasn't a normal goat."

My mind was elsewhere as I pulled up my sleeves and stepped over to the window. I was doubtful the creature was still there, but just in case I was hoping to catch a better glimpse at it. I was still looking out the window and into the darkness when Mary gasped.

"What… what happened to your arm?"

Shit. I had forgotten about my arm. Of course, my sister was going to have a lot of questions about that.

I grimaced and tried to keep us on task with the current problem. "Lights," I said. "Quickly."

She did as I asked, dousing the lanterns but leaving the fireplace lit. The light from the fire was less uniform, so it wouldn't give away our positions too much if we were careful. I felt her step next to me, but while I looked out the window, I knew her eyes were still on my arm.

I felt her hand touch it, examining the change. It had been almost a full year since the incident had happened, and I still hadn't told her about it. I don't know if it was to spare her or me, but it had only postponed the inevitable.

"It looks like your arm was cut off and someone glued a new one there," she gave a soft gasp. "Is that half of a tattoo?"

I put my finger to my lips and whispered. "That's exactly what happened."

Mary only blinked at me, processing what I was saying.

"This is a joke, right?" She sounded incredulous, but at least she was whispering now. She looked up from my arm and read my expression. "You're serious?"

I let out a sigh. "Now isn't the time."

My sister grabbed me by the shoulder and twisted me around. "You're always in the thick of it. It'll never be the right time, so tell me."

A grunt of frustration left my lips. Then the explanation did.

"When I lost my job as the dean, it was because an ancient god crossed over from another plane of existence. He was a god of nightmares." I still feared Icthosthau's return. Or worse: what he's doing with the survivors in his realm.

With Nancy.

I shook my head and continued. "He cut off my arm and, well, he killed me."

Mary's shock was almost thick enough to fill the room. "What? He did what? What do you mean he *killed you*?"

I stepped closer to the fireplace and pulled my collar aside to show the jagged scar in the side of my neck.

"He broke my sword in half and shoved it through my throat." My voice dropped as my mind drifted just a bit with the memory. "I still have nightmares about it. Metal scraping the bone."

"But, you're," she waved her hands at me, standing upright, "alive."

"I wasn't, though," I answered. "A small military group that was helping the campus defeat that monster used an experimental treatment to return me to life." I held up my arm, formerly that of another man. "That same treatment allowed them to graft a dead man's arm to my own."

My intelligent sister shook her head. "That's not medically poss —
"

A guttural, inhuman scream sliced through the night, silencing Mary.

I ignored the sound to finish this conversation as quickly as possible.

"The treatment they gave me was less than science," I shrugged. "Call it magic, but thanks to recent events, my connection to the Veil and the magic of our world has not been the same. At one time, I could call on spells I learned to defend us, or spirit us away to some other, safer location. Now, if I even try, I am sent into agony." I pointed at the door. "When that goat-thing slammed into the door, I felt it," my hand tapped my chest, "inside of me. That's how I know that thing isn't a normal goat."

"Besides the glowing eyes," Mary said, sarcastically.

I nodded. She had me there.

"The door shouldn't have stopped him," Mary said.

"Donny's sigils stopped him," I said. "He's warded the house with symbols from the *Al-Azif*. I think we're safe if we stay inside."

Mary exhaled slowly. "That's not a normal goat."

I nodded.

"I believe you." Mary said.

"What?" I asked, confused for a moment.

"I said I believe you." She looked me in the eyes, and I could see sadness and hope in there. "If anyone else had told me what you had, I would have thought they were crazy. Not you. Not my brother. You live in this world of absolutely horrible things and that terrifies me, but I believe you."

I offered a weak smile. "Thank you."

"Are you alright?" She returned her hand to my scarred arm.

"I have no idea. If I figure it out, I'll let you know. It scares me too."

"Now is not the time for that," she hit me in the arm that was still original. "I need Dr. Andrew Doran to rush in and save the day. Bury the fear, soldier, we've got work to do."

I offered a mock salute. "Yes, ma'am."

Returning to the window, I tried to find our aggressor. "I've been attacked by a lot of things in my life. This is the first goat."

"This isn't funny, Andy," Mary's annoyed sister-voice was coming through. I hadn't heard it in a while, and it comforted me that she had fallen back into it so easily.

"An ironic percentage of this is funny, but you're not wrong," I said. "Nobody should even know that we're here."

"Do you think that they are after Donny?" Mary asked.

I shrugged. That had been my first thought, but they could have taken Donny long before we arrived. He had admitted to being alone in the woods with that weird goat. That would have been the time. Instead, they waited for us to be here.

Mary gasped and then pointed out the window.

"What is that?"

Chapter Three

Mary's shock tore my eyes away from the window and to my sister before I followed her gaze back out the window and toward the still darkening woods.

I peered through the long shadows and thought that maybe I saw those same two red eyes from earlier, but I couldn't be sure.

"What did you see?" I asked my sister.

Mary shook her head and walked away from the window. "Nothing. It was nothing." She looked around in the dark, accentuated by the fireplace. "Do you have any guns?"

The question was also on my mind as it would have been a great time to have something that could forcibly repel supernatural intruders.

"I didn't think that we would need them," I said with clear disappointment. "Donny mentioned he might have something here if we need it. Stay low, just in case they have guns, and I'll go see what I can find in the bedroom."

Mary's eyes went wide when I mentioned that whoever brought the goat might have guns, and then she dropped to the floor but was close enough to the window to still peer outside.

"*Who* might have guns, Andy?" she asked in more of a harsh whisper than before.

I sighed. "Donny said he had been dealing with folks around here. Likely cultists like last time. He also mentioned that he had seen a weird goat. I can't imagine that both things this far from the town aren't related."

"Your collegiate level hypothesis is that we're being harassed by goat worshippers?" While our danger had clearly been real, I couldn't deny how incredulous her statement sounded.

I shrugged, not even sure if she could see it in the flickering light of the fire. "I am still piecing it together, but yes."

I took a moment to assess my thoughts before letting out a slow breath and saying, "The goat is a symbol of a particularly powerful and wide-spread cult. All the old Earth Mother deities ranging from Istar to Isis to Cybele and Gaia herself are but shadows of Shub-Niggurath."

To my surprise, Mary's eyes went wide with understanding, "Mother Nature is an uncaring bitch." Her eyes didn't meet mine as she turned her focus toward the fire.

Something about goat-worshipping cultists. Something about mothers?

I shook the thought from my head and focused on locating any of Donny's hidden resources.

The flickering of the fireplace left enough light to get me out of the main room and into Donny's old bedroom, but after that I was mostly fumbling around.

The layout of the small cabin was fairly simple. The living area and kitchen were all part of one room. The only other room was the bedroom with a small chest at the foot of the bed in lieu of a closet. The outhouse was about twenty to thirty feet from the back door from the kitchen area.

If we didn't get rid of this goat-thing, then our bladders were going to have a rough evening.

I went to the chest at the foot of the bed first. The lid fell back, and I did my best to feel around. Aside from some old blankets and a small bottle of something dark and certainly delicious, I closed the lid and resumed my search.

Even in the dark, it was clear that Donny was a minimalist or at least had moved everything to his newer home at this point and had only been using this cabin as a camping lodge or base for his hunting.

That left only under the bed to be searched. That was where I found a short crate, filled with various goods.

Digging through the dark, I found two canned goods that I couldn't read the labels of, more matches than I felt we would ever need, a hand-drawn map of the area surrounding the cabin with several more of Donny's sigils being used in relation to specific locations, and some old hunting gear in the form of a dull skinning knife and some shotgun shells.

The shotgun was nowhere to be found.

Picking up the crate, I carried it back to Mary in the main room while also trying to stay low and out of the light. It was becoming more evident as time passed that, whoever our goat-herding friends were, they hadn't come in peace, and I didn't want to find out the hard way that they might have brought weapons with them.

As I set the chest down next to where Mary sat against the wall under the window, I noticed that she was quietly crying.

"Mary," I was concerned, "did you get hurt? What's going on?"

She pointed up and over her shoulder, indicating outside the window.

"It doesn't," she tried to say before getting interrupted by her own sob. She tried again, "It doesn't make any sense."

I looked from my sister to the window, back to my sister, and then slid across the floor until I was under the window and peering out.

There wasn't too much to see, as the night had crept in and eliminated dusk while I was searching the bedroom. Shadows moved in the forest, and I could make out the silhouettes of trees and the log pile, but the reflection of the fire behind me made it difficult to see any details.

I crept closer and cupped my hands around my eyes to rid myself of the glare. Casting my attention into the darkness, I continued to scan the forest. If anything, I was mostly concerned over how still the woods had become.

Then movement caught my eye.

I focused on the area, about fifteen to twenty-five feet beyond the log pile, and waited for it to happen again.

When it did, I couldn't be sure of what I was seeing.

A tree, thinner than my torso, bent at an odd angle, the top remaining in place as the base rotated perpendicular to the stationary top.

Then the entire tree shot straight into the air.

I gasped but I couldn't take my eyes from where the tree had been.

"That wasn't a tree," Mary whispered from beneath the window.

I couldn't help but tear my gaze from the window to stare at my sister. What did she mean by that?

Finding no answers in Mary's terrified look, I returned to the window and saw another tree shoot up as another one slammed into the ground and resumed looking like a tree.

It happened again and dread told me what Mary already had.

It wasn't a tree.

"They are legs," I said.

Mary started to quietly cry again. "You see it now?"

"I don't understand," was all that I could say.

"There goes my last shred of hope," Mary's voice was almost inaudible.

I was witnessing my sister, a normal person in extraordinary circumstances, become deconstructed by her fear. That was what reintroducing myself back into her life was doing. Slowly, her concept of normal, her sense of peace, any quiet places in her mind were all being destroyed simply by being back in my life.

It was a world of nightmares and gods and things that looked like trees but clearly were not.

She didn't need logic, though, even when there was none to be found. She needed him. She needed her brother.

With a sharp motion, I yanked back the sparse curtain before spinning toward the lantern and relighting it.

"We're done hiding."

"What about the light?" Mary's voice was soaked in fear.

I grabbed both of her hands and pulled my sister to standing before grasping her in a tight hug.

"It doesn't matter anymore," I said, pouring confidence into my voice. "We might not know what we're up against, but Donny's door wouldn't hold up against a stiff breeze and it took the impact from that not-goat-thing like a champ. That means that while we're in here, we're protected by Donny's *Al-Azif* symbols."

"Alright, professor," Mary pulled away from our hug and I could see that she was smirking through her tears, "what do we do now, then?"

I returned her smile. "Right now, we need facts."

"And how do we get facts while safely locked inside this cabin?"

I shrugged, "I was going to go outside and ask them."

Mary's eyes went wide with fear again, this time for my sake. "You can't," she spun and scooped up the crate that I had brought from the bedroom. "Were there any guns in here?"

I shook my head. "No, none in the entire house. He must take those with him, as I found shotgun shells, but no shotgun."

"What's this?" Mary held up something that I hadn't seen in my cursory review of the crate in the dark of the bedroom.

In her hand was a cylindrical bundle of twigs and dried vegetation with a note wrapped around it. As Mary untied the string and unrolled the note, I saw that the bundle of plants was held together by a second bit of twine. The entire thing was tied together twice.

I looked over the bundle while Mary held onto the note.

"Normally, I would guess that this is sage, meant for cleansing a home of spirits, but this," I trailed off as I looked at the individual plants and fibers making up the collection. "This doesn't look like sage."

"And this doesn't look like any language that I know," Mary handed me the note, and I passed the bundle back to her to inspect.

The note was on old paper, but it wasn't ancient. From the weathering of the paper, I had to guess that it had been sitting in that crate for a long time. Mary was correct in that she was not able to read the note.

To some extent, though, I could.

It was written in one of the ancient texts that I had seen on the *Scroll of Eibon*. It wasn't Hyperborean, like the wizard of the same name was, but was instead a mix of Yithian and something else that I couldn't quite make out. My time with my former assistant, Nancy Dyer, and her Yith-touched father had given me some familiarity with the language and while I couldn't read it, per se, I could make out the general context of the note.

"It's Yithian," I said without thinking about how Mary would have no idea what the Yith even were. When I looked up, her eyes let me know my mistake. "Alien, but supernatural. The Yith are like," I struggled with a comparison, "observers. They watch us and try not to interfere."

Mary nodded toward the note, "That looks like interference."

"Kind of," I answered. "They send people here, usually in the minds of others, and they need to bring with them knowledge that can protect them while they are in our mortal shells. A lot of our superstition and knowledge of magic comes from them just attempting to survive our world."

"Is Donny one of them?" Mary's voice dropped to a whisper again.

In a knee-jerk response, I frowned and said, "No," and then paused and answered more truthfully. "Well, I don't think that he is. I think he found this somewhere, or someone gifted it to him as a protection against, well, I don't know what."

"Protection?" Mary asked. "Is that what the note said?"

Before I could answer her, a goat screamed outside. We both spun to face the door, staring at it with fear and confusion at the same time.

"I think they are calling to us," I said.

"For what?" Mary was beginning to panic again. "And why us? None of this makes sense." She waved the bundle at the door. "Will this thing work?"

I yanked it away from her and tied the note back to it. "No, it won't work like that, if it'll work against whatever that is outside at all."

"Then what do we do?"

I handed the recombined bundle back to my sister and turned to the door.

"I said we don't have any information," I said. "Now, I go and ask some questions."

Chapter Four

"Wait," Mary almost shouted at me.

"What?" I asked, checking her over again. "What's wrong?"

"Besides everything?" She tried to smile, but it didn't work.

"If you want all of the information, then I haven't told you everything," my sister blurted out.

"Mary, I don't know that we have time—" I started, thinking that this was some sort of fear, or thing she wanted to get off her chest in case she thought that I was about to die. I didn't want her last-minute confession regarding some old tragedy, or even a deeply felt moment of emotion just because she thought that I was going to perish. It would end up killing a lot of my self-confidence when trying to scare away a motivated cult.

"You told me about your dying," she interrupted me. "You told me something deeply personal, I would think, about things you didn't have any reason to believe that I would think were real." She was crying now, and I honestly had no idea what to do. I put my arm around her, deciding it was best to be close and let her say what she needed to say.

"You keep on trusting me," she continued, "but it's my turn to trust you with my scary thing. I wanted to tell you before the night was finished, but have you noticed? I haven't had any of the whiskey you've poured me."

Thinking back, I had noticed during dinner that she wasn't drinking anything. I assumed she was taking the evening at a different pace than I was. Why was this significant now? Oddly enough, it made me flash back to a previous encounter that I had a few years ago in which the person I had been speaking to had been completely fabricated from my memory.

Slowly, I reached forward and poked my sister. "You're really here, right?"

"What?" Mary stared at me completely confused. "Yes, I'm here you dummy. I'm pregnant." Seeing that I was still confused, she added, "Clarence's mother is a nurse, and she said that drinking when you're pregnant isn't safe for the baby."

"Clarence?" I said as the pieces, falling through the terror of everything else we were dealing with, started to drop into place. "Pregnant?" Realization struck and I pulled my sister into a hug.

"That's fantastic!" I shouted, forgetting our predicament and then flinching when I realized. Some moralists in Arkham would have reacted with more shock but we'd been at war since Pearl Harbor. Many husbands and beaus had been off while life went on. Unwed mothers, even when they were my sibling, were far down on the list of things to shock me. I was a man of the world not Puritan New England.

"Not really," Mary said, hooking her thumb over her shoulder to indicate the goat cult outside. "And, we haven't told anyone yet because we have yet to get married."

I pulled my sister into a hug so tight that she grunted.

"I'm going to be an uncle," I whispered with a huge grin as I pulled out of the hug. "I am going to have to meet Clarence," I looked back at the window. "Maybe before I leave back for Miskatonic if there's time."

Mary's eyes lost a hint of the fear that had been flooding them as she raised her eyebrow and aimed out the window. "If we don't die."

"Die?" I returned my attention to Mary. "Who said anything about dying?"

Mary just pointed at the door and said, "Goat?"

"It's a goat," I said, knowing full well that it was more than just a goat. "We've fought alien bugs from Venus before. Are you really afraid of a goat?"

Standing up, I straightened my shirt, grabbed the glass from the table and poured another whiskey, now knowing that I had a lot more booze to drink this weekend than I had just moments before. Tossing it back, I set the glass down and crouched again.

"Take the bundle of twigs and head to the room. If you see anything in the room with you, light that bundle and wave it in whatever direction they are." I handed her a book from our excess supply of matches.

"What are you going to do?" Mary asked,

I had no gun, no sword, and no weapon of any kind. I didn't even have magic. The only thing I had going for me was a memory in the back of my brain that wasn't making sense and a desperate need to keep my sister safe.

"We need more information, and we are both teachers." I shrugged, "I'm going to go ask it questions."

Mary didn't like this idea, but she allowed me to walk her to the bedroom and shut the door as she protested.

Then I walked to the front door of the cabin and opened it. I immediately shut it as I stepped out onto the porch. No matter what was about to happen to me, Donny's wards would keep Mary safe until her curiosity made her open the door. Not for the first time in my life, I found myself wishing that humanity wasn't so consistently curious.

Stepping over the threshold felt like stepping onto an alien world. The sounds were muted to the point where I had to focus to hear anything of the natural world. I could not see much further than the first line of trees. From dusk, I knew that the things in the woods were just on the edge, a few yards further than that first row of trees.

Donny had an old chair just to the left of the door to the cabin. I considered putting on a false front of being unafraid by having a seat and crossing my legs but decided against it. This wasn't a display of power, as I had none. This, I hoped, was an interview.

I cleared my throat and opened it to shout my questions into the woods.

A deep voice, melodic and masculine in depth, but clearly female, spoke from the darkness. "Bring us the woman."

I shook my head, "She and this house are under my protection. What do you want her for?"

They wanted Mary. Why would they want my sister? All my thoughts about why these cultists and this goat thing and whatever else were here just went out the window.

"Mother would like a word," the voice said.

"Mother? Who is..." That small memory in the back of my head was screaming now. I tried to focus on it while also trying to peer deeper into the darkness. "Mother? Do you mean the mother of..." I was struggling to remember, "well, a lot of kids? The goat mother, protector of the woods? Shub-Ni—"

"Do not speak the protector's name," the voice added no volume or pitch in cadence, but it was clear that this was a nonnegotiable order.

Their protector was Shub-Niggurath? I remembered nothing about that one. Goats were part of it and being a mother was a huge part of it. Mary was carrying a child, but how could they have known that? Their god must have told them. If that's why they wanted her. It could be they wanted her for her potential to be a mother.

"What does your protector want with her?" I repeated.

Red eyes flared in the dark. Good. Now I knew where the goat was.

"Not her," the voice said. "The child."

I let out a slow sigh. Not because I wasn't nervous, but because I *was*. I was preparing myself for... something. They wanted my future niece or nephew for something. The odds of what they wanted her baby for being wonderful were slim. I had not forgotten about whatever the thing that had trees for legs was. They had shown up in force for a baby. My doubts were running out of benefits to give.

"Why do you want her child?" I demanded.

"For the blessing."

In my history, I had seen a lot of blessings and have come to the conclusion that blessings tended to mimic the favor of the god giving them. I had no faith that the creepy goat with red eyes was looking to give a stuffed bear to my kin.

It was time to be Professor Doran. "Do you know who she is, the mother of the child you're looking to bless?"

There was a long pause before the goat or whatever was speaking through the goat-thing, answered. "We do."

"Then do you know who I am?"

"We do," the reply was quicker this time.

This time I smiled into the darkness and asked again. "Do you really?"

Red eyes appeared, but they weren't those of the goat-thing as its eyes were still open and just beyond the tree line. It was another set about twenty feet to the left of the first pair.

Then another pair.

Then more.

And more.

That was her name. I remembered the name that Shub-Niggurath went by when worshipped in the dark wood.

The Mother of a Thousand Young.

The kids were here, and they wanted to bless my sister's child.

Shit.

What I believed to be the first and original goat-thing stepped from the woods and into the shafts of moonlight peeking between the trees. He stood near the log pile.

The Young were like goats, and the moniker of goat-thing fit perfectly. It stood on all fours almost as tall as I was, dwarfing any other goat that I had ever seen. The thing was on all fours, but its front hooves were not hooves at all. Where hooves should have been were hands splayed in the pine needles and dirt that made up the forest floor. Its head was wider than any goat head, as if it had been flattened and then the goat snout pulled back out. It looked like some dark hybrid between an orangutan and a large black farming goat.

When it spoke, its lips parted to show animal teeth, flat like a goat's should be, but with incisors clearly meant for ripping flesh.

Its horns were the most normal thing about it.

"Mother wishes to protect the child," the beast said. "Mother knows of its great destiny. It will not be the disappointment that you were."

"That's rude," I said. "I will not let you near her."

"You cannot stop us," the beast replied. "Those who champion you are not here. The powers you once wielded are gone. You are weaponless against Mother and her Young."

"If I am so weaponless, why are you outside the house and not in there, already 'blessing' the child?" I demanded and suddenly a fear shot through my stomach as I realized the answer.

"We are."

Whatever effect Donny's wards had to keep out eldritch entities either had failed to do the job or had been useless from the beginning. The Mother only wanted to get me away from Mary.

I turned to run back inside, fear driving me as logic shouted that now would be when the goat thing tried to stop me. Instead of continuing to reach for the door, I twisted and stepped to the side.

The horn of the Young scratched my back as the beast charged through where I had been and hit the door again. This time, the Young didn't pull his attack and careened right through the door. Splintered wood shot into the air with the volume of crashing furniture.

I came in behind the Young and kicked it in the back of the head as hard as I could.

It was a goat, so that did nothing at all besides angering it, but it bought me a moment to rush beyond it and into the room with Mary.

Mary was lying on the bed with two of the Young standing over her and chanting.

Goats or not, I wasn't letting them touch my sister.

I dove at the first one and was slapped aside like a yapping puppy.

Come on, Andrew, think!

What did I know? Shub-Niggurath was a fertility goddess. Forest cultures worshipped her. I wasn't certain what happened to those blessed by her, but I had a feeling I was about to find out.

That was when I recognized some of their chanting. Before I started my next charge, I tried to listen.

Their words were a mix of languages. There was some Hyperborean, some Greek, and even some Egyptian.

Speaking in the worst dialect and using mostly the incorrect wording, as I hadn't spoken Egyptian in about a decade, I shouted, "Stop, before I summon the Black Pharaoh."

They halted their movements and turned to face me. It could have been just because I interrupted them, or it could have been idle curiosity at the human speaking in a language they hadn't expected me to know. I liked to think it was the threat of bringing someone here who was at least as powerful as the Mother.

To be completely honest, I knew the Black Pharaoh wasn't going to show up even if I were to perfectly summon him. The name had been used to associate it with Nyarlathotep, but recently I had discovered that it referenced one of his avatars. That realization had trashed a museum and sealed away the Black Pharaoh for… well, at least a really long time.

While it caused them to pause, it didn't stop them. A harsh bark from the one who had swatted me sent a wave of power toward me that picked me up and pressed me to the wall.

The pressure was intense, but nothing hurt me nearly as much as watching my sister being prayed over while I could do nothing to help her.

Our eyes met and I saw something in hers that I hadn't expected. Mary was clearly afraid, but she was trying to show me something. Her eyes kept darting down.

Following her gaze, I saw Donny's present from the Yith. It was about a foot from where I hovered against the wall and the matches were on a dresser right next to me. Next to the lit lantern on the dresser.

In all the commotion and rush to save Mary, I hadn't realized that she had turned the lantern on while she had been waiting for me. Judging by their proximity to each other, she must have just lit the lantern when the Young had grabbed her.

I watched the first of the Young—the one who had given us so much of our fear this evening—stride in and take up a place at the foot of the bed. His voice began to harmonize with my sister's other captors.

I started shouting in every language that I could remember. Languages long dead to human ears—earthly ears, or even the Mother's ears—for scores of millennia erupted from my mouth as I hoped to distract my captors so that their willpower would wane enough to drop me.

Helpless, I watched as they lowered their hands to my sister's abdomen and pressed their surprisingly human fingers to her shirt. The one who was pressing me to the wall with his mind touched the end of her shirt and lifted it up to give them access to her bare stomach.

Then they pressed their fingers to her flesh.

Then they howled.

I dropped to the floor both surprised by the fact that I was falling and in pain from the howl that not only filled the room but also the forest itself. Whatever was happening, it was happening to all the Mother's Young.

My eardrums were in enough pain to cripple my movements, but in the back of my mind I knew what I had to do: I needed to get the Yith ward and use it.

The Yith were time travelers that tended to interfere more than they claimed, and I felt like everything that was going on here might be something that they knew was going to happen. The odds of Bear having one of those that he chose to just leave here were thin.

The crippling pain in my head began to subside as their cries began to calm down. As I came back to myself, I jumped to my feet and grabbed the matches, having already scooped up the Yith ward.

I struck the match and lit the sticks. No sooner had the first wisp of smoke curled up from it than all three of the Young's heads spun toward me.

"Get the hell out of here," I said as I marched toward them with the false confidence of someone who knew what they were doing.

It had been an educated guess up to this point, but now that I was seeing their reactions, it was clear that this is exactly what the Yith and maybe even Donny had left this here for.

Like animals, they dropped to all fours, and each raced from the building.

Mary came to me instantly and we held each other while we watched the fire burn down the bundle.

"They will come back when that's gone," she was weeping into my shoulder.

"No," I pulled away from the hug to touch her stomach. "I don't think they want to. They left because of the smoke, but they were hurt by you."

"By me?" Mary asked.

"Well," I smiled, "both of you." I tried to explain. "Whatever just happened, I don't think they realize that your child's destiny has already been claimed."

"By who?" Mary's face was twisting up with anger.

"By the good guys," I smiled. "I hope." I held up the still-burning ward. "This was left here to push them back, but someone put wards on you to protect your child. I have only ever seen the reaction they gave when monsters are met with their counters. Runes of protection or spells of 'get away from me' tend to be the only thing that makes them howl like that. I think the next Doran kid is going to be a force to be reckoned with."

We hugged each other and didn't leave that room until morning.

The next day we reported back to Donny at his home about the damage to his cabin and what we experienced. Clarence was with him, but Mary distracted him while I told Donny everything. My friend said he didn't know what the stick bundle had been or how it got there, but he was happy that it was there. He promised me to keep an eye on Mary and report to me regularly even the slightest odd thing that might happen in the area.

Clarence met us next. Mary decided that the weekend's excitement wasn't for someone who hadn't been touched by the true madness of the world yet. Mary wanted to bring Clarence into this world that I was a part of but now was not the time.

He was an average looking man with glasses. He was bookish, but tall with a full head of hair.

I wasn't sure what to think about him until he asked me, "Do you ever watch any baseball games?"

After an almost obsessive conversation in which we both forgot that Mary was there, Clarence and I had become fast friends.

Finally, I gave my sister a hug with a promise to check in much more frequently.

"I could get you a job in Arkham," I nodded toward Clarence who was back talking to Donny, "and Clarence."

"That's not a discussion for today," Mary said. "I still have to tell him," she indicated her belly. "I just found out about a week ago. I wasn't even sure if I was going to tell you yet."

"Then goat-men attacked us," I smiled at the absurdity of it all.

"What's wrong with my baby, Andy?" Mary's face darkened.

I shook my head and pulled her into a hug. "Nothing. Absolutely nothing." I sighed but didn't let my sister go. "Time travel is horrible, and not because of how complicated it can get. But mostly because everyone treats it like history is a long line of inflexible stone. A pillar that can't bend or flex and that's just not the case. The Yith went to the future at some point and saw your little Peanut doing something that they think Peanut needs to do. Good, bad, or indifferent, they thought it necessary to save us in that moment. So, is your baby alright? As much as any of us. Your baby will be another cog in the machine that keeps this world moving and, more importantly, being that cog saved your life today."

That wasn't everything, but I knew less than I was letting on. The Yith had provided the bundle to scare away the Young, but whatever had hurt them when they had touched Mary wasn't the same power. It wasn't even the same technology. Someone had reached out and blocked their touch or, worse, had already blessed the baby.

That was tomorrow's problem.

Blessed Be Her Children

By Jessi Vasquez

The package was waiting on the porch when Liriope came home from school. The house was dark, even though her dad and stepmom had promised to be home early to take her out to dinner for her birthday. She ruled out the package being from either of them. It would have been given at dinner if it were.

Liriope picked up the box wrapped in plain brown paper and studied it as she unlocked the front door. There was a tag with her name in pretty cursive writing that was vaguely familiar. When she searched her mind for where she'd seen it before, there was nothing but hazy unease that urged her to hurl the package away from her. She ignored the impulse, chiding herself for being ungrateful for the gift, and brought it with her into the house.

In her room, Liriope tore the wrapping away from the box and uncovered a book. There was no writing on the cover, only an image of a woman with dark horns jutting from her hair, standing on hooved feet. She was the most beautiful woman Liriope had ever seen, but looking at the printed face sent cold chills down her spine. Liriope couldn't shake the feeling that the woman was staring back at her, pulling her into the black, bottomless eyes on the cover. The book smelled faintly of smoke and appeared very old, but when Liriope flipped through the pages she found that they were crisp and blank. She closed it and examined the cover again.

Liriope had a strange feeling she had seen it before, and that it had something to do with her mother. Though she'd spent most of her childhood with her mother, Cassidy, Liriope's memories of that time were patchy at best. She had one clear memory that she did her best to hold on to. It was from her tenth birthday, when Liriope, her mother, her Aunt Jude, and her Aunt Rachel had gone to an amusement park. They were in a spinning teacup, and Liriope and Cassidy were laughing wildly together while Jude and Rachel spun the little wheel in the center faster and faster. The next clear memory Liriope had was leaving late one night with her dad and coming to the house they lived in now. Beyond that, all she knew was what little she could get from her dad, Ryan. Which was that Cassidy and Jude had found Jesus and run away with some church. Liriope's therapist said the blank pieces were part of the process, that it was normal for things to come in and out.

Now, holding the book, Liriope was assaulted by an onslaught of fragmented images. In her mind she saw the book on what might have been the kitchen table in her mother's apartment before her mother snatched it away from Liriope's curious gaze. Then she saw it tucked in the crook of her mother's arm in a room that flickered with candlelight. Then Cassidy was hunched over it, scribbling frantically in the pages.

If the book was related to her mother, it must have been a gift from her Aunt Rachel. Last Christmas, Rachel had given Liriope a box of her mother's old high school keepsakes: a class ring, a yearbook, a bill from a play, and various other snippets from her life. Liriope had to hide it from her dad. She hadn't wanted him to take it from her, like he'd done with the one picture of her mother that she'd hung up in her room.

She fanned through the pages again. When she caught fragments of writing she flopped down on her bed and opened it to the beginning. Several pages appeared crudely sewn into the front at the seam of the book. The first was yellowed and filled with handwriting she recognized. She sucked in a sharp breath when she caught her mother's name and read the page eagerly.

July 29, 2021
Cassidy Silva
Log #1

I have no idea if I'm doing this right. I've been so anxious for my turn with this book. I could sense it would be some next-level stuff, but I'm not sure what to do with it or what it's actually all about. Maggie said that's part of the process. That's why I can't have the forbidden knowledge from the earlier entries yet. Okay, okay. Maggie didn't say it was forbidden knowledge. She said I could read it if I wanted to, but I probably wouldn't understand it. I need to have more one-on-one sessions with her so I understand the context of our Divine Mother. I tried to flip to the beginning anyway. The front pages are so worn out and delicate that I couldn't make out a thing. The first page I could read, I still had no clue what it said because it was in German or something. Even when I skipped ahead to the English bits, it didn't make any sense. Maybe I'll send over a picture of the older pages to my sister Judith. She loves stuff like that.

Maggie told me to state my name and to number the entries. But number how? It's my first entry, but it's not the first one in the book. I couldn't even guess how many there are. This thing is fat, and the pages in the front are hella old. It makes me nervous, to be honest. It looks fragile. I have a kid in the house, and while Liriope is pretty dang mature, she's still only twelve. This morning I tried to do a load of laundry and discovered I was somehow completely out of detergent. I went to Liriope to figure out what happened and found some sort of detergent science project on her dresser. Not an actual school project. Just one born from her own boredom and curiosity. I find lots of interesting "science projects" around the place. That's what she calls them. When I'm in a bad mood I call them messes. I can't actually be mad about it, though. She's so dang smart, and of course I want to encourage that. I don't know where she gets it. You'd never have caught me or her dad doing homework when we didn't have to. Maggie's only instruction was to write to the Mother and describe how I found my way to her church. But the Mother found me. I was just passing time on my phone when one of her church's Tarot readings ended up on my feed. I knew it was for me. I've been putting my energy out there looking for a way out of this mess, and lo and behold, there was Maggie on my phone, talking about how "This reading is for the single mother about to face an important court date" or something like that. I forget the exact wording. But it was specific enough that I knew it wasn't a coincidence. How else would she know I had a custody hearing on September 28th? I could feel such intense love pulling me in. So I sent the page a message requesting a more in-depth reading, and now I've been seeing Maggie and the girls for about a month.

August 1, 2021
Cassidy Silva
Log #2

Maggie is trying to prepare me for the road ahead. She gets how important it is that my ex doesn't get Liriope, and she believes the Church can help. I went in tonight for meditations and it's got me feeling better than I have in a long time. The other women there all started out like me. Alone with their kids, looking for their place in the world. Now most of them have found true happiness through the Church and are getting ready to grow their families. Caroline was the newest before I got here. She was the one who wrote in this book before me. I haven't read her entries yet. I feel kind of funny without talking to her about it first, and Maggie hasn't said I'm ready anyway. But Caroline told me some of her story, and it's pretty dang close to mine. Her ex treated her like garbage and took zero interest in their daughter after they broke up. Then he got remarried and suddenly he wanted to play the role of a loving father to impress the new woman in his life. That's exactly what Ryan is doing to me! But Caroline tells me I don't need to worry. The Church helped her get full custody of her kid and she says she can tell the Mother is going to bless me, too.

I know she's right. I can feel it every time I walk into the Meditation Hall. The Mother's statue is in the center of the room, and I can feel that same intense love that I got from Maggie's video, only now it's coming from the statue. It connects me to all the other women there, like the fabric of my being is all tied up in theirs now. I've never experienced a bond so deep, and I can't imagine my life without it anymore.

My sister Jude agreed to take Liriope on Wednesday nights, and to take her to school Thursday mornings so I can attend meditation sessions regularly. I feel like everything's coming together.

August 8, 2021
Cassidy Silva
Log 3

There's a girls' choir at the Church that Liriope's going to love. I brought her to the Saturday night gathering and she hit it off with the other kids. I think she looks up to Caroline's girl. She's taking Liriope under her wing like Caroline did for me. They're all shockingly well-behaved children. They'll be a good influence on Liriope.

August 9, 2021
Cassidy Silva
Log 4

Dear Mother,

I showed my entries to Maggie. She said I was doing just fine, but she suggested I write more directly to you, Divine Mother, and to write more about my relationships with Jude and Liriope. She said sisters hold a special connection to you, and three is a powerful number. My kid makes three, so....

That is how it's been since Liriope was born. The three of us in our own little bubble. I mean, her dad's around. That's why I have a mess now. But Ryan being there only started after he got engaged a few months ago to some lady who wants to take my kid to make a happy little family with him.

I'm getting off track.

Jude's always been my best friend. Cheesy to say about your sister, but it's true. It's the same for her, even though she does have other friends. Mostly people who were in drama club with her in high school. She reconnected with some of them when she moved back home after the accident. Her best friend Rachel even moved in with her for a while. I think her and Rachel dated or something, but I never could get the whole story out of her. Anyway, they're still tight, and Rachel helped a lot in the beginning when Liriope was little. She still gets Liriope birthday presents and comes with

Jude to all Liriope's school performances. I'm not sure if it's because she's still not-so-secretly in love with Jude, or because it reminds her of their theater glory days.

Me and Jude are five years apart, which seems like a lot, and maybe it mattered when we were little. But that's not how I remember it. It's only looking back as an adult that I realize Jude probably played dolls and make-believe games for longer than she wanted to for my sake. But man, she was good at them. Like I said, theater kid. Funnily enough, she wasn't big on actually being on stage. When she got older she was more about the stagehand stuff, and she said she wanted to write scripts someday. She went more that route after Dad died. Before that I fully expected her to be the star of some musical on Broadway when she grew up. But she got a lot more serious after Dad's cancer, like she thought she had to take up his role. Singing was something special they shared. I never got the silly side of Dad, the one that would make up songs with Jude, or exaggerate songs they heard on the radio together. Then Dad was gone, and all the silliness stopped for a long time. Rachel coaxed it back out of Jude when they met in high school. But still, she only acted that way around Rachel until Liriope was born.

I guess I should tell you about the accident. Jude went away for college, and I threw a big fit and told her I hated her for leaving me. I meant it, too. Me and Mom were close, the way Dad and Jude used to be. But Mom worked the night shift and was asleep most of the time she was home, so it was Jude who looked after me the most. When she left, I was alone. She called and checked in, but it wasn't the same.

She surprised us with a visit during her second year of college because she wanted to celebrate her twentieth birthday at home with her friends, but by then I was fully into my rebellious teenage party era. So I wasn't home when she and Mom got into the accident. If I was, I probably would have been in the car too. Maybe I would have died with Mom. For a while after I wished I did. Jude dropped out and moved back home to take care of me, but I'd just started going out with Ryan and we were deep into the party scene. When Jude got wind of how bad it was getting, she gave me an ultimatum. She said she understood why I was doing what I was doing, but she couldn't be around stuff like that because she'd been through enough of it with Mom and she wasn't going to let it back into our home. So if I stayed with her, I had to go straight for a while. No partying of any kind, not even drinking. I think I got where she was coming from. I was too young to know a lot about Mom's problems, but it got bad for a while after Dad died. So I agreed to her rules at first, but then the more I thought about it, the angrier I got. I felt like she was trying to be my mom when she wasn't, and like she was painting our real mom as a bad parent. The day after that talk, I told her she couldn't control me and I was moving in with Ryan. We didn't talk for a few weeks. Ryan's parents were cool about everything, but things got pretty bad with me and him. I ended up calling Jude one night after he shoved me and I fell down the porch steps. She came and picked me up, and I thought she might punch Ryan. He could see it, too. He looked pretty scared when she showed up and got in his face. A part of me thought that was funny, but most of me was stupid and still loved him so I got in the middle and asked Jude to just take me home. She did, and to her credit, she didn't say I told you so or act smug or anything. That lasted about two weeks, which was when I found out I was pregnant. When I first came to Jude with the pregnancy test, she got "the look." I wonder if she knows she gets "the look." That's what Mom used to call it when Dad would get it. It's sort of this snarky, fed-up, self-righteous thing they do with their eyebrows and the corners of their mouths. Like they're saying "You can't be serious" without actually saying a word. But once the initial shock wore off, she did get this little smile I'd never seen before and she said, "So I'm going to be an Auntie?" I was sixteen when Liriope was born, and we all lived together for a good while. Rachel moved in and helped the entire time I was in school, and even pitched in with food and baby things. Jude tried to get me to sign up for community college after I graduated, but it really wasn't an option. We were all coming unglued at the seams so I got a job bartending by lying about my age. Me and Liriope got our own place when she was three. Jude was pretty beat up about us leaving, but it was the right move. Now Jude has her privacy, and Liriope gets to sleep over at Auntie Jude's any time she wants. She even has her own room there. Me and Jude hang out all the time, and she's made it clear I can move back in if I want to. I keep holding out, thinking maybe she'll meet someone and start her own family. But I think she feels like she's invested too much in us. I know the fact that she can't have kids because of the accident doesn't help things. Maybe that's why me and Liriope are sort of surrogate children for her. I think she blames Mom for taking the chance for a normal life from her, and I'm afraid she blames me, too. She's my best friend. But I'm not going to pretend it's perfect, or like it hasn't been lonely for me. I dated for a while, but in the end it was always a bust and I'm not feeling the dating game right now. I just wanted to branch out some and maybe find my own space and community outside of my sister and my kid. Lord knows they both have a life outside of me. So that's another reason I reached out to Maggie and the Church of the Divine Mother. It's turned out to be so much more than I thought. I've found my place in the world.

August 10, 2021
Cassidy Silva
Log 5

Mother,

Me and Jude got into it last night. We're all good now, but it was a little ugly. I haven't told her too much about you or your Church because she can get judgy about stuff she doesn't understand. But I got caught up in some extra meditation sessions and lost track of time, so I had to call Jude to pick Liriope up from school. Then I wasn't able to get her from Jude's until pretty late, and Jude got all parental on me, talking about how "It's a school night!" and "You should have called!" blah blah.

Like I don't know my kid's school schedule, like I haven't been doing everything Liriope's whole life. I mess up one time and suddenly I'm a bad mom. I explained about the no phones rule, and how my phone died anyway, but Jude barely listened. I thought she'd hold a grudge against the Church after that. But I think she can see all the good you're doing me. She agreed to take Liriope on Friday and Saturday nights, on top of the Wednesdays, so I can study one-on-one with Maggie.

August 16, 2021
Cassidy Silva
Log 6

Mother,

I got too curious and tried to read the entries at the beginning again. I sent Jude a picture of the stuff I thought was German, but she said it was Old English. She was super interested in where the page came from and asked if it was what I was studying with the Church. I wish I'd told her no, because when I said it was, she got weird about it. I guess she does have it out for the Church after our last fight. She said the page I gave her creeped her out. She wanted me to send her more, but I lied and said I forgot it at meditations. I guess that's why Maggie said that the context was important. Anyway, this is what Jude could make out: *I watch my sisters dance And slip into their frenzied trance as we wild women have always done But I think this mother is not...*

September 2, 2021
Cassidy Silva
Log 7

Mother,

I messed up big time.

So last night Jude was blowing up my phone, but it was Wednesday so I ignored it at first. She knew I had a study session with Maggie. I turned off my phone, but then I got in my head and started to worry that something bad happened to Liriope, so I excused myself and called her back.

Jude answered right away and was all, "Where the hell are you? Do you know what today is?"

I second-guessed myself and checked my phone to make sure, but then I was like, "It's Wednesday. You know I have study sessions on Wednesdays."

Then she was like, "It's Wednesday, what, Cass?"

Her tone told me she had "the look." I searched my brain, thinking I forgot her birthday or something. Then it hit me. I said, "Oh, crap."

She started whisper-yelling, "You're damn right, 'Oh, crap.' What the hell am I supposed to tell Liriope? You missed her solo! She's been talking about this for weeks!"

I couldn't say anything, because of course she was right. I can't believe I got the dates mixed up. I've never missed a single performance, and this was a big one. I kept apologizing until Jude cut me off to say I could explain why I wasn't there to Liriope myself, and they were meeting Ryan at Porky's Diner. She ended the call with, "Meet us there if you can take a break from your chanting or whatever."

It figures Ryan would show up to the one thing I didn't. After I hung up, I went back inside and explained the whole thing to Maggie, and she ended up asking to join me so she could meet Jude. I was so stoked that Maggie wanted to go, but I didn't know how Jude would react.

I was right to worry. Jude wasn't terrible because she was trying to put on a nice face for Liriope and her friends, but she was still snippy with me and downright rude to Maggie. For a moment, I saw Maggie the way Jude probably did, as some intruder with mismatched, wrinkled clothes, dirty gray hair matted in places, and bloodshot eyes. But I shook it off. Maggie's so much more than Jude could possibly understand. Liriope was happy to see Maggie. And over the moon about her performance. She did seem hurt that I wasn't there, but she got over it quickly and broke down everything I missed anyway. I even got a little reenactment from her and her bestie, McKayla. Then she showed off the beautiful bouquet Auntie Jude and her dad gave her. I knew it was really from Jude. She was just letting Ryan have some credit since he no doubt showed up empty-handed. It would have been nice if Jude included me, too, but when I tried to say something to her when we had a minute alone she got all crabby and said she didn't realize I wasn't going to do my own thing.

Maggie was super gracious about it all, and in the end got Jude to agree to come to the Church's choir performance that Liriope's going to be in. I think that had to do with the way Liriope lit up at the mention of it, though.

The front door opened and Liriope's dad called out. Liriope shoved the book under her pillow as her dad came into the room.

"Aren't you ready? We're going to be late for our reservation."

Liriope sighed and put the book down to attend the meal with her father and stepmother. It was not something she was looking forward to. Liriope ordered her favorite dish, but the food left no impression on her. Her mind was tangled in things half-forgotten. The flowered wallpaper in her bedroom at her Aunt Jude's house. Singing in a room with other girls, the air hazy with incense. Waiting in front of her school for her mother, watching for her old Jeep.

Her dad said, "Something wrong with your enchiladas?"

"My mom loved enchiladas."

Her dad exchanged a nervous glance with her stepmom. "Did she? I don't remember."

"Cheese enchiladas, with red sauce. But I always wanted green sauce."

Her dad said nothing.

"Do you remember the first time you came to one of my choir performances? The one with Aunt Jude–"

"That reminds me," her stepmom said. "We need to go shopping tomorrow for your dress for the winter show."

The cold wind bit at her as children's voices rang out into the night. Shadowy figures danced around them under the shape of a horned woman. She inhaled the icy air, preparing for her part—

"Was I in another choir? With a church or something?"

"Let's not spoil the night. Look, we haven't shown you! Your stepmom had your favorite cake special-ordered."

After she was sure her parents were asleep, Liriope crept into the kitchen and cut herself a slice of leftover birthday cake. She took the plate back into her room, hoping she could actually taste it now. After savoring a few bites, she settled against her pillow and found her place in the book. The handwriting was more erratic and difficult to decipher. Liriope had to read several paragraphs more than once to understand what her mother was trying to convey.

September 6, 2021
Cassidy Silva
Log 8

> Mother,
> I feel like I'm going crazy.
> I don't think I really am, but it feels that way. Jude thinks I've lost it. When I told her what was happening, she was worried, but not in the same way I am. I feel weird even writing this stuff down. But I'm just going to say it here anyway.
> I've been getting this message. Over and over. I had this, like, dream. Well, not exactly a dream. I don't know what to call it. It's like I've been getting this message from my mom. And one of the things she told me... well. It's important because it's coming up soon. And it'll all make sense once I get the whole story out. So, a week ago I had this half-awake, not-awake dream where Mom was trying to tell me that Ryan's going to die. My hands are shaking so badly writing this. I know how it sounds. I've felt this heaviness ever since I got the

message. And I've been preparing for it and figuring out what to tell Liriope. When I told Jude that part she freaked out and told me not to say anything. And like, duh. I'm not going to tell her until it happens. But still. I gotta listen, right? It's you, isn't it? It's you helping my mom break through to me.

My baby is going to need me. She's going to need me to be strong. But does she have to go through this? I don't want her to feel what we felt when we lost our parents.

Jude tried to say maybe it was just a dream, but she doesn't understand the way you work. This message keeps coming up, clear as day. Either Ryan is going to die, or he's going to kill me. Jude never knew how bad things got with Ryan. She was mad enough when he pushed me off the porch, so I never wanted to tell her the rest of it. But I have to now.

I'm so scared. I feel like I can't breathe. I don't know why, after all this time. Why now? I haven't done anything. I don't understand.

The number of times I've received your message is what's scaring me. Okay. I have to get through this.

So, I've felt this tension escalating, and I'm not even doing anything. I can feel Ryan's hatred towards me and I don't know why it's coming up now. I'm minding my business, taking care of Liriope. But I never did anything to make him hate me so much to begin with. So anyway, I'm trying to live my life and ignore it. Tell myself they're just coincidences. But then, the day after Liriope's performance, I kept noticing the numbers nine-one-eight. September 18th was Mom's birthday, and whenever I see it, it feels like she's stopping in to say hello. The day after the choir performance, I kept seeing it everywhere. Nine-one-eight. Nine-one-eight. Nine-one-eight. On the clock, my total at lunch, the number when I pulled up to my gas pump. Way too much to be a coincidence. And the more I ignored it, the louder it got, like she was saying, "You can't ignore this!" Then, when I was scrolling on my phone, a reading popped up. A Tarot reading from the Church. Jude didn't want to hear this part, but I'm starting to believe nothing is a coincidence. It was one of Maggie's students, and she started with something about suffocating. And I was just listening, nothing clicking right away. Then she said she was seeing a significant number. Just guess what the number was. The reading went on and said there was someone who wanted to do harm to me. That they have a bad plan. And I got this feeling in my gut that I was supposed to listen. The spiritual world finds a way to reach you. Whatever they can use. And my mom is using you and the Church now. So, the reading said an evil energy has a wicked plan for me, but it's not going to go how they thought. It's going to work out and I'll be safe. I'm protected, and this evil energy didn't realize how protected I truly am. And they kept pulling cards and describing this bad energy, and I swear, it was describing Ryan. It mentioned someone with tattoos and a criminal record. Even the fact that he's a Libra. They pulled card after card, describing Ryan to a T. Then they said, "He's going to die. He's been warned to not go through with this, and he's going to face the ultimate karma." And I kept getting readings like that. All day. Not just from the Church, but from all kinds of accounts. The very next one called out Ryan by his freaking name. It's too coincidental.

I got another reading last night. Another one from the Church. This one was read by Maggie, and she said this was all going to happen by next Saturday.

I told Jude all this today and she wants me to stay

away from the Church. She doesn't understand. I told her I couldn't, that they were the only people who could help me. She thinks she's so smart, it's like she won't even consider someone else might know more than her. I tried to tell her to open her heart so she could get her own message from Mom, but she got incredibly nasty and said something about how all she'd hear was stuff about Mom's supposed drug problem. I don't know if she was trying to say I was on drugs, too, but I ended the conversation. Maggie tried to warn me Jude wouldn't understand your divine ways, and I may not get to take Jude with me on this journey. I'm heading over to the Church now. I just wanted to write this down first. Liriope gets out of school soon, and Jude wouldn't say for sure if she'd pick her up since it's not one of the usual days she does. I'm pretty sure she will.

September 7, 2021
Cassidy Silva
Log 9

Mother,

I feel a lot better after talking to Maggie. She explained this is all part of your plan. It's late. I just left Jude's house. I was going to pick up Liriope, but Jude told me to leave her since it's almost morning anyway. She was angry with me at first, but I could tell she was worried. I explained as best I could, but she still wanted me to stay away from the Church. I told her about how Maggie knew things she'd have no way of knowing. Even things about Mom and Jude, like how Mom's been trying to tell Jude how sorry she is about the accident, that she understands how much it took from Jude. She wants to make it right, and she's using you and Maggie to do that.

When I said that, Jude got all condescending and was like, "Make what right? How?"

Then when I told her Maggie believed she could help Jude have her own baby, she laughed. She actually laughed! I don't know what I expected, but it wasn't that. Jude said she wasn't going to take herbs and dance naked under the full moon, and I told her it wasn't anything like that. I asked her to come with me to meditations tomorrow and at first she flat out refused, but then she saw I had this book with me. Jude said if I let her look at it she'd consider it. I handed it over and she spent a long time looking at your picture on the cover. She asked me if I knew what a maenad was in Greek mythology and when I told her I didn't she asked me to look it up after I got some sleep.

She said she'd only go if I promised to really listen to what she had to say about it afterward. I gave her my word, but I know she's going to be surprised. It's not anything like she thinks it is.

September 12, 2021
Cassidy Silva
Log 10

Mother,

Maggie was completely right about everything.

At first, Jude was all snooty and judgy, even though she was trying to hide it for Liriope's sake. It's plain Liriope loves it. She was so excited to introduce her Auntie Jude to the other girls she sings with, especially Caroline's girl. Jude was all sugar to the kids and acted enthusiastic about their upcoming performance next Saturday. But there was something under her bright smile, like she was scared. I have no idea why.

That only lasted until Jude got to the room with the other women, where your statue is kept. It's the same divine image of you that's on the cover of this journal, the beautiful horned woman. I looked up what a maenad was, and I get why Jude made that connection. You look like pictures of those wild women, and sometimes meditation sessions get us all caught up in what probably looks like a "frenzied fervor" from the outside.

As soon as we got to the room, I could see the way the energy hit Jude, how her shoulders and eyebrows relaxed. Maggie greeted us and told us how happy she was that we were both there. She touched Jude's shoulder and Jude relaxed even more. She offered to give Jude a private reading, and when she took her hand away Jude looked different. I could tell she was filled with the need that only Maggie and the other women could fill, and to be honest it made me a little jealous. It took me so long to connect to the others like that, but of course Jude took to it right away. I felt her energy in the room with the rest of us, connected so fundamentally to us. Mostly I was just glad she understood now and I wouldn't have to grow without her.

Maggie led her out of the room, but Jude looked back at me and said, "I want my sister there, too."

Maggie nodded and beckoned for me to follow.

Once we were in Maggie's private reading room, she lit the usual candles and incense, and a feeling of safety settled over us. I sensed the way it affected Jude, too.

"Your sister tells me you're familiar with Tarot," Maggie said.

Jude shrugged. "I used to have a deck in high school. I did readings for my friends for fun, but nothing serious."

Maggie shuffled her deck and held it out. "Pick a card."

Jude did. She stared for a long time at the card before she flipped it over.

King of Pentacles, reversed. A man in a crown on a golden throne, holding a staff in one hand and a gold coin in the other. It was like a normal deck, but instead of golden bull's heads decorating the throne, there were black goats. And there was a dark forest behind him instead of a castle. The forest made me shiver if I looked at it too much.

Maggie said, "I think this is meant to represent you."

Jude made a face and was like, "Me?"

Then Maggie was all, "Oh, yes. You've watched over your domain carefully for a long time now, haven't you? You've always taken care of your family. Especially your sister."

I smiled, but Jude just shrugged and crossed her arms. I felt her trying to pull back.

Maggie went on to say, "But it wasn't always your seat. That's why it's inverted. To everyone looking on, you seem comfortable and content. But secretly you can see that endless abyss that could swallow you up at any moment." Jude stared at it, and my heart hammered because I felt the pull tugging at her, beckoning her to let go, to just give in and fall into it. Maggie told her, "The goats' heads represent your parents, both gone now. But you feel them watching your every move, don't you?" That snapped Jude out of it and she shook her head.

Maggie didn't seem to believe her, but Jude was stubborn about it. Maggie waited, and it was almost like something was uncoiling in Jude. She opened her mouth a couple of times but didn't say anything. I could feel her fighting it for some reason.

I tried to reassure her and tell her it was okay, but that seemed to pull her even more out of it.

She kept looking at me and said, "I don't feel them. I've tried, I'd love it if I could. But there's nothing there."

Maggie told her she only needed to open herself to it, and I could feel how much Jude wanted it. But she's too stubborn for her own good. She just shook her head. I knew she was lying. I could definitely sense Mom there, and I felt her calling out to Jude. Finally, Maggie said, "We'll move on for now. So, this card represents the path you've been traveling. But you've reached a crossroads, don't you think? I believe your next card will reveal your current transitional state."

Maggie held the deck out and Jude picked another card.

The Star. A naked woman with long flowing hair knelt next to a river. She had a vase in each hand, and one poured water into the river while she poured the other onto the earth. The water was like ink and was barely visible against a dark sky. The vases were decorated with two black horns.

Maggie said, "You've felt apart from nature. But now it's time for you to recognize your place in the world. You're being called forward to be a vessel."

Jude started to say something, but Maggie shoved the deck forward and Jude took another card.

Nine of Pentacles. A woman dressed like a princess stood in a garden with fat grapes. She was surrounded by nine golden coins carved with pentacles.

Maggie told us the goat was strong in the reading. That's what pentacles represent; they're related to Capricorn. She pointed out how the princess was admiring her garden and cultivating it. She said Jude needed to do the same. So, she could be a rich gardener, too.

She offered Jude another card. Jude shook her head but pulled one anyway.

A woman was seated on a throne, cradling a golden pentacle, a horned rabbit at her feet, and goat's heads carved into the chair.

Maggie said, "The Queen of Pentacles! This is what I mean. See the way she holds the coin at her womb? Can you feel her connection to Mother Earth? Feel your connection."

Then she placed her free hand on Jude's shoulder. Jude gasped and clung to Maggie's arm.

Maggie said, "This card is telling you your body can be healed. You just have to let go. You have to forgive."

Jude was like, "Forgive what?"

Maggie put another card in her hand. The Tower. Black flames poured out of windows, and lightning cut across the sky and burned the top of the shadowy tower.

When Maggie saw it, she was all, "An accident that left you scarred. Pieces of you broken. But it doesn't have to be."

She asked if there was a car accident where someone important to us was driving. It made me gasp, but Jude was like, "Cass told you."

When Maggie told her I didn't, Jude got mad and yelled, "She told me she did!"

"What exactly did she say?"

"That you... that my mother..." She kept blinking and shook her head. "That's not even what the Tower means," she muttered.

"Take another one. It'll give you clarity."

Jude reached for another card with a shaking hand, but then she pulled away.

"No. I'm done."

Maggie was surprised. She said, "I think you should take another card."

"I think I should go home."

"Well. If you're sure. But please, come back any time."

When Jude turned to leave, Maggie said, "Can you tell me the time, dear?"

Jude pulled out her phone and I could see it said 9:18.

September 13, 2021
Cassidy Silva
Log 11

Mother,

This is going to be my last entry for a while. Maggie wants the book to pass on to Jude. She says I'm ready for the next level, but she wants me and Jude to study together so Jude's got to get caught up. I was surprised Jude agreed. She seemed spooked by everything last night. But when I talked to her about it this morning and told her she'd be taking the book she sort of lit up. Jude wanted me to give it to her then, but I told her she had to wait for the ceremony at the Church tonight and she accepted that.

Maggie says it's important she gets it before the ritual on Saturday, when Liriope has her choir performance for the Church. She said Jude needs to write an entry or two before that, and then we can both access the truth of this book together.

I'm a little sad. I've liked writing these logs. But I know you are with me. I can feel you guiding us and bringing me and Jude closer to Mom. It'll be amazing to have Jude by my side for the next step.

Liriope noticed the handwriting in the book changed dramatically. Her mother's now erratic and corrupted pen giving way to a new writer's more forceful and precise style.

September 16, 2021
Judith Silva
Log 1

I owe you an apology, Cass.

I owe you many apologies, but we'll start with this one.

I'm not going to follow the rules.

I know what I said at the ceremony, and Maggie made it clear what was expected from me. But I'm not writing to "the Mother," and I'm not going to pass this thing on to the next poor woman who gets sucked into this mess. I'm hoping I can tell you all of this in person, but if I can't, I'm giving this back to you so you can read it for yourself.

I won't pretend I fully understand what's happening here, but I'm going to tell you what my experience with the "Church" has been and what I've learned on my own. From your entries, it's clear what I've been watching unfold is quite different from what you've been living.

Initially, I was excited when you told me you were checking out a single moms' meetup. I felt some trepidation when you were vague about any details, like where the meetups were located or who the women involved were, but I tried to keep an open mind. The changes in you were quick, and at first, they seemed positive. You had more energy, and you laughed more. You seemed connected and present with Liriope. There was a brightness in your eyes that I hadn't seen in so long, like I was glimpsing a younger version of you that

I thought was gone forever.

That lasted about a month.

While your overall transformation was fast, the pieces that set off alarm bells in me were subtle. Even now I have trouble pinpointing when my unease grew into something more serious. It might have been when you sent me that picture of the old page from this book. Or when I found out the meetings were focused on "growing a family." Or when you started calling the gatherings you were attending "meditations" and "church lessons" instead of meetups. In retrospect, I ignored that for longer than I should have. I have my own assumptions and biases regarding religion, and I didn't want that to cause me to make rash judgments. The first time I remember voicing my concerns to you was when you started drinking a supplement supplied by the Church, and insisting Liriope drink it, too. It's probably safe to tell you now. She's been dumping it out at school because she hates how it tastes, and I've been encouraging her to do it. I'm not sorry for that.

That's around the time you started pulling back from me. I asked you for a brand name or an ingredient list. I questioned you more about the Church. I think I lost you completely when I tried to get more background information about Maggie. Do you remember what you said to me? "You don't know everything, you know. There are people smarter than you. I've met them." I don't know how that managed to make me more suspicious and simultaneously more doubtful of my intuition. I held back on my criticisms, even though it felt like this "church" of yours was becoming an obsession. It came up in every conversation, and you carried this book with you everywhere. Liriope would tell you about her day, and I'd catch you thrumming the pages or stroking the etchings on the cover. That brightness in your eyes became delirious and gaunt. You picked up Liriope from my house later and later, and sometimes forgot to get her altogether. It was so unlike you.

I must admit when you convinced me to go to the Divine Mother's Church, I was nearly taken in. Well. Perhaps not right at first. You could see I was quite alarmed by the sheer mass of young girls who were dedicated to that place. Did you notice they were all girls? I wondered if any of those women had sons, and if so where they kept them. Now I believe the truth is the place draws in mothers of daughters, with very few exceptions.

I suppose that brings me to the draw the place had on me.

As I said, it wasn't immediate. When Maggie reached out to touch me I flinched before I could stop myself, taking a step back. Her smile didn't falter, but her eyes narrowed. I noticed how pale her hand was, and how impossibly long her fingers seemed in the flickering light. Everything in me screamed to pull away, to say something, anything. But then her hand clamped down on my shoulder, and the moment she made contact I couldn't remember why I'd been so distressed. I could feel threads weaving me into the fabric of the room, binding me to the women around me. They all thrummed with a vitality I craved. Once I was aware of my need, it consumed me on a molecular level. It was right there for me to take, a sort of belonging I'd only ever felt with you, Cass, so palpable I could trace it between every person in the room, reaching for me, caressing, calling me sister, daughter, mother....

When Maggie took her hand from me I was instantly hollowed out, the ache of loss making my knees weak. I wrapped my arms around myself as the chill of that emptiness assaulted me, and I became aware of every pair of eyes in the room watching me. I expected something accusatory in their gazes for causing dissonance in their harmonious web but found only warmth and sympathy on every face.

A small part of me still resisted it, but I wanted it so badly. I chased the feeling as Maggie led us into that smaller room, thinking she was the source. But as we walked down the hallway the thread grew taut, tugging me back to the room with the statue. It felt like it might snap at any moment, until Maggie pulled out those cards. I could see the image on the back of them was a replica of the statue. The woman was terrible in her beauty, with depthless eyes as dark as the horns on her head and the fur above her hooved feet. When the cards were offered to me, I had to touch the woman, and as soon as my skin made contact with her face I was brimming with her love. I wanted her to fill me completely, to use me in whatever way she believed best.

It quickly became clear what that meant.

And I ached for it; yearned for the things Maggie implied with each pulled card, nearly surrendered to it.

It's so strange when I think about it. Everything you say implies that for you, the pull to that place stems from your connection to our mother. Our real mom, not the Divine Mother. But that's the very thing that repels me. Maggie almost lost me when she said I could feel our parents watching me. I meant what I said. From the moment I knew they were gone from this world, I have never felt either of them. I don't think there's anything I want more than to believe they are here somehow, that they're saying hello in ways only I would understand, that they're watching. Even if it's to judge how poorly I've replaced them. I'd take it with gratitude.

Maybe you do have a connection to Mom. Maybe she sends you signs and speaks to you in ways most people can't see. I think it would be incredibly arrogant of me to say that's impossible. But she is not in that place. She doesn't know the Divine Mother. I knew it even in the grip of its thrall, and I know it beyond any doubt now.

When Maggie linked the last card to the accident, the thread reeling me in snapped. The illusion of warmth and belonging leaked out of the rip left in me, leaving repulsion.

And that brings me to my next apology.

Somehow, I gave you the impression my life is lacking. You believe I lost something more than our mother in the car accident, and I've been using you and Liriope to fill some void. And worst of all, you think you aren't enough.

I know as children when we played house or acted out our elaborate dramas with our dolls, I played with the idea of having a traditional family. We pretended we were grown and married with children. Sometimes we spent time dreaming up what our husbands would look like and inventing baby names. Maybe that's where you got the idea that I had some deep-seated desire for those things.

The truth is, the older I got, the more horrifying those things were to me. It probably isn't surprising if you think back to us growing up, past the games. Maybe you're too young to remember when puberty hit me and how appalled I was by every part of it, but I know you saw me strapping ace bandages over my sports bras more than once. And, I mean this next part respectfully. It's amazing you built a human being and pushed it out of your body. It makes you way tougher than me because I find the thought alone repugnant: something growing inside me, taking my nutrients and sustenance. Never mind the messy agony of it all.

When I was told I would never have biological children, the first thing I felt was relief. There would never be pressure for me to want that. Of course, it was quickly overshadowed by intense terror and grief at the memory of what caused my condition.

As for the rest of the idealistic traditional family concept, you know I never had any real interest in men. I guess I should have been more open about my romantic endeavors. I would have been, if I'd known you thought I was holding back for your sake. You suspected there was something with Rachel, and briefly, there was. There were also a few people in college of varying genders, and while I sometimes felt deep affection, I discovered I'm not terribly interested in physical intimacy. And I don't feel like my life is incomplete without it.

I love cake. I love cozy mystery novels and sad romance movies. I love my friends, I love Liriope, I love you. And that's enough. I wish I'd made this clearer to you.

I know Liriope has her part in the Church's service on Saturday, but I think it would be a mistake to let her participate. I'm going to pick her up from school tomorrow and I'm going to try to convince you to stay home from Friday meditations, so I can explain all of this to you. I hope your heart is still open to me and that you listen. That place isn't what you think it is, and neither is this book. I hope it's not too late to show you, and that writing in here doesn't make it worse for us both.

September 18, 2021
Judith Silva
Log 2

It's all gone to hell.

I don't know who I'm writing for anymore. I have small hope my words will still help someone. It's too late for us.

I know what this book is. Or what it was. I think I know how to destroy it. I've ripped out mine and Cass's entries in case I'm unsuccessful at stopping the Mother, so maybe someone will find them and finish what I've started. The rest I'm feeding to the fire as I write this.

I should burn Cass's pages, too. But I can't bring myself to do it.

As soon as I had the book to myself, I went directly to the page Cass sent me a picture of and tried to read the whole entry, but it was so faded I couldn't make much sense of it. So I flipped to Cass's entries and read those. Then I read Caroline's before her. Then the entries of a woman named Christine before that. Then Sarah's, and Lorena's, and Renee's, back and back until the words crawled from the pages onto my hands, up my arms, and etched in my skin. It didn't matter how old the words were, or what language they were written in. They poured into me and became a part of me. I feel them inside me now.

My sisters. Cass is there, and Caroline, and all the women from the Church. Even Maggie. They feel me, too. They know what I've done. Their pain is excruciating, and I can hardly bear it. But they needed to know the truth. The oldest names from the book tell me it was the right choice. The Elizabeths and Lucys and Maeves and Nazarias and Cenobias, and all the names I have no letters for cry out louder, demanding to be seen, dancing in ink across my skin begging to be set free. Each page that curls and crumbles grants them that release.

So much has happened since I last wrote. But I'm running out of time, so I'll skip over the agony of the last twenty-four hours after I discovered Cass had pulled Liriope out of school early on Maggie's instruction, so I had no choice but to come to the ceremony if I had any hope of saving them.

When I climbed out of my car and stumbled down the path crowded by trees, dimly lit only with moonlight, my only clue that I was even going in the right direction was the singing. It was outside the church in the forest beyond. I've never heard anything so lovely and so unearthly. I caught myself clawing at my ears. Then Liriope's voice rang out in an unrecognizable language, and I sprinted toward the sound. I was vaguely aware of my ankle twisting painfully on a root, and half my face suddenly becoming wet and sticky. I know now there's a deep gash there, probably from a low-hanging branch.

The first thing I could make out clearly was the statue. There was no doubt it was the same one I'd seen in the Church, though I had no idea how it could have been moved. It looked so impossibly heavy and like it had always been right where it was. It seemed to shift under the light of the moon, one moment the beautiful horned woman I'd been enamored with, the next a many-limbed, tentacled creature unlike anything I'd ever encountered.

Female bodies in various states of undress danced around her, some with faces I knew, most twisted and grotesque. There were several men tied to her legs, and I almost sank to my knees when I locked eyes with Ryan. I stumbled toward him, but my arms were wrenched behind me. My head was yanked back by my hair and someone poured a warm liquid into my open mouth. I choked and spit out as much as I could, even as Cass's voice crooned near my ear, telling me it was safe and I was loved. The children's voices echoed louder and my arms were released. The ground rumbled beneath me, and the bound men shrieked as the earth churned under them from the statue's base. They were being consumed by the Earth.

Living viscous black bile spilled from the statue's mouth and crawled onto each of the dancing women. I felt it webbing up my face and seeping in through my nostrils, my mouth, and even my ears, burrowing deep inside me. I could feel that connection again, the love of the Mother calling out to me, pulling me to her, an all-consuming need so close to being filled. And I felt something in me squirm and reach for her, undulating inside me, loving me. I knew if I let it, it would use my body to grow and then consume me, and I'd finally be whole.

Maggie caressed my face and took my hand. She placed it on my belly over the swelling ripple. Then I caught sight of the ink dancing up my arm.

"You know what you have to do," she said.

An ornamental dagger was placed in my other hand, and the crowd parted to allow me to see the statue and the men half buried in the earth. Ryan was directly in front of me, his eyes bulging.

The thing inside me quivered, hungry. *Yes,* it whispered in me. *His blood. Mother needs his blood to soak the earth before her. Then her children can come forth.*

I closed the distance between me and Ryan. He writhed and flailed, and I cupped his face. The being growing inside me rejoiced, telling me it loved me, that it was my baby, that the Mother was gifting me with her precious child and all I needed to be complete was to give her Ryan's blood. To feed my baby.

I lifted the dagger. The words that burned in my skin from the book flowed up and down my arms, demanding to be heard.

Tabatha and Annemarie and Matoaka and Savanna –

The thing that thrashed and twisted inside me was not my baby. It was an intrusion. A violation in my body, completely unlike the women who painted their stories in my flesh at my invitation, demanding my attention, begging for the cycle to be broken.

Bile rose in the back of my throat. The hand that gripped the dagger twitched in hesitation. I shifted and brought the blade down with all my force, over and over.

An unearthly shriek pierced the night sky and the women around me halted in their dance, wailing in agony.

I pulled the dagger from the statue, and viscous black fluid bubbled to the surface. It gurgled and spurted. The ground roiled and I sawed at Ryan's ropes. When his hands were unbound we clawed at the earth until he was free enough to crawl forward. He helped me with a second man's binding, but the women were on me then. They yanked and tore at me, while others tried to staunch the statue's ragged wounds. Cass's face was before me, contorted and covered in a black webbing. I gripped at her and called out her name, but there was no recognition there.

Then Liriope called out over the cacophony.

We both froze and Cass's expression flickered. Several other women halted and blinked in confusion as the children called for their mothers. Then Ryan was beside me, gripping both me and Cass hard. He screamed that we had to go.

Cass's eyes came in and out of focus. She said something like, "We're where we're supposed to be."

I told Cass she belonged with me and Liriope. She took my hand, squeezing so hard my tendons cried out in protest.

She said, "Take her! Get her away!"

The letters on my skin sizzled and I could feel her losing her fight, giving in to the cry of the Mother.

Cass screamed, "I have to save her!"

I didn't know if she meant the statue or Liriope, but she was gone before I could say anything more. Ryan tugged me to my feet and shoved me hard toward where we'd heard Liriope's voice. I looked back to see the man we'd freed struggling to release the others, but I knew he'd be too late. Ryan shoved me again and I forced it from my mind. We called out Liriope's name.

We found her, and she collapsed into Ryan's arms. His eyes were frantic and his movements jerky, but I was impressed when he swept her up and cradled her as if she weighed nothing. He'll probably feel all of it later. I tugged him down the path to my car, catching him when he stumbled on the same root I had. When we reached the car I unlocked the doors and helped him put Liriope in the back seat. Then I shoved the keys into his hands and told him to go. He looked at me like I was crazy and told me I couldn't help Cass. I said I had to try, then I pushed him into the driver's seat. He put the keys in the ignition and his eyes pleaded with me. I looked past him and when I saw the book resting in the passenger seat I practically climbed across his lap to grab it.

When I tried to excavate myself Liriope grabbed me and asked where her mom was. I pulled myself free and then opened the back door, crushing her in a tight embrace with the book smashed between us. My bare arms were alive with writing, their burn grounding and soothing. I could still feel Cass in there. I told Liriope, "I'm going to go find her."

I could hear footsteps and distressed voices on the path. I kissed Liriope's cheek and closed the door.

I stared hard at Ryan and told him to take care of her. I think he wanted to argue some more, but he nodded and started the car.

I stumbled off the path with the book clutched to my chest. I refused to look behind me, but I'm fairly certain I heard the tires spit up dirt and drive away over the cacophony of howling voices. I'm choosing to believe they made it out.

This is as far as I go. I knew when I lit the first page I was on borrowed time. Their voices get closer, and their agony is ripping through me. I can feel the Mother statue, her life force bleeding out. But that was never going to be enough.

I think burning the book will be. The pages burn unnaturally slowly, but each time one goes up, the Mother hemorrhages. The rest of us do, too. Something like blood is trickling from my ears and nose. I felt Maggie's pages go up in flames, and the thing that is not a baby now begs me to put the fire out. I'm crushed under the weight of its sense of betrayal, but I fed the flames the last pages anyway. Inside all of us, the Mother's children choke and strangle us. She's bleeding out of each of us, and I can feel the women fade one by one.

I know I should burn Cass's pages. The Mother's grip is still too tight on her. I don't think she'll survive it, either way. There's not enough of her left.

There might still be enough left of me.

Liriope stared at the words for a long time. Rage surged up inside her at how much her dad had kept from her; at what he'd let her believe. Her mother had fought for her, and Liriope hated him for driving her to Maggie and this "Divine Mother." Her chest ached for what could have been.

There might have been some version of her life where she had both her parents, working together to raise her even if it was in separate homes. She could have called up her Aunt Jude when her parents were both making her crazy. She imagined Jude and Rachel taking her out for mochas, where she'd vent her frustrations about being a child of divorce, instead of the fragmented visits Rachel now fought for alone. She envisioned her graduation and the gathering of people who might have been there cheering her name. Liriope wondered if it was too early to call her Aunt Rachel and see if she knew anything about the Church or the book. What had really happened to Cass and Jude. She stared at the horned woman, feeling the tug of her mother even more strongly than before.

She forced herself to put the book down and went to the bathroom. She splashed cold water on her face. Then she rummaged through the drawer, finding the lighter her stepmother kept there.

Back in her room, she opened the book and lit the lighter. Then she let it go out. She placed the book on her desk and set the lighter down next to a ballpoint pen. With a shaking hand she picked up the pen and flipped to a blank page.

Soulless Gods

By Patricia Macomber

Goat Island, 1922

There lay a secret in the forest where trees shimmered in the diamond-light of icicles and the birds had long since grounded themselves, the forest where boys tripped over long-fingered branches and ran from the shadows of things that weren't.

Word passed from mouth to mouth, in whispers and darkened doorways until gossip became truth and truth became lost. Then boys became kings, and the dead walked. All that mattered was the secret and the secret became reality.

The ground, hard-frozen and unforgiving, held the secret in cold, quiet solitude, keeping back those who would find it and those who would use it. When spring thaw came and the branches once more gave forth life, when the sun glowed instead of shimmered, when the birds returned, the boys also returned and the secret was theirs.

Joshua Lewis fumbled through the old book as the shadows danced across the pages, light dappling to darkness from the windows, his eyes adjusting but not seeing. From down the long hall came a soft squeak, growing louder as it drew nearer. Joshua closed the book quickly and slid it back into its hiding place beneath the stack.

"Sorry to keep you waiting, Mr...."

"Doctor. Lewis. Joshua Lewis." He stood and thrust out his hand, reaching a bit lower than normal to accommodate the man in the wheelchair.

"Of course. So sorry." Edmund Drake maneuvered the chair into position, directly opposite the sofa at which he waved. "Please."

Joshua retook his position on the sofa, his hands at once finding each other and kneading. "I suppose your butler told you why I was here. The interview."

"He did." Mr. Drake adjusted the lap robe and folded his hands neatly on his lap. "But I gather that's not the only reason you're here."

Beneath the scalding gaze of Mr. Drake, Joshua squirmed, his palms began to sweat. "I was told you could help me."

"And so I shall, if I can. But first you must tell me your problem." The first smile of the day, albeit disingenuous, flitted across the man's face.

"My wife, she's sick. She has a rather strong form of leukemia. I am a doctor and while I've tried…."

"You've tried everything, but it hasn't helped. And some poor soul, wishing only to save you the loss, has told you about me. How close am I to being right, Dr. Lewis?" That steely stare assaulted him again and Joshua paled beneath it.

"I'll be quick, Mr. Drake. I haven't much time and neither does my wife. An associate who used to live here while you were doing your research told me that you could help."

"They told you I know the formula for eternal life, yes?"

"Yes." He met the man's gaze with fervor and refused to yield.

"And so I do."

Stevie raced through the woods, his shoes digging ruts in the dirt, chased by his newfound pals. The boys who would be pirates tore through bushes and brambles, swiping away branches that lashed out at their faces with swords of twigs and daggers of wood.

Ahead of them, a large brown rabbit darted from side to side, cutting beneath the bushes and seeking safe haven.

As they cleared the thick brush and stumbled into the clearing, the rabbit made a hasty retreat under the roots of an ancient oak tree. Stevie lunged after it, his face red from exertion and his breath coming in short gulps. Never mind his father's strong admonitions to stay clean, stay out of trouble. The chase was on and he wanted that rabbit. His fingers touched fur as his chest hit the ground, driving the air from his lungs. He had been hauled up short by his new friend, Mike, he of the big brown eyes and the unruly red hair. "Don't go messing with that thing," he panted as he clung to Stevie's shirt. "Rabbits have long, nasty teeth and they aren't afraid to use them." "We need to dig out under those roots," another boy offered with a grin. "That old tree's nearly dead and I betcha there's quite a hollow underneath."

They nodded sagely and looked around for digging implements. In the absence of anything suitable, they dropped to their knees, praying at the base of that venerable oak, and digging at the dirt like dogs.

Several feet of earth disappeared beneath their grimy hands, piling up behind them, dry and wasted from lack of rain. Then, as suddenly as the digging fury had started, it ended when Stevie fell several feet into the hole, the ground beneath him collapsing, dragging his torso with it as though the tree roots themselves had grabbed onto him. In the face of such catastrophe, the rabbit did the only thing it knew how to do: it ran straight over Stevie's back and dashed away into the woods. "Holy…" "Hush!" Mike said. "Watch your mouth, pal."

Stevie eased himself out of the self-made cavern, his toes digging into the ground and his body inching backward like a worm's. When he had fully emerged, he turned his head to grin at the others, eyes twinkling in near-mad excitement.

Drake turned the chair deftly and shoved a snifter of brandy at Joshua. "I can help your wife, Dr. Lewis. But I'm not sure you'll like what you're left with when I'm done."

Joshua took a slow sip of the brandy and contemplated the look on the man's face. Caught between mocking and stern, it made him feel like he was nine again, being interrogated by his father over some petty school crime.

"How so?" he whispered.

"Would it surprise you to know that every single man, woman, and child in this town is really dead? A zombie, as it were?"

Joshua's head snapped back and he stared. "Dead? How can that be?" Suddenly, he needed a large gulp of brandy more than anything in the world. He took it. It burned all the way down and dug sharp claws into his stomach.

"You see, Dr. Lewis, my research wasn't just in the field of rejuvenation. It was also into physics. I thought that the approach to eternal youth had more to do with repair than prevention. Pay close attention."

"Your formula causes cell regeneration?" Joshua set the snifter on the table next to him and leaned forward at Drake's insistence.

"I developed a formula that would cause the body to repair itself. Every organ, every cell. And very quickly, too."

Joshua studied his face, searching for signs of faulty deception. "You're joking, of course. Nothing even close to that has been developed."

"Ah, but it has. By an old colleague of mine. Herbert West. But my formula works on the basis of cellular memory. If a liver is damaged, the body goes about repairing it. And the formula is not excreted from the body. It remains."

"There's something under here and it's moving." Stevie's voice echoed back at the others through small hills of dirt and clumps of roots.

"More rabbits," spouted another boy, his face red and freckled from the sun.

"Naw. Too big to be a rabbit. Not even a grown one." Stevie extracted himself from the small cavern beneath the tree and leaned back on his haunches. "I wonder what it is."

"Only one way to find out." A larger boy with more brawn than brains moved in to dig, slamming a blunt elbow into Stevie's ribs in the process and knocking him aside. "We'll see in a minute."

Drake drained his brandy and then turned to pour another. He proffered the bottle but was met by a shake of Joshua's head. His glass was still half full and already his head was swimming. He half blamed the brandy, half blamed Drake and his wild story.

"I don't appreciate you making light of this, Mr. Drake. I know that you lost your funding at Harvard for being what they considered a quack. And you were thrown out of William and Mary's for experimenting on live humans."

"Oh, I'm not making light, Dr. Lewis, I assure you. I can save your wife. But if I do, she'll live far longer than you. That is, she'll exist far longer than you."

"This is absurd. It can't be done."

The doctor moved suddenly, his brandy sloshing against glass in an effort to escape. "Dr. Lewis, my formula was meant only to regenerate lost or damaged organs. A one-time deal, as you young people say. But my colleagues and I discovered that it could have a much broader, long-lasting effect. They just didn't have the guts to forge ahead. I did. That's why I'm here. I came here to continue my studies. And I was successful, too."

Joshua knit his brow and spat out the word. "How?"

With a deep breath, Drake answered his question with another, completely unforeseen question. "What do you know of the Old Ones, Dr. Lewis?"

Joshua had heard of them, of course. The favored subject of paranoiacs, alien watchers, and deranged anthropologists everywhere. More fretting etched itself into Joshua's forehead and pressed his eyes into a squint. "The Old Ones? What have they to do—?"

"Everything." Drake washed down a sip of his brandy with another sip and smiled. "You have, perhaps, heard of Shub-Niggurath? The Black Goat of the Woods with a Thousand Young?" His interrogative was met with a slow shake of the man's head. "The description is nothing if not accurate. And I, Dr. Lewis, am the last of those young."

Joshua burst out in uncontrolled laughter, his eyes watering and his sides pumping as he heaved the laughs out from his body in bursts. "The son of an elder god? You cannot be serious!"

"Oh, but I am. I may look like an ordinary man, but I assure you, I am not. I am something else entirely. As the legend goes—and it is more than mere legend—Shub-Niggurath begat a Thousand Young, which she continually and constantly devours and spews forth. I was her last; born as a fully formed adult male. I was the only one to issue forth from her... and run."

Joshua was unblinking, mouth agape.

"Run," Joshua echoed.

"Yes. I ran straight away from her and hid. And I kept running until I found this place. Oh, she found me a few times, of course. In the beginning, I had the audacity to think I could hide among the mortals. I was adopted by a mortal family. That's where I met my brother and he has been after me ever since. All those years at university and my internships didn't leave me unscathed, either. But it was worth it. The people of this town knew all too well the story of Shub-Niggurath and her errant son. And so, they concealed me in their little hamlet. Have you noticed anything strange about the town at all? Its placement, its layout?"

Another slow shake of his head and Joshua finished his brandy.

"Ah, well, I shouldn't be surprised. In any event, the town is laid out in such a manner that the roads, the buildings, even the river that runs through it come together to form a giant sigil. That sigil keeps the elder ones out. If I remain inside this town, she cannot reclaim me."

Joshua blinked twice and snorted. "You're mad."

"I can't completely argue with you." Drake raised his glass in salute and then took a hefty draw from it. "Be that as it may, these people saved me."

"So, in order to thank them, you turned everyone in this town into a zombie." There was acid in his voice and a sneer on his lips. Joshua Lewis was just the straw that broke the camel's back.

"I had long known that I carried immortality in my veins. It took years of research to work out just how to extract it and make it applicable to my human counterparts. You see, when the people of this tiny island discovered what I was up to, they began coming to me for help. This one had a kid with cancer. That one had a beloved pet that they couldn't bear to lose. They begged. Finally, they threatened. And I gave in."

"And turned them all into the living dead." Whatever answers he had come there to find would not come from the lips of this insane man. Joshua had it in his mind to leap from the sofa, collect Stevie, and go back to the hospital. Still, something made him stay. Something in Drake's eyes made his heart double its speed and his mind trip over reality.

"Precisely." The chair moved again, rotating toward the door. "Giles, would you come in here?"

The tall, stately man who had let Joshua in entered the room. He bowed slightly and folded his hands in front of him.

"Giles, would you please let Dr. Lewis listen to your heart?"

Giles stepped forward and bent low, allowing Joshua to press his ear to his chest. Joshua listened and frowned, then felt for a pulse.

"You'll note no heart sounds at all. Neither is there the usual rise and fall of his chest associated with respiration. You won't find a pulse, either. He doesn't have one." Drake paused to offer up a self-satisfied smile, then turned a soft eye on Giles. "Giles, in what year were you born?"

"Why, it was eighteen-oh-three, sir."

"Thank you, Giles. You may go."

"I don't believe it." Joshua sat back hard against the sofa and sighed.

Mike shot backward from the tree and collapsed against the ground in shock. All eyes were upon him, faces pale and eyes wide.

"It is something alive. I saw toes. And they moved."

"No way! Maybe a corpse?" Stevie said as he watched the boy's face, concerned.

"Nah-ah! It moved."

"You just thought it moved."

"It moved," said the boy adamantly. "I swear to God."

Stevie bolted up from his position beside the boy and frowned at him. "Have some fun with the new kid. Sure! There's a real honest-to-God living guy under the tree."

"I didn't say it was a guy. I said it was alive and it had toes. And I'm not messing with you, neither."

"Yeah? Lemme see!"

Stevie dove to his knees at the base of the tree and shoved his head into the darkness beneath. His eyes adjusted slowly, his hands curling into the moist dirt. And then he saw it.

He launched backward with a scream, his head striking the ground and flashing bits of light across his field of vision. "For real! Toes! And they moved!"

"Dig him out! Dig him out!" They all began to yell.

And at once the pirates and soldiers, boys who would be kings, began to dig.

"Giles has been with me since I first started my research in college. I hired him on as a lab assistant, mostly because I felt sorry for him. A soldier's pension doesn't exactly pay the bills, you know." Drake chuckled at that and took a sip of his brandy. "Giles had been working for me for only three months when he had his first heart attack. Six months later, he had another. So, it was only natural that he become my first human test subject. He didn't exactly have a lot to lose."

"I don't understand. The man has no heartbeat. If your serum regenerates organs as you say it does, then Giles should have a perfectly functioning heart."

"Indeed. And in the beginning, he did. But the treatments—and their results—outgrew the need for feeble organs. The blood of the gods works very differently in the body of a man. All that was needed for a person to continue existence is a brain, and the frame to carry it around. He has all that."

"And a soul? Does he have that, as well?"

"Now you get into the realms of theology and philosophy. Those are not my fields."

"Neither are morals, apparently."

"A point well-taken. However, I can't be too much of a monster if Giles has been with me all these years. He stayed with me through several universities and hospitals and finally came with me here. Since he is not subject to my mother's wrath, he could leave at any time. And yet, he stays. I do have my suspicions that it was Giles who let the cat out of the bag. Off somewhere, bragging about his boss and the wonderful research he did. An old man's version of 'my dad can beat up your dad.' I don't blame him, of course. He had no way of knowing that the townspeople would insist on joining his ranks. And he had no way of knowing that I would pull a little trick on them."

"You see, when I injected them," Drake continued, "I gave them a different formula. I couldn't have a hoard of people running around, completely indestructible and able to live forever. So, I installed a safeguard. The people on this island are required to return to me every year for another shot. If they do not get it, they die."

"So, why not just stop giving it to them? Why not just leave?"

"Well, in the first place, I would fall prey to my mother the moment I stepped outside the wards of this town. Also, I don't want to be found out. Do you have any idea what the real world would do to me if they found out what I've been doing?"

"And perhaps they should." Joshua put aside his empty brandy and leaned back. "Playing God. Making people live forever." Somehow, Drake had woven his tale into Joshua's mind and made the unbelievable believable.

"Precisely the mentality the courts would adopt. They fail to see the benefits of it. So, I gave these people the serum. And every year I give them their booster."

"Really, now! Do you think anyone would believe their rantings? You could leave here, set up somewhere else. No harm, no foul."

"Except for one small detail. Since I am the only one who knows the formula, they couldn't risk losing me." Drake threw back the lap robe, revealing the hacked stumps of his legs. "You don't think this happened in a car accident, do you?"

"Dear God!" Joshua's face twisted.

"Yes, and to make matters worse, the whole devious plot was masterminded and executed by my own very human, adopted brother."

"It's really stuck hard," Stevie grunted from the hole beneath the tree. Just then, he wished his father would finish his business and come to collect him. He had long since passed the point where he cared what was living under the tree. He just wanted his daddy to emerge from the bushes and demand that he "come along."

"Pull!" The fat kid grabbed Stevie around the waist and added his strength to the effort.

"I am." Stevie pulled harder, feeling the sweat of the boy's arms soak through his shirt. "It's coming. Almost got it loose…."

Stevie slipped from the other boy's grasp and hit the ground with an audible "thud!" and the wind knocked out of him. When finally he regained his senses and saw what was in his hands, he nearly passed out again.

"Holy shit!" The fat kid abandoned all sense of propriety and screamed, his face red and his eyes stuck on Stevie's prize.

Clutched tightly in Stevie's closed fists was a leg, gripped at the ankle, toes wiggling. Stevie watched it, mesmerized, eyes traveling the length of it. It was normal and healthy enough, though something seemed to be growing out of the thigh end of it.

"There's another one in here." Another boy emerged from the hole beneath the tree and brandished a second leg like a sword. Covered in dirt but looking otherwise no worse for wear, the leg also sported a growth on its top.

Stevie stared for what seemed an eternity, the color running away from his face.

"So, in order to keep you here and keep themselves alive, the townspeople cut off your legs?" Joshua's face was a study in agony as he fought to wrap his mind around the tale.

"And that's not all. To make sure I could never leave them and deprive them of their precious formula, they injected me with the same formula."

"So, in order to live, you have to keep making the formula, eh?"

"Not at all. The formula they took from my lab and used on me was inconsequential. My own blood gave me immortality at birth. My annual 'booster' reacted quite differently for me, however. It made every part of me immortal. Every *single* part." His sparkling eyes hinted at a secret far darker than any other so far.

Joshua twiddled his thumbs for a moment and thought. When he spoke again, his face was slack, almost wan. "Did they inject you before or after they cut off your legs?"

"Before. Why?"

Stevie tilted the leg so he could see the top more clearly. It was definitely a man's leg, judging by the amount of hair on it. It was pale, as though it had been beneath the tree for a very long time. And something about it made Stevie's heart trip over itself.

At the top, where the thigh should have melded into a hip, the flesh drew inward, narrowing in circumference and puckering a bit before angling upward. As Stevie tilted the leg, the thing that grew from it came into view. The sight of that leg would prey on Stevie's mind for the rest of his life. His mouth opened and screamed and screamed.

"Then why have your legs not grown back?" Joshua glared at him from the corner of his eye.

"Ah, but they have. It's an annual ritual, you see. Once a year, my brother brings them all around for their shots. And when he leaves, he takes my legs. Seventeen years and seventeen pairs of legs. But that's my final revenge, don't you see. One of these years when my brother shows up, he won't just face just me. He'll face an army. It takes one year for a man's body to re-grow its legs."

In that one moment, many things became clear to Joshua... the man enslaving his brother, Drake plotting to kill his own sibling—if not by his own hand, then at least by proxy—and undead legs scattered about the town. Joshua's eyes glazed and his hand shook so uncontrollably that he had to clench his hands to make it stop. His skin itched, as though it was trying to crawl right off his body.

The expression of realization on Joshua's face pleased Drake. A smile crawled onto his face and a glimmer briefly lit his eyes.

Joshua stared at his hands, so tightly clenched that his knuckles had gone white and his fingertips had grown numb. When he looked up, he saw the foyer beyond filled with dozens of Drakes, each in a differing and more gruesome state of regeneration. This one with a missing arm, that one with a tiny head, still another with one leg twice the length of the other.

"And who knows how long for a leg to re-grow a man."

A Thousand Young

By Andrea Pearson

Emma Thomas had long since stopped praying for a miracle. Miracles were reserved for a specific subset of people — a group she and her husband had obviously been barred from, whether by God or some other deity, she wasn't sure.

After years of infertility, failed IVF cycles, and slowly decaying hope, she knew she was not one of the lucky or even one of the blessed, whatever that meant. She wasn't *meant* to have children.

So when she first heard the name Dr. Keziah Mason offhandedly mentioned in an online infertility support group, it felt less like salvation and more like an invitation to finally *belong*.

And yet, Keziah Mason was different. There was no website, no Google reviews, no social media presence. Her name didn't officially exist online at all. Emma could only find stories in infertility groups, and she had to dig to find even that much. But each of the women talked of results. Real results. One of them was five months pregnant after seven years of nothing. She swore by Dr. Mason. *She is so absolutely amazing!!! Literally the best doctor I've ever had!!!* The woman wouldn't stop gushing. *She doesn't guarantee results, and she was very specific about that when I met her. But the person who referred me was also pregnant... and, well, Dr. Mason gets results. She really does.*

For the first time in years, hope blossomed in Emma's chest. And so, clutching her husband's hand too tightly, she boarded a plane to Providence, Rhode Island, where something wonderful was already waiting for her. Where something wonderful *had* to be waiting.

As the plane landed, Emma scanned her infertility groups, searching, always searching, for another mention of Keziah's name. It was rare, but in every instance, the posts or comments were from pregnant women who raved about the doctor.

Emma lowered her phone, staring blankly before her. She sometimes had to shake off a weird feeling that crossed her about these women. They all had a sort of used car salesman personality—a little too enthusiastic, a few too many exclamation points. But Emma could *use* a little religious zealotry in her life. And obviously they were desperate for any shred of possibility to have what they each craved most. Their own child. Emma understood that. Her heart broke every time she thought of the years of *nothing*. Her arms ached to hold her babies.

Emma's husband, Peter, was more skeptical, but like his wife, he was tired of not having results. Tired of forking over cash for pointless treatments. Tired of the emotional rollercoaster. When Emma showed him posts that said Dr. Mason's fees were manageable, he approved immediately.

So did Emma.

She hesitated after stepping into Dr. Mason's reception area, though. It was old fashioned, as if it hadn't been decorated since Victorian times. A heavy feeling hung over the room, encouraged by the cracked oil paintings, faded leather furniture, and dark wood walls, ceiling, and floor. A strange, herbal scent was in the air. Dust swirled in the muted sunlight.

Houseplants filled the room—on windowsills, side tables, even the floor. Vines spilled from their pots and crept along the walls, some dry and withered, others overgrown and tangled. A few leaves were pale or spotted, sagging as if too tired to stand. They looked... forgotten.

Emma felt the heaviness of the room in her ribs, in the tightening of her jaw. She forced herself to look ahead, refusing to acknowledge how close the air felt, how close *everything* felt. She pulled her cardigan tighter around her shoulders, as if that might shield her from the weight pressing in on her chest. Nothing would get in her way of a family!

The front desk had no receptionist, and Emma and her husband looked at each other.

"Should we wait?" Emma whispered. "Or do we just go back?"

Footsteps sounded behind them, and a woman spoke. "Peter and Emma Thomson?"

Emma turned and nearly bumped into the small lady who had entered the room. The woman's eyes were dark, almost too dark for her pale skin and hair so blonde it was nearly white. Her skin was perfect, without a single blemish, wrinkle, or bump. Was this the receptionist?

The woman gave a smile that didn't reach her black eyes. "I'm Dr. Keziah Mason."

Peter extended his hand, but Dr. Mason only looked at it. Several seconds passed, and Peter dropped his hand, then fumbled, shoving it into his pocket. He glanced at the floor, his ears turning red.

Dr. Mason looked back and forth between Emma and Peter. "Please come to my office." She turned and walked through a door by the reception desk, not waiting for them.

Emma and Peter exchanged glances. Emma could see the same worry and hesitation she felt playing across Peter's face, but she turned and followed Dr. Mason anyway. Peter trailed a couple steps behind. They entered a lavish room with a massive, mahogany desk and more cracked oil paintings. Heavy drapes hung over the windows, blocking almost all of the natural light. More dead or dying potted plants decorated the room.

Peter and Emma sat at Dr. Mason's desk and listened as she talked about her practice and how she'd been helping couples have babies for decades. The fact she didn't look remotely old enough to have been doing that didn't register initially. Her protocol involved supplements taken four times a day for two months.

Her fee was only two thousand dollars. Exhilaration burst into Emma's chest. *Two thousand dollars?* It was even less than she'd read online! What a *blessing*. Were things finally falling into place for her and Peter?

Dr. Mason said she was looking for one more couple to help before retiring.

"And that could very well be you, if I decide to take you on." She smiled, showing perfect teeth. "Remember, I don't guarantee results... but I *do* get them."

Dr. Mason slid over several papers. "Now. How badly do you want a baby?"

Emma's breath caught. Her fingers tightened on the edge of the desk, knuckles whitening. "More than anything," she whispered.

And so, with hardly a glance at her husband to verify he was on board, she signed her name in all of the places Dr. Mason indicated. Peter signed too, but his hand was jerky and a tight line had appeared between his eyebrows. They left the clinic with a bag of supplements, Emma's heart lighter than it had been in a very long time.

"We should have discussed that before signing," Peter said. "I didn't like her. I wouldn't have gone through with it."

Emma apologized, but she barely even heard the words leaving her mouth. She had a hard time feeling sorry—she would do anything to get a baby. Peter would come around eventually. He always did.

Two months later, Emma stood in the bathroom, hand shaking, staring at her first ever positive pregnancy test. *Positive.* She couldn't believe it. Tears fell, splashing against the sink, and she rushed out of the bathroom, waving the stick, shouting for Peter to come see. He was as overjoyed as she. They were getting their baby!

The pregnancy was easy and uneventful. Far easier than her OBGYN told her it would be given her age.

"Every number is exactly as it should be," he said. "And still no morning sickness?"

Emma shook her head, smiling brightly. "Not a bit. I feel great!"

"You're incredibly lucky. Keep counting your blessings, Emma. It looks like your prayers are finally getting answered."

Her doctor was right, it seemed. Because he'd warned her that sometimes women who have easy pregnancies ended up having tough deliveries. But that didn't end up being the case for Emma. The labor was painless, and neither she nor the baby struggled.

It was a dream come true.

And that baby. Oh, was she perfect. The most beautiful infant Emma had ever seen. Even the nurses agreed—oohing and aahing over her, saying she was just like the poster of the Gerber Baby.

The moment Peter set eyes on his child, Emma knew he'd completely forgiven her. The hurt, the silence, the months of tension— gone. He let out a shaky laugh, brushing a tear from his cheek as he cradled the baby to his chest like something holy.

Macie, as they named her, brought joy and happiness to their home, completing their family. Emma bought house plants with tiny flower buds on them to go in the nursery. She tended to them as carefully as she tended her infant.

"Should we try for another?" Emma asked Peter two nights after Macie was born.

"Yes," he said immediately. "If we can figure out how to make it happen—I just don't want to hope our luck will continue."

Emma determined to talk to her doctor at her six-week checkup to find out how soon they could start trying.

"Give it a few months," he said. "Let your body heal." The doctor hesitated. "Though, I don't suppose you really need that, do you?" He smiled, shaking his head.

Emma knew he couldn't figure out why she'd had things so easy, but she was grateful. Those miracles she'd prayed for? She was finally getting them.

Four months later, Peter entered the bathroom as Emma was studying her profile in the mirror. "Shouldn't my bump be gone by now?" she asked, stretching her shirt over her stomach.

Peter frowned, studying her. "If I didn't know better, I'd say you looked pregnant again. I think your stomach is getting bigger."

Emma turned to him, feeling the backs of her eyes burn. Could it be? "Do you really think so? That would be wonderful."

Peter nodded, putting his arms around her. "Incredibly wonderful."

Emma beamed, relaxing in his embrace. She couldn't believe their luck.

Her OBGYN confirmed her pregnancy the next day. She measured at seven months.

"How is that possible?" she asked, wondering why she hadn't felt the baby move. "Macie is only five months old."

The doctor shook his head slowly. "We'll keep an eye on things."

This pregnancy wasn't as easy as the first, but still, things went well, and Emma and Peter were both overjoyed. They were even more overjoyed with Macie—she was the perfect baby. She rarely woke more than once at night, and she cooed and giggled all the time. In fact, during nighttime feedings, she would sit up in the crib and stare at the middle of the room, babbling and laughing. This despite the fact she shouldn't have been doing so until she was six to nine months old. Emma loved listening to her precocious baby so much.

The plants Emma had placed in the nursery didn't behave like normal houseplants. One of them seemed determined to die, no matter how carefully she tended it. Its leaves curled in on themselves, turned brittle and brown, and dropped one by one to the floor like tiny corpses. A few stubborn patches of green clung on, but they looked sickly, almost bruised. She watered it, rotated it, whispered encouragement—but nothing helped.

The other plant did the opposite. It grew too fast, too strangely. Thick vines snaked from the pot overnight, bulbous and knotted like veins, others thin and blackened at the tips. When she trimmed them back, more appeared by morning—longer and heavier.

No matter how she tried to ignore it, Emma couldn't stop thinking of the plants in Dr. Mason's office. These felt disturbingly similar.

The pregnancy came to an end, and Emma was disappointed to feel labor pains this time. They weren't bad, though, and the baby was born perfectly healthy.

The nurses oohed and aahed again as they took the baby's weight and checked her length, and Emma waited eagerly for them to place her child in her arms.

When they did, she stared at another absolutely perfect infant. Who was completely indistinguishable from her older sister.

"Wow—I can definitely tell she came from our family!" Peter said, smiling. "She and Macie could be twins."

Emma agreed, and they named the baby Maggie. Macie and Maggie—perfect names for a perfect pair.

When Emma went to see the doctor for her six-week checkup, she complained of feeling nauseated. Her doctor raised an eyebrow but didn't say anything.

He ordered a pregnancy test.

Emma protested. "I'm not pregnant," she said. "There's no way."

Still, she took the cup to the bathroom. Afterward, she paced her room, chewing the inside of her cheek. She kept her hands pressed against her stomach, trying to calm the fluttering that wouldn't go away. Emma paused, barely breathing, as footsteps approached in the hall, then sat on the edge of the bed, hands clenched in her lap.

Positive.

Emma stared at the doctor. Little bubbles of panic popped in her stomach. Her mouth was dry. She couldn't blink, couldn't think. "How is this possible?" she whispered.

"Well…" the doctor started, "Most of my patients aren't capable of waiting until the six-week mark."

Her mouth moved wordlessly as her thoughts tumbled over each other. "But… we… we didn't do anything—last time, we did. But this time, we were extra careful."

Emma could tell the doctor didn't believe her, which she understood. How was she going to tell Peter she was pregnant *again*? Macie wasn't even a year old yet, and Maggie only six weeks. And what about their friends and neighbors? What would people think? Emma drove home, the backs of her eyes burning the whole way.

Peter was understandably upset. He stormed back and forth, glowering. "How can I trust you?"

"I swear, Peter—I've never cheated."

"Then how are you pregnant?" he asked. His eyes narrowed. "It's that doctor and the supplements. *She* did this."

Emma blinked. She shook her head. "Don't blame Dr. Mason. She's the reason we have any babies at all."

Peter threw his hands in the air. "Fine. I'm getting a vasectomy, though."

Emma nodded, even though she still wasn't sure how she'd gotten pregnant. Better not to risk it, though.

Maybe something had released inside of her—maybe Dr. Mason had figured out how to get them extra fertile. While Emma was grateful for another little miracle, she needed a break. Because even though the babies were easy, they were still babies and required a great deal of time and attention.

What was she going to do with *three* of them? Should she... would she ever forgive herself if...

Her chest tightened and she practically heard her own voice say, "Don't fight this."

She wouldn't.

Finally, after Peter fell asleep that evening, Emma allowed herself to cry. She'd done her best all day to feel positive, but it had been hard.

And this pregnancy wasn't nearly as easy. Not only did she have morning sickness, but Peter started growing distant. Emma knew he didn't trust her, and it cut her to the heart to think of him pulling away. He never touched her and only rarely looked at her. It caused her so much pain, but she held on to the hope that she'd be able to prove herself, eventually.

Luckily, he was just as attached to Maggie and Macie as she was, and for now, that kept him from doing anything drastic.

Like divorce. Emma could barely think the words without pain and panic.

But when they learned they were having a boy, Emma found herself in Peter's arms, celebrating with him. He jerked away, as if remembering he didn't trust her, and rubbed the back of his neck, not meeting her gaze. But from that day on, he softened toward her. It wasn't as much as she wanted, but it was better than it had been, and for that, Emma was glad.

Maggie and Macie continued waking up at night, and an exhausted Emma would drag herself from bed to see to their needs. She would feed them a quick bottle, then kiss and tuck them back in. And each night, both of them would chatter and babble, eyes turned to the center of the room, grinning. Emma wished she could see the imaginary friend they were talking to, but she was glad they were happy babies.

When their little boy was born at seven months, Emma and Peter were astonished to find he looked *exactly* like his older sisters—same face, same birth weight and length, same big eyes that seemed to look into a person's soul.

"He's exactly like Maggie and Macie," Peter whispered. "How are we going to tell them apart?"

Emma smiled. There was an obvious answer to that question. "We'll let him run around naked."

Peter chuckled. "Luckily, they're different ages. That'll help."

"Good point." Emma felt silly for not thinking of it herself.

They named him Micah.

When Emma found out she was pregnant yet again at her six-week checkup, she sobbed uncontrollably. "How am I going to tell Peter? He got a vasectomy and everything."

Her doctor rolled his chair over, directly in front of her, a worried expression on his face. "I'm truly concerned, Emma. You aren't giving yourself enough time between these pregnancies. A better form of birth control is in order."

"Better than a vasectomy?"

He nodded. "Vasectomies aren't one hundred percent effective. Close, but there's still a very small chance the couple will conceive." He helped her lie down. "Let's check on the baby—see if we can find a heartbeat."

Emma cried even harder as the doctor got the ultrasound machine ready. How was it possible she and Peter were in the small percentage of couples who got pregnant after a vasectomy?

"What should we do?" she whispered.

"How do you feel about having your tubes removed?" The doctor pressed the ultrasound wand to her stomach.

"It doesn't matter how I *feel*—I can't do more of this. I can't even handle the babies I have."

He didn't answer—she couldn't tell if he'd even heard her. He cleared his throat. "Emma?"

"Yes?"

"You're having *twins.*"

Tears rolled from Emma's eyes again as she stared at the ceiling. "Okay."

She didn't know what else to say.

Telling Peter was hard, but he took it in stride. "If Micah hadn't looked exactly like his sisters, I would have suspected he wasn't mine. But he is—it's obvious he is. How soon after the twins come can you have your tubes removed?"

"The doctor is going to remove them the same day the babies are born. It won't be a fun recovery, but I'm willing to do anything, and he doesn't want to take a chance."

As it turned out, having her tubes removed wasn't enough because at her six-week checkup, she was yet again pregnant, and with another set of twins. Her doctor advised her to have a hysterectomy at the end of this pregnancy. Removing her tubes apparently hadn't been enough.

"Again, there's a very, very small group of women who get pregnant after their tubes are removed," he said, his tone flat, like he was reading from a script he didn't want to believe. "But the percentage of women who then get pregnant *and* their husbands have had vasectomies..." He tapped Emma's chart and looked up. "This... isn't supposed to happen. Your hormone levels are all over for someone who's getting pregnant regularly—you shouldn't even be able to conceive, based on those alone. And I removed your tubes myself, and I know I did an excellent job. The surgery was complete. There's no anatomical path left for the eggs to travel. And yet—" he gestured helplessly—"here we are."

Emma chewed her lip. Should she consider terminating?

The doctor studied her as he said, "I know what you're going to ask, and I'm telling you now—I don't recommend any termination procedures. Not with the way your body's reacting. Your hormone levels are weird for someone getting pregnant, but they're healthy for your age. You're basically entering menopause. You shouldn't even have any eggs left at this point. None of this should be possible."

He paused. "Whatever's happening... it's outside our understanding. And when the body starts doing impossible things, forcing it to stop can be dangerous."

Emma said nothing. She didn't have to.

Because even before the doctor spoke, she already knew. Every time the second line appeared on the test, that same chill swept through her body—the same pressure behind her eyes, the same tightening in her chest.

Don't fight this.

It wasn't a thought. And it didn't originate from her. She was coming to understand it was a warning.

Emma found herself developing trauma just from visiting her doctor's clinic, though, and after the hysterectomy and the addition of the new set of twins, she decided to switch doctors. Maybe a new one would have a better clue as to how to help her.

When her new doctor told her she was pregnant again, Emma gritted her teeth and explained to him everything she'd gone through recently. Tubes removed, hysterectomy, her husband's vasectomy. How could she be carrying babies—triplets this time—after all of that? How could she have even gotten pregnant?

The new doctor was clueless. He recommended she enroll in a research program, but he didn't even know which one. Emma knew he wouldn't have believed her if he hadn't had access to her charts himself.

This pregnancy was the hardest yet. By this point, she and Peter had separated the children into two rooms. Maggie, Macie, and Micah were in the same room and the two sets of twins in the other. Where were they going to put the triplets?

The nightly ritual of feeding the babies had become so very exhausting. Luckily, it was just the two sets of twins now, but Emma and Peter—who had started helping after Micah was born—barely had the strength to continue.

Like their older siblings, during the entire time Emma or Peter were in the room with them at night, the twins cooed and giggled, staring at the center of the room.

A month before the triplets were to be born, Emma found Peter at his computer and said, "I think we need to get cameras installed. I'd feel so much safer being able to keep an eye on the babies in every room they spend time in. I'm having a hard time keeping up with them during the day—I can't stop falling asleep." Being pregnant and a mom to so many young children was exceptionally challenging.

He agreed immediately. Mrs. Smith, the neighbor they'd hired to help with the kids during the day, referred them to the company she used.

The cameras were installed the next week. Emma loved how easy it was to use the system—as long as she kept her phone plugged in, the camera feed wouldn't turn off, and she could watch her babies all night and all day.

Soon, those babies had taken all of their focus. Not even Peter could stop watching them on the camera. They were so adorable and so special and so perfect.

One night, when one of the babies cried and an exhausted Emma opened the camera app to check on them, she screamed, dropping the phone.

Keziah Mason stood in the middle of the babies' room.

Emma scrambled off her bed and ran into the room. No one was there. But all of the babies were chattering and babbling. Emma stood there for a moment, watching as they turned their attention from the space in front of her. They all grinned—happy to see their mom—and she put a hand to her heart. Had she imagined what she'd seen? She was so incredibly sleep deprived. Had her brain played tricks on her?

But the next night, the same thing happened. A baby woke, she opened the camera, and there stood Dr. Mason, with the children giggling and cooing. Emma rushed into the room, but the woman wasn't there.

Horror clenched Emma's heart when she realized something. Her babies had been interacting with *that woman* from the very beginning.

When Emma told Peter what had happened, he asked her to wake him next time so he could see too.

She knew it would happen again because it happened all the time. She'd watched those babies countless nights, chattering at that same spot in the middle of the room.

The next night, when one of the babies started crying to be fed, Emma again immediately opened the camera app, this time, watching instead of rushing in. Same as before, Dr. Mason stood there. Horror clung to Emma as the woman smiled at each child, her face full of joy, the smile extending to her eyes. The baby that had started crying stopped and grinned.

"These are *my* babies!" Emma whispered. "How *dare* you invade my home!"

She saw Dr. Mason's mouth moving and turned up the sound on her phone.

"… see you," the woman was saying. "How is everyone doing?"

The twins—both sets of them—grinned. "We're all well," one said in response.

Emma gasped. The voice was young and tiny, but the words were clear. That child couldn't even crawl yet, let alone talk! She grabbed Peter's arm, jerking him awake.

"And how are the unborn babies?" Dr. Mason was asking.

"They're growing well," another twin answered. "But the mother suspects something. She has installed security devices in every room." The infant pointed at the camera that Peter and Emma were watching through.

Dr. Mason turned and smiled. "Thank you for your service, Emma," she said.

Peter roared, jumping from the bed and charging into the hall. Emma clutched her phone and watched as he entered the room and stood exactly where Dr. Mason had been before. But no one else was there. The babies stared at him, their smiles gone now.

He turned and left, rejoining Emma in their room.

"She wasn't there," he said.

"I know. I saw." Emma looked at her husband. "What do we do?"

Peter's face was grim. "We're flying back to Rhode Island. Tomorrow."

They made arrangements for Mrs. Smith to watch their children, then took the first flight they could find.

Dr. Mason didn't seem surprised to see them. "How are you loving the babies?"

Peter leaned over, his face red. "You stay out of my home! You leave our children alone!"

"*Your* children?" Dr. Mason asked.

"Yes, *our* children," Emma said. She stepped closer to Dr. Mason, glowering. "Do you realize I've been pregnant nonstop since meeting you?"

"I get results," Dr. Mason said, shrugging. "Isn't that what you wanted." She studied them for a moment, a satisfied expression on her face. "And besides, you agreed to it."

"When?" Emma asked.

"When you signed the contract." Dr. Mason bent and opened a drawer on her desk, pulling out a folder. She flipped through the pages in it, then pointed at a specific section.

Emma and Peter both leaned forward.

Be aware that unlimited fertility may result. By signing, you acknowledge this risk.

"I knew we should have read it more carefully," Peter muttered.

Emma shot him a glare, then turned to Dr. Mason. "How do we stop it? How do we void the contract?"

"You don't. It's binding until death."

Emma gasped. "Until *death*? Do you mean I'll be pregnant until I die?"

"Yes. Isn't it wonderful?"

Peter put his arm around Emma. "*No*, it's not," he said.

"Her womb belongs to Shub-Niggurath. The Thousand Young must be born. They will keep coming, generation after generation."

"Why couldn't you have chosen someone else?" Emma asked. "Haven't you worked with enough clients?"

The woman shook her head, clicking her tongue with disapproval. "None of them lived beyond three or four babies. Your body is uniquely attuned to having multiple children. I know how easy your pregnancies have been."

Peter shook his head. "The last few have been hard."

Dr. Mason stared at him, her dark gaze steady. "The current pregnancy still hasn't reached the difficulty a normal pregnancy would achieve."

"Are you serious?" Emma wailed. "I'm *miserable!*"

"Yes, well, my other patients were already dead at this point." Dr. Mason abruptly got to her feet. "Thank you for the visit. I have other matters to see to."

"Matters more important than this?" Emma asked.

"We need a copy of that contract," Peter said. "Because this isn't the last you'll be hearing from us—we're getting an attorney. You *will* undo the mess you've created!"

Dr. Mason waved him off. "Feel free to take pictures, but you'll find it's ironclad. No attorney can stop things from continuing." She glanced at Emma. "Thank you for your sacrifice."

Peter shouted obscenities at Dr. Mason and Emma sobbed, but the woman ignored both of them and walked to her door, gesturing for them to leave.

Dejected, disappointed, and crying uncontrollably, Emma stepped past the woman. She had sensed the truth in the doctor's statement—they wouldn't be able to cancel the contract. She remembered that voice—*don't fight it*. She absolutely knew horrible things would happen if she did.

Emma and Peter returned home, overjoyed to see their babies again, but full of sorrow.

It took her a day or two to get up the courage to do it, but finally Emma scanned through the contract Peter had taken pictures of. Her eyes widened in horror when she read a clause that said the babies belonged to Dr. Mason's agency. How was that possible? And *why* hadn't she read the thing before signing?

She told Peter about what she'd read. He asked to see it, and she opened the images again. But try as she might, she couldn't find the clause.

A couple of days later, she'd forgotten about it entirely.

Still, the feeling of foreboding and fear wouldn't leave. How was she to handle unlimited pregnancies? How would she survive? How would she survive a *normal* pregnancy, if this wasn't even that yet?

One morning the next month, when Emma went to get the older three children from bed, she found their room empty, their beds bare.

"Peter!" she screamed, staring at the room that should have been filled with laughter and cheerful conversation. "Peter!"

He rushed in.

"They're gone! Maggie... Micah... Macie. They're gone!"

"Check the camera feed. Did someone break in?"

Emma hurried to open the app on her phone and went through the recordings, starting with bedtime the night before when she and Peter had read the little children stories and kissed them, tucking them in. They fell asleep quickly, as they always did. Around three in the morning, a dark static filled the center of the feed. It grew, blossoming like a dead rose, its edges roiling with what looked like tentacles, until it filled the entire feed.

When the static disappeared, the children were gone.

Nothing else was touched or taken.

Emma turned to Peter, but he'd left the room. She hunted him down, finding him in the kitchen, doing the dishes.

"Aren't you concerned about this?" she asked, gesturing to her phone.

"About what?" he asked, glancing at her.

Emma looked at her phone. Her brain felt foggy. What had she been wanting to talk to him about? "I... I don't know. I guess it was nothing."

She turned, staring blankly out the kitchen window. Had she done laundry recently? Was that what had been on her mind? It must have been. Emma headed to the laundry room, hand supporting her belly, and transferred wet clothes to the dryer.

The triplets were born a month later. Emma and Peter named them Macie, Maggie, and Micah.

"I've always loved those names," Peter said.

Emma nodded. "They're so great—perfect for perfect babies."

She was overcome with exhaustion when she found out she was yet again pregnant with triplets.

And so the cycle continued. Years later, Emma no longer questioned how it was possible that she no longer had organs to conceive and bear and yet somehow continued. Dr. Mason had made it possible.

But Emma was ready to stop. The pregnancies had continued getting more and more difficult. Her nights were sleepless, her days filled with confusion and pain. Worst of all, though, was the constant feeling that she was missing someone. She only had eight children, and yet, it felt like she should have had more than that. Much more.

Hadn't she been giving birth every seven months, after all?

When she brought it up with Peter, he agreed—he too felt like something was wrong. But what?

Deciding to take matters into their own hands and knowing that Dr. Mason would likely come that night as she always did, they set up chairs in their babies' room. Peter wandered off while Emma grabbed several quilts and placed them on the chairs. He returned a moment later, two large kitchen knives in hand.

Emma's eyes widened.

Peter met her gaze with a grim one of his own. "Are you done with this?" he asked.

She nodded, accepting one of the knives. "I'm done."

Emma opened the feed to the camera in the room, and she and Peter stayed up, watching it. The air was heavy, the babies breathing slow and steady.

Around three in the morning, the feed went black. Emma glanced up—nothing was in the room. When she looked at the feed again, though, she screamed. It was full of churning black static with tentacles and eyes and mouths. She bumped Peter awake—he'd fallen asleep.

Peter reached over and turned the light on, then stood. Something shimmered in the air in front of him. He raised his knife and slashed at it but didn't connect with anything.

Emma jumped to join him as the thing began to solidify. She gripped her knife tightly, lunging and stabbing as the shape continued solidifying. The monstrosity pulsed before her—black tentacles whipping around, eyes and mouths emerging from the inky void. And there, in the middle, Keziah Mason watching, a gleam in her eye.

Emma screamed, slashing at the woman who had destroyed her life. She slashed again and again and again. Dr. Mason only smiled at her.

At Emma's last slash, Peter cried out. In a blink, Dr. Mason disappeared, and Peter stood there, Emma's knife embedded in his chest. Emma screamed, rushing for him, hands on his arms. Should she remove the knife? Leave it there? Call 911?

The chaos of tentacles continued undulating around Emma and Peter. Their chairs clattered, falling over. The babies began crying. Peter staggered back, clutching at the knife. His eyes widened as the tentacles and blackness converged on him, surrounding him, separating him from his wife.

The darkness swallowed him whole. It filled the room, the blackness smothering everything. Emma could barely see anything, but she knew—*knew*—he was gone. Her Peter was gone.

She fell to the carpet before passing out.

When Emma awoke the next morning, there were two knives on the floor next to her.

"Peter!" she breathed, getting to her feet.

Had she just had the worst dream of her life? Had she really murdered her husband? Emma searched the house but couldn't find him anywhere. She opened her camera feed and scanned through the events of the night before, watching as she and Peter staked out the nursery room. The feed was clear. They sat in their chairs, determined to stay awake. The recorded version of Emma kept an eye on her phone, watching closely.

The feed flickered, and Emma gripped her phone tighter. Peter and the babies had fallen asleep. The time clicked closer to three a.m.

Then the feed went out. Static and silence greeted her.

When the video went back to normal, there was only Emma, lying on the floor, the knives near her.

Emma stared at her phone for several moments before setting it down. Why did she bring the knives into the nursery with her? That was an odd thing to do. She picked up her phone again and stared at the second chair where someone had sat, then fell asleep.

Who had it been?

Peter. Someone named Peter. Who was Peter?

She couldn't remember.

And soon, she forgot the name itself.

Emma's life became a never-ending cycle. Against all logic and nature, she found herself pregnant over and over again. Delivering perfect babies, then losing them to a black void just a few short years later.

She understood her purpose. She understood why she existed.

She didn't fight it.

Emma was a miracle—a vessel for an important task.

The unending legacy of a Thousand Young.

None Shall Inherit the Earth

A *Cthulhu Armageddon* Prequel

By C.T. Phipps

"Pa?" asked my daughter, Samantha, looking up to the night sky. "Do you ever regret it?"

Samantha was a lovely seventeen-year-old girl with chocolate skin, deep soulful eyes, and raven hair which hung messily over her shoulders. She was also in a wheelchair, one which would need replacing as soon as we could scavenge the ruins of another hospital. Samantha was growing to look more and more like her mother every day and it only made me miss her more.

"Which part?" I asked, stabbing a can of peaches with a can opener as I tried to calculate how much I needed now versus later.

"Surviving," Samantha said, glancing around the old campsite. The trees around us were brown and sickly, having once been vibrant green conifers. That had been a different world, though, a world where madness and horror had been a distant thing on television or something that happened to other people.

I'd lost track of the days spent moving from empty town to empty town, scavenging whatever was available while trying to avoid the Goat Men and their worshipers. There was plenty of food to be had because most of humanity being killed freed up a lot of resources. But scavenging always carried the risk of attracting the Goat Men's attention. They didn't eat canned food or vegetables but the flesh of those humans who were still unchanged.

Like my wife, Samantha's mother.

"So hungry," Rebecca whispered, staring at me with the gore dripping down from her mouth: the remains of our dog.

I lifted my shotgun. "Stay back."

"Just a kiss," Rebecca said. "A nibble and you can both taste the Mother's love. She came to me in my dreams. Mother promised our daughter would be healed. We can be like the Old Ones, Pete. Wild, free, and untamed by the laws of false gods and men."

"I said stay back!" I shouted, the gun going off and blowing away half her face.

It hadn't stopped her.

Samantha could never know.

There were some who believed the Goat Men were the next stage of human evolution. That the naked beastfolk were humanity as it should be. At least if you listened to some of the babbling lunatics you ran into along the roads. Men and women who claimed special insight into what was going on because of the horrors in their dreams.

Cultists.

"No, of course not," I lied. "Every day is a treasure with you."

I tried to remember when things like electricity and fresh water were freely available. It was like a dream now, memories filled with endless faces I knew I'd never see again. Everyone I'd grown up with, my parents, wife, in-laws, schoolmates, and friends—gone. I wanted to share my secret that, yes, I regretted surviving. I regretted it every damn day.

Hell existed so surely there had to be a Heaven, or at least I told myself that, because the Goat Men being demons at least provided some form of hope that angels existed. I wanted to be there with fluffy clouds and a harp in hand. I would have settled for something other than a daily struggle to eat just the right amount of sugar so I didn't slip into a coma and leave my daughter unprotected. I was not the kind of hardened superman or even caveman who could survive an apocalypse. I'd been diabetic since my teenage years and the medicine I'd once relied on had all gone bad.

Even oblivion was starting to sound tempting. To not have to flee the sounds of the creatures in the woods that were infinitely worse than the wolves that had menaced my primordial ancestors. Yet, looking at Samantha, I couldn't bring myself to say it. Our survival depended on our desire—no, our will—to live because it sure as hell wasn't our bodies.

"I do," Samantha said, saying what I'd been afraid to. "You'd have a much better chance of surviving if I wasn't slowing you down."

I stared at her, realizing she was giving voice to the one thought neither of us could afford . "Baby girl, I'm a diabetic. How many times have you managed to get sweets or sugar down my throat when I'm senseless? I need you as much as you need me."

I couldn't live without her.

Wouldn't live without her.

"Other people can help you," Samantha said. "I'm just—"

"Other people don't want us." I gritted my teeth, forcing myself to say an uncomfortable truth. The last three groups of survivors we'd encountered wanted nothing more than to shake us down for supplies before sending us on our merry way. We were liabilities in their eyes, mistakes natural selection would soon sort out. It seemed the Rising had brought out the worst impulses in humanity. At least the Goat Men had an excuse for being monsters.

Of course, I would have been the same way had the situation been reversed. Probably. It was always easier to rue man's heartlessness when you weren't the one being asked to risk your survival on a diabetic with no useful skills and his crippled child. Mind you, those groups weren't exactly thriving either. In the end, they became like the Goat Men or became food for them. The lucky ones at least. It wasn't like famine, disease, and infighting had gone away after all. The stars had changed and anyone who looked at them seemed to hear the song of the Great Mother. Sometimes I did too.

Always it was my wife singing.

"Kiss me," Rebecca looked up, half of her brain missing and fresh leaves falling out of her skull.

"What the hell are you?" I asked, my hands shaking in horror as I held the shotgun.

"I am a nymph," Rebecca said, laughing despite the fact she should be dead. "A creature of the forest beyond. My blood, the Goddess' blood, runs through our daughter."

"No," I said, denying reality. You're just a thing impersonating her."

"Time will tell, Peter."

I fired again.

I reloaded.

Then fired again.

"We'll find someone," Samantha said, repeating her mantra. "A group of survivors somehow thriving in this chaos. People who won't mind taking care of us to whom we can contribute."

We'd heard from a survivor that there was a community of ex-military at Arkham Air Force Base and that was our present destination—it was hit or miss whether they'd shoot us, turn us away, or, by some miracle, have room for both of us. I wasn't holding my breath and that Samantha was speaking about finding "some place" proved that she wasn't too confident either.

I cut open a can of beans before handing it over to her. "I'm satisfied living with you, right here, right now. Think of this as an extended camping trip."

Samantha frowned. I could tell she wasn't content to travel with me forever across the back roads and highways of America. I couldn't blame her. We all needed people. Humans needed friends, lovers, and companions to get us through the day. I could live if my girl was alive. Taking care of her was my way of keeping my sanity intact.

But who did she have to take care of? No matter how hard I tried to convince her, I couldn't make her understand she was every bit as important to me as I was to her. Even then, little girls couldn't stay with their daddies forever. She was a young woman now with no prospect of love, life, or happiness. Only survival.

I forced down the thought that my wife might have been right. We were only two years into this nightmare—one that would not end until death, I was sure.

"We should get some rest," Samantha said, sticking a plastic spoon into her can of cold beans. "We have a long day ahead of us."

I smiled, thinking the moment had passed. "When isn't it long?"

"Yeah," Samantha said.

In my dreams my wife turned our daughter.

She changed.

She warped.

New legs replaced her old useless ones.

Samantha and her mother fed upon me to celebrate.

A feast fit for the gods.

I awoke to find our campsite ransacked and turned upside down. Our latched together shopping carts were overturned, our canned goods and backpacks were missing, the fire pit and its cover looked as if they'd been stomped on for spite, and Samantha's wheelchair was thrown to one side.

A little girl stood there, about twelve-years-old, with hair as white as snow. She was immaculately dressed in a private school uniform with cold, dead, white eyes and skin the color of obsidian. A pair of stag antlers sprung from her head despite her sex and I saw her legs were furry below her dress, with cloven hooves in place of feet. In some ways, she looked like one of the Goat Men's women but there was none of the savagery or animalism to her.

"Who are you?" I asked.

"The Black Maiden to the Mother," the girl said. "Just as there is a Crone. I am not one of my hungry nieces, though. Your flesh is safe with me, Peter."

"How do you know my name?" I asked.

The girl scoffed. "You've told me in your dreams. Such delicious dreams. That is the one lasting legacy of your race."

It didn't take a scientist to guess she was something wearing human form like a suit. The Goat Men had at least been human once before warping into the cannibalistic things they were. This? This was something else. Had this Black Maiden killed my daughter? If so, why leave me alive? I didn't want to live without her.

"You're not..." I started to speak, a horrifying chill passing over me. "What?"

The Black Maiden sighed. "You are blessed today, Peter. It is a day to fulfill your purpose."

I looked desperately around for Samantha but saw no sign of her. Had the Black Maiden eaten her? Had my daughter escaped somehow? What was going on?

"What *purpose*?" I spit out the word, wondering why the demon was toying with me.

"To pleasure the gods," the Black Maiden said. "To bring wonder and glory to our Great Mother's gardens."

I struggled to stand, feeling cold and empty as a drizzle of rain fell around me. "Where. Is. My. Child?"

"She has been taken," the Black Maiden said. "A sect of those who believe worshiping us will placate our wrath have dragged her back to their compound. There, they intend to offer her up for sacrifice." The little girl moved her sleeve in front of her mouth and laughed. "As if we cared about such things. It is as if the offering of an ant was laid before a man's foot."

I didn't care about any of that. This monster wanted to talk. Well, it could talk as long as it gave answers. "Can you point me in their direction?"

I didn't know why I expected it to help. Even if it wasn't one of the Goat Men, it was human enough to revel in my pain.

"Do you intend to rescue her? Go in guns blazing? Kill them all and claim your reward?" the Black Maiden asked.

"I don't have a gun," I said, biting my lip. I'd run out of ammo months ago. "Which you'd know if half of what you're claiming was true."

"*Pa, where's mom?*" *Samantha asked, terrified in the basement where I'd hidden her. "I heard gunfire."*

I stared at her, unsure where to even begin and my eyes wet with tears. "The things... baby girl. The things got her."

Samantha looked on in horror. "No!"

"We have to leave," I whispered, knowing she could never go upstairs. *"Now. It's not safe here."*

"But your medicine..." Samantha said. *"Our friends..."*

"There's no friends here," I said, thinking of how our neighbors had abandoned us when the first evacuation orders had begun. Even the gun in my arms had belonged to one of the people who'd not bothered to check to see if we had our own way out. They hadn't cared that any car with a computer in it was as likely as not to fail. In the end, their callousness hadn't saved them. All the places they'd fled to had been torn apart from the inside when the Goat Men had emerged. Hospitals and refugee camps had become abattoirs. "It's happening everywhere."

There was no safety in numbers, but just maybe I could keep the truth away from her for a little longer.

"I do," the Black Maiden said, smiling "The only reason you're alive, Peter, is because I decided it'd be more fun to hide you from them and see how you'd react."

I gritted my teeth, trying not to call the little girl a sadistic bitch. Desperation made me willing to grovel, though. I'd do anything for Samantha, even throw away what little dignity I had. "Would you *please* tell me which direction my baby girl is?"

"Ah, manners." The Black Maiden pointed down into the depths of the forest. "Over the river and through the woods to grandfather's house you must go. The Old Crone is in charge, but the granddaughter seeks her crown because her mother is dead. Hope is the weapon these people are vulnerable to, but bullets work too. Too bad you have none and they have many."

"Riddle talk? What is this, the fucking *Hobbit*?" I snarled. The prospect of losing Samantha kept me from thinking clearly. I couldn't survive knowing I'd failed her. I might as well just wander into a demon den and let them finish me.

In fact, I would.

Please God, let me get through this intact, I prayed. *I'll do anything.*

"My game, my rules." The Black Maiden shook her head and lifted her right hand to point. "Tick-tock, Peter. Your baby girl is waiting. I will feast well if you prove more beast than man."

I started to jog in the direction she'd pointed.

I jogged through the cold woods, frequently pausing to catch my breath. It was morning and a freezing drizzle was coming down. Adjusting my coat, I struggled to keep warm against the elements.

I hadn't had anything to eat and the thought of becoming senseless in the wilderness gnawed at me. When my blood sugar dropped below a certain point, I lost my mind and, effectively, became effectively drunk. Danger, horror, and the world around me ceased to be relevant.

Without Samantha to look over me and make sure I ate something sweet, there wasn't any way for me to recover. I could end up unable to help my child, losing my mind, and wandering aimlessly until I starved to death.

It was just the kind of twisted situation a monster would enjoy. Such thoughts were pointless, though. There wasn't anything I could do to change my diabetes and there were no fruits or snacks lying around on the ground. I was cold, alone, and the only person who could save my baby girl right now. Words couldn't describe how screwed I was.

By the end of my second hour of wandering, I was exhausted and ready to break. I had no idea whether the demon was telling the truth. Samantha might have been dead for hours and I was just following the product of my deranged imagination.

Falling to my knees, I decided to rest up against a tree trunk for a moment to try and regain my strength. I'd never been an athlete. Hell, I'd just barely avoided being an enormous nerd, but it felt like my body was betraying me now. I needed to be strong and that wasn't an option at that point.

Struggling to regain even the barest sense of myself, I heard water nearby. It was faint, almost inaudible in the mixture of insect chirps and rushing creeks which were a mainstay of forest life, but I could hear it. Climbing to my feet, I stumbled along and continued walking for what seemed like forever.

I came across a large rushing brook pouring its contents across smooth stones. Throwing myself to the ground, I cupped the ice-cold water between my hands and drank deeply. It wouldn't help my diabetes, but it was still a godsend. I reached over to my thermos, always keeping the metal cylinder tied to the end of my jacket and filled it. That was when I noticed the skulls.

Hanging from the trees nearby or impaled on spikes were over a dozen skulls. They weren't the only bones either. There were ribcages, skulls, fingers, and femurs all being used as decorations. It was a grotesque collection from a sick set of minds. The bones surrounded a pathway leading to an old trailer park I could just barely make out at the top of a nearby hill.

"Over the river and through the woods indeed," I muttered, taking a deep breath. My vision was blurry, and I had a headache. "I'm coming, girl."

This wasn't the sort of situation where I could just burst in and start punching people. I had nothing to bargain with and, as a threat, I ranked less than your typical feral dog. I didn't know how dangerous these people were but by their choice of decor, it was enough to kill their fellow man and scatter their remains about like it was Halloween.

I'd never killed anyone other than Rebecca—I'd never used a gun before that day—so violence wasn't the answer. Even if I did have a gun, they probably had more. I'd just end up getting myself killed and as tempting as that was, I wasn't about to give up just yet. Surrendering to a bunch of psycho hillbilly savages wasn't my idea of a smart plan but this wasn't an action movie. With no other options, I decided how I was going to play this.

Lie.

Lie like I had to my baby girl.

Repeatedly.

"Here goes nothing," I muttered. "Or everything."

Lifting my hands, I started walking towards the camp.

My only real survival tool in this hell we called life was my ability to talk and that would hopefully be enough. If not, well, then I'd at least have the chance to die for my daughter. That was better than some people in this world got.

The interior of the cultist's trailer park was a foul-smelling junk pit filled with scavenged goods, more skeletal decorations, and several "evil" symbols like pentagrams—not even upside-down ones—spray-painted on the side of their trailers. It was witchcraft and paganism for people who knew nothing about either, hoping to appeal to beings so far beyond us that we might as well have been shouting to the wind.

While the bones were intimidating and I was concerned about finding Samantha, I found my surroundings filled me with a sense of pity. Humanity was reduced to a bunch of people pretending to be on the side of the monsters in the vain hope they'd stop killing us. The Black Maiden's contempt of them was understandable but still depressing.

I didn't see anyone, so I decided to announce my presence, not wanting to risk getting shot as an intruder. I didn't have much of a plan, but I had the beginnings of one. "Fear not, Fellow Evil Doers! I bring a message from the Dark Mother! The Black Mother and her consort, the Horned King, speak through me, and you must all hear her wisdom!'

I was rewarded for this stupidity by someone slamming me in the back of the head with a hard metal object. I felt a sharp sting of agony followed by my body collapsing out from under me, then someone grabbed me by the back of my shirt and dragged me into one of the trailers.

After a brief patting down, I was shoved backward into a dog cage before a steel set of bars was shut on me. Shaking my head, I looked up to see I was in a claustrophobic chamber with a dozen other cages. A few of them were occupied, though their Rottweiler residents seemed sad and listless rather than angry or disturbed by my presence. I did a double take when I saw Samantha off to one side. She was looking at me with a mixture of disbelief, relief, and disappointment.

"'I bring a message from the Dark Mother'? That was what you went with?" Samantha said, leaning up against the side of her cage. She let out a gallows' laugh, closing her eyes so tight I could see tears forming on the edge of them.

"It was all I could come up with." I said, pressing my hand against the metal mesh over the iron bars between us. "I'm sorry, baby girl. I am so very, very sorry."

Samantha closed her eyes. "I didn't want you to die here with me, Pa. I'm so sorry I dragged you into this."

"How did you drag me into this?" I asked, raising an eyebrow. "Did you summon the hordes of Hell into the world? Did you—"

"Please, Dad, I don't want our last conversation to be about who is responsible for what."

I clutched the wire mesh tight. "This is *not* going to be our last conversation."

In the back of my mind, I swore I could hear Rebecca laughing.

Her voice sounded like the Black Maiden's at the end.

"Pa?" Samantha asked.

"Yes?" I asked.

"I know what you did," Samantha said, starting to cry. "I also know why."

I cursed myself. "Don't talk about it."

"Pa, I—"

"Don't! Ever! Please."

We were silent at that.

Two and a half hours later, my escape attempts proved futile. Despite the cage being made for dogs, my attempts to kick open the door failed. The door was padlocked as well, something I couldn't deal with. Samantha was silent throughout my struggle, except for giving small encouragement, and it was only when it became clear that I wasn't going to be able to do anything she began to talk about how we were going to die.

I couldn't comfort her, though, because my strength had left me. With no food in my belly or anything sweet to drink, my mind began to leave me. I don't recall anything more until I awakened to the taste of rehydrated orange juice being poured down my throat.

Gulping it down, it was several minutes before I realized I was being helped by a woman who wasn't my child. She was Caucasian, mid-thirties, and had stringy blonde hair which hung far down over her shoulders. Her clothing was dirty, much like mine, with a straw hat on her head. There was also a holster carrying a pistol at her side, something which caused me to do a double take.

I was just outside of the dog cage they'd locked me in. Looking to my side, I saw Samantha's cage was missing and night had fallen out through a side window. Only the fact I was exhausted kept me from bolting to my feet.

I choked on the orange juice, forcing her away. "Who are you?"

The woman glared at me. "The Black Maiden said you were coming. She did not say you were a weakling."

I almost laughed, sick of being manipulated. "Yeah, well she keeps her own counsel. Are you the granddaughter she mentioned?"

"I am the granddaughter of the High Witch, granddaughter of the Crone, and rightful leader of this coven. Satan and Lilith have come to claim this Earth for a thousand years! I have seen the Eternal Moon and heard the beautiful songs from distant Carcosa. The Black Man is my grandfather and I am of the true gods' blood. You can call me Keziah the Third."

I tried to ignore my skepticism. Especially as I believed she was completely human from a glance. Also, the title of High Witch struck me as something they'd made up. It reminded me of the ridiculous titles the KKK gave the leaders of its branches. These were witches alright, but they were about as real in their magic and knowledge as Sabrina or Glinda.

"The Black Maiden told me you were going to overthrow your grandmother," I said, deciding to continue lying my ass off. "That you were the one meant to be immortal, not her."

"Yes!" Keziah said, clasping her hands together. "I knew it! The Great Mother favors *me* rather than my witch ancestor! The Black Man wishes me to be the Earthmother's voice! Praise the Black Goat Queen! Praise Shub-Niggurath! The time has come!"

I'd have laughed if not for the fact I was dealing with a genuine cultist willing to kill people for her dark gods. If the last two years hadn't prepared me for the horrible fever dream which my life had become, I would have mocked her decree.

"Yes, it has," I said, trying to play on her vanity. "However, it can't happen if my daughter is killed. She's... special."

Keziah stared at me. "I'll make my move at the High Sabbath then. The Great Mother will show us her favor once I offer my grandmother to her. As for your child, though, you'll have to be the one to free her."

Keziah reached down and handed me her pistol. I stared at the weapon. "Alright. Thank you for your trust."

Keziah snorted. "Those the gods favor are immune to mortal weapons."

The Black Maiden said otherwise but I didn't mention that.

"Right."

Hiding the pistol in the back of my pants, I felt slow and confused but tried to force my way through the fog. I couldn't lose myself now, not when I so close. At least the cultists fed me, even though they forced me to use the bathroom in my cage. I had no idea what they were doing to Samantha and just prayed sacrifices had to remain pure.

"Focus," I muttered, crawling towards the trailer's door. "Focus."

Outside, a massive bonfire blazed in the center of the trailer park. There, the residents were gathered around Samantha's cage. She was inside, her fists wrapped around the bars and mesh, screaming her head off and yelling obscenities.

"Fuck you, you sick psycho fucks!" Samantha's screams echoed around us. "I hope you burn in hell along with the rest of humanity!"

I had to admit that I was a little proud of her. Yet the trailer park cultists didn't look in the slightest bit rattled. In fact, they looked calm and normal. Well, what passed for normal after the End of the World.

There was no chanting, no robes, or ritual knives amongst the cultists. Instead, there was just a group of normal-looking survivors gathered around a seventy-year-old white woman in a plain summer dress holding a crucifix upside down as she spoke words that I assumed were her attempts at Latin. They prayed to the Black-Eyed Man, Satan, the Horned King, Lilith, Gaia, Demeter, and gods I'd never heard of that she'd either made up or conjured from the nightmares we'd all shared.

I couldn't tell how many cultists there were or maybe I was simply too upset. Still, there were a lot of them. Easily a dozen. Worse, I could tell the ones closest to the old woman all held cans of kerosene. They were going to burn my daughter alive.

It took all my willpower to not start shooting into the crowd. I'd probably miss everyone, but it might have scattered the crowd. I held off my firing, though, because I noticed damn near every single one of the cultists was carrying a firearm. The last time I'd seen anyone so well armed was a group of militiamen holding a road hostage in exchange for canned goods and women. Samantha and I had escaped by pretending to be deathly ill.

Taking a deep breath, I scanned the crowd for some sign of Keziah. She wasn't present and it took me a second to realize she was sneaking up from the side with several teenagers all carrying shotguns. I didn't have time to react before Keziah gunned down the old woman while her fellows started opening fire into the crowd.

Feeling a rush of adrenaline, I stumbled to my feet and ran headlong into the crowd. It was stupid, insane even, but the cultists were too busy shooting at each other to do much. I stumbled over the bleeding form of the grandmother in front of Samantha's cage and the elderly witch reached over to me, her mouth dripping blood. It was one of the most disgusting sights I'd seen since the early days of the invasion when demons warped humans into unrecognizable masses of flesh and used them like toys.

"Back off!" Kicking her in the head, I found myself by Samantha's side.

"You're alive!" Samantha called, staring at me like I'd appeared from nowhere.

"Scoot to the back!" I shouted, aiming the gun at the lock, and praying I didn't miss as I pulled the trigger. The recoil was intense. There were loud bangs which deafened my ears as I felt a sharp whizzing past my cheek that I really didn't like to think was a ricocheted bullet. The lock, however, fell to the ground in pieces. Dropping the gun, I opened the dog cage door, while Samantha reached for the weapon. I pulled her out of the cage while Samantha clutched the pistol tightly against her chest. Despite not being the strongest of men, I managed to lift her up and carry her.

Adrenaline was a hell of a drug. I passed by bloody bodies and dying men, ignoring them to focus on my escape. I had no doubt everyone present wanted my head, but they wanted each other's lives even more. I couldn't have cared less. If they wanted to kill each other, that was their own business.

Trying to navigate down the trailer park in the middle of the night carrying a one hundred- and thirty-five-pound woman with people shooting at you was not what you'd call easy. I stumbled and the two of us went rolling down into a pile at the bottom of the hill. I ended up banging my shoulder against a ribcage-covered signpost.

"Samantha!" I called over, trying to see in the dark.

A flashlight appeared at the top of the hill, and I could see a blood-splattered Keziah III standing at the top of the hill carrying a shotgun as she directed one of her teenage followers. Possibly her daughter to make this whole generational power struggle even weirder. That was when there were two more shots in the darkness as Samantha fired the pistol in her hands, killing them both. I could hear the sounds of things in the air and Goat Men in the woods. Our actions had brought the attention of the otherworldly and my only hope now was that they went to feast on the cultists rather than us as we fled.

"We can't outrun them, Pa!" Samantha cried out.

"We don't have to," I replied, making an old joke. "We just have to outrun the others."

The Black Maiden's laughter filled the woods as I heard the dying screams of those being eaten alive.

None of the Goat Men or their bat allies pursued us.

I don't recall the rest of the night but, somehow, I got Samantha in my arms again and carried her two miles to an abandoned 7-11 where we rested for the next evening. There was a little food there despite looting, some of it still edible. Enough to drive back the fog since it was processed sugary bullshit. The monsters didn't come our way. Not for tonight and I had a flash of insight: I didn't regret surviving at all. Neither did Samantha.

I did, however, regret failing to protect her from the choices necessary for us to survive. Requiring her to become a killer to save me when I just flubbed it all up. However, she was tougher than me. Stronger. Able to forgive me for killing the thing that her mother had become when I wasn't able to forgive myself. The two of us were strong in different ways which complemented each other.

I didn't believe the so-called strong would inherit the Earth like so many of the crazed Darwinists or mad fanatics out there. But I didn't believe we would survive much longer either. I accepted that our time would be measured in days, weeks, or months, but not years. So was the rest of humanity doomed.

Still, it was only a mile and a half to Arkham Air Force Base, and we'd make our way there to try to survive for however long that could be. Getting another wheelchair was difficult but not impossible and I'd carry her if I had to. It was better than trying for my old alma mater, Miskatonic.

The meek would not inherit the Earth.

None would.

But we could live until we died like humanity was always destined to.

Maybe I'd make it the Booth family motto.

The Mother's Gifts

By Eric Malikyte

My shop has been empty for months.

The holidays in this town used to be bustling. Now, they've slowed to a crawl. Turns out, two boys drowning thanks to a riptide will do that for the tourism trade.

If it weren't for the crowds the festival is promising to bring, I'd be questioning why I even moved here to begin with.

Questions, all of them in my dad's rasping voice: *Why try to open an antique store in a hundred-year-old building that ain't seen a lick of maintenance since the Seventies?*

Why take your son away from his daddy? Why not try to make things work?

Was it just to get away from him?

Was it really that *bad?*

And my favorite: *Are you sure it wasn't all in your head?*

The questions are superfluous. Of course, I *know* why I moved here.

I take one look at my son—smiling while he digs through his tiny backpack for things to entertain himself—and I know I've made the right choice.

The chimes over the door ring, and my excitement at the idea of having a real customer today fades when I see Janice standing there, the sunlight beating down on her hot pink hair—this time cut in an asymmetrical bob—as she holds the door open, eyes zeroed in at the new sign I put up outside.

"So, you kept Jacob's Things?" Janice says, giving me the "you're crazy, you know that?" look. "I seem to remember telling you it sounds like a toy store."

"Hey, before those kids…" I look at Jacob, he's too busy playing with the Legos he brought from downstairs to care what we're talking about (yet I still censor myself). "You know. *Before*. This place was bopping."

Janice approaches the counter and leans over it. "Bopping?"

"Well, I was able to pay my bills comfortably and had plenty of time to work on the restorations."

Janice flips her hair out of her eyes and turns around to look at the plastic sheets gating off the back section of the store. "And how's that going?"

"Lots of time," I say. "No money for supplies."

Janice grins. "You know what might fix that?"

"I'm *not* changing the name."

Janice laughs. "No! We're doing a gallery night this weekend for the art community."

"I…" I avoid her gaze. "I don't know if I'm ready for that yet."

"Come on, girl! You're killing it! You should come, show off your new sculptures, and get absolutely shit-faced. Who knows, maybe you'll sell a few pieces while you're at it."

For a moment, I can imagine it. I can smell the faint aroma of cannabis in the air, of whiskey and rail vodka. The lingering smell of cigarette smoke clinging to the clothes of people coming in from outside. I can feel the lights focusing on me, on a round table featuring my latest work. I can feel their eyes on me, and the liquor in my veins giving me courage. I can…

My eyes find Jacob, playing with his Legos. "Who'll watch Jacob?"

"I know a girl," Janice says. "She's fantastic. Has amazing reviews on Nextdoor."

Maybe she's right? I've always wanted to have a gallery…

"Every Breath You Take" by the Police bounces off the walls of my shop.

"Shit," Janice says, looking down at her phone. "That's my beer supplier, I gotta go handle this, but you're coming right?"

"I can't promise that!"

"You're coming, babe!" Janice laughs as she puts the phone up to her ear. "I'm coming to the door right now, don't go anywhere."

The chimes ring as Janice rushes out the door.

What should I do? Is it smart to trust a stranger with my son?

Especially after what happened…

I'm getting the strong urge to journal about this. Maybe make a list of pros and cons?

Doctor Patton did say it'd help me if I felt stuck, if I was spiraling, or any of the other bullshit that comes with having ADHD as an adult. Well, that and the new medication she prescribed…which I forgot to take this morning.

Goddamn it!

Okay, I'm going to do at least one thing right today!

I take out the journal and set it on the counter, grab a pen from the cup of them I keep next to the register, and put the pen to page.

I'm halfway into an entry and Jacob's pulling on my pants, trying to get me to look at what he's built with his Legos.

I'm about to write about all the things I haven't done today. How the antiques are gathering dust, and how that makes me think of Mom before she went to hospice when her MS got bad. How I keep hearing Dad's voice when things don't go according to plan, telling me that there's nothing wrong with me that a good ass-whippin' wouldn't fix.

And I write about how good it would feel to let loose for a night, show off my art, and just…

Did I just hear the bells over the front door?

I don't even have to lift my head from the page to tell it's not Janice.

Which means I have a real customer!

YAY!

But, when I look up, my excitement fades almost instantly. Instinct takes over. My hand is under the counter, gripping the wooden bat I store next to the mini fridge with all of Jacob's snacks and juice boxes.

And then I catch the reflection off his glasses.

They have the same eyes!

Or, at least, that's my initial thought.

My eyes find Jacob on the floor, having gone back to his Legos to build his next masterwork.

I want to get him out of the store without raising any suspicions.

"Jacob," I whisper. "Why don't you go upstairs and play on my tablet?"

Jacob's eyes are so sharp, his lips pursed; he knows something's wrong with how I'm talking. "But you said I could only have an hour of screen time."

"Just do it for Mommy, okay?"

Jacob nods and goes through the door behind me. I watch him make his way back up the stairs to the apartment, checking through the wooden rods of the banister as he makes sure Mommy's okay.

I hear the door close, and I can finally focus on...*him.*

The morning sun casts bands of light through my store's windows. It reflects off his brown hair and his beard, and creates a glare on his glasses, hiding the dark eyes that keep glancing my way.

I watch him walk up and down the aisles. He's tall. Heavyset. Not exactly the kind of person I would expect to be exploring an antique store. My hand remains on the handle of the bat as he pretends to be interested in an old china set, and then a grandfather clock.

The more I look at him, the more I'm sure I've seen him before. And that thought alone is enough to make me want to call the cops. Not that it would do any good.

Oh God! What if he sees all the dust on my shelves and decides to leave a one-star review? Dad would tell me I should have prioritized the business instead of goofing off with Janice and scribbling my feelings down. A couple of times I catch his eyes hovering around my chest before turning back to whatever he's doing—like I don't notice.

His eyes. The desperation in them as he looks at me. It's impossible not to think of Clint standing over my bed, breathing heavily and clenching his fists. Makes me realize I'm all alone here and keeps the traditional "Can I help you" from reaching my lips.

I look out the windows.

The street's empty. It's Monday. Day after Thanksgiving weekend. Of course no one's around. Everyone's at work. Even Janice is busy with her beer delivery.

Now that I think about it, he looks a bit like a lost puppy.

A puppy that could easily overpower me and... God, I sound like my mother.

I grip my pen tight. I hope Doctor Patton doesn't want to see my journals.

He's stopped.

All he's doing is staring at something on the shelf.

I mean, not the pretend interest like in the china or the grandfather clock. He's *really* focused on it. Like when I hyper focus on sculpting or pottery...

Come to think of it, I can recall a few people stopping to look at that statue over the last month or so.

A few more minutes of this shit and I'm calling the fucking cops. They might not do shit, but the red and blue lights might make *him* think twice about pulling something.

I dig my phone out of my purse. I'm about to dial when he stops staring at whatever the hell was so interesting on the shelf and storms right toward me.

My anxiety is through the roof. I hear my Dad's voice again. This time reciting his favorite prayer.

Here I lay me down to sleep.

He's close. My heart is racing. I can smell the cheap cologne he sprayed himself with. I swear it's the same as Clint's.

To thee, O Lord, I give my soul to keep—

When his eyes meet mine, I suddenly wish I'd caved and bought a gun for the store like Dad suggested.

Wake I ever, Or, wake I never—

And then he hooks a left and walks right through the doors, saying "Thank you" as they slam closed.

To thee O Lord, I give my soul to keep forever.

My hands are in the clay. Molding and kneading it. Carefully shaping it.

Creating a foundation for the statue burning like stars in my mind's eye.

My tools glimmer. Reflected light from streetlamps.

Jacob is asleep in his bedroom.

That knowledge is all I need to allow myself to sink into my work. To allow it full control over everything I am or will be.

My hands caress the armature. It's a skeleton made of aluminum wire. It's so cold, lacking life.

I will give it warmth. I will give it a piece of me.

Her flesh will need something to cling to. I pick up the floral wire and wrap it around the legs and arms.

I take the clay and slowly mold it around the torso. Then the head. Then the arms and legs, until what stares back at me is a poor approximation of a human figure. An imitation.

There is still much work to do. It's the furthest thing from the figure I can see as clear as day in my mind.

Her soft skin. The wonder in her bold, striking eyes.

The way the light filters through the trees.

How the tree limbs shoot out from the ground and envelop her like flower petals.

How she balances on them.

How it all makes her feel alive.

The rough, uneven human form. I take my torch and baptize her flesh in fire. "And why shouldn't you go this weekend?" Doctor Patton asks.

My eyes comb over her features. Her hair is short and dark. Her features are sharp. Fierce. But youthful. She wears a pantsuit. Something I'd sooner see on an FBI agent than a therapist. I'm sitting across from her desk in a leather chair designed to be just comfortable enough to lower my guard. It always smells so strange here, so sterile. Part of me wants to go back to doing this over the app. I'm playing with a piece of paper in my pocket, staring out the window as the tree limbs swing back and forth in the wind. Her eyebrow raises. I've seen that look before. Often on Dad right before I was about to get an ass-whipping. It means, "Don't make me repeat myself." "I...it feels irresponsible," I finally say. Doctor Patton lifts my journal. "Seems like Janice has thought of everything. The babysitter is well reviewed on Nextdoor." "I know, but she's still a stranger." Patton lowers the journal back to her desk. "And you're worried a teenage girl is going to beat your son like Clint did? I'm not sure I'm seeing the connection." "It's stupid...maybe it's my dad's voice. I know what he'd say." "Family comes first, except when he's out drinking himself stupid, or gambling, or cheating on your mother?" I avoid her piercing gaze. "Yeah...that part." I hear her sigh. "Time's almost up, so I want you to consider going to this event. Do something normal and selfish for once." I'm a little surprised to be hearing her saying something like this. Doctor Patton always seems so... stern. Responsible. I nod. "Okay. I'll think about it."

Alarm bells.

Fog.

Ugh. What time is it?

My 8:30 a.m. alarm is blaring.

How long has it been going off?

I silence the alarm and check the time. It's 10:25 a.m.

What's at 8:30 a.m.?

What day is it?

I glance around my bedroom, out the windows. Seems like all I see now are the stores across the street from my shop.

Could have sworn I closed the curtains last night.

SHIT!

The date on my phone's screen finally registers. It's December 5th, and it's Thursday.

Which means I'm over an hour late opening my store!

I jump from my bed and rush into the kitchen. Jacob is on his tablet playing games.

"Honey," I say, trying to keep the panic from seeping into my voice. "Why didn't you wake Mommy up?"

He doesn't respond.

I worry he'll inherit my ADHD. I need to get him tested. If he's having trouble focusing at five years old, who knows—

"I did," he finally responds.

"Then why—"

"You said go watch cartoons, you had a sculcher to finish."

I stop what I'm doing. "What do you mean... do you mean sculpture?"

He nods. Doesn't take his eyes off the tablet.

Maybe it was a mistake to get him that thing?

"Honey, Mommy was probably having a dream."

"A dream?"

I glance at the clock on the wall. It's thirty minutes fast. The logic being that it's supposed to help me be on time. Joke's on *past-me* for that one, my apartment's right on top of my shop and I still can't get to work on time.

Right. The time. It says it's 11:00 a.m., which means it's 10:30 a.m. already and Jacob needs to be at preschool today, which is across town, which is why I was supposed to be awake at 8:30 a.m. at the latest so I could go take him and—

"Honey. Sweetie. Dearest child of mine."

"Yeah, Mommy?"

"Get your shoes on."

"I don't wanna."

I'm about to lose it. I don't want to yell. Not like his dad. He's a sweet boy. I don't want him turning into...

We're in the car. Jacob is in his car seat. I had to force him to get his shoes on. But! I did it without raising my voice, and that's a victory. Isn't it?

The radio. It's droning on and on and on about the weather and the upcoming festival. The one that is going to make or break me.

"Caprae Island residents are ecstatic about the quarterly fertility festival. Vendors, performers, and locals are all gearing up to usher in the winter season."

Ugh. I need YouTube. Why doesn't this island have 5G? I've heard that even the Virgin Islands have it. So why not here?

And, not to look a gift horse in the mouth, as Dad would say, but who the hell has a fertility festival in December? Don't these people know Christmas is right around the corner?

"Caprae Cathedral is putting on a very special performance you're not gonna want to miss."

By the time I get to Jacob's Daycare, it's already 11:00 a.m. The real one this time.

I try to remind myself no one comes to my store on a Thursday afternoon as I smile, kiss him goodbye, wave to the nice man who runs the daycare (I forget his damn name cause I'm terrible at all the things) and rush out the door.

I think twice about stopping for coffee like I usually do before opening up the shop. I'm late as it is, but the caffeine withdrawals are already setting in.

I say fuck it and stop at the corner shop.

Dad's voice echoes in my head: *If you can't afford your rent, you can't afford a thirteen-dollar cup of coffee.*

Deep sigh.

You know what? I'm gonna get some damn breakfast today too. You wanna know why? Because I *deserve* breakfast.

I'm standing in line, waiting to place my order, when I feel a tap on my shoulder.

I turn around, confused, and resist the urge to scream for help when I see those smoldering eyes.

His eyes.

It takes me a few panicked moments, but I come back to my senses and realize it's the creep from the other day.

He's wearing a jacket the color of a manila folder, jeans that run a little too high on his gut, and a white polo with a pocket protector.

Now he's standing in front of me, smiling at me through crooked teeth.

And the look in his eyes…it's like he's eye-fucking me and I hate it.

I can feel a pit slowly forming in my stomach, can feel a flash of heat across the back of my neck.

"Hi," he says. "We met the other day at that shop, didn't we?"

"You mean *my* shop?" I ask, trying desperately to keep the snark out of my voice.

"Yeah, sorry, I…" He pauses, his eyes drifting to the counter. "Sorry again. It's your turn."

I turn around and sure enough the owner of the coffee shop—an elderly man everyone calls Old Arty—is waiting patiently for us to finish our conversation and for me to order, AKA get my damn shit together.

"Oh, right," I say, laughing like a moron. "I'll have a large black coffee and a blueberry muffin."

Old Arty smiles wide, hands me my coffee, my muffin, and says, "May the Mother smile upon you, child."

He must be Catholic. I *think* Catholics say stuff like that, right?

With coffee and muffin in hand, I scoop up a fist full of sugar packets and Half-and-Half and I take a seat at the window.

Sure enough, when he isn't staring at my tits, smiling-beard-man finds himself standing over me, breathing heavy and eying the open seat across from me.

"Umm, we didn't get to talk the other day," he says.

"We didn't talk at all," I say. "Unless you count awkwardly shuffling out the door while saying 'thank you.'"

He chuckles awkwardly. "Well, do you mind if I join you?"

Fucking hell no. "I'm late as it is, I should really be getting back to the—"

"But you just sat down."

"I..."

I look around the coffee shop for... I don't even know what. Support? Someone, anyone, willing to jump in and throw me a lifeline?

The whole coffee shop seems like it's frozen in time. Everyone is staring at us. Waiting for me to say yes. For another one of their cheesy goddamn love stories to unfold before their eyes so they can put it into their brochure to lure desperate women seeking solitude from their exes to...

Oh look, he sat down while I was monologuing to myself.

"Come on, I don't bite," he says.

This is *not* going in today's journal.

"Why not." I lay on the sarcasm as I gesture to the chair he's stolen. "It's a free country. Or, at least that's what my dad always says."

I figure, *Hell, it's a public place. He can't murder me here, right?*

"Haven't tried the coffee here yet. Is it good?"

"Are you new to Caprae Island?" I ask, before taking a sip of sugary-caffeinated goodness.

He shakes his head. "No, not really. But I just got back from Scotland."

"Interesting. I'm guessing you're not from there, either, since you don't have an accent."

"No, no, I was in the Navy."

"Past tense?"

"Yeah, I got out. I'm working at the new Applied Sciences building."

"Who?"

"The guys who work for NASA?"

"Ah, you're a scientist?"

That would explain why he's so damn weird. Maybe. I don't know many scientists. Any, actually. I don't know any.

"No," he says. "I just work on their computers. Well, we assume that they contract with NASA, but none of us are really sure."

"Less exciting."

"Yes." Smiling-beard-man sniffs at his coffee, then takes a sip. "Not bad."

"It's coffee."

"Yes."

My mind starts to wander. It's about then that I realize that, on top of everything else I've screwed up this morning, I forgot to take my damn medication. Again! Not that this would have prevented my brain from going on sabbatical—imagining smiling-beard-man wearing a naval uniform while riding the Loch Ness Monster—but there you go.

"I have a confession," he says.

Never a good thing to hear a random stranger say, unless the confession is "I like *Bridgerton*." Okay. That would be worse. *Bridgerton* is terrible.

"I saw you in here from the window and I just had to come say hi," he says.

"Uh, huh…"

My heartbeat. I can feel it in my ears. I glance at the exits. When I turn back to him, he's staring at my chest again. When I put this blouse on, I thought it looked cute, but now I wish I'd worn a hoodie or something instead.

"I'd love to…" He looks down at his coffee, sighs, furrows his brow like he's got broken marbles for brains, and adjusts his glasses. "I'd love to take you out to dinner and a movie."

"What's your name?" I ask. I need a name to put on the restraining order, after all.

"Ch-Chester," he says.

At least it's not Ted. Ted would be a *real* red flag.

"And why do you want to go out with me, Chester?" I ask.

"Because…" He looks up. His forehead is practically drenched in sweat. "Well, you're the most beautiful woman I've ever seen and…"

"And?"

"And I just got out of the Navy?"

A wave of relief passes through me. I tell myself he's only so awkward cause he probably enlisted when he was young. Maybe right out of high school. Maybe he avoided talking to enlisted women? Maybe this is the first time he's talked to a real girl since high school?

"I don't think that means what you think it means," I say.

"What do you think it means?" Chester asks, smiling nervously.

I look over my shoulder and lean forward when I'm sure no one is too close to overhear me. "I think it means you're just horny."

"No, no, not at all. Well, I suppose maybe a little."

"A little?"

"A lot. Definitely a lot. But, no, what I mean is that I've been gone a long time and I don't really know anyone except for old Navy buddies, and Mother, so I'd like to…"

"Oh, shit, look at the time!" I look at my phone, keeping Janice's contact ready just in case I need someone to pull my ass out of here. "It's time for me to go to work!"

I duck out the front door and hurry to my shop.

I'm practically running down the street. But when I arrive, I'm shocked by the sight of an old nun standing at the front door.

A nun who is looking at her watch.

"Hello," I say. "Can I help you?"

When I get closer, I notice she isn't wearing the typical black and white stuff nuns wear on TV and movies. Hers look… older. Like monk's robes or something.

"It says here you were supposed to open several hours ago."

"I'm so sorry," I say, fiddling with my keys and the lock. "Normally, there aren't many customers at this time of—"

"We must keep our appointments," she says.

"Right, yes, you're right, I should be here on time."

I open the door, the smell of dust slapping me in the face, and wave for her to come inside.

The old woman is slow to enter. She's pale. I mean, I'm a red-head and even I'm not that pale. No rosary or cross visible. But, she is wearing something around her neck. I try not to be obvious about sneaking a peak at whatever it is. She notices and tucks it inside her robe.

I have the strangest thought. *Nosferatu*'s Count Orlok pops into my head—goofy teeth and everything—when I look at her. Maybe it's the way she moves?

I'm sure it's just my imagination running wild again.

Doctor Patton would have a field day with that one. Another thing to avoid in my journal. Finally, the nun enters my shop and peruses my shelves.

"I see you enjoy antiques," she says.

"I mean, that is why I opened an antique shop," I say, immediately covering my mouth. "Sorry. I didn't mean to sound snippy. There was this guy at the coffee—"

"I, too, share an interest in the ancient."

The way she's staring at me. Eyes like shadows. Focus honed like a knife. Like a butcher sizing up a piece of meat. To say it makes me uncomfortable would be an understatement.

"T-that's great!" I say, smiling nervously.

The old woman nods at me and continues browsing the aisles.

I'm happy to do some journaling instead of contributing to whatever this conversation's becoming. I dig my notebook out and set it down. I pray to the universe that she loses interest in me and leaves. But then I realize I'm writing with my left hand and stop. Put my hands in my pockets.

"I was told by Elder Clarence that you had many rare pieces," she says.

God, her voice. Like one of those shrill old schoolteachers from black and white films. I imagine her with a ruler, slapping the hands of small children for daring to be left-handed.

I can practically feel the sting on the back of my hand...

"Elder who?" I ask.

When I look up again, she's standing in front of me, holding a statue I picked up at a yard sale months ago. A stone idol, I guess you could call it, of a pregnant woman wrapped up in the twisting limbs of a willow tree. The original owner caught me staring at the thing for way too long. I bought it more out of embarrassment than anything else.

To be honest, it was a bit creepy looking, with those black eyes and weird vines that wrapped around the base. But... I don't know, there's also something beautiful about it.

"Oh, found what we're looking for?" I ask.

She leans forward. "Do you know what this is?"

I shake my head.

"A rare idol of the Mother," she says, leaning back and examining it closely, brushing it with her hands like someone caressing their cat. "It must be at least a million years old."

"I'm sorry?" I don't think I heard her correctly. "Did you say a million?"

She smiles, and I suddenly feel the urge to make sure spiders aren't crawling over my blouse. "Yes. A million. Quite an exquisite piece."

I think about my rent coming due. The restorations that have stalled.

"Well, how about five thousand dollars to take it off my hands?"

Her expression sours. "Do you realize what this statuette means to the people of Caprae? It would be profane to sell it."

"Well, honey, I gotta keep the lights on somehow."

She's silent for a time, staring at the idol. "Well... I suppose an arrangement could be made."

"A what now?"

That worked?

"Come to my church this Friday evening. I will give you an address and you will bring the idol with you. Elder Clarence simply must be allowed to appraise it."

"I'm..." I shake my head. "I'm sorry, are you a *nun* or something?"

"You could say that. You will join us?"

"I really don't think—"

"Perhaps, in just this one instance, a cash sum could be approved by the church. It would be fair, I think."

"You think it's valuable?"

Her lips curl into a smile. "Oh, immensely."

"Great!"

What am I thinking? I know what Janice would say if she saw the way this woman is behaving. It reminds me of the woman who co-leads Heaven's Gate.

The next thing I know, I'm staring at an empty shop.

My eyes find a note attached to the statue.

When the hell did she leave?

I snatch it up. It reads, "Don't be late." Followed by an address and a time for Friday afternoon.

I'm not telling Janice. She'd say I'm nuts.

Though, it could translate into a sale. The nun did say it needed to be appraised.

That could keep the lights on! Doctor Patton opens my notebook and frowns. "You're not journaling as often." I nod and lean forward, hands clasped together. "I know, I'm sorry. It's just…" "And I see you mentioning this person named Chester a lot." "I…what?" I haven't journaled about him…have I? Doctor Patton scans through the few journal entries I made since our last session faster than I can finish a muffin. "I saw him staring at me at the grocery store, I don't think he knows I saw him." "I don't…" I don't remember writing that. "He was at the coffee shop again this morning, standing a few spots behind me. I got my coffee and left as fast as I could. Old Arty even pointed him out and asked if I wanna stay and join my sweetheart. I could have vomited." "Are you…" I stop myself from saying the thing that's on the tip of my tongue.

Are you sure that's my journal?

I didn't write that.

Are you messing with me?

A wave of silence passes through us. Something changes in Doctor Patton's demeanor. Her eyes drill through me, like she's trying to read my thoughts or something. I avoid her gaze, my attention darting around the room.

I focus on a stack of files on her desk with a strange logo on the top folder. At first, I think the logo is for some kind of government agency, but when I try to get a better look at it, Patton's hand slaps down on the stack of files.

"Ahem," Doctor Patton grunts. "Ms. Ward, you seem to be having trouble focusing, so I'm going to assume you're not taking your medicine."

"Umm…" I hang my head in shame. "I've been remembering more lately."

"Well, I suppose that's an improvement, but remember what I said about doing everything that's necessary?"

"I'll set another reminder."

"So, you have an admirer," Doctor Patton says, setting the journal down on top of the stack of file folders.

"That's not exactly how I'd describe it."

"But I don't see anything about your friend's gallery show. Have you made a decision there?"

"I..."

Patton sighs. "I'm going to assume that's a no."

"I know it would be good for me."

"Then go. Maybe getting out of your apartment and shop will help with your memory problems."

I nod. "Yeah…maybe."

I excavate her eyes.

Digging into her flesh like people dig pits in the earth.

Those pits run deep. They reveal nothing but darkness.

Two wombs that swallow the light.

Like spiderwebs, veins spread out from them, coating her skin with Her gift.

Her mouth. In my mind's eye it is gaping and wide.

A scream flows from her that awakens the cells of the dead and transforms that which is already living.

With my stylus, I stab into her featureless chin. I remove her flesh and form her screaming mouth.

The rage in her. It gives me life. Purpose.

With the rake tool, I scrape away at her naked form. Running it over her skin. Evidence of her sacrifice.

I trace the muscles up and down her anatomy, making sure to hint at the flesh underneath her skin. Hands answering gravity's call, bracing against the tree-limbs.

Her mouth and eyes drink the light.
Take in its warmth.
Nurturing what grows inside.

I talked myself out of going like three or four times.

Janice said I was batshit for even thinking about it.

But somehow, I end up at the address provided on the note.

The property is near the edge of town, where the forest takes over.

I park the car outside the gate.

The gate looks like something a Silicon Valley billionaire would put outside their mansion.

Except...the design is strange.

Black iron vines wrap around each of the bars, all of them flowing to the arched center of the gate. They caress a symbol I'm not familiar with, a silhouette of a woman, wrapped up in those branches.

When I stare at it, it creates a strange sensation in me.

Something familiar.

When I approach the gate, it opens, as if it has a will of its own.

I don't see any wires or an intercom, but I assume I'm just not being observant enough. ADHD and all that.

I find myself wandering up the path, enjoying the breeze. Part of me hopes that nun doesn't show.

She does, though.

The woman, nun—whatever she calls herself—is just *there* on the path. Like she appeared right out of the damn ether.

"You're late," the woman says.

"It took five minutes to walk up the path."

"It is unbecoming of us to make excuses for our shortcomings."

"You're right. I'm sorry. Is your elder still willing to meet with me?"

"Follow me."

The nun leads me down a path on the side of the crumbling stone building. I can't guess how old the church is. The stone walls look like a sculpture whose clay has been raked, revealing the flesh layer by layer. I tell myself it's just the island air, like beach homes that suffer from the salt in the air.

By instinct, I head for one of the church's doors.

The nun's gnarled hand wrenches at my wrist. "We will not be in the main temple today."

She points at the fork in the trail leading into the forest, a canopy of dense trees that remind me of the Amazon Rainforest.

As we move up the path, the trees look...off. I'm not sure how else to describe it.

Like they're the wrong kind of green. The wrong shapes.

This late into the fall season, I expect the trees to have lost their leaves.

Still, their bare branches twist and stab into the air like dead rosebushes.

The sound of our shoes crunching on dirt and gravel is deafening as we approach a gap in the canopy where the path penetrates the forest.

The opening is like a mouth agape, waiting to swallow us whole.

It's probably an understatement to say I'm nervous.

I hold myself, shivering, and wishing I brought a coat.

It is surprisingly cold.

Growing up in Southern California, there weren't too many places that got legitimately cold. Living on an island in the Atlantic has been a major adjustment, but I could have sworn the weather apps all showed temperatures in the high seventies this week.

Despite my better judgment, I follow this woman deep into the forest, where no one will ever find my body.

As we walk, I notice how little light there is. The artist in me studies the silhouettes of tree limbs and trunks in the distance. It's almost like they're embracing. Their snaking limbs climbing over each other like serpents.

But, as I study, I get the strangest feeling that we are being watched.

I clutch the idol statue tight.

And when I do...

The briefest of flashes. Like a dream.

Twisting, black branches.

Enveloping, caressing something deep within the soil.

When I snap out of it, part of me wants to turn tail and run the other direction, to get back in my car and go home.

But it's too late.

We emerge into a clearing with a stone altar at its center. The altar is a raised platform about the size of a twin bed. I can see fire pits to the right and left of it. The pits are full of charcoal and burnt things.

The detail on the altar is exquisite. Whoever sculpted it was a master of their craft.

"Impressive, isn't it?" the nun asks.

The only response I have is to nod. What the hell else can I say?

"Like the idol in your hands, it too was carved in the days long before us. The same is true of the courtyard at the center of our town, in fact."

"You…" I swallow hard. "You said this statue was a million years old, right?"

The nun nods.

"But, how can that be when we're the only intelligent life that's ever been on this planet?"

"And who told you that?"

"Umm…science?"

"Your science and history may be right about a great many things, but there are things beyond them, waiting to be discovered. How lucky are we to live in an age when such things are at our fingertips?"

I'm about ready to abandon this old hag and leave her with her creepy-ass statue and her dead trees, when I hear the voice of an elderly man calling.

That's when I see him. Like he appears from the trees.

I'd be lying if I said he isn't handsome.

Like if Bruce Campbell had a lovechild with Mitt Romney.

I resist intrusive memory of myself on the floor of my parent's apartment, kicking my legs in the air as I lay on my stomach watching

Evil Dead II: Dead by Dawn, admiring Ash's smoldering eyes and hairline and…

He smiles at me and the woman bows to him.

"Is this the young lady you told me about?" he asks.

The look in the nun's eyes as she looks at the elder is not what I would call submissive. "You will appraise the statue she has brought with her," she says.

The elder bows to her. "Yes, Matriarch."

The Matriarch gives her subject a nod and retreats down the path we came from, never making eye-contact with the elder once.

"Mrs. Ward," he says, extending his hand to mine. "It's a pleasure to finally meet you, I've heard so much."

"I thought you were the one in charge of the church?" I ask.

"I can see why you'd think that, growing up on the outside," he says. "Our faith is a matriarchal one. Agatha is the eldest of us and the wisest."

"You're not Christians?"

He smiles and extends his hand. "Mrs. Ward, we have no use for fairy tales in our faith."

I go to shake his hand, but he pulls my wrist up to his lips and kisses the back of my hand. When I finally get my hand back, the noises in the forest are drowned out by my racing pulse.

"Fairy tales…" I say. "And, it's Ms."

"You're not married?" he asks, his eyes studying me in the same way Agatha's did. The pit in my stomach has returned. "I was certain I saw a child at your shop."

"Divorced. Anyway, you wanted to see the statue?"

"Ah, yes!" His laughter is boisterous…unnatural. "Forgive me, I'm a people person. Can't help getting to know a member of our community. Please, do show it to me."

I realize I'm still clutching the idol. I release my death grip and place the statue on the altar, making sure to keep it between us. If he tries something, it'll make a wonderful club.

"Oh, it is quite exquisite!" The elder runs his hands over the idol, like someone shaping pottery clay. "The Matriarch's description hardly does the piece justice."

His fingers trace each and every branch. Fingering the empty spaces and caressing the idol's breasts.

I realize that the woman's mouth is open. Why didn't I see it before? Her eyes, dark pits. Lines, like veins coating her naked form. Like little canals. Several of the tree limbs seem like they end where her feet begin. As if they are one.

The elder basically zones out, continuing to fondle the statue for an uncomfortable amount of time.

Like I'm not even here.

"How much are you offering?" I ask.

His eyes open wide, like globes. "I-I'm sorry?"

"Your Matriarch, Agatha told you to appraise it?"

"Oh, yes, I'm sorry…" He chuckles. "Old age and all that, you know how it is."

"Will it take long?" I ask.

"What?" He seems surprised. "Oh, I'm going to need to keep it overnight."

"Oh…"

"I trust that's all right?"

"Oh, sure. And you think you'll have an answer tomorrow morning, or…?"

"Oh, yes." He smiles. "I promise."

"We should probably have a contract drawn up," I say.

"Of course. I'll have my assistant send one over by the end of the day. For now, let's just treat it like a handshake deal, yes?"

I nod.

I glance down the path. For some reason, my eyes don't want to focus on the shadows. Don't want to linger.

"Is it easy to get out of here?" I ask.

"Oh, it's quite easy to get lost in these woods." He loops his arm through mine; I try not to show my discomfort. "Allow me to escort you."

I nod, and he walks me down the path.

And as we travel, he runs his mouth some more.

"We're having a service tonight," he says. "I'm sure our dear Matriarch already told you. But it's a fantastic ceremony. Really, the whole island's going to be there, so it'd be an excellent opportunity for you to get to know the community."

"I have to pick my son up at daycare…"

"He'd be more than welcome. There are lots of boys and girls his age he could play with."

"Right…" The path. For some reason, the more we walk, the darker it gets. I check my phone for the time, but the screen is black.

I swear I charged the battery.

"Is something wrong?" he asks.

"My phone…it's dead."

"Ah, I see. This forest can sometimes have strange effects on electronics, which is why we leave ours in our rooms."

"Will I have to replace it?"

"It should be fine after you charge it."

I return my phone to my purse.

"No, I'm getting to that," he says.

When I turn back to face the elder, he has the strangest look on his face. Like he was just making eye contact with someone else.

"Did you say something?" I ask.

"Oh, it would appear we're close to the end of the trail," he says, pointing back down the path.

I saw nothing but darkness along the path this whole time. I was half convinced the sun already set. But now, instead of darkness, I see the end of the trail leading to the grassy hillsides outside their cathedral, and the unmistakable light of the blazing winter sun in the distance.

As if the forest decided to open itself up and let us go.

"Well, thank you for taking a look at the statue." I wave goodbye to the elder and attempt to leave. "But I've got to get my—"

The elder grabs my arm. His grip hurts.

"We also have a service on Sunday evening," he says. "You will join us then?" It isn't a question.

His eyes. I don't like the way he's looking at me.

I force a smile on my face. "I'll...think about it."

He releases his grip. The feeling comes back into my arm.

"You will," he says.

I nod and power walk my ass out of there.

Twisting, black branches.

Enveloping, caressing something deep within the soil.

Where the heat is perfect and nurturing.

Something that pulses with a pale, otherworldly light.

And feels like it's drawing me closer to it.

Calling to me.

Always calling.

The spotlights above my exhibition bake down on me and the sculpture I chose for this night. The intermingling smells of cannabis and cigarette smoke from people coming in from outside, how the smells cling to everyone's clothes, suffocate me. The chatter of everyone in the bar as they mingle and make the rounds to every exhibit except mine makes me wonder why I even came out tonight. Why I went through all the trouble to put on my most expensive dress and earrings... I wonder about the babysitter. Whether she's doing okay. Whether Jacob is being a good boy. And I wonder if all this, being in a bar at 11:00 at night makes me a bad mom. Clint would certainly say so. Dad's words are as real to me now as the indie music coming from Janice's speakers. He tells me a child should never be far from his mother or God's wisdom. Well, joke's on him, because I'm right next door, and all I have to do is run out the front— "You look like a fish out of water, Lisa!" Janice's touch shocks me out of my head. "Sorry..." I tilt my head away from the chatter and music. "I just feel a bit out of place here is all." "You're doing great!" "No one's come to my exhibition yet and—" She pats my shoulder. "They'll come! You're amazing!" Janice's head whips to her right, as one of the servers rushes up to her and whispers in her ear. "Something wrong?" I ask. Janice shakes her head. "I gotta take care of something in the back." And just like that, she's gone. I'm left to mingle on my own. I don't even want to look at the sculpture I chose for tonight. Janice thought I should bring more than one piece, but I didn't think the rest of my portfolio was ready just yet. I curse myself for not being ready. For letting Clint take a bat to my work. For... "This is an exquisite piece," a woman says. "You must be so proud." I smile and nod. "Thank you. It took about a month to finish it." "Well, the detail is incredible, you should be proud." "I agree," a man says to my right. "What does the piece mean? I especially love how the vines and how the tree limbs wrap around her arms." "You know," the woman says, rotating around to face the man to my right. "I want to say that the woman probably represents the goddess Aphrodite as she is dragged down by man's world." "Oh, interesting, is that true?" I'm about to explain that the woman's interpretation is all wrong, that it's not a goddess at the center of it at all, when... "Is this the piece you were mentioning the other day?" a familiar voice calls to me from my left. The blood drains from my body as I turn to him, and spot that smug smile plastered beneath his glasses.

"You're especially distracted today."

"Umm, sorry?"

I cradle my head in my hands. Why does my head hurt so damn much?

It takes me a few moments to remember where I am. My eyes find the framed inkblots behind Doctor Patton's head.

I remember picking Jacob up at preschool and then dropping him off at the kid's area here.

And then...

"You're doing it again, Ms. Ward," Patton says. "Have you been taking your medication?"

"Umm…"

"I'm going to take that as a no," Patton says. "And what about the nightmares you mentioned in last week's journal?"

"Huh?" That's funny… "I don't remember writing about nightmares."

Patton holds up the notepad.

"And I quote," she says. "'Twisting, black branches. Enveloping, caressing something deep within the soil. Where the heat is perfect and nurturing. Something that pulses with a pale, otherworldly light. And feels like it's drawing me closer to it. Calling to me. Always calling.'"

"I… I don't remember writing any of that!"

"And another entry… 'Chester woke me up late. He knows not to let me snooze my alarm, that I'll sleep all day if he lets me. Guess he thought I needed my beauty sleep.'"

I… I didn't write those words!

"So, our admirer has graduated?" Patton asks. "Is he a new boyfriend? Did you meet up at the exhibition?"

"I…"

The bar… Janice… I can remember the spotlight and my sculpture, people talking, mingling, how good it felt when people finally started to notice me, but then…

"Ah, here's another one." Patton clears her throat and holds up the journal. "'Chester is so good with Jacob. He's offered to take us both to tonight's ceremony at the main temple, and afterward we'll all go out for ice cream.'"

"I didn't write that!"

Patton is quiet for a while. Her cold stare makes me wonder how crazy I just looked. *If they institutionalize me, who will take care of Jacob?*

"This is going to sound a bit unorthodox," Patton says. "I'm going to have my assistant bring in some paints and a canvas, and I want you to paint whatever comes to mind."

"I..." I look down at my hands and try not to think about the scars. About that final night. "I haven't painted in so long... not since... I'm not sure I'll know how anymore."

"I have a feeling you will, whether you realize it or not."

"What does that mean?"

The doors behind me open and I'm sitting there, frozen, watching Doctor Patton's assistant set up an easel and a canvas.

I'm trembling when she places a palette, a cup full of brushes and a set of paints in my lap.

Why do I feel like a lab rat all of a sudden?

I shake my head. "I can't..."

Patton's eyes are full of fire as she towers over me. "I didn't ask for your opinion."

My hands grip the rake tool. I begin the meticulous process of dragging it along each of the tree limbs.

When I'm satisfied with the details, I set the rake down and retrieve my stylus. Carefully, I insert it into one of the tree limbs. When I'm done, I've created a hole. A hidden place. A dark place.

I repeat the process for all of the tree limbs.

And I make sure to include the things hidden in those dark places.

The things that watch us all.

Finally. My creation is finished.

The elders say something. Their words seem to hang like whispers around the mouth of the pit.

I rise as the whispers command and place my offering outside of it. Where She reach it.

More whispers.

And then my hands are on my gown.

It puddles around my feet.

And I kneel.

I blink.

Where the hell am I?

The first thing I notice is how cold it is. The feeling of goosebumps spread all over my body. Then, I notice something else. A smell that makes me gag and cough. One that reminds me of mold, of infected wounds, of vomit, and maggot-infested dead things.

Then I see candles and torches and men in black robes standing around me. Their bare feet touching a dirt floor. Their eyes—all of them—on me.

A glance down at myself.

I'm naked.

Five other girls are with me, naked and kneeling around a giant hole in the earth.

Their eyes are blank, like nobody's home.

I try to demand answers.

But the words fumble out of my mouth. Twisted and wrong.

I stumble to my feet. I feel…high. Like I've been drugged.

And I scream.

And no sooner as the noise leaves my lips, a man is at my back. His hands wrench my arms. His sandpaper skin grinds against me, his fingers digging into my flesh like a stylus stabbing into clay.

As he holds me, my heart races. My mind plays out every gruesome ending to this scenario it can conjure up.

How no one will ever find my body.

No one will be there for Jacob.

The man pushes me forward. I kick and scream. My eyes find the edge of the pit again. Each of the girls has placed small clay statues in front of them.

Familiar ones that mimic the look of the stone idol I was going to sell to the…

The man's breath.

It's hot on my neck.

It's hot and familiar and wrong.

"Elder Clarence, she's awake!"

Elder?

His eyes. From within his hood, I can see his piercing eyes.

Still studying me.

Sizing me up.

And then...his eyes are looking elsewhere, for approval...for...

Her.

She's wrapped up in black robes, a familiar symbol draped around her neck. The one she tried to hide from me.

But it's her.

The Matriarch.

Agatha.

"Return her to the pit," she says.

I'm struggling. The man's grip is too strong.

He pushes me back toward the pit in the floor. Back onto my knees.

That disgusting, oozing smell is so potent that I think I'm going to throw up.

I can think of only one thing to do.

I ram my fist backward into the man's balls.

When he crumples to the floor, I realize his face looks like Chester's.

He's glaring at me through broken glasses.

And then, I'm running. Falling, picking myself back up, stumbling, and running again. Scrambling through the cathedral, hunting for an exit. But, where I expect to find worn stone walls, I find nothing but darkness.

No matter how far I run, all I can see is dirt floors and cobwebs and endless shadows.

The men don't do anything to retrieve me. Even when the man I assaulted rises from his place on the dirt floor, all he does is watch me.

All he does is wait.

What do they want from me?

The words. I can feel them forming in my mouth.

I ask them where my son is.

Still, my words come out jumbled and wrong.

"I believe she wants to know where her child is," the man says.

The other figures turn their heads in my direction.

"Your son is here, my dear," Agatha says, her lips parting into a crooked smile. "He is enjoying the service, just like the rest of the community."

Their arms point to the pit.

"Return to your place, and he will not be harmed."

My heart.

I can feel it quaking in my chest.

My pulse in my temples.

So much blood rushing to my head I feel dizzy.

When my eyes find the pit again, my breath is short, my skin is flushed.

I trace the edges of the pit.

And I think of Jacob. His bright smile. The funny way he pronounced grandpa.

In my mind's eye, I see him waiting.

Always watching the door.

Waiting for Mommy to finally come home.

To play with him.

To protect him from the things lurking under his bed.

I swallow my fear.

And take a step toward the pit.

One step at a time.

"That's right, dear, you don't want your son to lose his only mother."

And another.

Until I am standing before the sculpture of a pregnant woman trapped within a prison made from my own hands.

"Kneel."

The rotting earth is cold against my knees.

"Each vessel will offer their gift to the Mother, and the Mother will bless you with gifts of Her own choosing."

I watch the others scoop up their sculptures and drop them into the pit.

The Matriarch's gaze is piercing.

"Now you."

Reluctantly, I pick the sculpture up and hold it over the pit.

When I hesitate.

When I don't let it go.

The weight.

It becomes unbearable.

And it drags me forward, and I nearly tumble into the pit.

I watch it fall into the abyss.

And when it's gone…

Six serpents pierce the dark, climbing the walls.

Once again, I scream, falling on my back. Crawling away from the pit.

And they rise, dripping, oozing with something that reminds me of pus. And they stare at me. Right through me.

I scramble, fighting through the fear. Pushing away from the pit with every fiber of my being.

The serpents slither along the dirt floor.

A glance at the other five girls, and they have all laid flat on their backs. Their legs spread for Mother's gifts. Like they actually want it…

And I wonder, Why? How could they?

Sandpaper hands wrench at my limbs.

And I see the anger in his face when he whips me around to face him.

And it is Clint's face I reel back from as I collapse in the dirt.

Agatha's words feel like a foreign language as he stalks over me, removing his broken glasses and tossing them onto the soft, rotten soil.

I see Chester's face as he grunts and wrenches at my limbs.

I see Dad's as he drags me back to the waiting serpent.

I feel Clint's hands as he slaps me when I try to crawl away.

When he smiles, it's Chester's smile.

And the pain that radiates from my gut is too much…

The world fades from away from me…and I see all three of them…Dad, Clint, and Chester…

I let the void take me.

Anything is better than this.

Anything.

I'm standing in line at the coffee shop.

There is an ache pulsing in my stomach.

Old Arty is smiling at me.

The other customers…

They're all staring at me.

I get my coffee and muffin from Old Arty, and he tells me, "May the Mother smile upon you."

I take my seat.

And I sip and stare at my muffin.

The next thing I know, someone is sitting in the seat across from me.

I didn't see him sit down.

He smiles at me with crooked teeth. Stares at me through cracked lenses.

My fist clenches up.

My stomach rumbles, spreading the ache to my back and up my spine.

"You really should eat something," he says, scratching at his beard. "You need to keep your strength up."

I don't reply. I don't know what to say. *What kind of a hint will it take for him to leave me the hell alone?*

Instinct takes over, I'm about to put my arms out in front of my chest when I realize I'm wearing a black maternity dress.

I don't remember putting it on.

"I'd like you to meet my mother," he says. "Well, I guess you've already met, but an official dinner as a family couldn't hurt, right?"

Already met?

"What are you talking about?" I ask.

"We're gonna need a ring too. Don't worry, I'll handle that. Mother's more than willing to let us use hers. It's a family heirloom after all."

"What the hell are you talking about?"

"When the baby comes," he says, as if I'm supposed to know what the hell that means. "You don't want to live improperly, right?"

I'm standing. Holding the coffee in my hand. The whole cafe is staring at me. Smiling. Waiting for me to concede. To say yes to the strangest proposal in the history of proposals.

"I'm not pregnant," I say.

"Of course you are!"

And then, they're all around me. Disembodied hands caressing my protruding stomach. An old woman I've never seen before is rubbing my shoulders, easing me back down into my seat. An old man, congratulating the greasy son-of-a-bitch sitting across from me.

They won't let me leave.

"Congratulations, Chester, we're so proud of the man you've become."

The bruises on my arms. They ache.

"Have you looked at houses yet?"

"Well, Lisa's got the apartment above our store, I'm sure we could stay there while we look for a buyer."

"Oh, I know a fantastic real estate agent. I'll give him a call and tell him to set something up with you."

"That's too kind, truly."

"Do you think she'll want to keep the shop?"

"Oh, nonsense, it's fine for a woman to stretch her legs once in a while, but her place is in the home, in the kitchen, and raising Her children."

"She'll sell it, of course. Settle down just as the Mother intended."

I think about Daddy. Sitting at the table with his newspaper, just as his daddy before him did. Learned behaviors and all that.

How the conversations changed over the years.

Mom would wait on him hand and foot.

What Daddy complained about in the paper changed year to year. One year he was complaining about the war in Iraq and Bush Jr., and the next it was how the homeless were ruining the city, and then a few more and it was how much he missed the good old days when women weren't allowed to vote, and how unions were bad and regulations held back true progress.

Daddy stopped listening to his music.

Stopped watching movies with me.

Stopped caring about who I would become.

Started asking when I'd finally settle down with a real man.

"Don't you agree?"

I snap out of it. I missed everything they were saying.

They're all looking at me, expecting me to say yes.

The exit. There's only one.

And they're surrounding me. Suffocating me. I can smell their perfume and cologne mixing, creating a noxious cloud.

I can't breathe.

He's staring at me through those broken lenses again. Sweat dotting his forehead. Lips twitching, transforming from smile to frown.

I'm not sure what to do.

Not sure how to get away.

Not when he knows where I live and work.

"Dear," he says, "answer the nice lady."

I can't breathe and the cafe is spinning. There's a pain inside me, coming from deep within my stomach. A pain so complete that all I can think about is how it shouldn't be there.

I feel... I feel violated...

My thoughts are racing. I think about how bad things will be for me if I snap. If I say what's really on my mind.

Sandpaper hands wrench at my limbs.

I see Clint as he slaps me.

"I'm not your goddamn girlfriend!"

The whole cafe goes quiet.

"And I'm not pregnant!"

They're shocked. I'm cutting through the cafe's patrons. Ignoring their bewildered expressions. And I charge through exit.

I don't give a damn what they think.

No way in hell I'm gonna end up in another situation like that.

I swore, never again!

I'm halfway up the street, breathing heavily.

Every step becomes a struggle.

The empty street and its lies. They swarm around me. Like a storm of ever-watchful eyes.

Always watching. Always waiting.

Just like the forest...

I'm staring at my own reflection. Finding where my dress's collar meets the skin of my neck.

In the reflection. I see it. My bulging gut.

Instinct takes over. My hand stifles my screams. Black tears carve trenches in my cheeks.

And I feel it kick.

Like serpents, writhing beneath my skin.

Jacob is running circles around the store today.

I was four hours late opening up.

No customers.

But every time someone walks by the windows, I freeze up.

I have my appointment with Doctor Patton today after work.

Hopefully I can keep it together until then. I'm sure she'll have a field day with all this.

Maybe she'll give me something for these panic attacks?

When the door finally rings, I scream.

But when my eyes dart up to see who's come through the door, I see her. Agatha. The Matriarch.

My breath seizes in my chest. My fingers clawing into the counter.

"Mrs. Ward," she says, scowling right through me, "I was here promptly at 9:00 a.m. You weren't here. In fact, I came back at 10:00 a.m. and 11:00 a.m. and you still had not kept to your appointment and opened your store."

I want to respond. But I can't.

She's coming toward me.

The pit in my stomach…it's transformed into a dull ache.

I don't want her near me. I want her to leave!

To leave and never come back!

I'm hyperventilating.

"If you expect patrons to frequent this establishment, then you should really keep to your appointments."

Store hours aren't an appointment you fucking hag!

My fingers...soon they're covering my ears, digging at my scalp.

"Mrs. Ward, are you listening to me?"

Then, her hands are on my wrists, pulling them away from my ears—

It happens so fast.

One second, she's grabbing me...

The next, she's lying on the carpet, and covering her face.

And then I'm alone.

There's an envelope full of money on the counter and I'm sobbing into my hands, wondering what the fuck is wrong with me.

Jacob is watching from the other end of the store. His face is full of confusion.

I don't know what to say to him.

I tell him Mommy's okay, she just had a little freak out is all. Mommy's fine. Just needs her coffee.

That's right.

That's what she needs.

I pick up the envelope and open it.

It falls from my hands when I see what's inside.

The cash spills out on the counter.

Thousand dollar bills. So many of them.

With this, the rent'll stay paid for years...

But then my eyes catch something else inside the envelope. I tip the envelope over and let it fall into the center of my palm.

It's a diamond engagement ring.

My eyes. They drift to the windows, to the stores across the street.

For some reason, I start thinking about how I never see anyone in them. No owners. No customers.

Even Janice has stopped coming by. No text messages. No calls. Like she never existed at all.

In fact, I can't recall any customers here other than...other than...

My text message ringtone goes off.

I drag my phone out of my pocket.

Chester: Why haven't you been returning my calls?

The second my brain registers the name I toss it on the counter and scream like it's gonna give me a disease.

Jacob's at my side, doing his best to comfort me as I curl up into a ball and sob into my hands.

But my phone...

It doesn't stop.

Text after text comes through.

And against my better judgment, I'm fumbling for the phone and opening up the messages and...

You better fucking answer me.

I know you're reading this!

You think you can ignore me? Get rid of me?

You're mine. Body, soul, everything!

Mother said so!

Just wait! You can't get rid of me, no matter how much you try!

Answer your fucking phone, you whore!

My own screams wake me.

But I can't move.

It takes me a minute to realize I'm not fighting for my life.

I'm in my bed. My heart is racing, my cheeks flushed, and...

When I glance down, my sheets are covered in blood.

Did I get my period last night?

Confused, I check my calendar. I'm early. By two weeks.

I make a note to call my doctor and spend the first part of my morning putting my bedsheets in the wash.

The time. I should have noticed the time.

It's 12:00 p.m.

What day is it?

Tuesday?

How is it Tuesday?

The cold touch of a faux marble countertop makes me scream.

I don't know why I'm so jumpy. Why I can never seem to get enough air.

Why I feel like my insides are being ripped apart.

Why the sound of the washer spinning is deafening.

Why my legs won't support my weight.

Why I'm embracing the floor.

"Mommy?"

I'm having a panic attack.

I can barely turn my head. Feels like the bathroom is spinning.

But when I do, I see Jacob standing in the doorway, holding his stuffed purple octopus. His favorite.

Seeing him is enough to calm me down.

I stretch my arms out to him, and we embrace.

He's okay.

I'm okay.

But then...then I see someone else in the doorway.

He's got new glasses, but everything else about him is the same.

He comes into the bathroom and wrenches Jacob away from me with his monstrous hands, smiling as he does.

"Jacob, you need to let your mother do her chores," Chester says. "Come on, we'll play some videogames or something."

"Okay..."

My heart's racing in my chest.

Watching him put his hands on my kid.

Leading him away. Smiling. Laughing.

As if he's some kind of father figure for him!

I'm scrambling to pull myself together, to force myself to stand and scream and fight. "Let go of my son and get out of my goddamn home!"

Chester hardly seems phased by what I've said. He turns slowly to me, a dark look in his eyes. "Oh, dear. You're not yourself. It's okay. I'm not offended."

Jacob's pulling on his manila jacket. "Is Mommy okay?"

"Oh, she's just fine. Must be the medication that nasty therapist of hers prescribed."

I'm crawling, fists clenched.

The pain in my guts…

What's wrong with me?

Why can't I move?

"She shouldn't be taking bad stuff like that."

"No, no I think you're right. Especially not with the baby on the way. In fact, I think it's time for her to stop seeing that nasty lady, don't you think, Jacob?"

"Yeah!"

My palms are on the floor.

They come together.

Ball into fists.

I stare at the man who is wrapping his arm around my son.

And I tell myself not to forget this time.

I scream myself awake.

The room is a blur.

It was all a dream.

I remind myself over and over.

My vision begins to clear.

I reach for the water I always keep on my nightstand.

Sandpaper hands wrench at my wrist.

And there he is.

Smiling through crooked teeth.

Staring through broken frames.

"I've got you, Lisa," he says, returning my hand to my stomach. "You took a nasty fall."

I can't speak. Can't get my breathing under control.

The door is cracked. I panic, wondering what he's done with Jacob. Where is my little boy?

"Jacob is fine," he says, smiling like he knows something I don't.

I can barely get the words out. I feel like I've been drugged.

"Don't worry, he's with the other children at the cathedral."

No matter how far I run, all I can see is dirt floors and cobwebs and shadows.

"I told them we'd be absent tonight, but they'll be expecting us tomorrow night." He stands up. His glasses reflect the light from the hall, hiding the evil I'm certain is lurking behind his eyes. "So, rest up."

When he leaves the room, I try to scream. I try to move. But my limbs, my voice…they're not mine anymore.

My shop is empty.

Always empty.

I am an unwilling participant, watching from across the street. Staring through the windows as the dust collects on the shelves, on the merchandise.

My reflection stares back at me.

My mouth, forever open. Screaming silently as I watch the world forget everything I ever was or wanted to be.

The serpents. They have spread. Wrapping about my appendages like floral wire around a metal armature. And now that they have, the clay is ready to be added.

My eyes rot within my head.

My skin sweats white and viscous.

My hair is stringy, as though it's always wet. Always slimy.

And my stomach.

It bulges and it breathes and it grows with each passing breath.

My silent screams wake me.

My eyes wander. The only things that are still mine.

I'm sitting in a pew, surrounded by what I assume is the entire town.

Sandpaper skin caresses my hand. Thick fingers coax my clenched fist open. My hand obeys.

"Daddy?" Jacob's voice is a comfort as long as I don't think about the thing that just came out of his mouth.

I force my eyes into the peripheral.

And there he is. Sitting next to *him*. Tugging on *his* sleeve.

"Is the Mother going to cure Mommy?" Jacob asks.

His free hand pats Jacob's head.

"Of course," he says. "Of course She will, son."

Son?

When did that happen?

What is going on?

Why am I here?

How much time has passed?

An organ plays. Its sound bounces off unfamiliar stone walls.

Ancient stone, yet youthful.

Built in the time of man.

As Elder Clarence takes to the pulpit, I know it's a lie.

These walls are just a facade.

A wall meant to hide the true temple that lies beneath. In the earth.

How do I know this? Why am I so confident that these things are true?

"Welcome, my community," Elder Clarence says, his voice booming thanks to the stone walls. "Soon, our fertility festival will commence. And this one is truly special, my friends. For this one will bring about a new era. A new age."

The congregation cheers.

Elder Clarence holds his hand up. "For too long, we have been a small island in the middle of a vast, dreaming sea. Drifting between what is real and what is made of dreams. But as our sacred books tell us, the Mother's touch is ever-changing, and no mortal mind can resist her truth. The true, powerful change that is possible from her touch is undeniable. As the six mothers in our congregation would attest, if they had not taken a vow of silence."

The elder's gaze falls on we six. On those that have been cursed and robbed of our most precious gift.

Our voices.

My eyes. They find the others.

A woman with black hair, blue eyes. Her eyes find mine. Though my mind is swimming with knowledge that isn't mine, I don't know her name.

It's not important.

Another woman, this one is black. I remember her as having an afro. Now her hair is flat. Sweaty. Sickly.

Another is blonde, with sad brown eyes.

Another has light brown hair and Salvadorian features.

Another is young. Too young. Her skin was once smooth, her hair brilliant and blue in the island's setting sun.

She came here to get away. A vacation from her life. From school.

Funny how I know these things.

Funny how I don't know their names.

I know they'll never know mine.

"You all were lied to by the outside world. When they told you the meek would inherit the Earth. No. The meek will inherit nothing. They will be devoured and remade in Her image in the coming dawn.

"But *we* will be shepherds of the Mother's changing hand. With our Matriarch's wisdom as our sword, we will restore sanity to this insane world. We will make it right. We will all make it right again.

"As our Matriarch teaches, the common woman's place is not to think of a life outside of her household. No. It is in her home, by the bedside, where she will foster our future.

"Never again will a child be without a father. Without their mother.

"And never again will a woman forsake the gifts of the Mother. May she reign forever."

The congregation agrees. They show it by cheering for Elder Clarence and their Matriarch.

My head is full of knowledge.

It swims before my eyes. Shadows whispering to me like black goats lost in the woods.

But they are not lost.

No.

And they tell me secrets.

We six know.

And yet, our curse is to never be able to warn the others. The others who listen, who believe their lies and drink of their venom as if it's wisdom.

But…we know something else.

Something even Agatha doesn't know.

They think they can control what's coming.

To bend it to their will.

But they're wrong.

SHE. IS. WRONG.

My store is empty.

Always empty.

I'm staring at my reflection.

I don't recognize myself.

My body is bulging. My limbs are tumorous and wrong. My skin is gray in the torchlight that lines the streets.

Thick, black, snaking webs cover me head to toe.

The pain is a dull roar. I know if I were myself, it would be excruciating.

I can hear voices.

Singing, chanting, melodious ones.

The serpents pull at the armature beneath.

They guide me up the torch-lit street.

My heart is calm. My mind is not.

They can't take that from me.

I'm standing in the dark before a crowd in the town courtyard.

The island's population is gathered, some of them holding tiki-torches.

They have no idea what's about to happen.

They turn to me, and five others.

We're naked.

Naked and fat and growing. Festering.

Ready to burst.

Their eyes are uncertain as they gaze at us.

I can feel their doubts, their fear that everything they've been sold that has led to this night is a lie.

But it's too late.

Their fears erode as they remind themselves to obey the Matriarch.

As they remember to deny what their eyes see.

The crowd separates. They make a path for us and turn their attention to the elevated platform at the center of the courtyard.

My eyes scan the crowd for Jacob, for the man who stole him from me.

But they find nothing.

Did they escape?

Why is it so hard to remember?

At the center of the courtyard is a hole in the earth.

It wasn't there before.

I'm sure of that.

Elder Clarence tells us to approach the pit.

Tells the crowd that now is the moment.

They're about to enter a new dawn.

A new age.

My only comfort is that it will be an age without them.

The elder's words are hollow, filled with lies and platitudes for a future that none of these fools will see.

But, then Agatha ascends the stone altar and extends her ring finger.

And Elder Clarence bows.

And he kisses her hand.

The next thing I know, Agatha has taken his place, and he remains on his knees.

"My community," Agatha says, her voice booming through the courtyard like a dark goddess rallying her seraphim. "Tonight is a special night. Long have I waited for the six vessels who stand before you now, ready to bear the gifts of the Mother unto the world. You have all waited so patiently as we studied the hidden truths in the *Cultes Des Goules*. As we devoted ourselves to the Mother, hopeful that we would one day be worthy of receiving the Her gifts.

"And now, on this night of immense cosmic significance, She will cure the sickness in this world and return humanity to its rightful place.

"But—" Agatha's lips twist into a smile, one that reminds me of rotting, ancient wood. "I'm afraid none of you are quite prepared for what is to come. In order for our world to be reborn, many of you will have to suffer. But worry not. This suffering will not be in vain, for it will lead to a new age. A golden age where humankind is transformed with the power of the Mother's gifts.

"Now, I must know. Are you ready to sacrifice? Are you ready to do your part?"

The gathered masses cheer.

My eyes trace the grooves in the stonework, leading to the pit. They're everywhere. Beneath their shifting feet, like geometric veins carved into the surface by a forgotten sculptor.

We're all standing on an altar.

And none of them have figured it out.

"Wonderful," Agatha says, her dark eyes sweeping over them. Her tongue lashing out, licking her lips. "Join me in prayer!"

And they obey. Their inhuman words fill the courtyard, and tower up to pierce the island's churning, boiling skies.

To peel back the veil to reveal the Mother's hand.

"Iä! Iä! Shub-Niggurath!" they chant. "*Ph'wgah'kul, mak'k'io lw'nafh, shaf'ra, Mor'tia! Iä! Iä!*"

The pain in my guts.

The burning, seething, spreading sensation.

It travels up my spine and caresses my brain.

"Iä! Iä! Shub-Niggurath! Ph'wgah'kul, mak'k'io lw'nafh, shaf'ra, Mor'tia! Iä! Iä!"

And I fall. My legs unable to support my own inhuman girth.

I am on the ground, my eyes focused on the churning, boiling sky.

It is now that I see Her.

Twisting, black branches.

Enveloping, caressing something deep within the pit.

Where the heat is perfect and nurturing.

She pulses with a pale, otherworldly light.

She's calling to me.

Always calling.

Telling me to come closer.

It is deep within the pit. The place where She waits for the stars to be made right.

Where She will emerge to remake us in her own image.

Our true Mother.

My thoughts are shattered by a stabbing, drilling, seething pain in my guts.

With a mind of their own, my legs spread.

The pain…all consuming…

It's nothing like Jacob. Nothing at all.

Their dripping, hoofed appendages come out first. Their birth-cries mask our collective screams.

"Iä! Iä! Shub-Niggurath!"

With cloven feet, they take their first steps. Our children. Her gift to us for suffering so.

"Iä! Iä! Shub-Niggurath!"

They stand tall, taller than any man.

Their tendrils rise to the sky, curling and stabbing at the air around them.

Fools would mistake them for trees.

Their dark eyes sweep over the gathered flock.

As if they are an offering presented by Her bosom.

"Iä! Iä! Shub-Niggurath!"

Their appendages lash out like gnarled, wooden scythes, rending their victims limb from limb. Spilling their blood upon the stone altar.

Their inhuman mouths, adorned with human teeth, gnash and grind into their flesh.

"Iä! Iä! Shub-Niggurath!"

The chanting quickly turns to screams as their life's blood flows through the small canals built into the altar.

The canals run red with their blood.

And flow into the waiting pit at the center.

The Mother's womb.

Their screams transform into a panic, and they scatter like cockroaches, fleeing for the edges of the altar.

It is a comfort to see them reap what they sow. The result of playing with forces they did not understand.

A shadow falls upon Agatha. Her arms raised to the boiling sky.

Her gnarled smile fades.

I watch in delight as my offspring rends her flesh and splits her in half.

As she falls into the pit, her eyes full of shock and betrayal.

I return her smile.

To think she thought she would be exempt.

Soon, though, the screams die.

And our children, the Mother's gifts.

They march.

March back to the forest where they belong.

Where they will stand like sentinels.

Their eyes ever watchful.

As they wait for the stars to be made right.

When they are gone, and my blood has almost drained into that waiting pit.

I crawl toward my destiny.

To embrace Her deep within.

And I wonder if Jacob made it to safety.

And I pray.

That the Mother will spare him.

Beyond the Gardens of Good and Evil

A *Cthulhu Armageddon* Story

By C.T. Phipps

This takes place between *The Tower of Zhaal* and *The Tree of Azathoth*

Chapter One

"In-A-Gadda-Da-Vida" by Iron Butterfly was playing on the old jukebox in the Wages of Sin. The Wages of Sin was a brothel, bar, inn, and Sheriff's office all in one. Mostly because it was one of the few buildings left standing from before the Rising as well as one of the few places in town that had electricity. It had been a cheap motel with four levels before the end of civilization and the upper two levels had collapsed but the lower two still stood and were the center of social life in the tiny cattle town that was full of the lost.

Most communities remaining in the New England Wasteland were isolated, suspicious, and inbred. They turned inward rather than outward and gradually fell one by one in the face of a world transformed by the Great Old Ones into an endless ruin-filled desert. New Ulthar was different and not just because there were hundreds of cats everywhere, somehow living unchanged despite every other animal being extinct or strangely mutated.

It was, simply, a town of outcasts. Every one of its citizens was an exile from one of the other communities here, either fleeing the consequences of some crime they'd committed or driven out for reasons known only to them. There were children of cults, half-human hybrids, petty wizards, and lovers whose choice of partner was forbidden. People minded their own business in New Ulthar and it was perhaps the last place on Earth a man like me might feel welcome.

So, with that established, understand how peculiar one has to be to draw the attention of the various customers of the Wages of Sin. It was only the afternoon and the crowd consisted mostly of those who required alcohol more than sex. It had been a slow day with only one murder this morning—two cattle men getting into a fight that ended with one dead—so I'd just been sitting at the front desk with a battered copy of a Countess Zorzi novel from before the Rising. I'd found the book while looting an office building populated by mindless, blind ghasts.

It was fun.

Hearing the usual mutterings and casual profanity cease, I looked up to see the newcomer who was standing in front of me with a broad smile on her face. She had pale white skin, bright brown hair cut in a page boy style, and perfectly straight teeth. Clean too. Smelled vaguely of lilacs. The woman looked to be in her early thirties and was wearing a bright blue jumpsuit with overalls that seemed fresh from the laundry. A beaten newsboy's cap was resting on her head, the only thing looking like it came from the Wasteland.

"Good morning, barkeep!" the woman said, cheerfully. "I wish to partake in your wares as well as hopefully peruse your mind for information."

"Uh huh," I said, taking out a clay mug for her. "And you are?"

"Doctor Brianna Lethder," the woman said. "I am a scientist."

"You don't say," I said, noting that her words were immediately indicative of using a fake name but only one in a hundred thousand of humanity's survivors would probably get the joke.

Brianna Lethder was also known as the Mad Nun, a twelfth century Medieval French novitiate who suffered from visions, probably epilepsy, and periods of amnesia. She wrote her visions down in a book that eventually became known as the *Re'Kithnid*. The book contained many of the creatures from the *Necronomicon* and *Book of Eibon* but reframed in alchemical terms with each of the Great Old Ones envisioned as an elemental that was part of a larger family. Hastur was

Cthulhu's half-brother and so on. It furthermore envisioned the Great Old Ones as engaged in a cosmic battle of good versus evil with the Elder Gods (the Elder Gods being the good). The late Doctor Alan Ward had owned an English translation annotated by English magician and skeptic, Titus Crow.

I poured her a drink of mud beer, noting she hadn't asked for anything specific, and passed it to her. "Here you go."

"Thank you, kindly!" The woman said, drinking the entire thing in one go. Something that would have knocked out most people since mud beer bordered the line between beer and spirits in terms of potency. "Ah, earthy. The fecund taste adds an interesting flavor. Mushrooms?"

"They grow in the dark and feed on shit," I said, simply. "Much like people."

"Yes, it is a rare staple item that humans are still able to cultivate," Brianna said, nodding as if making an especially profound observation.

"We manage," I said.

"Yeah, too bad about humanity's imminent extinction," Brianna said, tapping the side of the bar.

I grimaced. I had heard that everyone on Earth would be dead within sixty years from no less a source than an avatar of Nyarlathotep. That had been close to ten years ago and the very substance of reality was breaking down into the Dreamlands or Yog-Sothoth (it's not like I could do scientific tests). "What do you want, Doctor Lethder?"

"So respectful!" Brianna said, smiling. "Most people leave off the doctor."

"That's because the only doctors left are either the ones from the university, a den of madmen and cultists, and those who know how to saw off a gangrenous leg. Which are you?"

Brianna grimaced, the first expression I recognized as common in the Post-Rising world. "The former. I am from Miskatonic University."

"Ah," I said, as if that explained everything and it did.

My Pre-Rising knowledge was higher than most humans, assuming you qualified me as one, but it was still limited regarding matters beyond the esoteric. Still, I knew that Miskatonic University was one of the centers of learning from before the Great Old Ones destroyed almost all of human civilization a century prior. The university retreated into the steam tunnels and bunkers beneath it made during something called the Cold War. They'd expanded and built a strangely functional city with the aid of several alien races.

Neither of us said anything after that.

"We're not as strange as you might think!" Brianna said after an impressive silence.

"I see," I said, lifting a clay pitcher of mud beer. "More?"

"Sure!" Brianna said, holding up her mug. "I don't suppose you know where a Mister John Henry Booth is. Former Captain of the New Arkham Rangers?"

She was either testing me or legitimately had no idea what I looked like. "I might."

Brianna waited for an answer, not yet seeming to know how the Wasteland worked. One time a man died in the bar and it was three days before anyone removed him because no one cared enough to bother. That and the fact I'd been waiting for his family to clear his debt when they claimed his body.

Probably why they hadn't bothered.

"Ah," Brianna said, once more noting that there was an impressive silence between responses. "You require payment?"

"I'm not sure what you think passes for currency these days," I said, about ready to just walk off. The last job I'd done for the university had been trying to save the world from the Unimaginable Horror. It had gotten all of my friends killed but one and also had revealed I was part monster. There was nothing I wanted from them anymore.

"I have New Arkham dollars, Kingsport coins, and Dunwych script," Brianna said. "I also have trade goods with your associates."

I sighed. "I'm John Henry Booth. What do you want?"

If she was an assassin or cultist after me then at least I'd be able to shoot her in the face. I doubted it, though. Most of the people who wanted me dead knew what I looked like. The others were dead themselves. A six feet two inch tall black man with black eyes and no mutations was strange enough in the Esoteric East to be easily recognized.

"I want you to save the world," Brianna said, raising her mug.

"Let's see your money. You're now getting charged extra."

I heard her story.

I laughed in her face.

Then I told Mercury, my business partner and lover.

She found it less funny.

In the end, I found Doctor Lethder still hanging around the Wages of Sin's bar hours later as if she knew I'd return. Virtually all the other customers had been driven away by her strange but cheerful presence. Also, she'd decided to help herself to the mud beer and had drunk enough to put down a Deep One elder with no noticeable effects. Not that we ever had the (dis)pleasure this far inland.

"Are you ready to hear my proposal?" Brianna asked.

"No," I said.

"Absolutely," Mercury replied, standing by my side. She was wearing a pair of tight pants, boots, and a plaid button-down shirt despite being the manager of the brothel. As far as I knew, her wares were for sale and she was more useful as their doctor and manager than fellow harlot. It was a lateral career change from serving as the chief torturer of New Arkham, a job she'd been involuntarily forced into by her late husband. Late because she'd killed him.

Mercury was uncommonly lovely for the Wasteland with a peculiar combination of short red hair, freckles, and Asiatic features. Even so, the harsh living outside what passed for civilization had taken its toll. Her eyes were sunken and perpetually restless. Callouses had long since covered her hands from even the minor amount of hard labor she had to do compared to New Ulthar's other residents. Around her waist was a strange belt containing various powders and bits of bone, the meanings of which I questioned not. Instead of a gun, she simply wore a ring with an Elder sign and it had so far done more to intimidate people than any firearm.

"Are you a religious man and woman?" Brianna asked.

"I used to be an atheist. Now I believe the gods are out to get us. So I would have been Catholic Pre-Rising. Now I'm just polytheist. Propitiating the gods so they leave us alone is as close to hope as I have these days," Mercury said, making a joke I didn't really get.

"I was baptized in dirty water," I said, annoyed. "My mother was one of the last remaining Christians and my father was agnostic. He eventually murdered her and tried to kill me before I put him down. I believe in the gods, Ms. Sunset. I believe they are indifferent and those that are not are not worth worshiping. You don't want to hear my opinion of religion as a whole."

It was a great deal to unload in the first meeting with a stranger but I was hoping my confession would drive her away. There was something about the falsely named scientist that was off-putting, triggering something in the back of my alien-tainted mind. She was not right. Like recognized like.

Instead, Brianna just nodded her head as if our answers were not unexpected. "Well, I *am* religious. The Mother of Life, Shub-Niggurath, is worshiped not just on this world but by nearly all sapient races. The Fungi from Yuggoth, the Yig, the ghouls, and humanity are all beings that venerate her glory. It is by her—"

"If this is a sermon, you can go," I said, gesturing to the door.

Mercury, by contrast, walked up to the table and sat down. "Tell us about the project."

"Project: EDEN," Brianna corrected her.

"Yes, tell us about the incredibly unoriginally named government conspiracy," I said, taking a seat beside Mercury. "A government that hasn't existed for a century or more and couldn't do anything against the Great Old Ones in the six or seven minutes that it lasted before the end of humanity's capacity to fight back."

"Well, I explained it to your friend, Captain Booth—" Brianna started speaking.

"Sheriff or just John," I said, less because I was being familiar and more because I didn't want any association with my soldier days. That life had ended in betrayal and death, though I couldn't tell you who betrayed who.

"Thank you, John," Brianna said, smiling awkwardly. "Well, as I explained to you—"

"Please just start from the beginning," I replied. "I'm sure I lost some of the subtleties."

"In between mocking the very idea, yes," Mercury said. "I'm not as incredulous as John at the prospect of saving humanity."

I didn't respond because there was nothing to respond to. Mercury still believed there was hope. It was not a belief that I held. It was better to accept the coming doom of mankind—particularly one's own—with grim determination.

"Of course," Brianna said, nodding. "The story starts before the Great Rising."

"Obviously," I muttered.

Brianna ignored my response. "There were people who knew of the Great Old Ones before the end of the world, even while the vast majority of humanity remained blissfully ignorant of the coming end of everything. A fraction of humanity has always been aware of the true origins of life on this planet. Cults existed dedicated to Great Cthulhu, Yog-Sothoth, and beings like Yig or the Unimaginable Horror. Usually, these cults were incredibly wrong in the finer details, though. However, one might argue the very concept of gods was inspired by—"

"We know," I said.

Mercury seemed to pause for a moment as the name Cthulhu caused her to dig her fingernails into the side of the table before her. We'd joined the ranks of a precious few who had seen the miles-tall monster and survived. Whereas I, inhuman as my soul might be, survived with my sanity intact, the experience had driven Mercury irrevocably mad. Well, perhaps not irrevocably, as an associate had destroyed the memories that she'd gained of the experience. It was a horrific procedure but had allowed her to recover. It had also awakened her latent talent for sorcery and created a great lust for the secrets of the arcane.

"Not all of the people who knew of the Great Old Ones thought of them as enemies to fight or gods to worship, though," Mercury said.

"Some of the individuals who knew of them thought of them as indifferent cosmic forces that could be harvested for good or evil. One of them, Doctor Ruthanna Bloom, was an associate of my... ancestor. She believed that the only way for humanity to survive was through using the Old One's power for mankind's benefit."

"So, she was a fool," I said, unwilling to let that statement go.

Brianna's entire demeanor changed, and her eyes became cold, intense, and furious. Her teeth clenched. "She was a genius."

"John won't speak again," Mercury said, elbowing me. "Will you?"

I shrugged and crossed my arms.

"Doctor Bloom became familiar with the religion of Shub-Niggurath and its many variants during the 1960s. Combining LSD, hallucinogenic plants, and the mystic practices of several cultures, she believed she made contact with witch ancestors dating back to the Pre-Hyborian Valusian age."

I kept my thoughts to myself.

Mercury, by contrast, seemed enraptured. "Fascinating. Was she a student of the university?"

"No, she was actually from Hall School that had gone on to form its own university branch after an endowment from Eleanor Roosevelt. They were always more open-minded due to its founder, Jezebel Bowen, being the daughter of Church of—"

"Go on," I said, breaking my silence already. It was deeply suspicious she had so much knowledge of a time period buried by the seas of time and disaster. Very few records survived from the time before the Great Old Ones.

"Doctor Pears and my ancestor formed Project: EDEN with the help of a variety of incredibly wealthy sponsors over the course of the next few decades. They were aided by Project: Blue Book and UFO watchers as well as Christian fundamentalists with a belief in the apocalypse that provided the funds. The American President, Ronald Reagan was an especial believer in the occult so that when—"

"What is Project: EDEN, really?" Mercury, for once, was the one to interrupt.

"It is an extra-dimensional space that contains an ark of the Pre-War environment," Brianna said. "A place where humanity is capable of living and growing outside the Great Old Ones. I know where it was created. It might even contain humans."

That was when the wall exploded and a green, ivy-covered tentacled thing went for Brianna Lethder's throat.

Chapter Two

Well, that was unexpected.

I must admit that when living in the Wasteland you must be ready for things to go to shit suddenly with no warning. New Arkham has been one of the biggest and strongest settlements yet ended up being demolished by a random Cthulhuoid smashing through the place like a man walking over an ant hill.

In this case, the man walking over our ant hill seemed determined to go after Brianna Lethder specifically, and she called out a rather theatrical scream while trying to protect herself with her arms against the monstrous plant-thing. At least, I thought it was a plant-thing. Some things were beyond description and humanity just had to muddle through as best they could in making poor comparisons. Sort of like how the color fuchsia didn't exist in nature but was just the brain attempting to fill in the blanks.

The plant-thing—for no other name came to mind—seemed like it was a mixture of flora and fauna with its green, vine-like tentacles coming out of an eight-legged plate-covered body that was animal in nature. Its hideous mouth was a gaping pit surrounded by a pair of Venus flytrap-like mandibles. It was at least the size of a jeep and looked like it had exploded out of the ground outside the Wages of Sin. I couldn't help but imagine it akin to a plant and ant-hybrid that could possibly be the forefront of a vast colony of them about to rise among us.

"*Ich Ve Al-Pharaza! Ack Mett Un Cthugha! Ack Mett Un Hastur! Ack Mett Un Re'Kithnid!*" Mercury shouted, raising a green stone amulet from beneath her shirt. The object burned brightly and caused the creature to rear back as if blinded despite having no visible eyes.

I recognized the incantation from the *Re'Kithnid* and wondered where Mercury had managed to find a copy. It was an idle thought that was disrupted by two near-simultaneous moments of staggering pain. The first was the light of Mercury's spell that had left a horrifying burn on my arm and the side of my face, which I only registered seconds after they had happened. It was a reminder that the magic of the Elder Gods—or whoever was behind Mercury's magic—hated me as much as they hated the other supposed creatures of the Great Old Ones.

The second was that the plant-thing had reached out its tentacles—more prehensile vines really—and they bit me. Yes, the vines had mouths and very sharp teeth that bit into my burned flesh like lampreys. It was a more horrifying experience than the burning because of the primordial fear of being eaten alive which every living organism capable of thought has.

I was not someone who went down easily, though, and with my other arm I pulled out my revolver and aimed the weapon into the center mass of the creature's maw. The gun had been made by Mercury and blessed with every single invocation to what Small Gods of Earth might lend a portion of their power to humanity's survivors. As for the bullets? They were made of Deep One gold, mined from the reef beds of R'lyeh, and carried some of the strange radiation of Great K'Tulu's homeworld in its impurities.

The plant-thing let out a distinctly painful roar as three of the bullets penetrated it, searing holes where they struck and burying themselves into its extradimensional skin. The parts struck by Mercury's spell started to wither and if it had any sort of intelligence, it must have realized that we were hardier prey than it expected.

Unfortunately, that did little to aid our situation as whatever intelligence it possessed did not see retreat as an option. Instead, the creature reorientated itself and came after me directly. The massive things vines enveloped me and I found myself pulled towards its gaping maw.

Surrender to your true self, echoed in my mind. More as a concept than direct words.

"No!" I called out, struggling vainly as the plant-thing's mandibles prepared to crush me into pieces. *I can't. I won't!*

I will guide you.

Survival instinct won out over my desire to never give in to the monster within. I screamed as my bones morphed within my arms, shooting out as black steely tendrils and impaling the monster around me. Raw fury took me over as my body grew a hideous exoskeleton that formed into armor around me. My sight transformed from human into something wholly alien that detected the creature as an intruder on this level of 4-dimensional space.

I was not human, not truly, but a savage alien thing that just so happened to have been merged with a half-human babe before becoming the thing that could pass for a man. What I became did not think like a man, but it was similar enough to turn the primordial urges on the plant-thing.

I *fed*.

"John, John!" Mercury's voice echoed inside me.

Awaken, Kastro'vaal, the voice spoke in my mind. *Your power is not needed now.*

I fell to my knees and spat out the plant-flesh in my mouth. I was covered in gore and viscera with my clothes torn to shreds. The creature before me was dead, torn to pieces, and both Mercury and Doctor Lethder were beside me.

Who are you? I spoke to the voice with my mind.

You know, the voice replied.

I looked at Doctor Lethder, who just smiled as she pulled out a strange starfish shaped metal object which she ran over me. "Interesting."

I batted her hand away. "What the hell is that?"

"A scientific instrument," Brianna said, blinking. "It's fascinating what you are. Do you know—"

Mercury picked up my gun and pointed it at the back of Brianna's head. "You didn't see anything?"

Brianna seemed less concerned than a woman in her situation might have. Both at being around an inhuman monster in human form, and at having a gun pointed at her head. Then again, if she was the voice in my head then she wasn't exactly human herself.

"What are you?" I asked.

"A person with a vested interest in humanity's survival," Brianna said. "Perhaps the only one who still does who can make a difference."

I can help you control what you are, the voice spoke in my mind as she narrowed her eyes.

I don't want to, I thought back, looking at my hands. I want to be human.

That's possible too, Brianna lied. *I can make you whatever you want if you help me reach the Goddess' sanctuary.*

But I was willing to believe her. "Tell us *everything*."

"When you agree," Brianna said, calmly.

I looked at Mercury. She was staring at me with a pleading look in her eyes.

"I agree," I said, sighing.

"Good," Brianna said, looking down at the creature with a disgusted look on her face. "Then allow me to reveal something since we are now friends."

"That's going a bit far," I muttered, disgusted with myself. Even so, I couldn't help but feel a sense of power and pride. I had transformed voluntarily for the first time without losing control, even if I had been "helped." If Brianna Lethder had psychic powers, magic, or some hidden science then maybe it meant I wouldn't have to worry about becoming a monster. I would swear my allegiance, life, and whatever was left of my soul if it meant that I would not be a threat to those I loved.

"Put on some clothes, John," Mercury said. "I'm pretty sure we're going to be mobbed by visitors in a bit."

I looked to the giant hole in the wall and shook my head. "The people of New Ulthar are survivors. They see a monster emerge from the ground; they aren't going to run to it."

Nevertheless, I did go to my nearby office and cover myself in a blanket before coming back out.

"I repeat John's question. What are you?" Mercury asked. "Because you're certainly not human. No matter what you appear to be."

Brianna's expression didn't change. "My body is human. I would not share this except for the fact you just saved my life and demonstrated a certain kinship. My people are as old as the stars and from long before this time. We will also be far in the future."

"You're Yith," I said. "The body snatchers."

The Yith were not the first sentient race on Earth, at least according to what I knew of ancient Earth history, but they were close to it. They'd lived during the Cretaceous Period among the dinosaurs and their heyday had lasted millions of years. What little I knew of them beyond this was that they had mastered the power of time travel and were psychic beings versus physical ones. They wore the bodies of other races and species like suits of clothes and seemed wholly unconcerned about the ethics of possession. Which, admittedly, was a good idea not to confront them with.

Brianna blinked. "My, you are well informed. Yes, I am of the Great Race. I have held dozens of bodies of women and men across the short millennia of your species' history. It is through my mind that I have provided a context for your people to understand much of this world."

I narrowed my eyes. "Why?"

"Why should I show compassion to a less-developed people?" Brianna asked.

"Yes," I said, bluntly.

Brianna frowned. "This is not the future that was promised to our race. Humanity was eventually supposed to live a long—at least by your standards—life then pass to oblivion. My race would then take the next species to dominate this world as its own. That will not be possible, though, because this world is ceasing to exist."

Spoken bluntly. "So, you're not seeking this Project: EDEN because it's a home for humanity. Instead it's a home for *your* people."

Brianna smiled. "You keep seeking a cynical reason for this to happen. No, the Yith will simply seek a home beyond this one. Either this dimension or another. Project: EDEN depends on Yithian technology. I know because I taught Doctor Bloom it. Well, the elements that could be understood by humans."

She was lying.

Or, worse, selectively withholding the truth.

"Why would you say that?" Brianna asked, looking at me and making it clear she was reading my mind.

"What?" Mercury asked.

"Why was that creature after you?" I asked. "It wasn't here by chance. Even in the Wasteland, random monsters do not pass through half a village to go after a trio of people in an empty bar. It knew who you were and wanted you."

Brianna blinked slowly. "You're right."

"He is?" Mercury asked, confused.

Brianna looked at Mercury with a chiding, almost parental look. "I know Project: EDEN exists because I have been there. It's a place defended by creatures of both science and sorcery. Well, if you can call the primitive superstitions of mankind to be science. I mean, your race still believes in germs."

Mercury, who was a doctor educated in New Arkham's education system, opened her mouth before closing it. "That the people we'd be seeking out don't want us there is a pretty significant detail to leave out, Doctor Lethder. Perhaps more so than the fact you're not human."

Brianna shrugged. "Humanity is overrated. Not even *most* of humanity was human during its prime."

I wasn't in any place to argue, especially if her claim of making me human was true. "What happened when you visited?"

"The automated—for lack of a better term—defenses of Project: EDEN prevented me from getting close," Brianna said. "The creations of the project's genetic engineering keep away any individuals that might try and break in."

"I suddenly see why you want us," I muttered. "What do you really hope to find?"

"Like I said, an escape," Brianna said. "The university plays with stupid plans to live underground with the ghouls or seek asylum in the Dreamlands. A few even believe that mankind can be altered into becoming like the Old Ones. No, the only options are through Yith technology. To live in a preserve of a dead world's ecology. The Great Mother is your only hope as a race."

It sounded very much like she considered what she was doing to be akin to a that of a Pre-War conservationist. "You want this world to be a zoo for mankind."

"It *is* a zoo for mankind," Brianna said. "I cannot return to the past. My fellow Great Race members do not accept what I have been doing as necessary or wise. However, I am willing to keep moving forward. I believe the Great Mother blessed Doctor Bloom with immortality and her people are still there with her. It is my desire to join her and I offer to you the same."

"Will we have to deal with more of these creatures?" I asked, looking over at the deceased plant-thing.

"Yes," Brianna said. "It is also a long journey across punishing wilderness and strange environments. Project: EDEN was constructed past the Canadian-Chicago border. I was able to make it here from there, but I lost my original crew of six."

I exchanged a glance with Mercury. It was clear her enthusiasm for this mission had waned with all the revelations that had occurred in short order.

"John?" Mercury asked.

"I said I would," I said, pretending that it was a matter of honor versus reckless hope. Brianna was clearly a liar and if she really was a Yith—telepathy pointing to that being the truth—then she was even more likely to view us as expendable pawns. Yet, I would do anything to be human, and this was the first hope I'd had in years.

A fool's hope or not.

"I dunno," Mercury muttered. "Maybe if you could—"

"I'll share some of my race's magic," Brianna said, handing the starfish device to Mercury. "Knowledge of the higher mathematics that your race would have to make a pact with the Dark One to achieve."

"I'll do it," Mercury said, too quickly.

It seemed everyone had their price and the Yith in the body of some poor young woman from the university knew how to pay them. One thing I'd learned in my time in the Wasteland, though, was that if someone was willing to pay any price in their promises, then they probably did not intend to pay anything at all.

Brianna chuckled at that thought. "Oh John, you say the funniest things."

Yeah, this was a bad idea.

But we were committed now.

Chapter Three

The city of Pnakotus was beyond beautiful, at least to the strange compound sensory organs that my new body possessed.

I was no longer a human being but a rugose cone standing at least three meters tall and possessed of two forward-facing tentacles that ended in crustacean-like pincers that, nevertheless, possessed fine tool-like tentacles along their interior. I moved with a kind of sloshing back and forth. Indeed, I would not have been surprised to learn I no longer possessed a skeleton. My head and another organ that I could scarcely imagine the function of were at the ends of two more tentacles that brought my total to four.

Such a radical change of physicality would perhaps have driven another man to madness or denial, but my Kastro'vaal blood provided a bulwark against panic. They were shape-changers and flesh-sculptors who inherited distant blood from the Unspeakable One and the Black Mother. It had allowed them to take husbands and wives from hundreds of other races while slowly transforming their mates from within into more Kastro'vaal.

A race of interstellar gene pirates.

Or perhaps cuckoos.

In this form—which some distant racial memory told me was a Yith of Earth—I struggled to adjust to all the new sensory input coming in. I could see it in five dimensions for example. I focused on the beauty of the city to give something to center me. Built in layers of space that humans could only guess at, the city was made of floating crystal pillars and spinning portals that tunneled through space like an ant colony. It was interwoven with gigantic vines that were kilometers-tall and wrapped around trees that passed through dimensions.

The Yith were not alone in their colony here in the part of Pangea that will eventually be Australia. They shared the community with shoggoths as well as the still-young Mi-Go. The Elder Things had retreated to their cities and Cthulhu's people had entered a million-year-slumber.

How do I know this?

WATCH, a chorus of voices spoke. *LEARN.*

Who are you? Brianna? Whatever the hell your real name is?

WATCH. LEARN. HUMAN-THINKING-SHOGGOTH.

I am not a shoggoth.

YES. STUPID. WATCH. LEARN.

I tried to figure out where the voices were coming from but they seized control of my mind and directed my attention to two Yith standing before a black oily statue that dwarfed them like children. It was as hideous as the city was beautiful, with horrific mouths, tongues, sexual organs, and tumorous growths throughout. If it was a religious statue, it was to a god that repulsed me in an almost primordial fashion.

You must abandon this superstition, [Incomprehensible gibberish], the first of the Yith spoke in its strange psychic language. It made a noise with its secondary organ that I assumed was it speaking a name aloud.

The second Yith spoke with Brianna Lethder's "presence", though. It was her in her original body. *It is not superstition. The Black Mother is real, unlike so many dream creations of less developed species. Beings like the Vhoori, Great Cthulhu's people, and the Mi-Go worship her. She is the source of all life in the cosmos. Her seeds are the birth of every intelligent planetoid's life. She is the consort of Yog-Sothoth, who is the Key and the Gate. Their children, Nug and Yeb, are the parents to other Great Old Ones. She is the goddess of a billion races that worship her.*

Yes, they worship her, the other Yith said. *A worship that attracts her spawn's attention and warps the body as well as mind. The higher dimensional beings are as alien to us as we are to the species we study. Those who seek them out doom themselves to madness and death. Nothing good comes of involving themselves in the Outer Gods' activities.*

Learning is its own reward, Brianna replied. *The Yith have become tired, weak, and resigned to immortality from stolen lives! We flee from planet to planet, stealing race after race's future, only to do the same again when circumstances change. The Black Goddess offers a chance to change and grow our bodies' connection to our minds. A thing we have forgotten!*

You would have us become degenerate flesh-creatures cavorting in the name of your depraved fertility goddess, the other Yith said. *To be wild and free like the Old Ones cultists that have brought down every civilization they've lived in.*

Brianna just laughed aloud.

I woke from my dream—if that's what it was—with a blinding headache as the sunlight came in through the flaps of my tent. My bedroll was empty except for me, and that meant Mercury was already awake. I could hear her outside, chatting with Brianna, though not what they were discussing. Brianna had attempted to grow friendlier with us over our past month of travel across the Great Barrier Desert and New England Wasteland. There were a dozen other individuals outside, people we'd hired as part of an expedition across the remains of the Northern United States.

Brianna had been insufferably friendly the entire way. I had met some truly insincere people in the hellholes and hives that passed for human civilization after the Rising, but Doctor Lethder had established herself as one of the most. Her every action over our journey had been cultivated to manipulate, misdirect, and control us. Mind you, she wasn't human and the fact she was constantly reading our minds to know what we wanted to hear didn't help matters.

Was this journey just another attempt of a madman to lead us to our doom? Doctor Alan Ward, Katryn of the Dunwych, and Marcus Whateley had all led us on merry chases. Perhaps this one was the Devil leading us rather than doing the chasing. My dream might have been just that, a conjuration of my fears, or perhaps it was the Old Yith sending me a warning. Either way, I needed to push it down to the recesses of my brain to hope that it could not be sensed by the woman who was our guide.

"John!" Mercury's voice called through the tent flaps. "You need to come see this."

There was excitement in her voice that surprised me since we were only two days past the ruins of Chicago. The Great Lakes had become fetid swamps filled with hideous mutated creatures as well as mixed communities of humans and Deep Ones. The locals had taken to worshiping Cthugha with an ever present need to appease their evil sun god. We'd survived but just barely and two of our team had been lost to the bloody knives of the Chi-Town priests.

"I'm coming," I said, climbing out of my bedroll and getting dressed. I took the time to arm myself as well. There was nothing I could do to harm Brianna Lethder. After all, her body was only a poor innocent victim whose consciousness had been displaced. But I still preferred to have the option of banishing the psychic entity from this time.

However temporarily.

You are a deeply distrusting man, John Henry Booth, Brianna's presence filled my mind. *Has the Wasteland truly beaten out all trust from you?*

Yes, I replied. *I'm only here for your promise.*

It will be fulfilled and more, Brianna said. *Have I not already shown you wonders during our time together?*

I didn't respond as I left the tent, covering my eyes to avert the punishing sunlight of Earth's corrupted orange-black orb.

Brianna had done things that had warranted a certain amount of trust, so to speak. Her powers had suppressed the beast within me to the point that I'd felt more like myself than I had since I'd made the awful discovery about my conception.

She'd even shown me how to control the darkness inside enough that I'd been able to do minor adjustments of my form while staying "myself." But that had been at the cost of letting her into my mind and I had no idea what sort of changes she had done inside my consciousness while there.

If I was able to affect a shoggoth's mind, then I wouldn't be bothering with you, John, Brianna taunted me. *I'd have much higher ambitions than recruiting a semi-human sheriff and his hedge witch ally. But if you doubt that I am leaving your free will intact then just think about how hostile and untrusting you are. Why would you feel that way if I could change it?*

Maybe that's so you can claim that I am free through that method, I said, looking around our camp. *As long as I distrust you, that means I still think I have free will.*

The camp of the Garden Expedition Company—original name I know—was a makeshift collection of tents and carts that we'd managed to pull here using horserats. Horserats were exactly what they sounded like: giant rat creatures the ghouls had domesticated as pack animals ages before they'd escaped to the surface during the Rising. Our workers knew very little about what we were seeking but couldn't have cared less.

We'd paid in food and other necessities that had lured them from Kingsport, New Arkham, and even the ruins of Boston. We'd set up camp on the end of a broken highway bridge that dropped off overlooking a fetid jungle swamp that glowed in the night. Mercury and Brianna were on the edge. They'd set up rappelling chords over the side, which would take us down when we were ready. It said perhaps everything you needed to know about the world we lived in that I distrusted green land and worried more about my survival in it than I did the blasted deserts around New Arkham.

Ugh, Brianna expressed a mild disgust via our bond before looking back at me. *I wish you'd have let me demonstrate my softer side. You and Mercury would both make very gifted lovers, I'm sure.*

I'm surprised your race has any interest in that, I said, disgusted at the thought of lying with someone's body while they weren't in it.

Most of my species don't. All our reproduction is done via pods. But this body has needs.

I doubt the original Brianna Lethder would enjoy you using it that way, I said, not bothering to hide my revulsion.

The original Brianna Lethder maintained enough knowledge of her time in Pnakotus to write her deranged manifesto and perhaps save a few human lives, Brianna said. *At least until she committed suicide to avoid the church murdering her. This body was a volunteer. The university's students welcoming the chance to learn in the past and, for a time at least, escape Earth's doom. I go by my first host's name simply because you cannot hope to imagine my true name. To speak it requires organs you do not have.*

I involuntarily thought back to the incomprehensible gibberish I'd heard in my dream before pushing that thought away.

If Brianna had any reaction to the thought, she didn't show it.

"What is it you wanted to show me, anyway?" I asked, walking up behind them.

"This," Mercury said, pointing just above the vast swamp.

I blinked, turning my head to one side. "Is that a... trapezoid?"

It was and it wasn't. What we saw was a building-sized metal object that rapidly shifted in its shape while hovering fifty feet off the ground. It was one of those incomprehensible sights that you encountered in the Post-Rising World. Things the curious died investigating, the wise avoided, and the deranged worshiped.

"It's Project: EDEN," Mercury said, pointing out as if she was a child seeing something new for the first time. "The Yithian technology has created a true space between spaces."

"There are entire universes in the space between atoms," Brianna said, as if this was something profound rather than simply nonsense. "Even so, this is not so much Yith technology as magic compensating for ideas inspired by Yith technology. It was the math magics of Salem witches combined with Mi-Go technology with a dash of Ruthanna's genius."

Brianna was contemptuous of humans in ways both overt and subtle but that never seemed to apply while discussing her associate. If I didn't think the Yith incapable of it, I would have said that she'd been in love with Doctor Bloom.

"This wasn't here yesterday," I said, desperate to change the subject from the utter madness being discussed.

"No, it's only available to see within an hour of sunset," Brianna said. "We've got thirty or forty minutes left before it disappears again."

I shook my head, shocked to discover the object existed. I hadn't really believed it until now. "The others in the expedition won't willingly go in. Men and women of the Wasteland don't live long if they poke places like this with a stick."

I remembered my horrific journey into the Black Cathedral, an Elder Thing temple to the Outer Gods, and how it had ended with the loss of everything I cherished—including my humanity. Mercury knew this and opened her mouth to speak.

"They don't have to," Brianna spoke before Mercury. "I have recruited some aides."

"When?" I asked, wondering when she'd managed to pull this off. I looked at Mercury, who seemed as perplexed as I did.

"Before I recruited you," Brianna said, amused. "They accompanied my original team here. Obviously, we failed. However, now we have newer and more talented individuals to replace those we lost."

I silently cursed myself and wondered just how much of a fool I was for going along with this scheme.

"I see," I replied. "So, you crossed a quarter of the country to find replacements."

"Of course," Brianna said. "I'm sure you'll get on swimmingly."

I looked at Mercury and said, "Please tell me you're at least getting something out of this."

"Knowledge beyond my wildest dreams," Mercury said, looking uncomfortable. "Unfortunately, that knowledge doesn't change me from being a bug on the shoe of beings who will live epochs," Mercury said. "You?"

"We'll see," I replied. "I take it these other recruits are nearby?"

"Yes," a voice said, sounding like someone speaking through an air filter. "We are."

The figure speaking was not the most hideous thing I'd seen in the Wasteland, not by a longshot, but wasn't going to be winning any prizes for beauty either. He was, in simple terms, a walking corpse with a face that looked like it had been mummified before someone had shoved piping up his nostril holes and through the right side of his skull. He had a skintight black suit of some kind covering most of his body which also had piping running in and out of it, as well as a backpack that hummed with unrecognizable noises. Some sort of exoskeleton was attached to his knees and arms that gave the corpse-man a weird jerking motion.

Behind him were a shaggy man that seemed caught between half-ghoul, half-man. His body was covered in fur almost like a pelt, and he wore a coat and bloodstained denim pants, but no shoes. His posture was twisted and hunched over, giving him the look of at least something akin to a werewolf.

A third figure was an ordinary-looking, brown-skinned woman with her head shaved, dressed in the traveling attire of a Chicago Wastelander: cotton shirt, leather vest, leather boots, and homespun pants. She was carrying a rifle that looked like it had been manufactured on Mars, though, and had a handle welded to its side to provide a grip for human hands.

It seemed we were just part of the freak show rather than its central attractions. "I see."

The other members of our team gave these individuals a wide berth and probably with good reason. They had the aura of casual killers. Something I recognized in Mercury and myself.

"This is Doctor Julio Munoz," Brianna gestured to the corpse-cyborg. "He's a former cryobiologist from before the Rising. When Atlanta was destroyed, he was one of the many individuals turned into inexhaustible labor by the City-that-Walks, Iterraxan."

"My ancestor invented immortality in 1905," the half-corpse, half-machine said. "Unfortunately, the City-That-Walks put my attempts at improving on it to unfortunate use. Atlanta's people are now simply gut bacteria in a deranged K'n-yan device."

"This is Roland," Brianna said, gesturing to the wolfman. "He's a mutant."

"Charmed," the wolfman said. "Who do I kill?"

"And Leslie Sharp," Brianna said. "She's a Loop slaver, but one that knows how to get into Project: EDEN."

I narrowed my eyes.

I hated slavers.

"It needs a shoggoth," Leslie looked at me. "Or something close to one. We hunt them for the Elder Things' agents."

"We've been waiting a month, Lethder," Roland said, opening and closing his clawed fists repeatedly. "They had better be worth it."

"Real bunch of winners you've got yourself here," Mercury said, shaking her head. "All this to break into a garden from before the Rising?"

"The Fruit of Knowledge was something Adam and Eve partook of," Doctor Munoz said. "But humanity was never able to taste of the

Fruit of Life. God himself was terrified of what humanity would become if they did."

That was when the plant-things attacked.

Hundreds of them.

Chapter Four

The plant-things were coming up the ruined highway bridge forming a disgusting swarm of deformed genetic abominations. Few of them closely resembled the original we'd fought, and I could see the remains of other animals that had been absorbed into collectives of strange green growths. The heads of stags, wolves, and bloated humans stuck out of moss and vines while crying out in agony.

I'd prepared our expedition as best I could to deal with the plant-things. They had crude flamethrowers made from the methane-based fuel that powered most of humanity with the absence of crude oil. My expedition moved efficiently and with courage to defend themselves, deploying their weapons rapidly. However, there was no hope against the numbers we faced, assuming that the flamethrowers would even put the monsters down.

I'd only been guessing.

"This way!" Brianna shouted, gesturing to the set of ropes she'd set up to rappel down the side of the broken bridge. "We need to get to the forest!"

"The plants are coming *from* the forest!" I pointed out, picking up my rifle and firing enchanted rounds into the monsters. The runes inside them exploded when they struck home and covered the monsters in fire. The monsters reared back, thrashing harder, but they kept coming.

Great.

"The only sanctuary from them is in the forest!" Brianna said, starting to rappel down the ropes she'd set up on the broken bridge's edge.

It seemed awfully convenient that Brianna Lethder's goal was our only sanctuary but I also didn't believe she could control this many monsters. No, it seemed more likely that the creatures sensed their enemy and were now descending on her like a tidal wave.

The rest of us were just in the way.

The first wave of the plant-things was held back by the rest of the expedition even as members were dragged to screaming death by vines or eaten in their horrible mandibles. It was clear that the flames were an annoyance to them rather than a genuine threat, though. Perhaps I was the only hope they had but even if I transformed fully, they would probably attack me as much as the monsters.

"John, we have to go!" Mercury said, grabbing my arms.

"I'm not abandoning my men," I shouted, preparing to transform and let the dice fall where they may.

"They're not your men," Leslie the slaver said, lifting her strange sci-weapon and firing glowing green blasts that disintegrated the plant-things as if they were smudges being wiped away from a window. "The job is to protect Doctor Lethder."

I was about to object when I noticed that Julio and Roland had already descended the ropes with Brianna. Then I noticed how the plant-things assaulting the fifteen or sixteen remaining members of the expedition reacted to her absence. They started falling back and moving around the bridge.

They were definitely chasing down Brianna. "Our best way to protect everyone is to lead her away."

Mercury glared. "Sure, John, if that's what it takes to get you to go."

I turned to speak to Leslie the slaver, so far the only person who had displayed any ability to fight the plant-things. Instead of standing there, she'd already started falling back with the others defending Doctor Lethder. I had to wonder what she'd offered the others to make them so interested in her defense.

And whether any of it was true.

"We need to go," I said, watching the lines of the remaining expedition members break as the monsters retreated. They were fleeing in every direction away from the highway and I didn't blame them.

"That's what *I* said," Mercury growled, heading to one of the ropes and descending downward in an awkward but effective manner.

I moved to try to join the others when one of the plant-things—an eight-legged thing with a malformed canine-skull covered in chthonic bark—came charging at me. It had long tubes stretching out of its sides and each of them ended in pincers. The creature came directly at me and before I could move, I was struck by it and sent flying over the bridge's edge.

The drop was ten meters and I would have been crushed underneath the monster were I to strike it head on. Instead, I abandoned myself to the beast as I fell and gave it full freedom to survive.

Kill.

When I awoke on the ground, I was covered in gore and the plant-thing was in pieces around me. The smell was oddly piney and contrasted with the usual smell of guts and viscera. Bones snapped back into place and healed even as I felt claws made from the tips of my fingerbones retreat into my body. My clothes were damaged but not torn to shreds. I'd only changed a small bit for my survival. It made me wonder if I'd been lucky, that this particular plant-thing had been exceptionally weak, or if I was becoming more powerful as Brianna Lethder altered my mind.

"So, should we shoot him or not?" Julio asked, behind me.

My attention was brought back to the others who were standing behind me and I realized I'd only been in a beast-like state for a few seconds. It was a new record for me and one that suggested I might someday have true control over my body. The Kastro'vaal took centuries, even millennia, to master their shape-changing but I didn't have that kind of time. I didn't have minutes if I died here.

Especially since Leslie had her strange gun pointed at me.

"I say we risk it," Leslie said.

"We need to move!" Brianna gestured. "The plants are coming!"

Mercury pointed and shouted a warning I didn't hear over the noise of the floral horde gathering around us.

"Right," I said, realizing I'd been distracted at a crucial time. I had no idea whether it was possible to outrun the horde but I wasn't about to survive being tackled by one of them off a small cliff only to be eaten here.

"Leslie, Roland, provide a distraction," Brianna said, gesturing for the two to address the oncoming plants. "John, Mercury, Julio, run."

I expected Leslie the slaver and Roland to disobey or hesitate, but both moved into position to defend Brianna. It was suicide but they didn't hesitate. I would have questioned their decision, but I wanted to live and seeing Mercury take off toward the floating trapezoid, I followed. The strange undead cyborg followed our rear, making bizarre rumbling noises as he did so.

Leslie fired her energy cannon again while Roland, much to my surprise, turned out to be a sorcerer. He called out in his ghoulish language and storm clouds filled the sky, raining down lightning.

"Is there any chance of their survival?" I called out, feeling my bare feet slosh through mud and against rock as I ran through the swamp jungle around me.

"Their survival isn't the mission," Julio responded, coldly. "We all have our reasons for being here, John Henry Booth of the Kastro'vaal."

"How did you—" I started to say, only to be grabbed by some of the tree branches around me.

I should have expected more resistance from our environment, but my mind was slow. Trying to deduce Brianna Lethder's game while unravelling the mystery of Project: EDEN was hard enough with all the pressures of leading an expedition across the former United States. The trees coming alive to grapple us was just another display of how outmaneuvered we were.

"*Vak mal' tak Ut' Shub-Niggurath!*" Mercury shouted, trying to cast a spell on the fly. It seemed to cause a horrific screaming throughout the forest around us as the tree branches thrashed and pulsated.

"I don't think they liked that," Julio said, lifting up his wrists before releasing freezing cold jets of pressurized air. They didn't function like anything from the normal laws of physics but more like something out of an old Pre-Rising story. The trees cracked, froze, and fell to pieces around us.

One of the plant-things managed to catch up with us but I tore into it, assuming the armor and blades of before as if they were as natural as breathing. Brianna's influence was everywhere and I was terrified I could get used to it. That I'd come to enjoy her power and the sense of freedom it bestowed.

I barely registered what followed as we continued to fight our way through the forest. Most of the horde did not pursue us or we moved faster than them. I saw no sign of Brianna Lethder and privately hoped she'd succumbed to the monsters chasing her even as I knew that was a selfish and unworthy desire. A part of me couldn't shake my distrust for the Yith, though. She was too casual in her lies, manipulation, and willingness to cast aside those who had served their purpose.

Then there was my dream.

What did it mean?

Argh.

Either way, we managed to find our way underneath the trapezoid that was now the shape of a torus. The plant-things pulled back abruptly, and we found ourselves covered in a shimmering blue-gray light once we were underneath it. A strange humming noise was all around us, coming from no particular direction. The air was charged and I saw the water ripple around our feet.

There was no sign of Brianna.

"Goddammit, where is she?" I asked, looking around rapidly.

"Here!" Brianna shouted, surprising me. Somehow, she'd fallen behind us and was now helping Leslie into the circle we'd found ourselves. The slaver was still clutching her strange weapon and was bleeding badly from the side despite attempts to hold her guts in. Apparently, she'd managed to carve a way through the plant-things and follow the path we'd cleared.

"What happened to Roland?" Julio asked.

"He didn't make it," Leslie said, looking up. "The distraction worked, though. The Heartroot's army is outside of the habitat."

"The what in the who now?" Mercury asked.

"It doesn't matter," Brianna said, dismissing her. "We just need John now to serve as the key to the gate."

That was ominous. "I don't know what you want me to do."

"You're playing this awfully close to the chest, Lethder," Mercury said, looking at the circle of creatures gathered around the circle we'd been forced into. They weren't moving or making a sound, which was more frightening than they'd been making howls of agonized fury.

"*Doctor* Lethder and that's my prerogative," Brianna said, looking at me. "One of the doctors in the project was one of your kind, John. Perhaps even a previous incarnation. It provided the information necessary to make the space between this world and others. The Kastro'vaal are, after all, known as the Eyes of Yog-Sothoth. They exist in-between space-time with rare exceptions like you."

I stared at her. "I repeat: I don't know—"

"We don't have much time!" Brianna said, suddenly shouting.

"Fine! OPEN SESAME!" I shouted up at the sky before looking back at her. "There, happy?"

Much to my surprise, the trapezoid assumed a pyramid shape and the bottom opened like an iris, revealing blinding light. A set of rings descended to the ground and hovered in the air in an ordered fashion with approximately one meter between each.

"Huh," I said, dumbfounded.

"Don't worry, John, you didn't actually trigger the building's AI that way," Brianna said, smirking. "It just needed to finish scanning you. You were the missing link the first time I was here. It should be smooth sailing from now on."

"Let me treat her," Mercury said, going to Leslie's side. "I'm a doctor."

Leslie collapsed into her arms, not responsive.

"That won't be necessary," Brianna said, pulling the strange weapon from her dead hands. The long silver tube looked ridiculous in her hands but somehow, she lifted it like a children's toy. "She also served her purpose."

I half expected Brianna to blast us all at that point, but she gestured instead to the ring with the gun. "Your reward is inside."

Mercury and I exchanged a glance. Both of us were thinking the same thing: that we had made a terrible mistake in trusting the Yith woman.

"Right," I muttered, more certain than ever that we weren't going to be receiving any reward other than death.

"We'd better go in," Julio said, showing no concern for the death of his comrades or the ominous way this mission had gone.

"What are you getting out of this?" I asked, wondering what sort of hold a Yith might have on a living dead man.

"None of your goddamn business," Julio responded, which was a fair reaction.

"The trapezoid is stalled and the defenses of the Heartroot are laid bare, John," Brianna said, sounding more tired than afraid or mournful. "You need only to step into the rings to bring this journey to an end."

Pure simple stubbornness almost had me refuse. I was sick of being lied to and exhausted from this entire ordeal. Unfortunately, surrounded by an army of surprisingly hesitant plant-things was neither the time nor place to bring up my objections. To paraphrase Winston Churchill, when going through hell, one should keep going.

"Alright," I said, heading to the rings. "Let's see just how far down the rabbit hole this journey will take us."

So, I entered, never once considering how I was going to get back out again. Hmm, maybe I needed to stick to the Genesis parable.

But was I Adam or the Serpent in Paradise?

I soon found out.

Chapter Five

There was a blinding blue flash of light as I stepped into the rings, followed by a sense of movement before my eyes cleared to see something distinctly different from what I'd expected. I'd expected some sort of alien planet, really. A kind of otherworldly garden in a box that they'd somehow created. Possibly a place that was filled with humans who absolutely didn't want anything to do with us due to Brianna's selfish desire to invade their home.

Instead, it was more like an overgrown tomb.

The air was musty and warm, so thick with water that it covered my face. We were in a metal corridor with a circular platform underneath us, surrounded by consoles that were projecting holograms in the air. It was technology that humanity had never developed before its extinction but the kind of thing humans would eventually come up with.

The walls, however, had been eaten through with a corrosion I didn't recognize, like rust except as effective as industrial acid. Black branches crawled through these holes and extended throughout the chambers without shutting down the machines. There were desiccated corpses spread about the place, old and decayed with the branches growing through their chests and into their eyes. Their insides looked like they'd been sucked out. Someone had put up a bed sheet on the side wall with words painted on it in crude sludge, "DO NOT ENTER. THE MOTHER IS NOT GOOD."

"Well, this isn't worth an angel guarding the place with a sword," Mercury said, appearing behind me in a light that formed into her person.

"It appears humanity has been cast out of this garden," I said. "I'm sorry."

"Honestly, this is pretty much what I expected," Mercury said, surprising me.

"What?" I asked, doing a double take.

"I checked the corpse of the first plant-thing thoroughly," Mercury said, looking behind her as if waiting for Brianna Lethder to appear any second.

"And?" I asked.

"There was a face in its lower chest," Mercury said. "Locked in a scream. I wouldn't be surprised if we found vestigial human traits on all of them."

I stared at her. "The plant-things were *people*?"

"It surprises you?" Mercury asked. "No one can touch the Great Old Ones or their gods and not be affected by the experience. All the races that can interbreed with mankind are mutated from humanity's base. Deep Ones, Serpent Men, and ghouls are just people with their taint. That's why they can still breed with us. Well, all except shoggoths. They're able to breed because—"

"Let's put a pin in that," I said, cutting her off. "Why bother coming if you thought that?"

"Because there might be something worth stealing," Mercury said, looking around, careful not to touch anything. "We're running out of options, John. If we're going to save humanity, then we need a miracle and that requires the gods: even if that god is Lilith."

"We can't save humanity, Mercury," I said, sighing. "I'm not even sure we can save ourselves."

With that depressing statement, the platform around us glowed and both Brianna and Julio appeared beside us. I wondered what the two had talked about before deciding to follow us or if they'd simply waited an inordinately long time in silence.

"Talking about me? Brianna asked, cheerfully. "Possibly sexually? Did you know that the fertility rites of Inanna, Isis, and Demeter were often used as covers for the veneration of the Black Mother?"

"This isn't exactly the kind of place that puts one in the mood," I said, looking to the corpses around us.

"Ooo, a mummy," Brianna said, sarcastically. "I am aghast."

It was a reminder the Yith was not nearly as easily shocked or naïve a person as she pretended to be.

"Hmmph," Julio grunted, looking aside. "A few pipes, an air conditioner, and an engine and they'll be fine. People underestimate just how cool air can preserve a body."

"It's humid," I said.

"I know," Julio said, confusing me. "But I can't feel it in this suit. You know, what with it being a refrigeration unit and me being undead."

What a strange fellow. "You knew this is what we'd find."

"Of course I did," Brianna said. "I also know that Mercury figured out the plant-things were the original staff and their descendants. They're a collective hive-mind linked by telepathy based around the Heartroot. They live by photosynthesis and water in the air. They can eat dirt. Really, they're an improvement on homo sapiens in every possible way."

I prepared to kill her, stupid as that might be since she was carrying a weapon that could disintegrate me even at my strongest. "Is this the salvation you were thinking for humanity?"

"No," Brianna said, dismissively. "Though I lack your small-mindedness about what is a worthwhile path of evolution to take. Especially when dealing with superior levels of it."

"Evolution is about adapting to your environment. There's no such thing as a superior evolutionary level," Mercury said, annoyed.

Brianna smirked. "See what I mean? It's so cute the way you talk about science. Like a dog explaining leeches and phrenology."

Mercury looked about ready to go for Brianna, too.

Julio cleared his throat. "Let's be honest, none of us gives a shit about what happened to these old scientists. They rolled the dice on trying to ride out the apocalypse as something more than human and got snake eyes. This body has some familiarity with that itself."

I stared. "I don't see much reason to keep assisting our employer since everything she's told us so far has been half-truths at best."

"Really, John? You'll stop right at the finish line?" Brianna asked. "I may have omitted certain details—"

"What most people call lying," I replied.

Brianna smirked. "But you have benefited from my efforts already. You've gained more control over your condition than you would have in a dozen centuries and without losing what you mistakenly believe is your humanity. Mercury has been taught things that would have made my Zamoran lover, Salome, rich with desire. The barest arts of dream-weaving I've shown Mercury are beyond the measure of most sorcerers."

"And Julio?" I asked.

"Still none of your goddamn business," Julio said.

Brianna chuckled. "The Black Mother's blessings can benefit you both, personally, not just your race. Immortality, healing of the most grievous wounds, and the ability to survive on this world as well as others. Perhaps even children that will outlive you or, better still, live alongside you for ages. But I don't need to promise you any more of that."

"Why?" Mercury asked, frowning.

"Because I know you'll come because you're a curious monkey and shoggoth," Brianna said. "Do you know what 'shoggoth' means in the Elder Thing language? Why you hate it, Kastro'vaal?"

"It means slave," I replied. I'd learned that from Doctor Curwen's writings in the Black Cathedral when I'd gone back to try to make sense of them all.

"Multi-purpose organic tool, really," Brianna said. "You will come simply because when the Elder Things injected a bunch of ape brains with shoggoth DNA to make better slaves, they instilled it with curiosity. A trait you cannot deny."

Both Mercury and I stared at each other, silently agreeing we should kill her but neither of us making a move.

"I can't imagine why people don't like you," Julio said, sarcastically.

"What do you mean?" Brianna asked, confused. "People love me."

"Show us what you came here for," I said, staring at her. "Because I am curious."

Brianna chuckled as if I'd said something hilarious.

Travel through the remains of Project: EDEN provided a story of mad hope and dashed dreams. It had been an advanced facility far beyond the normal individuals of humanity with plans of serving less as an Earthly paradise and more as an ark. There had been families here, cultivated to provide a maximum genetic diversity, and the strange facility was powered by machines that seemed to need no fuel.

There were no signs of the plant-things and no resistance from the creatures within. There was scurrying animal life, but they were deformed lizards and rat-like creatures belonging to an ecosystem far removed from humanity.

The scientists' choice to transform themselves had apparently not been universal as the human corpses spread around included many who were armed, with a handful of plant-things among the dead. The worship of Shub-Niggurath had seemingly been practiced as we came across several makeshift altars made of bone and a full chapel that had been defiled with bodies tossed in a pile.

"I guess a cult is a cult," Mercury said, shaking her head. "In the end, the plant-things won."

"The plant-things as you call them—I prefer Edenics—were not the aggressors," Brianna said. "Still, I'm a bit ashamed of Ruth, she should have cleaned up. I suppose such things became irrelevant once she made her change."

I didn't even need to ask for an answer because it became apparent in a few moments. Brianna headed through a series of broken decontamination rooms before entering a massive thirty-meter-tall geodesic room whose ceiling provided artificial sunlight from glowing plates over a stadium-sized chamber. The chamber was a garden built around a singular organism that I suspected was the master of this supposed hive-mind.

The organism was an enormous twenty-meter-tall tree that stretched to the sky with its trunk growing around a hideously mutated human being. Its human core seemed to have its mossy red flesh merged into the plant like a fungus growing on its surface. The tree had thick slimy bark that seemed to ooze bright orange ichor as its limbs stretched out with thick branches that hung down like a willow's leaves. It was breathing, making humanish noises that chilled the soul. Worse still, the Heartroot—for it could be nothing else—was a mother.

The bark was covered in pustules of orange, glowing, pod-like growths within which I saw deformed fetuses growing. I could feel a presence radiating out from it with what little psychic potential I possessed. A presence that I knew hated Brianna Lethder with every fiber of her being.

"Huh," Mercury said, looking up at the Heartroot. "That is fucked up."

"I've seen worse," Julio said, unfazed.

"Oh, Ruthanna, you have become so beautiful," Brianna said, approaching the Heartroot and putting her hand on its side. Leslie's weapon was on her back now, held there by a leather strap I'd paid little attention to earlier. "This is what I have come to acquire, John, Mercury. It is an organic computer that rivals the shoggoth in its genetic perfection. The Great Mother's blessing has created a machine that will save the Yith and humanity both."

"What are you going to do with her?" I asked, wondering if I should just shoot Brianna right now and put an end to this madness. That would kill the woman the Yith was occupying, though.

"Transform the Yith and humanity both," Brianna said, enraptured. "I could not achieve the spiritual perfection that Ruthanna with her simple human love could. The Great Mother rejected me but Ruthanna was reborn. Now, I will combine her with our race's technology to create a new world. One that will have the world's ecosystem, and its inhabitants live in harmony with one another. Humanity's remnants will be the seeds and the Yith will possess them, creating a new race that guarantees the survival of both."

"I don't think that's going to happen," I said, pulling out my gun. "We're not just a pair of suits for your race to wear."

"You won't harm me," Brianna said.

I tried to shoot her but found I couldn't raise the gun at her. I looked to Mercury, who raised her hands to cast a spell only to lower them.

"Or more precisely, you can't," Brianna said, grinning. "Don't worry, John. You will have a place here as well once I've merged you with the Heartroot. A shoggoth's biological flexibility is the missing link to enhancing the tissue. Our previous shoggoth ally, Doctor Campbell, fled before he could accelerate the project's growth to cover the entire planet. That had been my original plan, but the Rising interrupted it. You, John, will be free of your inhuman nature and

334 / C. T. Phipps

become the father of a new race. Don't worry, Mercury, you will have immortality too. After all, we'll need a human womb to impregnate as the new Heartroot. Julio? Don't worry, I will transport your consciousness to a Pre-Rising human body to live out its life as promised."

"I'm afraid he already made that deal with another," Julio said, his voice dry but amused. A psychic presence other than Brianna's filled my mind. *You've done your part well, John Henry Booth.* I recognized it as the one from my dream.

"What?" Brianna asked. "No!"

Julio pulled out a small silver pyramid from his jacket. "Your crimes against the Great Race have been noted, catalogued, and judged. It is time to return home. You have done immeasurable damage to the war effort across multiple incarnations of this universe."

I stared at him. "You're Yith."

"What gave it away?" Julio said.

Brianna glared. "John, kill him!"

I felt an immense pressure against my brain and every instinct in my body wanted to terminate the zombie cyborg. He was a Yith after all, wasn't he? Why not? Maybe I could kill them both. Then I forced down that thought, focusing on one single idea: Lethder wanted me to so I damn well would not.

"No," I said, finally.

Brianna stared at Mercury and I felt a shimmer in the air before my lover fell to her knees. Mercury held her head tightly before smiling. "Yeah, I decided to put this on for today."

Mercury pulled out her Elder stone necklace from under shirt. "Apparently, this works against the Yith too."

Brianna stared. "Primitives! I'm surrounded by primitives!"

The Julio-Yith lifted his silver pyramid, and the top opened in four directions. A small ball of light emerged from it and shone throughout the room. Brianna's body collapsed like a puppet whose strings had been cut. The pyramid's top closed and Julio put it back in his pocket.

"It's over," the Julio-Yith said. "The Great Race thanks you for your assistance. If not for her being here in a space outside time, the High

Priestess you know as Brianna Lethder might have been able to escape again. Perhaps even reset events as she's done in the past. The Great Race also needed to know what her plans were in order to see what her allies have been up throughout the timestream. The Cult of the N'gasha'too or Egg-Laying Queen is a source of great unrest in Pnakotus' final years."

"Huh," Mercury said, looking at Julio then back at me. "Well, didn't see that coming."

"What will happen to her?" I said, wondering if we'd have to fight Julio now.

"The entity you know as Brianna Lethder, our sister, will face punishment for her deviant actions," the Yith calling itself Julio said.

"What do you consider deviant?" I asked, looking at the horror show around us.

"Interfering with the normal flow of time in this universe," the Julio-Yith said. "Her puerile interest in your species' survival is merely distasteful rather than forbidden."

Suffice to say, my opinion of the Yith did not improve. "So what will happen to her?"

"She will be rehabilitated," the Julio-Yith said.

"Rehabilitated," I said. "After all the lives she destroyed."

The Julio-Yith scoffed. "How many animals have you eaten? How many people have you killed? Our society is more civilized than yours. If it is any consolation, the process will probably take millions of your Earth years."

"Yay for civilization," Mercury said. "Just make sure she never crosses our path again."

The Julio-Yith scoffed at the idea. "I sincerely doubt that is likely. You may be rocks thrown in the river of time but the ripples you create are of no concern to me."

I looked over at Brianna Lethder's body. It sat motionless. "What will happen to her?"

"Return it to the time stream of your world and we will be able to send her original consciousness back to it," the Julio-Yith replied.

"Consider it a reward for the mild service you have done the Great Race. That is, unless you require payment in other methods."

His contempt was so thick that I was surprised he didn't offer to pay us in shiny beads.

"We don't need anything from you," I said, sneering.

"We'll take it," Mercury replied, going to Brianna's still form. "If we can save one life here then it will have been worth it."

The Julio-Yith snorted before turning around. A glowing slit the size of a man appeared in front of him that opened itself to the city of my visions. The Julio-Yith departed through it and abandoned us in the cursed chamber.

"We should have asked for a ride back to New Ulthar," I muttered.

"He'd probably have dumped us in Pangea," Mercury replied, checking Brianna Lethder's pulse. "Or Mars. Maybe when it had hot alien princesses instead of endless barren wastes."

Mercury was such a strange woman.

"We could have asked to be dumped Pre-Rising like Julio apparently did," I replied, shaking my head. "We'll have to find our way back."

"What will we do about her?" Mercury asked, looking up at the malformed remains of Ruthanna Bloom.

I looked up at the mutated figure grown in and out of the Heartroot, her face frozen in a masque of horror. No longer was she a mad scientist who had unleashed a horrific plague to me. No, instead, she was just another victim of Yith arrogance. "What do you want, Doctor Bloom?"

Much to my surprise, the corpse-thing managed to speak in a low rumbling tone from a dozen orifices around the chamber. "Kill me. End the dream of survival. All things die. It is the natural order. The Mother has forgotten."

I closed my eyes and picked up Leslie's gun before aiming it at her. "Alright."

It was a long trip home.

Epilogue

Black Goat Goddess

By C.T. Phipps

My mind filled with images and dreams of a thousand different people experiencing the glories of Shub-Niggurath and her children. Some of them were confusing, others were structured like movies, and a few ridiculous. Still, as I stood there in the body of my daughter, Asenath, I sought some secret revelation or truth that would elevate me to the mastery of the cosmos.

None came.

Instead, I found my consciousness returning to the moment when I'd sacrificed poor Wentworth on the altar of Sentinel Hill. I was naked and vulnerable as storm clouds poured down rain that I'd long held the power to summon at will. One of the many gifts I'd learned from the Deep Ones.

Before me was the Dark Young I'd summoned. The gaseous, tentacled, blob-like thing chilled me to the bone even before its blasphemous adoption of my daughter's face. Asenath had been a disappointment in her birth, carrying the Deep One genes from her mother as well as a prodigious intelligence, but was ultimately unable to provide me with what I coveted most: immortality.

I had sought the secrets of magic through the Church of Starry Wisdom and my own studies of that hoary institution of Miskatonic University. That demented hillbilly, Old Whateley, had mocked my desires. He was more priest than wizard and happy to condemn the world if it meant his god might become one with it.

"Hello, Father," the monstrous thing said to me. "It has been a long time."

I stared at the features so perfectly replicating dear Asenath's, mirroring the one I now saw every time I looked into a mirror. "You are not Asenath. Asenath is dead, cold and buried in my old body in the Innsmouth cemetery. She sacrificed her life to give me a chance at eternity. To cross the lines between life and death, man and woman, to unite them in one being."

The Asenath-thing laughed in a way that was a perfect replication of my child as a girl. "Sacrifice implies willingness, dear Ephraim Waite. You murdered your daughter and stole her body that you wear as a suit."

"A child should be willing to die for their parent," I said, defensively. I could not believe this creature, this thing, was trying to shame me. The Dark Young and their Mother were beyond such things.

Should be beyond such things.

"A parent should be willing to die for their children," the Asenath-thing spoke. "It was her destiny to dwell in wonder and glory forever among the children of R'lyeh. But you never could have that destiny, Ephraim. The other Deep Ones would sense the monstrous crime you had committed and offer you as a sacrifice to their god. That is why you fled Innsmouth."

My rain-soaked face burned with her words, primarily because they were the truth. The transformation into a hybrid of man and merfolk had not gone as smoothly as I'd hoped. Whether it was because the female brain frustrated the male consciousness within or because the Deep One blood fundamentally changed the way one thought was immaterial. The Children of Dagon were a superstitious, clannish bunch who clung to primitive notions of morality even as they violated every taboo that so-called civilized society held sacred.

I covered my breasts as I glared. "I come as a supplicant! I have offered blood and flesh to your offspring, yet you insult me with this grotesquerie! Asenath is gone! Cast into the void and shadow! You show me nothing but stories of cowboys and Indians like a child's radio play! Where is the truth? The secrets promised!"

"Poor Ephraim, still clinging to thy prejudices even in the face of the Great Mother's Daughter," the Asenath-thing mocked. "So certain you were that stealing the body of a woman and debauching with both sexes would provide you the power you desired and satisfy the lusts that you have always held. Had you come to the Black Goat with eyes downward, she would have provided you such delights and wisdom that death would have held no succor. Never in your wildest dreams did you imagine that your daughter was initiated into the craft, learning your secrets from your book and others from her mother before her retreat under the sea's waves. That as your daughter lay there dying in your old decaying body that she might offer herself unto the goddess."

I blanched, realizing just how much danger I was in. "You... no. Impossible. You are just some *thing* that is drawing from my memories. Trying to lull me into some guilt-driven fugue state to feed upon me. You're an angler fish, nothing more! Some sort of psychic parasite that wants my flesh! Well, you can't have it."

I backed away from the horrifying monster before me, for the first time feeling true dread and fear at what would have driven most normal men to insanity already. My eyes darted to the altar where the goat-babies had already finished their cannibalistic feast of poor Wentworth.

I'd been profoundly foolish in my summoning and broken the most sacred rule written down by that old warlock Joseph Curwen: "Doe not call up Any that you cannot put downe." I'd been so tantalized by the summoning ritual I'd found in the Masonic letters as well as amused by how much my adopted body affected Wentworth that I'd made no real protection against the things around me. Even my Elder sign amulet—the one I'd kept despite how it repulsed Asenath's body—was in my discarded clothes.

"Perhaps," the Asenath-thing said, writhing her tentacles and moving across the wet grass around the stone monoliths. "Perhaps this is just a conjuring of your diseased mind that I am feeding on. The spells that reach across the Dreamland take forms that can read the oh so pitiful mind of murderous little cravens like yourself. But I do not

340 / C. T. Phipps

think this is the case, Ephraim, because you would be required to be capable of guilt and shame in order for me to feed upon such."

I found myself pressed against the stone pillar I'd unwittingly backed myself against. Stark terror filled me as I struggled to think of some spell to banish the Asenath-thing from my presence. None came to mind as my words caught in my throat. Instead, I tried to appeal to emotion. "Mercy, please, daughter."

No answer, merely a familiar half-smile that I'd copied many times to seduce men as well as women.

The goat-babies moved around me, and I worried they would soon pounce upon me. "What... are... you going to do with me?"

I closed my eyes and waited for oblivion.

Or worse.

Wentworth, it seemed, had the last laugh.

"Nothing, Father," the Asenath-thing said.

I blinked my eyes in confusion. "Nothing?"

"Nothing," the Asenath-thing said, pulling away on its tiny goat legs that somehow supported its vast girth. "You have learned absolutely nothing from the tales that have been shared with you. The consort of Yog-Sothoth could have been your salvation if you'd allowed yourself to be reborn from her womb like these little kids."

The Asenath-thing lifted one of the foul abominations with her tentacle as the bloody-mouthed cannibal-monster brayed in my direction. The Asenath-thing absorbed it into one of its orifices and I wondered if she'd eaten it or put it back into her womb. The other monster children laughed as I saw they were now about the age of six or seven.

I wretched. "I am destined for a greater immortality."

The Asenath-thing laughed. "You are destined to die twice more. Once at the hands of one who loved thy body and not thy mind, and again to another who loved thy murderer. You will meet thine end surrounded by madmen and doctors."

I bolted from the pillar to my discarded clothes, reached into the pockets and grabbed the talisman I'd prepared from star stone with the Elder sign scribbled on it. It caused me to look away as even Asenath's diluted Dagon heritage was repulsed. I vomited to the side even as I managed to start spewing out the spells to banish a Greater Daemon. I had no idea if it would work but prayed to whatever deity that would aid me.

"*Ach-Thule, Ach-Thule, Iä Nodens! Iä Bast! Iä Kithnid!* I invoke thee, Elder Gods and enemies of the Great Old Ones..." I trailed off as I realized I was alone on Sentinel Hill.

The Asenath-thing was gone.

So were the goat-babies.

I breathed a sigh of relief before I realized that such was perhaps premature. I moved with the speed of Atalanta, never more grateful for the female body's endurance of pain than when I was running down the rocky paths of Sentinel Hill. By the time I presented myself to a poor farming couple, claiming assault and worse, I was reduced to a bloody disheveled mess that eliminated all the body's sultry allure.

I cared little.

Edward, my pathetically devoted husband, had his driver bring him out from distant Arkham to pick me up. The scandal of my story would have ruined my reputation and his, so he'd paid the Good Samaritans to keep their silence before agreeing to take me back home. A reputation as a harlot and an adulteress was tolerable for a woman of means, but a victim? No, that would never do. I informed Edward I'd let his driver go, though I'd disposed of him with a single pistol shot in the back of the head the next evening. Arkham's swamps were filled with victims of suicide, Prohibition, and lovers' quarrels. I'd simply added his body to their number. The Lady Derringer was just as lethal as its more masculine counterparts at close range.

Edward hadn't yet questioned his disappearance. I suspected Edward was also fully willing to take all my lies about that night as the truth: that Sebastian Wentworth had lured me out to Dunwich for discussion of his theory that the Natives had used Sentinel Hill's circle to study the stars, only to assault me. I would not be associated with the facts that Sebastian's bones had been picked clean, and he was missing. Edward's money would guarantee that.

His only redeeming value.

Well, that and providing a male form I could use.

A thought I'd been exploring.

Even a week later, I was still suffering from shivers and terror from the encounter with the Asenath-thing. It made me want to dig up my old body and burn it. I dared not possibly invoke whatever that thing truly was, though. I was sitting in my bathrobe on the couch in the foyer drinking coffee in the middle of the night to avoid sleep. I was staring out the window into a rainstorm that I'd conjured while Edward was preparing pancakes. (He was experimenting with cooking as a hobby.

"I don't blame you," Edward said from the kitchen. "You can always depend on me. I never liked that sleazy bastard."

"Let's never speak of him again," I muttered. "But yes, Edward, you are someone I can rely on. Perhaps now more than ever."

My encounter with the Dark Young had proven to be fruitful even in its failure. It made me realize that I didn't desire the same sort of immortality promised to the Deep Ones. I had no desire to abandon the pleasures of humanity, transient as they might be. To become a monster, however powerful, was a fate worse than death. Nor did I intend to surrender myself to the eternal void that all mortal creatures succumbed to.

No, there was another option.

Life eternal.

As a man.

And perhaps a woman after it.

I was sure now that Shub-Niggurath was a hermaphroditic organism, both man and woman as well as other. Perhaps someday I would try again to unite the magic of both man and woman, but until then, I would seize myself a new body while discarding this tainted one.

I had no blood or spiritual connection to Edward Derby so it would be a long and involved process to claim his body. It would months, if not years, to slowly drive him out of his consciousness. Possession of his body would be akin to digging a tunnel through the immature fool's brain and hollowing him out.

Still, I had time.

I refused to believe the Asenath-thing's prophecy, so clearly designed to unsettle me. I would die, yes, again and again. However, I would continue to move my mind to new bodies for as long as the Sun existed.

Perhaps longer.

The Black Mother had no hold on me.

The female animus was mine to command.

That was when I caught a glimpse of one of the goat-babies in the window, staring at me with its bloody teeth and too-wide grin.

I screamed for the rest of the night until Edward called a doctor to sedate me.

The Black Mother's influence could not be escaped.

She was inside me.

She was inside us all.

Bonus Short Story

The Maltese Cthulhu

A *Cthulhu Armageddon* Story

By C.T. Phipps

This is set during the events of *The Tree of Azathoth*

"You want me to find your missing idol," I said, sitting behind my desk and staring at the woman sitting across from me.

I had been working as a private detective in the Dreaming City for the better part of a year now, and the realities of the business were clear. Most cases dealt with smut, broken trust, missing items, lost relatives, or suspected fraud. A not insignificant portion of them dealt with magic and the best solution in those cases was to consult a wizard or witch.

However, one element of my relationship with my clients was that it was very rare that any of them could be described as glamorous. In a city of illusions and magic to cover up your horrific true appearance, only a few could afford to be beautiful. This woman was beautiful. Too beautiful in fact.

Standing roughly six feet tall in heels, she was pleasantly shaped in a way that wasn't quite natural. I'll spare you the private eye ogling and simply state that I was no stranger to gorgeous woman, but her appearance exceeded all but a handful. Her skin was the color of coffee, and her eyes were the most magnificent shade of black. She was wearing a red sequined dress that looked more like it was for a party than handling any sort of business in the city. Then there was her wide brimmed hat that seemed designed to make her seem more exotic and mysterious. She also had a handbag larger than a lady's usual purse, large enough to carry a gun or wand.

"My missing Cthulhu idol, yes," the woman said. "You can call me Marceline. Marceline de Russy."

An obvious pseudonym.

Marceline de Russy, AKA The Medusa, was a famous Witch Queen of the Pre-Rising Earth down New Orleans way. She had been a Cthulhu cultist who had made the mistake of falling in love with a rich, bigoted man who had ultimately murdered her after discovering her heritage before killing himself. The legend, like so many others in the city, had taken a life of its own. It was generally told as a cautionary tale about why followers of the Great Old Ones and Outer Gods should avoid marrying those who worshiped the Small Gods of Earth. Or just bigoted white men, no matter how rich.

I crossed my arms and tried to avoid looking directly at her. There was something hypnotizing about her and that wasn't always a metaphor. "You should know, Ms. de Russy, that I have not had the best of experiences with the Cult of Cthulhu."

"It's a religion like any other," Marceline said.

"One that promises the cultists that when their god rises, all of their enemies will be destroyed and they will dance on the ashes," I replied.

"So does Christianity," Marceline pointed out.

"Another religion that has tried to kill me a few times," I replied. "Most New God churches in the City consider me a demon."

"Are you?" Marceline asked.

"Demon, jinn, spirit, detective, soldier," I said, shrugging. "It's why I generally don't do religious cases."

The woman reached into her handbag, causing me to move for my pistol hidden in a holster taped under my desk. She pulled out a wallet from which she produced ten crisp century notes which she placed on the desk.

"I am at your disposal, ma'am," I replied, dryly.

"Money is all it took?" the woman asked, questioningly.

"What have you heard about me?" I asked.

"That detective John Henry Booth is a man of honor, nobility, and willing to walk the mean streets of the City without being mean himself."

"Good." I nodded. "Then my publicist is doing his job, as I am none of those things. I am, however, quite willing to do the job for cash."

Capitalism had not been a concept with which I'd been intimately familiar when I'd first come to the City. I'd swiftly adapted to the concept when it became clear that credit, paper, and coins were the driving currency (no pun intended) for determining whether a person should live or die. Indeed, I might have avoided many of the people trying to kill me if I'd been wealthy, alien blood or not. It seemed the rich could get by worshiping alien gods, practicing bloody atavistic magic, and consorting with unclean things as an eccentric hobby. It was only the destitute and working class who were considered anathema.

"Good," Marceline said. "The statue is made of clay, about eight inches tall, and depicting an image of the Great Old One's oversized head with a representation of its body underneath. It is several thousand years old and of great value to my family."

"Is it magical in nature?" I asked.

"Absolutely not," Marceline said, obviously lying to me. "Its nature is purely sentimental."

"Mm-hmm," I replied, deciding to take notes. I took out a pen and began writing on the crisp yellow paper on my desk, the letterhead proudly reading KING PAPER COMPANY. "Do you have any idea who might have absconded with this object?"

"I know *exactly* who has taken the idol," Marceline said.

That was an unexpected and suspicious bit of good fortune. "And who is that?"

"The Ecstatic Order of Shub-Niggurath," Marceline said, frowning her pretty, black lips.

"The *Ecstatic* Order?" I asked.

"It's a sex cult," Marceline said.

"I guessed," I said.

Shub-Niggurath was a less popular cult than those of Cthulhu, Yog-Sothoth, or the New Gods, but still had a powerful following—for perhaps obvious reasons. A fertility goddess, Shub-Niggurath was usually worshiped in conjunction with Aphrodite, Bacchus, the Morrigan, Inanna, and Pan. Wild revelries were the order of the day, and it was why her religion was banned even in a city where monsters walked freely.

"They stole it from my family for their rituals," Marceline said.

"And you want me to steal it back," I replied, finally getting down to brass tacks.

"Yes," Marceline said, not denying it or engaging in euphemism. I appreciated that. "There will be an even greater reward for you once you bring it back."

"More money?" I asked.

"Ten times as much," Marceline said, positively slinking over to me. It was not so much alluring as a predatory movement of her body. "And still greater rewards."

Like a snake.

She pressed herself forward, putting her face-to-face with me, before kissing me on the lips. My mind grew somewhat foggy.

"I see," I said, trying but failing to pull away.

"Until next time," Marceline said, departing and leaving me tingling all over.

Oh yeah, she was going to betray me.

Tracking down the Ecstatic Cult of Shub-Niggurath proved easier than expected.

"It's a goddamn sorority?" I asked, staring at the pleasant Victorian building across the well-manicured green lawn.

It was a two-story structure sitting in a row of a dozen others that formed their own city block. Only the very rich and very gifted could attend college in the City, but that didn't prevent people from creating their own little secret societies to help guarantee their futures once past graduation. Notably, the building had iron bars on its windows, behind which were thick curtains. There was also a large stone wall around the place and several wards with real magic to them.

In retrospect, I shouldn't have been surprised. A wise but cynical man once said that cults were what big religions called the little ones. The truth was a bit more complicated. A religion was allegedly open about its doctrine and truths that it was supposed to share with everyone. A cult, by contrast, was at heart about secrecy as it kept its higher truths to devotees that proved themselves worthy of such power.

When magic was involved, inevitably cults formed around the power that its leadership was reluctant to share. Wizards and witches were a surly and jealous lot that always wished to expand their knowledge but were reluctant to share it. Apprenticeships were like slavery, and it was the rare conjurer who would let his student learn as much as himself. It was why colleges like New Miskatonic were gathering places for the arcane as a college was meant to share everything, even when it was perhaps better that such truths were kept hidden. Who knew how many secret societies and would-be magicians had found their footing in New Miskatonic's occult library? Many, I'd wager.

"I mean, it certainly fills some men's fantasies," Jackie said, staring at the sign. The muscular redheaded woman was only a bit shorter than me. She was also dressed in a trench coat and fedora that were more men's fashion in the City. Her glamour was slipping a bit today and her teeth were unusually sharp with prominent dog-like canines as befitting a ghoul-human hybrid. Still, she could look like a twenty-year-old, someone who could fit in among these upper-class twits. I admitted, I'd expected to find the cult a bit further afield, though.

"Please don't make jokes," I muttered, having raised Jackie since she was an adolescent and not able to deal with the fact she was an adult. Arguably centuries older and looking no older than twenty-eight.

"A good chunk of them are New Miskatonic U cheerleaders, too!" Jackie said, giving me an elbow nudge. "Go Squids."

I stared at her. "Please tell me you're joking."

"I never joke for the twenty-five bucks an hour you pay me," Jackie replied. "Two of the ladies here, the Crampton Sisters, are the minds behind the Ecstatic Order. They recruit over the city's internet and host raves that include many after-parties where the drugs and sex flow freely."

"Fascinating," I said, dryly. "The internet is the telephone service that sends pictures and written messages, right?"

Jackie sighed. "We're never going to get you caught up, are we?"

"I don't believe in Yithian science," I said.

Jackie sighed. "You're hopeless, Dad."

"Well now I just have to figure out how to get inside," I muttered. "If they've got the Horror in clay then they're probably keeping it in their sacred place—so to speak."

"Yeah," Jackie said. "Are you sure this client is on the level?"

I struggled to throw off thoughts of Marceline. The kiss she'd planted on me had put me under some sort of spell and, worse yet, I knew it. She was an extremely attractive woman, but she hadn't needed to put some sort of geas or curse on me to get me to bring back her idol. I would have done it for the money alone.

Unfortunately, the aftereffects were leaving my blood on fire and thoughts constantly drifting back to the witch. I wanted to bring the statue to her, and I could tell that unnatural hunger was imposed on me. I also knew that there was no way it would be a simple transaction and that anyone who used that kind of power on another to control them only intended to end it in blood.

"John?" Jackie asked, sensing my discomfort.

"No," I answered her earlier question. "She is not. Did you pick up any dangers?"

"You mean are they actually just a pair of party girls, or are they genuinely dangerous?" Jackie asked.

"Yes," I replied.

"I don't know." Jackie frowned. "It seems like there are easier ways to justify college hedonism than invoking forces mankind does not understand. There are rumors."

"There are always rumors," I said.

"And some of them are even true," Jackie said, slyly. "However, unfortunately, these rumors also come with missing persons reports. Never students of New Miskatonic University, but other invitees, poorer and not supposed to be there in the first place. Maybe it's unrelated. Maybe they just ODed."

"Or maybe they're paying a tithe for their pleasures," I said, grunting. "Real magic always has a price."

"And the trick is getting other people to pay it," Jackie said. "The magic in the walls says that someone inside this place knows the real deal, though. The cult is only starting out but it's eager to expand its knowledge base."

That gave me an idea.

Laying out the breadcrumbs had only taken a few days but worked like a charm among the more credulous of the city's supernatural enthusiasts. Jackie had created a false profile on the internet for me, a reputed book seller and former student at Miskatonic with a master's degree in alternative religion.

"Mr. Henri de Marigny" had apparently run into some financial difficulties and was now willing to part with his occult library of originals as well as the translations he'd done. Fragments of the *Necronomicon*, *Book of Eibon*, *Pnakotic Manuscripts*, and so on.

This was already a big warning sign for any serious occult collectors because true practitioners wouldn't sell their copies. If you had access to such a treasure trove, you'd rob and kill or make deals before parting with them. It was enough to appeal to amateurs, though, and that was what I was hoping the so-called Crampton Sisters were. We'd received hundreds of inquiries over the next few days. Then our fishes had taken the bait, if you don't mind some Innsmouth town slang.

"We're so glad to see you, Mr. de Marigny," Babs Crampton said, answering the door in a Miskatonic U sweater and knee length skirt.

Babs was a beautiful blonde girl with a headband and girl next door looks that nevertheless smoldered with an understated sensuality I couldn't entirely disregard as the lingering effects of Marceline's spell. It had been three days and I was still suffering from its influences.

"Thank you, madame," I said, affecting an upper crust City accent. "I am very pleased to make your acquaintance. Is your sister here?"

Disguise wasn't my forte, but it was amazing how a pair of glasses, a change of clothes, and an adjustment to one's demeanor can alter one's entire position in society. In this case, I'd put on a jacket with brown elbow patches over a plain dress shirt, beige pants, and almost slipper-like dress shoes to distract from my bulky, muscular form.

"Oh yes," Babs said, cheerfully and opening the door to reveal the second of the Crampton sisters.

Raquel Crampton was the opposite of her sister with barely any resemblance between the two, having tanned skin and pretty, orange hair, and wearing a lime green jacket. She looked like she'd just stepped in from the rain despite it having been bone dry for several days. Both she and her sister, together, looked like actresses playing college students as opposed to college students themselves.

"I've heard so much about you!" Raquel said, cheerfully. Which was quite impossible given I was a fictious construct that hadn't existed a week ago.

"You flatter me, miss," I said, smiling as I held tightly to my briefcase. "Will we be alone this meeting?"

"Why, are we not enough?" Raquel asked, her innuendo-laced joke strangely lacking in sexuality.

"Our sisters are away," Babs said, quickly. "This is a private matter for the leadership of our coven."

"Coven, eh?" I asked politely.

Babs moved to the side, allowing me to pass. "Oh, yes. We teach in the Ecstatic Order of Shub-Niggurath that the word 'witch' is actually a word for the wise. We seek to appropriate it from the patriarchal, oppressive, religious forces of Yog-Sothoth and Hasturian religious structures. Ones that accent the male idiom over the feminine. Don't you agree?"

I was of the opinion that the Great Old Ones did not remotely give a shit about humanity, let alone our genders that probably didn't correlate to anything their species possessed. I also felt it ridiculous to worship beings that considered us equivalent to termites on a good day, but that wasn't going to help my position.

"That sounds fascinating, though I admit I am here primarily to discuss our business arrangement. I want my library to find a good home and that requires a face-to-face meeting to hash out our details."

I walked past the sisters and found myself in a stately looking study with a set of winding stairs leading to the second floor, and walls full of books, mostly lesser volumes of the occult mixed in with a variety of cheap romance novels for strange contrast. The place had a lot of light coming in from the windows and well-appointed antique furniture — or excellent reproductions.

They'd gone to some elaborate lengths to make themselves appear respectable and it was entirely possible they were, at least by City standards. None of that could hide a darker cast to everything, though, as my honed senses detected something unholy beneath me. I could sense a terrible power thrumming under the floorboards and guessed something or someone was gathering mystical forces for some nefarious purpose. It always was nefarious with magic. Call me premature, but I'd have bet my PI's license that was where the Cthulhu idol was.

"Of course, Mr. de Marigny," Raquel said. "We just thought you might like to acquaint yourself with the intimacies of our religion since you are going to help us so greatly — profit motivation or not. Would you care for a drink?"

I smiled. "I don't drink. Deadens the mind."

How stupid did they think I was?

So, I was an abject moron.

I was presently tied with ropes around my wrists against a Saint Andrew's cross in the middle of the sorority's basement. A large green balefire was burning in the center of the chamber. The walls were covered in a noxious smelling pinkish fungi and smeared with other more identifiable fluids. Both the walls and fire seemed to be feeding strange artery-like vines that crisscrossed the floors, walls, and ceiling.

There was a general sense that the building's foundation was alive, and the earth had been dug out to allow the unnatural meat-plant growing around me to live. Worse—at least for my peace of mind—there were countless animal bones and more human-like ones scattered among the bizarre underground garden. There were a few fresher bodies that looked like they'd been drained of blood, with large, circular, sucker-like wounds on their bare sides.

How I'd managed to enter this unfortunate situation when I was so cagey and determined to keep the upper hand over the Crampton Sisters is a fascinating story. However, I'm not going to tell it because it makes me look bad and you'll just have to use your imagination. Let's pretend it was something semi-dignified like knocking me over the head with the Cthulhu idol when I wasn't looking.

The Crampton sisters moved into the chamber, both wearing extraordinarily revealing attire whose sexualized effect was somewhat blunted by the fact they were now hairless, nose-less serpent-women. Their bodies were covered in thick scales, and they had eyes of the most malign yellow, and long tails sticking out from the lowest point of their backs. Which, technically, I suppose made them resemble lizards more than serpents, but taxonomy wasn't my strong suit. How did I know they were the Crampton sisters? They were still recognizable in their general shape, which was troubling on its own way.

Babs Crampton held a purple pillow bearing the Cthulhu idol. It was very different from the way Marceline described it as instead of clay, it was constructed of R'lyehian gold. Perhaps it had been covered in clay and the Crampton Sisters had cleaned it off. Raquel was carrying a large sword with a serrated blade that had a carving of a snake along its side. That was not a good sign.

"You sought to steal from us, Mr. Booth," Babs Crampton said, her voice now carrying the inhuman throaty rasp of a serpent woman. Apparently, I hadn't fooled them and my reputation had preceded me. "The idol to Great Cthulhu is something that is ours by right of conquest."

"Marceline de Russy disagrees," I replied, working against my bonds as I tested both the wood and rope. The rope was strong, but the wood of the cross was old and probably bought for purposes other than bondage—at least of human sacrifices.

"Ha!" Babs sneered. "You don't even know her real name."

"No, I admit I do not," I said, wondering if I had any magic that might aid me down here. I was a hedge wizard and the cost of even the lightest spell was one paid in blood or souls—if such a thing existed—and I was always hesitant to open my mind up to those terrible cosmic forces.

Once there had been a time I could have just torn through the creatures like wet tissue paper, ripping flesh and bone like they were nothing. I had been a creature that could have been worshiped by foolish mortals. I'd traded it for my humanity and some days—like right now for instance—I wondered if I'd gotten the better part of the deal. Instead, I focused my strength on one spot and hoped I'd be able to break the center of the cross.

"We were her apprentices," Babs said, placing the statue at my feet. "She opened our minds to the true nature of the cosmos but refused to give us real power. So, we took what was ours!'

"Uh huh," I said, staring at her. "Was this before or after you became snake women?"

Raquel hissed at me, actually hissed. It was *ridiculous*.

"You will die, Mr. Booth, and your seed and blood will be offered up to Shub-Niggurath," Babs said. "The Mother of All and Nothing shall feast upon you, and we shall drink of her ichor."

I was less than impressed with their pulp magazine villainy and wondered how much their evil witch act was how society had educated them that evil priestesses were supposed to act. This was strictly amateur hour sorcery and they'd obviously ditched Marceline—if she was the real deal—well before they'd learned anything useful.

"The seed giving part wasn't so bad, but I've had better," I replied, referring to how they had gotten me here. "At least now that the beer goggles are off."

I was referring to their illusion magic.

Raquel lifted her sword and shouted. "Iä! Shub-Niggurath! *Yig-Seth! Bla'ata'al mack!*"

Raquel was close enough that my recklessness had a small chance of success. Forcing even every bit of strength into my limbs, I snapped the Saint Andrew's cross in half at my back and maneuvered my body so that the sword buried itself into the wooden beam binding my right arm. Striking it, the area gave way to free my upper arms and I grabbed Raquel and lifted her into the air.

"Ahhh!" Raquel shouted. "What are you—"

Raquel was cut off by my hurling her into the balefire behind her. What followed was a nightmarish scream accompanied by alien and not-so-alien obscenities. The flames licked at the serpent woman, and she thrashed in its magical light, the forces inside the fire tearing at whatever spells she'd cast upon herself to make her immortal. Raquel reached out to her sister, calling in some ancient tongue to be rescued.

"I can't!" Babs shouted, horrified by her sister's burning. Looking as if she wanted to go into the fire or work some magic to save her, she instead grabbed the Cthulhu idol on the ground before rushing to the door at the other end of the makeshift temple.

"Bitch!" Raquel's final word was entirely understandable. The burning serpent woman then exploded and became a flying spectral will-o'-the-wisp that bolted out of the balefire and rushed through the doorway past Babs. It reminded me of something out of a fantasy barbarian story. The remaining Crampton sister was thrown to the ground and the Cthulhu idol skipped across the ground away from her.

My legs were still bound to the remains of the Saint Andrew's cross, which was bolted to the ground. Reaching down to grab the late Raquel's sword, I started cutting myself free. The sword was incredibly sharp and freeing myself was fast but not quite fast enough. Because I noticed the room was *moving*.

The vines on the ground and wall detached themselves, revealing lamprey-like suckers that made disgusting noises as they began to descend upon me. A large, tumorous, fleshy growth descended from the center of the roof, revealing the evil heart of the creature the Crampton Sisters had cultivated here.

"The Great Mother's Daughter shall devour you!" Babs shouted, raising the idol that she had retrieved into the air. "Feed, mighty one! Feed!"

I finished cutting myself free and slashed my way through the vines as they came for me, spilling a noxious ichor where each was struck. Running toward Babs, I gave her a punch to the jaw that was perhaps not my most chivalrous action but it managed to achieve what I was hoping for: knocking her flat on her tail. Grabbing the Cthulhu idol from her arms, I made a break for the door as I left the sword clattering on the ground.

"You will never be able to outrun the Great Mother!" Babs shouted at me as I started up the stairs.

"I only have to outrun you!" I shouted back, a quick glance having confirmed the vines in the basement were starting to wrap themselves around their former master.

I tried not to listen to the sounds I heard as I reached the first floor. They were infinitely worse than screams.

I grew sicker and weaker with the passing of the days. Within two days, I had lost twenty pounds and every moment I was covered in sweat from a fever that seemed always on the verge of taking my life. I also found myself carrying the Cthulhu idol wherever I went, unable or unwilling to let it leave my sight save with the strongest of efforts.

Marceline's spell was more clearly something designed to kill me unless I returned to her the property she thought was rightfully hers. It was bad client manners and yet I had to admit I only cared that she undid the magic when I finally arranged for the meeting at the docks near midnight.

I, of course, didn't believe for a second that she intended to remove the curse once I'd delivered her property, though. One thing I'd learned about wizards over the years that had held true with virtually each I'd met was that they were all assholes.

I was standing on the edge of pier 13, holding a large package wrapped in brown paper with a little wax covered rope around it. I was once more dressed in my trench coat and fedora, glad to have a set of clothes again even if covering the cost of my lost disguise would be a blow to my profits. I was armed but I didn't think that would make a large amount of difference with Marceline.

Not if she saw it coming.

"I'm glad to see you're a man of your word," Marceline's voice filled the night air, just a few strokes after midnight. She'd changed from her flamboyant red dress to a blue trench coat that was complimented by a similar blue hat.

"You promised me ten grand," I replied, now shaking with the pain of her presence. I wanted to throw myself on the ground, present the Cthulhu idol to her, and offer my life up for sacrifice. It was behavior so out of character that I wanted to put a bullet through my brain just to make sure I died as myself.

"I'm afraid that part of our deal is cancelled," Marceline spoke, stretching out her hands. "Give me the idol."

Her voice had a compelling, almost hypnotic quality. "Not until you fix whatever you've done to me."

Marceline's eyes narrowed and she repeated herself. The power behind her words became all-encompassing. *Give me the idol.*

Instead, I unwrapped package and revealed the Cthulhu idol. It had a grenade wrapped in duct tape around its side. I pulled out the pin and squeezed the safety lever. "I'll happily give you the idol. But unless I'm cured, I guess we'll be finding out if it's explosive-proof."

Marceline stared at me.

"Impressive, Booth," Marceline said, her voice sounding familiar in that moment. However, I couldn't quite place it.

"It seems you haven't lost all of your Wasteland cunning in your time play-acting as a detective."

"Make your choice," I said, struggling for breath. "My hands are really shaky."

Marceline waved her hand over me. "May the dark gods cease feasting on your soul."

I fell to my knees, a sudden sense of relief filling my body. "Thanks."

"Give me the idol," Marceline said, slowly walking forward. "Put the pin—"

Of course, I obeyed her command this time and threw the idol into her arms. Marceline began screaming several commands in a guttural inhuman language before I drew my gun and put three rounds into her head. Her body collapsed into a bunch of writhing snakes that fled into the water beneath the pier. I wasted a few bullets, blowing up as many as I could before they disappeared. I got maybe half in the end, leaving bloody snake parts and bullet holes all over the wooden pier's planks.

Jackie, my backup, ran up to me with a shotgun in hand. "Did you get her?"

"I have no idea," I admitted.

Jackie looked down at the Cthulhu idol and pulled out the wooden grenade I'd carved and painted with shoe polish. "Glad she fell for the bluff."

"I wish I could have acquired the real deal," I muttered. "No matter, I suggest we take this thing down to the nearest foundry and smelt it."

"That'll really piss her off," Jackie muttered.

"I got the impression she already hated me," I muttered. "But hopefully she'll take time to recover."

"Ex-girlfriend?" Jackie joked.

It wasn't funny to me. "To be honest, for a second there, she sounded a lot like my ex-slave master, Katryn. Does no one stay dead anymore?"

I looked down at the Cthulhu idol, whose four ruby encrusted eyes twinkled back with the glow of an alien power that would hopefully fade once it was melted down. A part of me considered keeping it, but I knew it would just make me a target for every two-bit magician and wannabe sorcerer in the City. I had enough enemies as it was.

"He's not the one to ask," Jackie said, joking. "He's not dead, only sleeping."

"Yeah, and this world is the stuff dreams are made of."

About the Authors

Matthew Davenport hails from Des Moines, Iowa, where he lives with his wife, Ren, and daughter, Willow. When his scattered author brain isn't earning weird looks from the ladies of his life, he enjoys reading sci-fi and horror, tinkering with electronics, and doing escape rooms.

Matt is the author of the *Andrew Doran* series, *The Trials of Obed Marsh*, *Satan's Salesman*, and the *Broken Nights* series (with his brother, Michael), among other titles. He's also a self-styled student of the Cthulhu Mythos and exerts that influence in his stories and as an editor at the blog Shoggoth.net.

David Hambling lives in darkest Norwood, South London with his wife and cat. He is a journalist and his fiction, starting with the collection *The Dulwich Horror & Others*, explores the Cthulhu mythos in his own locale. He continues the theme in a number of novels including the popular Harry Stubbs adventures set in the 1920s, and the epic fantasy *War of the God Queen*. He has contributed to the anthologies *Black Wings V* and *VI* (PS publishing), *Tales of the Al-Azif* and *Time Loopers: Four Tales From a Time War*.

Keep track of his fiction at the Shadows From Norwood page on Facebook: https://www.facebook.com/ShadowsFromNorwood/

Amazon page: https://www.amazon.com/David-Hambling/e/B0034QC7OO

Patricia Lee Macomber is the former editor-in-chief of ChiZine. She has been published in *Cemetery Dance* magazine and such anthologies as *Shadows Over Baker Street*, *Little Red Riding Hood In the Big Bad City*, and *Dark Arts*. Along with her husband, David Niall Wilson, she has written *An Unkindness of Ravens* and *Stargate Atlantis: Brimstone*. Her first solo release, *Zombie - A Love Story* is now available. Currently, she lives in North Carolina with her husband and their children.

Eric Malikyte is a neurodivergent author, illustrator, science communicator, and video editor. He has published works in various genres, including Lovecraftian horror, dark fantasy, and cyberpunk. He has written for YouTube channels such as TopTenz, Geographics, and Biographics. He lives in Richmond, Virginia with his wife and two cats, where he spends his spare time exploring used bookstores, Irish Pubs, and terrorizing the neighborhood children on Halloween. Get a free copy of Eric's debut novel *Echoes of Olympus Mons* here: https://dl.bookfunnel.com/1cw07o2uyb

Tim Mendees is a rather odd chap. He's a horror writer from Macclesfield in England's northwest who specializes in cosmic horror and weird fiction. A lifelong fan of classic weird tales, Tim set out to bring the pulp horror of yesteryear into the twenty-first century and give it a distinctly British flavor. His work has been described as the lovechild of H.P. Lovecraft and P.G. Wodehouse and is often peppered with a wry sense of humor that acts as a counterpoint to the unnerving, and often disturbing narratives.

Tim is the author of over one hundred published short stories and novelettes, seven novellas, and two short story collections. He has also curated and edited several cosmic horror-themed anthologies. When he is not arguing with the spellchecker, Tim is a goth DJ with a weekly radio show on The Feelgood Station, and the co-presenter of the *Innsmouth Book Club Podcast* and *Strange Shadows: A Clark Ashton Smith Podcast*. His latest Lovecraftian novel, *Zone 51: Shadow of Chaos*, is out now from Eerie River Publishing.

He currently lives in Brighton & Hove with his pet crab, Gerald, and an ever-increasing army of stuffed octopods.

timmendeeswriter.wordpress.com/

Andrea Pearson is a *USA Today* bestselling author of several series including the Kilenya, Mosaic, and Koven Chronicles. She lives with her husband and children in a small valley framed with hills. She graduated from Brigham Young University with a Bachelor of Science degree in communications disorders. Her Mosaic Chronicles has been lauded as "a little bit Harry Potter, a little bit HP Lovecraft," and most of her books exemplify an appreciation of the works of Lovecraft and his peers.

Andrea spends as much time with her family as possible. Her favorite activities include painting, watching movies, collecting and listening to music, and discussing books and authors.

C. T. Phipps is a lifelong student of horror, science fiction, and fantasy. An avid tabletop gamer, he discovered this passion led him to write and turned him into a lifelong geek. He is the author of *Agent G*, the Bright Falls Mysteries, *Cthulhu Armageddon*, *Lucifer's Star*, The Supervillainy Saga, *Wraith Knight*, and others. He is a regular blogger on *The United Federation of Charles*.

http:// unitedfederationofcharles.blogspot.com/

Jessi Vasquez is a queer writer who resides in Washington with her spouse, her band of misfit friends, and their correlating pets. Her short horror story "Emergency Contact" was selected as part of Indignor House Publishing's 2024 annual short story competition and subsequently published in their 2024 *Fear* Anthology. She has written several scripts for the YouTube channels Science Get and Geographics. Fueled by her love of dark roasts and reading, she devotes her time to crafting speculative fiction and creative nonfiction.

David J. West and his not-so-secret pen name of **James Alderdice**, write dark fantasy and weird westerns because the voices in his head won't quiet until someone else can hear them. He is a great fan of sword & sorcery, ghosts, and lost ruins, so of course he lives in Utah. He has written the 10-book *Brutal Sword Saga* series under James Alderdice; while the *Dark Trails Saga*, *#SAVANT*, *Cowboys & Cthulhu* series are regulars in the best seller list for western horror. There is always more to come.

Curious about other Crossroad Press books? Stop by our website:
http://crossroadpress.com
We offer quality writing
in digital, audio, and print formats.

Subscribe to our newsletter on the website homepage and receive a
free eBook.